Can't Stop

Can't Stop

Clifford "Spud" Johnson

www.urbanbooks.net

Urban Books, LLC
300 Farmingdale Road, NY-Route 109
Farmingdale, NY 11735

ISBN 13: 978-1-62286-558-1
ISBN 10: 1-62286-558-8

First Trade Paperback Printing July 2017
Printed in the United States of America

10 9 8 7 6 5 4 3 2 1

This is a work of fiction. Any references or similarities to actual events, real people, living or dead, or to real locales are intended to give the novel a sense of reality. Any similarity in other names, characters, places, and incidents is entirely coincidental.

Distributed by Kensington Publishing Corp.
Submit orders to:
Customer Service
400 Hahn Road
Westminster, MD 21157-4627
Phone: 1-800-733-3000
Fax: 1-800-659-2436

Prologue

With tears streaming down his face, Jason Gaines stood in front of the mausoleum that held the remains of his parents and his baby brother. Though it had been over six months since their brutal murders, he felt as if it had just happened. He thought back to the day he found out that his immediate family had been slaughtered and asked himself again, for what seemed like the millionth time, *why?* Why would someone do this to his family? No one seemed to know anything other than the fact that his mother had been shot twice in her head, her beautiful features destroyed to the point where they had to have her casket closed at the funeral. His father had been shot twice as well, but twice in the heart at point-blank range. Last was his brother, who also was shot twice, once in the throat and once in his heart. Why? Who would want to do this to his family? Nothing was stolen from their three-bedroom home, so robbery wasn't the reason. No one in his family was into anything illegal, nor had any drug problems or anything going on in their lives for this to happen to them. This is what caused the confusion on top of the pain he felt because it ate at his core every hour of the day. He was slowly losing his mind. The only thing keeping him somewhat sane was that he had to avenge their murders. He had to get the people who were responsible for killing his family. That was his sole purpose in life.

Right now, he had to get things in motion to make sure that his money was right, and he knew the only way that would happen was for him to make some major moves out of town. He had all the time in the world to find the killers of his family, but for now, it was time for him to get focused on the tasks at hand. He sighed, stepped to the mausoleum, kissed each nameplate, and promised his family he would find the people who murdered them. As he turned to leave, he saw that there was a black Range Rover with dark tinted windows parked directly behind his car. *Here we go*, he thought as he walked toward the Range. As soon as he made it to the truck, the rear door was opened for him from the inside. He climbed inside of the truck and stared at the two men sitting in the backseat and waited for one of them to speak.

"How ya doin', Hot Shot?" asked JT, a country-sounding white man from Pikeville, Kentucky.

He was a man Jason knew was serious about everything when it came to their business. One of the few men who he respected other than his father, who was no longer breathing. A man who was as dangerous as he was. A man who was cold-blooded, exactly as he was.

In a world where everyone has a nickname, Jason's was "Hot Shot." He smiled and said, "What's up, champ? You good?"

"I'm always good, even when I'm bad. Seeing you out there at your family's final resting place has me worried about you, son. The question is, are *you* good? Or should I ask, are you ready to handle this business and move forward with your life?"

Hot Shot frowned when he spoke. "My life will move forward when I find the people responsible for murdering my family. Until then, I'm just here. As for handling the business, when have you ever seen me not ready to handle a mission, JT? Have I ever failed before?"

"You don't know what the word 'fail' means, Hot Shot."

"That's good, because we're about to get serious, and it's vital that you handle your business and not let your personal situation get in the way," said the other man inside of the truck, dressed immaculately in what looked to be a very expensively tailored suit. "Everything you need is already in Texas. Once you arrive and get settled, give JT here a call and put things in motion. Whenever you need anything or any assistance of any kind, get with JT. Understood?"

"Yes."

"Any questions on what's expected of you?"

Shaking his head, Hot Shot said, "No. I know how to get money, and I know how to handle myself. As long as I have what I need weapons-wise, everything else will fall right in place once I get situated out there."

"Listen, I don't want you out there being a loose cannon with it. Get the money and make any new connections you can while getting it in."

"I'll get the money, but if anyone gets in my way, they will be dealt with in whatever manner I see fit. I will not jeopardize the money, but I will do what I deem necessary in order to keep breathing."

The man sighed and said, "Understood. Take care of yourself out there, Hot Shot."

Seeing that he was dismissed, he gave both men a nod, and then climbed out of the truck, followed by JT.

"Now, why in the fuck did you have to go and say that shit for?"

"Wanted it clear off the top how I'm going to handle things. I'm out there with no one, straight solo, so if I feel the need to get deep in someone's tail for trying me, then that's my decision to make. You will be there if I need you, but you won't be on the front line with me, JT. So let me do me, huh?"

"I got you. I guess there will be some things we might have to keep just between us. Just don't screw this up for us. This could be the beginning of something special, son. I know what drives you, Hot Shot, and that worries me some, but it scares me more. Don't take the pain you're feeling from the loss of your family out on the men and women you come across out there in Dallas. Control that rage inside of you, son."

With a grin on his face, Jason "Hot Shot" Gaines asked JT, "Have you ever heard of anyone being able to control their rage, JT?"

With a smirk on his face, JT answered, "You know what I mean."

"Yes, I do. I will handle what needs to be handled, and everything will be good. You do your part for me and put all the ears you have out here in these California streets and get me some information on some kind of leads on the killer who took my family away from me. Don't worry about me and those Texas jokers. I don't lose, and I will not lose. I know how to get paper and make all the right moves. I won't stop because I can't stop, JT. Never forget that."

They shook hands and parted ways for the time being. It was time for the fun to begin.

Chapter One

Three months of living and hustling in Dallas had paid off big time for Hot Shot. He met most of the serious hustlers in the city and conducted a few deals with some who felt comfortable with him since he was fairly new to them. Some of the men he met were skeptical and chose to fall back and watch the new guy who says he's from California and see what he was about. Hot Shot respected those who didn't get right at him. That showed him they were cautious, and being cautious while dealing in the streets, no matter what state one was in, was a good rule to hustle by. Those who had been hesitant to deal with him would soon come around. That was something he was positive of.

The money was good, and the product was great. No matter what was requested of him, he delivered nothing but the very best, whether it was cocaine, marijuana, X-pills, oxycodone, and the ever-popular-in-Texas, codeine syrup. That was his best seller at the time, and he couldn't order enough of it. This seemed to make JT extremely happy, and as long as JT was happy, Hot Shot was happier.

Most things were good. Though money was right, Hot Shot couldn't shake the day-to-day depression that was eating inside of him from the loss of his family. Every time he flew back west to Los Angeles, he would check with a few of his family members to see if they heard anything on the streets about what happened to his family, and every time he received the same answer: nothing.

The streets weren't talking, and that bothered him. The streets always talked. Why not in this case? What would make someone want to hurt his family? Checking with the police was a waste of time as well, so he gave that up quick. He would find out no matter how long it took. He would find out who took his family away from him.

Right now, he was in Dallas, Texas, getting money, and that was his main agenda. He pulled out his smartphone and called Cotton. Cotton was who Hot Shot referred to as his "little helper," though there wasn't anything "little" about Cotton, who stood six foot three and looked as if he could get on anyone's basketball team and work it something fierce. When Cotton answered the phone, Hot Shot, in his normal, slow, and calm way, said, "What up, champ? What you got going on your way?"

"Same ole shit, Boss man. Waiting on you to hit me off with a little something, 'cause you already know I'm out here getting that bread."

There was an extended pause before Hot Shot spoke. "You won't be satisfied until I stop messing with you, huh? How many times have I told you not to speak about anything on the phone?"

"Damn, what I say? That I'm waiting on you to hit me off with a little something? You need to chill out, Boss man." Quickly changing the subject before he further irked Hot Shot, Cotton asked, "You coming out to play tonight? It's Friday, and I'm trying to hit the club up and have some fun. You with me, Boss man?"

Letting Cotton off the hook for the time being, Hot Shot smiled into the receiver and said, "Yes, I'm with that. Tired of staying at the pad playing games on PlayStation 3. Where you trying to get at tonight?"

"Beamers. It's supposed to be real live on Friday nights."

"Where that at? You know I still don't know my way around this city all that good yet."

"It's right off I-35, on Walnut Hill Lane. Put it in your GPS and you should find it with no problems. If you want, we can hook up somewhere and roll together."

"I have a few errands to run before I get out that way, I'll meet you there. I think I'm going to have that amigo, Juan G., meet me there so we can chop it up. He sent word through that amigo that you hooked me up with last month that he wants to holla ta me."

"That's serious. He's doing his thang right out there in Oak Cliff. You gon' do some big thangs if you get him on your line."

Hot Shot sighed heavily but decided against checking Cotton some more for talking on the phone. Instead, he said, "I'll see you at the club later on," and ended the call.

After taking care of his business, Hot Shot went to his downtown condominium so he could relax for a few hours before he met up with Cotton at the club. As he relaxed back on his comfortable king-sized bed, he thought about what Cotton said about him hooking up with Juan G. That would be a major accomplishment. The money made from dealing with the top Mexican in South Dallas could get ridiculous. That thought put a smile on his face as he slowly drifted off to sleep.

Hot Shot woke up feeling refreshed and ready to handle some business and hopefully enjoy himself at the club. He knew that Cotton would be in full floss mode, meaning he would be trying his best to outshine every hustler in the club tonight. Trying to buy the bar and pop as many bottles as he could to impress the ladies and stunt. Hot Shot couldn't care less about any of that. All he was concerned with was money. So, after the sit-down with Juan G., if he didn't find a female that he deemed worthy of his attention for the night, he was out of there with a quickness.

After deciding on a pair of jeans with a crisp white dress shirt and some Air Force Ones, he smiled at his reflection, something he rarely did in public. When he was out and about, he felt there was no time for smiling. Smiling was for happy people, and he was not a happy man. Also, he didn't want anyone thinking he was there to be friends or to make friends. Business only was his rule while he was in Texas. All he had was money on his mind. He knew he was a handsome man, but he wasn't the womanizer type. He kept it way too real when it came to women so there would never be any type of misunderstanding. They want to spend some time together, then cool; relationship stuff, no way.

He stood six foot one, with brown skin and a smooth bald head and a body that screamed "workout fanatic!" Abs to kill for and cut and chiseled like a hard piece of stone. After grabbing a red blazer out of his closet to match his Nikes, he grabbed his phone and keys and caught the elevator downstairs to the underground parking lot to choose which vehicle he would be driving to the club tonight. Since he was hoping on obtaining some female company, he skipped over his brand-new Ducati Panigale R. *No need for speed like that tonight*, he thought as he stared at his two-year-old GMC Denali. He shook his head no at the SUV and smiled. *When you want to let your swag speak for itself, you can never go wrong when you foreign*, he thought as he stepped quickly to his Audi S8. Nothing like the 130K-plus automobile to show that your swag was really on point. He laughed at that thought as he climbed inside of this car.

Twenty minutes later, he pulled in front of the club and stared at the large crowd waiting in line to get inside of the club. Not cool. Hot Shot don't do lines at all. So, he bypassed the club and gave Cotton a call. When he didn't answer his phone, he sent him a text asking him where he was. Cotton responded back and told him he was already inside the club and would meet him at the door and to text him when he was there. Hot Shot texted back that he would be at the door within the next five minutes, and then quickly made an illegal U-turn and came back to the club.

He pulled into the valet parking and eased out of his clean, sleek vehicle looking real good as he reached back inside of the car and grabbed his blazer from the passenger's side and slid it on and began to stroll confidently toward the entrance of the club where he saw Cotton standing next to one of the humongous security guards posted at the door. Without saying a word to the security, Hot Shot strolled right past him because he knew Cotton had already taken care of things.

Several females watched as the tall, slim brother with the bright red jacket and matching Air Forces on his feet strolled confidently inside of the club without anyone saying anything to him.

"Girl, whoever that man is, he sure as hell got it going on," said a female who watched Hot Shot enter the club.

"You better say it! Did yo see that new whip he jumped out of? What's that, some type of new Benz?" asked another female onlooker.

"Benz? You stupid! Girl, that's that brand-new Audi, and it looks like the top-of-the-line one at that. I'm definitely trying to get close to that perfect piece of male specimen tonight."

Laughing along with her friend, the other female said, "Not if I can get to his fine ass first!"

Each lady gave the other a high five and giggled like schoolgirls instead of grown women as they waited impatiently to enter the club.

Inside, Hot Shot was led straight to one of the VIP sections by Cotton who hadn't stopped running his mouth since they entered the club.

"I'm telling you, Boss man, that dude Juan G. is already here, and he got like two superbad Mexican broads with him. Shit, you about to make some boss moves up in here tonight, Boss man. Do you want me to tell Juan G. you're here now?"

Hot Shot gave Cotton a look as if he was stupid and shook his head. "No. What I want you to do is calm down some and chill. I'm in no rush to get at that Mexican. When the time is right, it will be right for business. I want a drink first, and then I want to check out the scene some. I cannot do that properly with you running your mouth nonstop, Cotton."

Cotton nodded and shut up as he waved and got the attention of a waitress who was taking care of everyone in the VIP section. When she approached their table, she smiled at Hot Shot, totally ignoring Cotton, and asked, "What can I get you, sir?"

"A bottle of Peach Cîroc, darling."

"The entire bottle? I'm not sure we sell by the bottle, sir."

Hot Shot pulled out his wallet, took out his Black Card, and gave it to her smiling. "I'm sure once you explain to the management that I'm going to spend a nice chunk of change in here tonight they won't mind selling me the entire bottle one bit. As an added incentive to make sure, you take a $500 tip for the work I'll have you doing for me in here tonight. I also need you to send your best bottle of champagne over to that table on the other side of the club where those Mexicans are. When you deliver the bottle, please tell the Mexican gentleman sitting in between those lovely ladies over there that Hot Shot is in VIP and will be waiting for him whenever he would like to chat. Do you think you can handle all of that for me, darling?"

The waitress smiled brightly at him and said, "I'm sure I can make everything you want happen, sir."

"Hot Shot. Please call me Hot Shot or Shot if you like."

"Okay, Hot Shot. I'll be right back with your bottle of Peach Cîroc."

Hot Shot watched as the waitress left and smiled at her thickness and wondered if he should let her be the lucky lady of the night. The night was young, no need to pick hastily, he thought as he turned and faced Cotton. Before he spoke, his words were caught in his throat when he saw one of the most gorgeous women he had ever seen in his entire thirty-one years of life. Scratch that. The most gorgeous *women* he had ever seen in his life. The two lovely ladies were following a man who looked at best to be about five foot seven. The little man was being led toward the stairs to the VIP area by two chubby brothers who were also twins. This seemed really strange to Hot Shot; two sets of twins, male and female. *Hmm, interesting.*

Following his gaze, Cotton's smile turned into a frown when he saw who Hot Shot was staring at. He shook his head and said, "Not a good look right there, Boss man. These females you checking for are strictly off-limits."

"Is that right? Who are they?"

"They belong to that boss nigga, Tiny Troy."

With a frown on his face, Hot Shot said, "You are really trying my patience today, Cotton. How many times do I have to tell you about using that N-word around me? Respect yourself and respect the black man by not using that degrading word in my presence."

"My bad, Boss man."

"Now, tell me more about Tiny Troy and those females."

"Like I was saying, they are way off-limits. No one messes with those two. You see those two gigantic cats watching over them like hawks as they lead the way?"

"Yes."

"Keeta Wee and Weeta Wee are some dangerous cats and well known around Dallas as some serious head busters. When it come to Tiny Troy and his girls, Nola and Lola, they will smash something with no hesitation."

"Keeta Wee and Weeta Wee, huh? You got to be kidding me! Those chubby jokers look more soft than dangerous to me."

"Don't let their looks fool you, Boss man. I'm serious here."

"Whatever. So, what's the deal with the females? Are they Tiny Troy's girls or what? And I must say, those nicknames are really, and I mean *really,* killing me!"

Cotton shrugged and said, "That's how it is out here, Boss man. But yeah, they belong solely to Tiny Troy, and I've never heard of them fucking with anyone else."

"Is that right? Hmm . . . Which one is which?"

"Nola is the one with the short haircut in that blue dress, and Lola is the one with the long weave."

"Okay, my little helper. It's time to make some changes around Dallas. This is what I want you to do. I want you to go upstairs to the VIP and respectfully ask the female twin in the blue dress if she would like to join your peoples for a drink. No, scratch that. I'd better make this move myself. When the waitress returns with the bottle of Cîroc, pour us some drinks. One for me, my new friend, and one for yourself."

"Come on, Boss man, you can't be serious. Haven't you heard anything I've just told you?"

"Loud and clear, but something tells me everything isn't what it seems to be, Cotton. Watch my work. I'll be right back, and I won't be alone," Hot Shot stated confidently as he stood and stepped out of the VIP and headed toward the stairs so he could go up to the VIP area.

Cotton watched in horror as his Cali connect, the man who was helping him make a whole bunch of bread, headed toward a fucking wreck, and there was nothing he could do to stop him.

Fuck!

Chapter Two

The two female admirers of Hot Shot had just entered the club when they saw him headed upstairs. They quickly followed in hot pursuit, determined to get some of his attention. Actually, each was hoping for more than just some. By the time they made it up the stairs, they stopped and watched as Hot Shot approached Tiny Troy's table in the VIP section. Knowing the notoriety of Tiny Troy gave both females pause. They were definitely not trying to get on Tiny Troy's bad side. His reputation for having people punished was solid all around Dallas. Without saying a word to each other, the two ladies turned and went toward the bar to wait and see if they would get an opportunity at Hot Shot later.

Hot Shot stepped boldly to Tiny Troy's table and was about to speak when he was stopped by either Keeta Wee or Weeta Wee with a chubby hand placed firmly on his right shoulder. Hot Shot frowned as he looked to his right and stared at the man's hand on his shoulder.

His first instinct was to grab the man's hand and break it, but that would defeat his purpose, so instead, he took a deep breath and said, "My bad, my man. Not trying to disrespect in any way. I came over here to ask the lady right there for permission to buy her a drink and have a dance with me," Hot Shot smiled as he pointed toward the twin Cotton said was Nola.

Laughing, the blocky shouldered, chunky torso twin said, "You are either not from around here or are one stupid-ass nigga. You need to get the fuck on before you get your ass hurt. That's the only warning you're gonna get, nigga."

Hot Shot sighed. He hated the N-word with a passion, and no matter what, he refused to be called it.

"Twice. You called me the N-word twice. Please don't make the mistake of calling me that again, my man. Like I said, I'm here to speak with the lady right there. Now, if this is a problem, then please accept my apology. There was no disrespect intended."

The other twin security stood next to his brother and was about to make an aggressive move toward Hot Shot but was stopped by Tiny Troy. "Hold up, Weeta Wee, let me have a few words with this man who has the nuts of a gorilla." He then stared at Hot Shot for a few seconds, and then said, "So, you're trying to holla at Nola here, huh? Even though you saw her come into the club on my hip, you have the nuts to come to my table and disturb us by trying to get at her? Like my man said, you either not from around here or you're one stupid dude. Which is it?"

"I have never been known to lack intelligence, so I would rule out being stupid. Your first assumption is correct. I'm not from around here. I'm from California. Inglewood to be exact. Where I'm from, we're known for going after something we like. And, yes, I watched you enter the club with this beautiful woman here, and I instantly liked what I saw. What I saw was not a woman on your hip, but following you inside of the club. Her body language showed me that you two aren't intimately involved, and that assumption prompted my actions that brought me here to your table. If I'm wrong, then again, please accept my humble apology and let me buy you a round of drinks."

Impressed with Hot Shot's courage, Tiny Troy started laughing. "What's your name, dude?"

"Hot Shot."

"Hot Shot from Inglewood, huh?"

"That's right."

"How long have you been in Texas?"

Hot Shot stared at Tiny Troy for a moment before responding. "Check this out, champ, I think it may be best that I take the advice from your man here. I don't get off on speaking my business to strangers. So, again, I apologize for interrupting you all."

Without another word said, he turned and left the VIP area and went back downstairs to his own table in the downstairs VIP where Cotton sat with a drink in his hand nervously waiting for him. After Hot Shot was seated and poured himself a glass of Peach Cîroc, he smiled and said, "Well, that was interesting."

"Man, I'm surprised you even made it back to the table. What did they say to you, Boss man?"

"Missed. Tiny Troy asked a few questions but didn't receive any answers. Tell me more about his get down. What he on out here?"

"A little bit of everything. He fucks with the work, but don't fuck with too many people. I've heard he was into the yay yo and pills, not sure, though, 'cause no one has ever really been able to honestly say they've fucked with him. His money seems long, and he comes out flossing around town at every hot spot. Some say he's into pimping too."

"Are you saying those twins are his hoes?"

Cotton shrugged. "I don't know for certain. I do know every time he comes out to play, they're with him along with his bodyguards, Keeta Wee and Weeta Wee."

"Those names kill me. How could two grown men call themselves something stupid like that?"

"Those two men are killers, Boss man. They don't fuck around."

"Yeah, right. Those jerks are nothing."

Damn, this nigga is crazy, Cotton thought to himself. "Whatever you say, Boss man. Look at those females that just came from upstairs. They got us locked in."

Hot Shot turned a little in his seat and watched as the two females who had watched him enter the club were staring at him as they slowly approached the VIP section. He let his eyes roam all over the two ladies and instantly lost interest when he saw how cheaply dressed they were. He smiled suddenly because coming down the stairs was the twin, Nola, and she too had her sights locked on him. "Looks like I didn't miss them after all."

"Yeah, I know. Them fine-ass females are making a beeline right toward us."

Hot Shot frowned and said, "Good. Make sure as soon as they get here that you stand up and take them to the bar on the other side of the club and buy them something to drink. I'm not trying to waste any of my time on those broads."

"You tripping, Boss man."

"Nah, you're tripping, Cotton. When I said looks like I didn't miss, I wasn't talking about those two birds. I was talking about *her,*" he said as he pointed toward Nola who was maybe ten steps behind the two females approaching their table. "Do as I said and get those females away from me as soon as they get here."

Cotton saw Nola was, in fact, headed toward their table and said, "Damn! I'm on it, Boss man. But remember what I told you. This could be some sneaky shit being put down."

"I feel you. I doubt it, though. I could tell how she was looking at me when I was at their table. She was feeling my vibe, and I'm about to see exactly how much."

Before Cotton could speak, the two females made it to their table. Cotton stood and spoke before either of them could say a word. "Hello, ladies. Why don't you let me take you to the bar and buy you a drink?" Without letting either reply, he grabbed them by their hands and turned them around gently and led them away from the table and Hot Shot. Cotton noticed that Nola had a smile on her face as they walked by her.

Nola stopped in front of Hot Shot's table and asked, "May I join you for that drink?"

"Only if the dance will come afterward."

"Let's have the drink first and see if you can impress me some more before we get to that dance."

"Some more? So, I impressed you up there? Sure didn't seem like it being that you didn't say one word to me while I was being lightweight interrupted by your—"

"Associate," she finished for him. "Sometimes silence is golden. One can learn a lot by observing instead of speaking."

Nodding his head in agreement, Hot Shot stood and stepped around the table and pulled out a chair for Nola so she could be seated. After he was back seated, he said, "Not only are you beautiful, you're smart. That's a deadly combination."

"Compliments are nice, especially when they're on point."

"I see you're not modest."

They both laughed as Hot Shot grabbed an extra glass and poured Nola some of his Peach Cîroc. "Modesty is a waste of my time. I'm a bad bitch. You know it just as I do. My name is Nola."

Hot Shot sipped his drink. "Hi, Nola. I like you."

With a smile on her face, she took a sip of her drink and said, "I know. It remains to be seen if I like you, though."

"I hope I'll have the time I need to get you to like me."

She checked her watch and said, "It's early. We shall see."

As they sat and stared at each other, Hot Shot took his time to admire her in greater detail. She was wearing that blue dress as if it were a second skin with some simple pumps and very little jewelry. Her short, pixie haircut fit her small, shaped head perfectly. Though she was a twin, he could tell the difference between her and her sister simply by their different styles. Nola gave off that classy look, whereas her sister looked as if she was more chic. Both were gorgeous, but both were totally different. Hot Shot could see that a mile away. Smooth brown skin complexion with some light brown eyes that seemed bright, intelligent, and energetic. Slim waist and a nice ass. A *really* nice ass. *Mmm,* thought Hot Shot as he set his drink down and said, "Do I need to speak first or do you want to take charge of this conversation?"

"Since you don't like to be asked questions, I figured I'd let you take the lead."

"It's not that I don't like being asked questions. I don't like to be made as if I'm being interrogated, especially by someone that I don't even know."

"I can understand that. Tiny Troy is somewhat overprotective. He was merely being cautious."

"I cannot blame him for that. I mean, I would be too when it came to your well-being."

"Sweet. You're sweet, bold, and cute. Keep on, Hot Shot, you're doing well at impressing me right now. Don't overdo it, though."

"Cute? Cute is for puppies, baby. I'd prefer handsome over cute."

"Okay, handsome, it is then. Can you tell me what made you come out here to Dallas to get money?"

"Get money? What makes you think I came out here to get money?"

"Come on, everyone knows how you Cali dudes rock. When you come to the South, y'all come out here to get money only. Either that or gang bang. Do you bang?"

"Never banged a day in my life."

"With all that bright red you got on and you being from Inglewood, I would have thought you were a Blood."

"What do you know about Inglewood?"

"I know that's where the Bloods get down at. You know all of Cali's gang culture has migrated all over the South. You guys ain't a mystery to nobody. Shit, most of these Texas streets are Bloods or Crips."

"I feel that. Like I said, I don't do the bang thang. I'm more into making money."

"That's what I thought. Like I asked, what made you choose Dallas to come get some money?"

"Let me correct you so you can truly understand. I don't *get* money out here. I *make* money out here."

With a shrug of her shoulders, she said, "Get money, make money, it's all the same thing to me. When you're out here handling your business right, your money will be right."

"No, you're mistaken. There is a difference between the two. I take care of business, no doubt, but I don't get money. I make money. I supply people who supply people who drink, sip that syrup, snort, shoot, or smoke. Whatever is ordered from me I deliver as long as my fees are met. I also supply weapons, big or small, for those who wish to cause extreme amounts of pain to those they deem enemies. I make money in various ways, and there's no limit to my means of making money. That's why, in my eyes, there is a difference."

"I can respect that. You just added another notch to my liking-you meter. I respect a man who makes money," she said smiling. "Please, continue to impress me, honey."

"Actually, I've just broken several of my rules with you, and that is somewhat confusing to me. I don't normally speak on my business to anyone who is not in my immediate circle, let alone a total stranger."

"I'm no stranger, honey. I'm Nola."

"Yes, you are Nola, and as far as I know, you could have been sent by your 'associate' to see what you could learn about me since he was unsuccessful with his attempt at it. You could be setting me up for a jack or something like that."

"Is that what you really think, Hot Shot? Are you scared now?"

"Scared? Baby, I don't understand the meaning of scared or any other word associated with it. Facing fear is way better than running from it. I embrace it. That's why I'm never scared."

"Sometimes fear can break a man. What if it's a fear you can't beat?"

"Then I'd rather be dead. Take, for instance, when your associate's bodyguard grabbed my shoulder. I was seconds away from hurting him because I felt like he was going to try to cause bodily harm to me. I felt some fear, just enough to prepare me to seriously hurt him and his twin if it would have come to that."

Smiling, she said, "Okay, tough guy. You want me to sit here and believe that you at, 195–200 pounds tops, was ready to hurt Keeta Wee and his brother, Weeta Wee, who both top 290 pounds easily?"

"That's exactly what you should believe. Those men are big, yes, but they possess no real skills in combat, whether it's hand-to-hand or anything else, for that matter."

"And how do you know that? You don't even know them. I do, and I know they are some very dangerous men. You shouldn't underestimate. That could get you twisted, Hot Shot," she said as she sipped some more of her Cîroc.

"Underestimating or overestimating one's ability could be fatal, that is a fact. I've never been one to do either. I'm extremely good, and I know that. I know what I'm capable of, and very few men can match me when it comes to being violent in any form. There are men out there better than me. Not many, but a few."

"Oh my, you not only added two more notches to my liking-you meter, but you've turned me on tremendously!" They both started laughing. "Seriously, that wasn't a smart move by telling Keeta Wee not to call you a nigga. You could have caused a whole lot of problems for yourself."

"If that's true, then why didn't things get crazy up there?"

"Because Tiny Troy was intrigued by your direct approach. Believe me, none of these locals would have had the courage to do what you did. Tiny Troy knew instantly that you were someone that he would like to get to know better."

"Is that right? So, that's why you came down here, for Tiny Troy?"

"I came down here because any woman who can make a man come up to Tiny Troy's table in VIP and request a drink and a dance would know that that man was worth getting to know."

"I'm feeling that. Now, where do we go from here, Nola?"

Before she could respond, Cotton returned to the table and said, "Excuse me, Boss man, but Juan G. sent word that he'd like to holla at you."

"Go get at him and let him know that I'll be at his table in a few minutes."

"But he—"

"I said, tell him I'll be at his table in a few minutes, Cotton. I'm currently occupied at the moment."

"Okay," Cotton said and left the table to deliver the message.

"Juan G.? Should the fact that you are meeting with Juan G. impress me too?"

"Not really. I don't want your liking-me meter to raise because of any of my business dealings. That would be a waste. I want it off the meters only because of me."

"I can dig that, honey. Believe me, you're on point for blowing it off the charts right about now."

"Why is that?"

"You have displayed everything I look for in a man. It's been a real long time since that has happened to me. You have my interest piqued, and I'm really wanting to get to know more about you, Mr. Hot Shot."

"That's a good thing. So, shall we exchange numbers first?"

"No problem, but what's the second?"

Hot Shot looked toward the dance floor and said, "That dance I asked for."

"What about your business with Juan G.? I'm sure you don't want to make a powerful Mexican like him think you're not on top of your game."

"Maybe it's a character defect, but I've never really cared about what people say or think about me and how I do things."

"Oh, my. Yes, you are blowing the lid off my liking-you meter, honey."

"Baby, when I first laid eyes on your fine self, you blew my meter sky high. That dress you're wearing has been driving me crazy all night."

"Then I chose the perfect outfit tonight. Trust, these goodies I got under this dress can make you fantasize in the day and make you sweat at night, wondering how much pleasure they can provide you. And FYI, Hot Shot, the pussy is that great!"

"Will you marry me?"

They both laughed.

"Slow down and go handle your business, honey. Hook back up with me after you've handled Juan G."

"How do I do that? Go back up to VIP and get you?"

Shaking her head, she said, "Uh-uh. Just send me another one of these," she said as she held up her glass of Cîroc. "When the waitress brings me a glass of Peach Cîroc, I'll come meet you on the dance floor to let you get that dance you want so badly."

"That's what's up, Nola."

"Don't."

"Don't what?"

"Don't disappoint me, Hot Shot. I'm stepping way out of my comfort zone here."

Staring directly into her light brown eyes, Hot Shot said, "I've never disappointed anyone in my life."

"Don't you fucking start now either," she said as she stood and left him staring at all of that ass as she walked out of the VIP section.

He shook his head, downed the rest of his drink, and muttered, "Man, that woman is fine."

Chapter Three

Even though he left the club by himself, Hot Shot woke up the next morning feeling as if he accomplished more than he intended. The fact that he wasn't able to enjoy the softness of a lovely, country Southern belle was somewhat disappointing. The mere thought of the sexy and desirable Nola made him moan as he climbed out of bed and went to go relieve the pressure from his early-morning hard-on.

After he finished handling his business, he brushed his teeth, washed his face, and then went back into the bedroom, threw on a pair of sweats with his favorite USC tee, and began to stretch.

When he felt he was ready, he started his workout in his living room that consisted of 500 push-ups, 500 sit-ups, and 500 jumping jacks. This was his normal routine every morning, and as usual, he completed the workout within one hour.

After he finished working out, he went into the kitchen and downed a bottle of water and sat down in the dining room while he cooled down. He checked his e-mails along with his text messages to see what he would have to take care of for the day. He smiled when he saw that Nola had sent him a text asking him to give her a call. *Now that's a good way to start a day*, he thought as he continued to go through his texts. His smile disappeared when he read a text from Cotton. He quickly tapped the keys on his smartphone and called his little helper. When

Cotton answered the phone, Hot Shot wasted no time with a greeting.

"Don't talk because I know you will say something stupid, so just listen to me. Meet me at the IHOP off 635. I'll be there in the next thirty minutes, and we'll discuss this Juan G. business. Understood?"

"Yeah, Boss man, I understand."

"Good," Hot Shot replied and ended the call. He then went back to reading his text messages and saw that he had one from JT. He sighed because he wasn't really in the mood to deal with the old man, but he knew it would be best to get that out of the way, so he called JT.

"What up, champ? You good out there?"

With his deep Kentucky drawl on full blast, JT said, "Shit, I should be asking if you're all right, son, especially since I haven't heard from you in a damn week, boy. What you been up to out there in the Lone Star State?"

"Doing what I do best. I haven't had any reason to get at you. So no news is good news, right?"

"That depends. I need to know at all times that you're aboveground and doing well, son. Don't make a habit of giving me this disappearing act. My ulcers can't take that type of shit."

Laughing, Hot Shot said, "You need to quit it. You know you don't have any ulcer problems. You're as healthy as ever."

"Yeah, I guess you're right. So, don't give me any. I assume things have been slow for you since you haven't made any requests?"

"Not really. I've made a few more contacts that will bring in some good money. As a matter of fact, I'm about to meet with my little helper and see what's with something that could be real good for us."

"Now that's what I need to hear. I'll be waiting to hear from you. Stay safe out there, son. All money ain't good money, remember that."

"You just a lie. When it comes to the paper out here with these country fools, I'm getting it in. I'm doing what I need to do, JT. Let me do me, huh?"

"You know you got the green light to get it. I just want you safe. Something wrong with that?"

"Nope. I feel you. I need you to be more focused on getting me information on my family than worrying about me out this way. I'm good."

"You stay good out there, and I'll stay on top of things out this way. When I know something, you'll know something. Until then—"

"I know, stay safe. I'll hit you when I need you, JT," he said as he ended the call and went to take a shower to start his day.

Hot Shot entered the restaurant to see Cotton stuffing his face with a variety of breakfast foods. He sat down, and a waitress quickly appeared at the table ready to take his order. After ordering pancakes, scrambled eggs with cheese, bacon, and orange juice, he turned toward Cotton and said, "Now, what has gotten your panties all in a bunch this morning?"

Cotton wiped his mouth with his napkin and said, "I know you do things the way you want to out here, Boss man, and I respect your get down. I mean, you got me eating good on these streets, and I love that. But there are just some things you can't do out here. I'm out there making moves trying to get ends on a daily grind. I've shown I can move whatever, whenever. Shit, I could get even better for us if you just listen to me sometimes. It's like you be saying fuck what I have to say. Now, I may be a pond in your eyes, but actually, I'm a stronger piece than you're giving me credit for."

Nodding his head in agreement, Hot Shot said, "True. *We* getting this money, and it's going to get better. I can see that. So, what's wrong?"

"What's wrong? You don't arrange a sit-down with one of the top Mexicans in the state, and then basically say fuck him by not giving him the proper respect. Juan G. requested your presence, and you chose to ignore him. That's fucking nuts, Boss man! You can't do shit like that if you trying to really blow and lock shit down out here."

"There's levels to this game, Cotton. You have to understand that I've dealt with all types of levels in this game, and no one, I mean, *no one,* dictates how and when I move. I don't jump when someone calls or requests a meet with me. When I was done getting at Nola, I had all intentions of getting with Juan G. I was walking to his table, and the fool held his hands up to me, signaling for me to wait. So, I went back to the VIP and had another drink. When I saw that that clown was still sitting down there talking on his cell and holding court for all his Latina groupies, I was like, forget that stuff. That's when I hooked back up with Nola and enjoyed the rest of my evening. By the time you came back and told me he was ready to meet with me, I was like, screw him. That's why I left."

"But what if that shit fucked up the money we can make with that Mexican?"

"So what? We move on and get money from someone else. That Mexican runs stuff in the south part of the city. He don't run the entire city. We find more money to make in Dallas. Screw him."

"You're the boss. I'm just saying, that shit could have been avoided."

"You right. If that joker would have treated me with the respect I deserve, then we would have made some positive business moves last night. One thing you have to do is trust me, Cotton. I been doing this a good minute. We gon' be good, and eventually that Mexican still gon' get at us."

"I hope you're right. I'm trying to get me as much as I can and get the fuck outta this game. This shit ain't a long-term thang for me, Boss man."

"I know that's right. You got to be built to last, and some just ain't made for that type of life."

"Are you made like that?"

The waitress came and set his food in front of him. When she left, he said, "Absolutely. I'm going to keep getting money and making these moves like a boss is supposed to. Now tell me, what exactly is Tiny Troy into?"

Cotton rolled his eyes and said, "Come on, Boss man. Damn, you done cracked the fool's family. Now what you trying to do?"

"I told you, I'm trying to get all the money out here. So, what's up with the little man?"

"He fucks with the pills mostly. X and oxy. I heard he was with the pimping too, but I'm not sure. Like I told you last night, he used to fuck with the yay yo too. Don't know too many people who have fucked with him on that tip, though. I do know that Keeta Wee and Weeta Wee are his main men and handle most of his business in the streets."

"All right, I want you to check and see if you can get me some more knowledge on his get down."

"Why?"

"We might be doing some business together in some capacity, and I want to be ready to rock when he gets at me."

"How do you know for sure he will get at you, Boss man?"

"Nola getting at me last night wasn't because she digs my swag, Cotton. If my hunch is right, Tiny Troy gave her the go-ahead to come and check my temperature and peep if I was a solid dude. That, plus she is definitely feeling me."

"What about you? You feeling that broad like that?"

"You better believe it. She is too bad for me not to feel her vibe. As a matter of fact, she already got at me and told me give her a holla, and that's exactly what I'm going to do today. So, if you need something, get at me via text. Don't call me unless it's important."

"I'm good right now, finishing up the tail end of that last package you blessed me with. I do know some of those Bloods out north have been asking around for some heat."

"All right, check and see if their paper is correct. If so, let me know, and we'll put something in motion."

"Cool. Watch yourself with that broad, Boss man. She may be on some grimy shit."

Staring at his helper as he nibbled on a slice of bacon, Hot Shot said, "If she even thinks about crossing me, she will die a slow and painful death. Her, her sister, Keeta Wee, Weeta Wee, and that little man, Tiny Troy. I have yet to display my violent side, Cotton. Mainly because everyone in these streets of Dallas has been straight up with the business, and that's cool, just the way I like it. But trust me, when and if I have to get wicked, I'm nothing nice."

Cotton stared at Hot Shot but couldn't come up with a response suitable, so he chose to remain silent and finish eating his breakfast.

As soon as Hot Shot was inside of his SUV, he activated his Bluetooth and called Nola. He smiled when she answered the phone and said, "Hey, my private dancer. How you doing this morning?"

"Private dancer, huh? That's my label for dancing the night away with you last night?"

"Yep. I hope you enjoyed yourself as much as I did."

"I did. And to answer your first question, I'm fine this morning, honey. You?"

"I'm straight. Just finished having breakfast with my people and now about to bend a few corners. What's on your agenda for the day?"

"Actually, I was hoping we could get together."

"Damn, that quick? You must really be feeling me. I guess my dancing blew the lid off of your liking-me meter."

"Take some off all that swag you got, Hot. Shot," she said and laughed.

"Mmmmmmmm."

"Mmmmmmmm, what?"

"I like how you said my name with that pause in between each word. Say it again for me just like you just did."

"You are too silly."

"No, I'm not. Say it."

The demanding tone in his voice did something to her that made her get a tingly feeling all over her body. "Hot. Shot."

"Yes, I like that. Can't wait either."

"Can't wait for what?"

"I can't wait until I make you say my name just like that while I'm making long, slow love to you."

"Oh, you need to slow your roll, for real there, mister."

"Okay. Everything good comes in time. I'm a very patient man." Switching subjects, he said, "So, you wanted us to get together and . . .?"

"Talk some business."

Just like I thought, he said to himself. "Business?"

"Yeah, like making money type of business."

"Does this business involve your 'associate'?"

"Does it matter?"

"Maybe it does, and maybe it doesn't."

"All of my business concerns him, so if that's a problem, then we can skip that, and you can treat me to an expensive lunch somewhere."

"Even if I'm not interested in doing business with you or your 'associate,' you're still wanting to see me?"

"I don't mix business with pleasure. I like you. Fact. I want to do some business with you because both myself as well as my 'associate' feel we may be able to make some things happen that would benefit us all. Fact. What we do personally, if we do anything on a person level, will have absolutely nothing to do with the business, if there, in fact, is any business handled between us."

"I'm feeling that. I just finished a hearty breakfast, and I don't normally do lunch, so let's get together and do some shopping. I'm in the mood to look for some new gear."

"Now you know that's the real way to capture a woman's heart. Taking her shopping is always a plus."

"You need to hold up there, woman. Who said anything about taking *you* shopping? I said *I* was in the mood to do some shopping, and that *I* needed to look for some new gear."

"You just lost some valuable points toward getting me to say your name. Hot. Shot," she teased flirtatiously.

"You're good, you're really good."

"Honey, you have no idea how good I can be. So, where do you want to meet? I'm twenty minutes outside of Dallas, so we can hook up within an hour or so."

"Meet me at the Grapevine Mall. We'll do some shopping there first and chop it up along the way to see if we can do some business. You never know, I may give in and buy you a few things."

"That's the least of my concerns, honey. You know the perks that can come from that there gesture, so I'm sure I'm going to have a good day shopping with you, Hot. Shot."

"Meet me at the food court, and we'll see, Nola."

"One hour," she said and ended the call.

"Man, I am digging that woman," he said aloud as he turned his SUV onto the highway and headed back toward his downtown condo. He wanted to switch cars. He felt the S8 would be more appropriate for Nola to be riding in with him. Or was he trying to impress her? *Good question*, he thought with a grin on his face.

Chapter Four

Five hours and four malls later, Hot Shot was starving. The meal he had earlier had been totally walked off from strolling around the mall with Nola. Not only could the woman get her shop on, she was expensive! He couldn't front, though, he loved every bit of it. Even though he put more on the Black Card than he intended to, he did enjoy himself watching her do her thing. What touched him most was how after every purchase he made for her she would smile and give him a kiss on the cheek and say, "Thank you, Hot. Shot."

Hot damn, that turned him the hell on! It was time to eat now, and since she had been dropped off at the Grapevine Mall where they first met up, he asked her where she would like to have a late lunch.

She checked her watch and saw that it was close to five p.m. and said, "This will be more like an early dinner, don't you think, honey?"

"Whatever you say, I'm just ready to eat."

"What are you in the mood for?"

"Food, Nola."

"I was going to see if you could impress me more by choosing some place expensive and nice, but since you're so hungry, I'll let you off the hook. Let's do some Pappadeux's. I'm in the mood for some of their fried frog legs and shrimp."

"Fried frog legs and shrimp? Really?"

"Yes, really. Just drive, and you'll see how good they are once we get to the restaurant."

"I highly doubt if I'm going to like that," he said as he turned the car toward the highway, headed to the restaurant.

By the time they finished eating, Hot Shot had to admit that he enjoyed his meal. He refused to eat the fried frog legs but enjoyed several different shrimp dishes that Nola suggested he try. This day had turned out even better than he hoped. Here he was enjoying a nice dinner with a gorgeous woman after enjoying a day of shopping with her. The only way this day could get any better was if he could get Nola out of that sexy red sundress she was wearing, he thought and smiled.

As if reading his mind, Nola smiled and said, "You're close, Hot. Shot. But not *that* close. Be patient."

"What are you talking about?"

She stared at him for a moment before replying. "Nothing. All right, let's get the business side of things out the way so we can see if you'll be interested in what we need."

He relaxed back in his seat and said, "Okay, holla at me."

"Kush, by the pounds. Can you get us that at a good price?"

"Definitely. The best the West has to offer."

"Oxycodone and X-pills?"

"No problem."

"Cocaine, powder only, at least five–ten kilos a month?"

Hot Shot stifled a yawn and asked, "Anything else?"

"That's it, smart-ass. Now, what kind of prices are we talking about here?"

"Depends."

"On?"

"On how much you trying to get. My money comes from several different ways. I get love for the prices on all of the drugs, but I charge for the transportation and delivery. So if you spend good, the prices will be good. The cocaine I can get you for 22,000 a kilo. The Kush a little over 2,000 a pound. The oxy and X, 5,000 a bundle."

"Those are some nice prices."

"I know. But you will add $2,500 to every delivery for getting it out this way. That, plus paying my people who bring it to me, which will be another $2,500 per delivery. So, let's say you get five kilos of cocaine, five pounds of Kush and ten bundles of oxy and X, that would be five Gs for the delivery of the oxy and X, then another five Gs for the delivery of the cocaine and weed."

"That's fair. I'm sure Tiny Troy won't have a problem with that."

"Okay, cool. Now that we've had this discussion, we need to set up a time for me to have a sit-down with Tiny Troy so we can have a face-to-face. I don't deal with go-betweens. No matter how gorgeous they are."

"I figured you'd say something like that. That's why I had Lola drop me off at the mall. When we're finished here, let's go to DG's."

"The strip club?"

"Yes."

His eyes lit up when he asked, "You're into that type of thing?"

"Every time you take my liking-you meter to a higher level, you say something stupid to decrease your momentum. Though I do admire a beautiful woman, I'm not interested in them at all other than looking. Tiny Troy, Lola, Keeta Wee, and Weeta Wee are going to meet us there; that is, if you don't have any other plans."

He checked his watch and said, "Let me check with my mans and see." He then pulled out his phone and called

Cotton. When Cotton answered, he asked him, "Say, how did that thing go with you and the red team?"

"I was just about to call you, Boss man. They want to holla at us for sure and what they trying to cop is major."

"When?"

"Whenever you're ready."

"They understand that I have to get half before I can move?"

"Yep, and they ain't tripping."

"Where are you?"

"Out south at Big T's Bazaar."

"All right, meet me at my place in twenty minutes. We'll finish this discussion then and decide how we will move with them."

"Cool. Oh, Juan G. got at me. How he got my number is beyond my ass, but he said that he wants yo to give him a call."

"I told you."

"Yeah, I guess you had that one right, Boss man. But you still got to lighten up sometimes."

"Whatever, you extrasensitive clown. See you in twenty minutes," he said and ended the call. "We need to make a quick stop by my place, then we can head to DG's."

"That's fine," Nola said with a grin on her face.

"What's the grin for?"

She shrugged and said, "Nothing. Just check you out, Hot. Shot."

He rolled his eyes and said, "Whatever. Come on, let's shake this spot so I can handle some business."

By the time they made it to his condominium, Cotton was already there waiting. When he saw Hot Shot's car ease into the underground garage, he got out of his car and met them at the elevator bank. They rode in the elevator in silence mainly because Cotton was shocked to see Nola with him. His demeanor showed this, and that made Hot Shot laugh out loud.

"What's so funny?" asked Nola.

"My mans here is uncomfortable with me letting you know where I rest my head. He looks like he has a bad case of gas, huh?" Hot Shot said and laughed some more.

Cotton said nothing as he continued to stare at the doors of the elevator. *Your ass gon' wish you would have listened to me when that grimy bitch gets you twisted*, he said to himself. To Hot Shot, he said, "Did you get at the Mexican?"

"Nope. After I change clothes real quick and we chop it up, I was going to take care of that. Hopefully, I'll be able to set up a meeting with him tonight so we can get that going as well. It looks like we're going to have a busy week," he said as the elevator made it to his floor and the doors opened. Hot Shot led the way to his condo and was followed closely by both Nola and Cotton. Once they were inside, he told them they could have a seat while he went into his room to change clothes real quick. He wanted to put on something more comfortable for the strip club.

Nola smiled as she sat down on what looked like an expensive Italian leather sofa. She noticed some of the tasteful pieces of artwork that hung on the wall and had to admit that Hot Shot had some class about himself. *Yeah, he's going to get some pussy. I just don't know when*, she thought as she relaxed on the sofa.

"So, you're feeling Boss man, huh?"

Nola gave Cotton a look as if he were beneath her but chose to remain cordial and said, "Yes, he seems sweet. How long have you two been friends?"

"We hooked up when he first got out here a few months back. Ever since then, it's been all about getting that bread."

"I see. Where are you from? I think I've seen you around the way before."

"Yeah, I've seen you out and about. I'm from North Dallas, but I get around the town a lot," Cotton said confidently.

Before Nola could respond, Hot Shot returned to the living room and said, "You know you wrong for trying to question my mans. Stop that, Nola." Without giving her time to speak, he turned to Cotton. "Come in the back room with me real quick." He turned and stepped toward the back without saying another word to Nola.

Well, that was nice and rude. Shit, actually, it was a damn turn-on. It's been a long time since I've met a man that can handle me and be about his business. Yeah, you definitely getting some pussy, Hot Shot, she thought as she continued to relax on his sofa.

When they made it to the back bedroom, Hot Shot closed the door behind Cotton and said, "You know better than to be answering any questions from that broad."

"I thought you was feeling her, so I figured it was cool."

"Nah, you let me handle that end of that, whether I'm feeling her or not. Never let anyone check your temperature, Cotton, especially when it comes to how you and I get down. Our business is our business, and if I ever hear about you running your mouth excessively about our business, we will no longer have any business for you to blab about. You got me?"

"Yeah, I got you, Boss man."

"What's up with those Bloods?"

"I spoke with the main dude, Tone. He outta Abilene, but he runs shit down this way with the red team. He wants the heavy shit. He spoke of some guns I never heard of, so I wrote them down, and he said if we can get this, then he would rock with us for certain," Cotton said as he pulled out a list and gave it to Hot Shot.

Hot Shot accepted the list, read it, and grinned. *This dude is serious about his choice of weapons,* he thought.

"I can handle this. It will take me about a day or two, but there shouldn't be any problem getting him any of these guns. What the heck does he need all these weapons for? Are the Bloods out here about to go to war or something?"

"I don't know, and honestly, I couldn't care less. All I'm interested in is that bread."

"You better say it, champ. Okay, make the call and let them know we need to set a time and hook up. Get back at me and let me know what we gon' do. I'm about to go hang with Nola and Tiny Troy. Looks like they want to do some business so I'm going to have a meeting with him to see what he talking about."

"You called that one right on the money, Boss man."

"Yes, I know. I knew when she came to get at me it wasn't only because she was feeling me. She was checking my temp on the cool. No way would that little guy send her to me for any other reason. Anyway, go on and handle that business and get at me later on."

"What about Juan G.? You gon' make that call or what?"

"I'll get at him after I see what's what with Tiny Troy. Do you need anything, 'cause if you do, you need to get at me before I make this next order so we can tackle all of this at one time?"

"Might as well hit me off with at least four bundles; two of the X and two of the oxy. And about three gallons of syrup."

"All right, you make sure the ends is right from the last round, and everything you want will be on deck."

"I gotcha, Boss man."

"Cool. Now, let me go entertain my guest so we can see what's with the notorious Tiny Troy." They both started laughing as they stood and went back into the living room.

When the men returned to the living room, Nola was still sitting on the sofa, but now she was having a conversation that seemed to be somewhat heated on her phone. When she saw Hot Shot and Cotton, she brought the conversation she was having to an end.

"Look, I'm getting ready to go now. I'll see you in a little bit, bye," she said as she ended the call. She then glared at Hot Shot and asked, "Are you finished with your business because we have business that needs to be addressed like pronto, honey. Certain people are getting on my damn nerves, and that has fucked off my mood."

"Sorry to hear that, Nola. Let's roll," Hot Shot said as he grabbed his keys and waited for her to stand. As they left the condo, he couldn't help but stare at all of that ass she was packing in that sundress she was wearing.

Sensing his eyes were on her ass, she stopped abruptly, turned around, and faced both men. Shaking her head, she said, "You two need to keep your minds on your money and not my ass. Especially your ass, Hot Shot, because at the rate you're losing all your bonus points, you won't be able to recoup the losses from my liking-you meter. Now, come on!"

Watching her storm off toward the elevator gave her ass even more sway when she walked, and both Cotton and Hot Shot smiled. "There is nothing sexier than an angry black woman with a big booty, Cotton, never forget that."

"You got that right, Boss man!"

Chapter Five

By the time they arrived at DG's, which stands for Dallas Gentlemen's Club, the parking lot of the popular strip club was packed. After finding the closest parking space to the front of the club, Hot Shot turned off the car and faced Nola. "Listen, just because I'm feeling you doesn't lock in whether I'll do business with your 'associate.'"

"Ugh! Brother! He's my *brother*, Hot Shot, so we can kill that 'associate' crap. He's my older brother. And Keeta Wee and Weeta Wee are my cousins. Yes, we're one big happy friggin' family, okay? And for God's sake, don't speak of this to them when we have this meeting. I'm already highly irritated by the fact that they feel it's up to me to make this all go down just because your ass is feeling me. I'm so not needing this kind of pressure right now. So, if you do or don't, that's on you. I feel we can all win, and you and I can really win, but that is two totally separate issues. If you do get down with us, then cool; if you don't, then that's cool too. We will make whatever we make work, regardless. Now, come on so we can let my brother try to impress your ass."

"From what I heard, he has shit on lock. Why would he need to impress me?"

"I told him about your plugs in the West and your prices, and he feels the timing for this happening is perfect. The last people he's been dealing with are acting funny style, so he wanted to get away from them. That's why he feels that we need to impress."

"We, huh?"

"Yeah, we."

He reached across the seat, grabbed her hand, gave it a squeeze, and said, "You impressed me when I first laid eyes on you, Nola. For what it's worth, you will be the reason why I do business with your brother, so don't trip. And don't insult me by even thinking I expect you to give me anything for making that decision. Business is business. Anything else that comes to be with us is because we both want it like that. Feel me?"

She smiled at him and replied, "Yes, I feel you, Hot. Shot."

"*Sssss,* see, there you go with that again. Come on, woman, let's go holla at your brother. By the way, I knew that Tiny Troy was related to you in some way. Didn't figure he was your brother, though."

"And how did you figure that out?"

"Like I told Tiny Troy at the club last night, when you walked into the club you weren't walking in as if you two were intimately attached. So, it was a basic feeling I had from that observation. That, plus your sister was peeping at every other dude in the club that she seemed to like while in his presence."

"Mmm. Are you always that observant?"

He stared at her as they walked toward the club and answered honestly. "Always. I play this game to win, and I have to make sure that I remain on point in all facets of it."

She smiled. "Okay, you're really back to impressing me here. Stop that."

"Why? I thought impressing you was a good thing."

"It is. But not right now 'cause you're making me have thoughts that don't pertain to business, and that is somewhat disconcerting right now."

"Disconcerting?"

"In other words, you're making me wet."

With a grin on his face, he muttered, "I hope we can do something about that."

"I heard that. Come on, Hot. Shot." She led the way inside of the club and quickly spotted her brother, sister, and her two cousins sitting at a table at the back of the club. Once they were at the table, Nola frowned at her brother and said, "All right, here he is. I need to use the bathroom. Why don't you come with me, Lola, so Troy and Hot Shot can talk."

Lola smiled at Hot Shot and said, "You do know what they say about female twins, right? When one is attracted to a man, the other twin is even more attracted to him. That then makes them real aggressive. On top of that, female twins are known to share everything."

"Everything?"

Looking him up and down and smiling while licking her lips, she said, "*Everything.*"

"Bitch, would you bring your nasty ass on!" Nola said and pulled her sister away while both started laughing.

Tiny Troy shook his head and pointed toward the seat across from him and said, "Have a seat, Hot Shot. Please excuse the girls. They can get wild at times. You know how it is, huh?"

"Not really, never been with a set of twins before. She did make it sound enticing, though."

There was a flicker of change in Tiny Troy's facial expression, but he quickly smiled to mask this, just not quickly enough for Hot Shot not to notice. *Mmm, an overprotective big brother, huh?* he thought as he sat back and waited for Tiny Troy to speak.

"Yeah, I know what you're saying. Look at this, though, Nola told me the prices you gave her, and as long as your work is on hit, then I want to fuck with you."

"Just like that? You don't know me from Adam. I could be an informant, police—anything. A jack boy for all you know. You get down with people you don't know that easily?"

Laughing, Tiny Troy said, "Nah, I'm a tad bit more thorough than that, Hot Shot. I have plugs in several key places, and one thing you gotta know about Dallas, Texas, is, the people talk on these streets. You've been out here for a little over three months. Since that time, you hooked up with Cotton, who is from North Dallas. Cotton e-moved everything for you from Kush, yay, X-pills, and oxy. He also lets it be known that you can even get guns on a large scale, if requested. Since you've hooked up with Cotton, his hustle game has elevated greatly. The few dudes you do deal with have spoken highly enough of you that I feel comfortable with us doing some business together; that is, if you *want* to do some business with me."

"You've based your decision on dealing with me because of Cotton's moves since I've been in town?"

"That, and the fact that I had your name run through the NCIC by some of my people who work for Dallas PD."

"Really? So you're saying you know my real name and all?"

Taking a sip of a bottled water he had in his hand, Tiny Troy said, "Yep, sure do, Mr. Jason Gaines from Inglewood, California. Age thirty-one, one prior conviction for possession of cocaine for sale, accepted three years' summary probation, and had the felony knocked off your jacket down to a misdemeanor back in 2007."

"Impressive."

"Tell me, are you trying to let me spend my money, or what? I'm a busy man, and this part of the hustle is key to some major business that I'm a part of. Shit goes good for the both of us, then maybe I can pull you in on the bigger scheme of things."

Nodding, Hot Shot said, "I'm feeling that. What exactly do you need?"

"Twenty pounds of Kush, five kilos of powder, five bundles of X-pills, and five bundles of oxy."

"I assume Nola gave you my figures along with my taxes and delivery fees, so let me see, that would mean for twenty pounds of Kush, five birds of yay yo, five bundles of X-pills, and five bundles of oxy, you will have to come off $370,000."

"Damn, you added that all in your head that fast?"

"This is what I do, Tiny Troy. You do know that I need half of the money up front, right?"

"Nah, I didn't know that, but I don't have a problem with it. You don't strike me as the type to play games with my paper."

"I sure hope not, because that would mean me and my brother here will be sent to get dead on your ass, nigga," said Keeta Wee.

In a flash, Hot Shot was out of his seat and in Keeta Wee's face with his right hand locked in a death grip around his throat, choking the shit out of him.

"I told you the last time we spoke not to call me that N-word ever again. Just because you have the size and numbers here does *not* mean you will win messing with me. I can crush your windpipe right now, and then handle your brother as well as Tiny Troy without breaking a sweat. Do. You. Understand. Me. Keeta. Wee?" Hot Shot asked as he squeezed the man's throat a little tighter.

After Keeta Wee gave a slight nod of understanding, Hot Shot pushed him away and calmly sat back in his seat facing the other twin who remained seated throughout that brief encounter with a shocked expression on his face.

"If you even think of trying to make a move, Weeta Wee, your fate will be worse than your brother's." He turned and faced Tiny Troy and said, "I am very big on respect. I give it, and I demand it in return. I don't curse at people, nor do I refer to any black man as that N-word. I'm about my business in every way, and I will stand on my product. If you have any issues, you will get your money back for whatever you bring me. I stand on everything I say, and believe me, I have no problem getting violent. I prefer to handle business on some real time, but if it's time to get gangsta, I can take it there better than any man you have ever seen. If your security/bodyguards here ever tries me or think they can move on me in any aggressive way after this minor altercation, understand that they will put themselves in a situation that will cause them some serious pain. If they continue to push the issue after that, then you might as well get them suited for some black suits. Am I understood, Tiny Troy?"

With the same shocked expression on his face that Weeta Wee had, Tiny Troy shook his head and said, "Damn, I've never seen a ni—I mean a man move that fucking fast. I feel you, though, Hot Shot. These are my bodyguards/security. They will go above and beyond for me and my girls."

"They should know when and when not to speak. Two big men seems like overkill to me, but that's my opinion. I'm sure they have your best interest and safety at heart, but they have to understand that just because of their size, they don't intimidate everyone, especially me."

"I feel that. But it's always better to have them around when some suckers might think they can try me. I'm a small man, so I'm used to having big things or big men around me. I must stay safe at all times."

"I understand."

He stared at Weeta Wee whose shocked expression had turned to one of anger. "Are we going to have a problem, Weeta Wee? If so, we might as well get it out the way right now."

Before Weeta Wee could answer his question, Nola and Lola returned to the table, and each of the twins could sense that something had gone wrong. Nola went to Hot Shot's side and put her hand on his shoulder while Lola went to her brother's side and asked, "What's going on, Troy?"

Tiny Troy started laughing and said, "Everything is all good. Ain't that right, Weeta Wee?"

"Yeah, everything is all good. I heard you loud and clear, Hot Shot. We good, just understand that all big men ain't easily got."

"If you say so, my man," Hot Shot said as he turned back to Tiny Troy and said, "Well, it's understood then, the quicker you get me that 185 racks, the quicker I can make the call and have your order filled."

"I'll have Nola bring it to you in the morning then."

"No, you won't. You'll have Lola bring it to him. I'll already be with him in the morning," she said as she gave Hot Shot's shoulder a squeeze.

Laughing, Tiny Troy said, "Dammit, man, you done stole my girl!"

"Stop it, Troy, he knows. He figured that shit out at the club last night. He's far from lame like these Dallas niggas."

When hearing his sister say the word "nigga," Tiny Troy tensed as he stared at Hot Shot.

Hot Shot looked up at Nola from his seat and said, "Could you please not use that word around me, Nola. It's offensive and very insulting to us as a people."

She was about to say something slick but saw the look of fear on her brother's face as well as her cousins' faces and said, "My bad, honey. Now if the business has been handled, let's get up out of here. Or do you want to go get a couple of lap dances from some of the girls here first?" she asked with raised eyebrows.

"No, I think I'm ready to go too," he answered sheepishly.

"Great idea, Hot. Shot." She turned and faced her brother and said, "Give me a holla when Lola is ready to bring me the money, and I'll come meet her."

"That won't be necessary. She can come to my place," Hot Shot said as he jotted down his address on a napkin and passed it to Lola.

"I respect you and how you rock, Hot Shot. Since you know that Nola and Lola are my sisters, I hope that you will respect her. You've displayed some real shit tonight, but don't think that you're the only man here that can get wicked. Feel me? 'Cause when it comes to my family, I am willing to go all out."

Hot Shot stood and reached out his hand across the table and shook hands with Tiny Troy and said, "Like I said earlier, I am a man of respect. I give it at all times, just as I demand it in return. Now if you will excuse me, I'm now placing myself in the very capable hands of your little sister here."

"That's right, Hot. Shot. Let's go!" Nola said laughing as she pulled him away from the table and out of the strip club.

After they left the table, Weeta Wee grunted and said, "I cannot wait to look at that nigga."

"Me too," added Keeta Wee.

"You two niggas need to shut the fuck up. That nigga checked the fuck outta all y'all's asses. Makes me wonder if I need to hire me some real muscle for my bodyguards/security."

"What happened while we were in the bathroom?" asked Lola.

Laughing, Tiny Troy stood and said, "Ask your big, scary-ass cousins! Come on, I'm ready to go. We got some money to count and get ready for Hot Shot."

Chapter Six

"Oh my! Yes, honey, yes! Just like that, honey, right there! You licking me something good, honey, please don't stop! You! Are! Making! Me! Come!" Nola screamed as she held on tightly to Hot Shot's head as he fucked and licked her pussy to a very satisfying orgasm.

Without letting her catch her breath, he quickly mounted her and eased his dick inside of her soaking wet pussy. She moaned as he filled her up with his more-than-ample-size tool and quickly wrapped her long legs around his waist and tried to help him get even deeper inside of her.

"Oh, I knew you would be packing, honey, I knew it! Give it to me! Give it to me! Give it to Nola real hard. Hit this pussy, honey! Hit it!" she screamed as she dug her nails deep in his back.

Not being much of a talker during sex, Hot Shot couldn't hide the fact that she was turning him on even more with her heated words. The more she talked, the harder and deeper he tried to bury his dick inside of her pussy. When she reached around and grabbed his ass cheeks and squeezed, that was what did him in. He came so long and hard that he felt faint. Nola was sweating so much that she soaked the sheets, not caring at all as he rolled off of her right onto the wet sheets and sighed.

"Wow," he said as he tried to catch his breath.

"Wow is right, honey, that was sooooo good! You worked me right, Hot. Shot. But you do know that we're far from done. That was round one, and I intend to go the distance, ya hear?"

"Whatever you say, Nola. You just have to give me a sec to catch my breath."

"No problem, catch your breath. I'll be right back," she said as she got out of the bed and went into the other room.

Too tired to even think about where she went, he smiled as he watched her leave the bedroom naked. Tall, slender with all that ass, plus some great pussy. . . . A deadly combo if he'd ever seen one, he thought as he relaxed and closed his eyes.

"Oh no, you don't! Wake up, Hot Shot!" Nola yelled as she stood next to the bed staring down at him. When he opened his eyes, she smiled and said, "Here," and gave him a bottled water that she grabbed from his refrigerator. "This will rehydrate you for the work you put in and the work you're about to put in."

Sitting up and accepting the bottle of water, he gratefully started drinking. When he finished, he said, "That was what I needed. Now come here."

She smiled and slid next to him, and he wrapped his arms around her, and they shared a tender kiss that instantly turned passionate. Nola broke from their kiss and slid down to his crotch and pulled the used condom off of him and tossed it on the floor and quickly put her mouth around his semihard dick. She then began to give him some of the best fellatio he'd ever experienced in his entire life. He closed his eyes and enjoyed her warm, wet mouth as she sucked away. He was so hard and turned on now that he knew he would be coming soon so he tried to pull her up so he wouldn't explode inside of her mouth.

Nola stopped for a moment and looked up at him from his dick and said, "I just came like gangbusters inside of your mouth, so it's only right I reciprocate. Hold on tight,

Hot. Shot, 'cause it's about to go down. Don't you take your eyes off me, ya hear? Don't close them. I want you to see what I'm about to do to you," she said as she went back to sucking and licking his dick. She stared at him the entire time as she licked up and down his shaft slowly. When she put his balls inside of her mouth and began to hum, he moaned loudly. She worked her way back to his dick and sucked him hard as she took him deep inside of her mouth. When she felt him hit the back of her throat, she took it like a pro, no gagging or choking. She inhaled deeply and breathed through her nose as she sucked every inch of him, all the while never once taking her eyes off him. When he tried to close his eyes, she stopped sucking his dick and said, "No, honey, you have to keep your eyes open and watch me." She then went back to work sucking him faster and faster and pumping his shaft with her right hand until he moaned louder, signaling that he was about to come. "That's right, now bust for me, Hot. Shot. Bust," she said as her hand worked him faster and faster. Just as he started to come, she wrapped her mouth back around him and caught every last drop of his semen.

"Ugh! Nola!" he screamed as she gave him the best feeling he ever had. When the last tingling sensation ended, he shook his head and said, "Whoa. You gots to marry me!"

Laughing, she said, "Come on, honey, we've just gotten started. If you thought that was something, wait until I put this pussy on you right. You ain't seen nothing yet."

Almost two hours later, he realized that she wasn't just talking noise. She put that pussy on him so good that he was ready to do whatever she wanted him to do. He knew that he was in love, with that pussy, that is. Those were his last thoughts before he fell into a deep sleep.

***

When Hot Shot woke up the next morning, Nola was gone. He got up and went to use the bathroom. After getting himself together he went into the living room and began to stretch for his morning workout, even though he felt he could skip it because Nola gave him one hell of a workout just a few hours ago, and he was sure that that was some serious cardio he put in. He laughed out loud as he turned on his music and let the lyrics of Tupac and The Notorious B.I.G. consume him as he started to work out. As he was finishing his last set of push-ups, Nola came walking through his front door as if she lived with him for years. She jumped and dropped the brown leather Gucci bag she was holding and screamed, "Don't shoot me, honey!"

When he had heard the key being turned in his front door, he stopped instantly and grabbed the H&K .40-caliber pistol he kept close to him at all times when at home and aimed it directly at the door and waited to see who was opening it. When he saw that it was Nola, he lowered his weapon and calmly said, "Never do that again, Nola. You almost got shot."

With her right hand across her chest she sighed and said, "Shit, I see that. Who did you think I was? You had to know it was me, honey. I took your car to go get with my sister to get that money. Didn't you notice your keys were gone?"

"Nope. Was kinda out of it when I woke up. Didn't pay that any attention. Sorry for scaring you, but I'm not used to anyone walking in that door with my key but me."

"I see you like packing big guns. . . . That one right there as well as that big ol' one between them thighs."

"Always. I take my security serious, just as I take my sex game equally serious. I take it you enjoyed yourself last night?"

"Yes, pat yourself on the back, honey, because you did good. Real good. Now come over here so you can count your money. I don't need my brother calling and irritating me asking me if everything has been handled."

"Toss it on the table. It's all good. No need to count it. It'll be counted when my people get it. I'm about to take a shower, and then we can go get something to eat; that is, if you don't have any other plans."

"None whatsoever. Want me to join you?"

"No. I need to save some energy. If you get in that shower with me, I will end up getting back in that good of yours, and that will sap what energy I have left. I need food in me before I can even think about trying to get something started with you again, Nola."

"Okay, go on and take your time. I'll make you something to eat while you're in there."

"And she cooks as well. What else do you have in your bag of tricks?"

"Oh, honey, you ain't seen nothing yet. You know they say us Texans are known for doing everything big. Keep that in mind, so when we get into that sack again, you can at least be somewhat prepared for me and my big old appetite. Now go, shower and get yourself together. The food will be close to done by the time you're finished."

He turned and went and did as he was told with a silly smile on his face. He was definitely enjoying Nola's company and wondered if he would be able to keep on seeing her. That thought shocked him. "Never thought I would ever seriously think about being with a female out this way," he said out loud to himself as he entered the bathroom.

When Hot Shot came into the kitchen, he was shocked to see that Nola had prepared him a breakfast fit for a king. She had home fried potatoes, scrambled eggs with bell peppers and onions, bacon, sausage, and he could smell some biscuits baking in the oven.

"My God, woman, that smells good. Who else is joining us for breakfast, because I know I can't eat all of this food, Nola?"

She smiled sheepishly and said, "Sorry, honey. I don't know how to cook no other way. Used to cooking a lot of food. Don't worry. If we don't eat it all, we can save some and warm it up later on. Now come sit your butt down. The biscuits should be done in a minute. Sorry, I didn't have enough time to bake you some from scratch. I had to use that Pillsbury Doughboy stuff you had in the fridge. I swear, you city boys just don't understand," she said laughing as she pulled the pan of biscuits out of the oven and set them on the table in the dining room. By the time they finished eating, Hot Shot felt as if he were going to burst. The food had been delicious.

He pushed away from the table and said, "Okay, you've officially ruined my entire day. All I want to do now is go back to bed and sleep the rest of the day away."

"You know you can't be doing none of that stuff, honey. Don't you got to handle that business for my brother?"

"Yes, I guess you're right. Plus, I need to check with my mans and see what he has up for me today. As a matter a fact, I wonder why that joker hasn't called me by now." Right on cue, Hot Shot's cell rang. When he saw that it was Cotton, he said, "I guess I spoke that one up. Excuse me, Nola." He then answered the phone. "What up, champ, you good?"

"I'm straight, what about you?"

"Everything is everything. About to get the day started and take care of some B. T. What you got going?"

"Need to get with you this afternoon so we can hook up with those Bloods."

"All right, I'll hit you around two. I'm going to make a few runs, and then we can put that in order. I'm also going to give that Mexican a holla too. Anything else?"

"Nah, that's it."

"I'll hit you when I'm ready," Hot Shot said and ended the call.

He then called JT and told him that he had some that would be coming his way. "I got a pretty big order I'm about to blast your way in the next hour or so. When do you think you'll get back?"

"Twenty-four hours after I get that from you."

"Cool."

"Everything all right out that way, son? Any problems?"

"Nope. Making the necessary moves as always."

"Keep up the good work then."

"Will do. You got anything for me, JT?"

"Stop asking me that. When I have something for you, you will be the first to know, Hot Shot. Stay focused on the money."

"Whatever," he said and ended the call. He turned and faced Nola and said, "This is how it's going to happen. I'm about to overnight the ends to my people in the West. Twenty-four hours after he gets it, I'll get everything your brother ordered."

"How in the hell are you going to overnight all that money, honey?"

He stared at her with a blank expression on his face and said, "Through the mail. Package it up and mail it express mail, and its guaranteed to arrive within twenty-four hours."

"Just like that? You take almost $200,000 to the post office and mail it overnight express mail? It's that simple?"

"Most things in life are that simple, Nola. People tend to make things more difficult than they really are. Tell me, if you were the people, would you expect for anyone to mail that kind of money through the post office?"

Shaking her head, she answered honestly, "No, I wouldn't."

"Exactly. Simple. Believe me, Nola, simple is good."

"I feel you, honey. Can you tell me something?"

"What's up?"

"Why do you have a problem with the N-word, for real? Lola told me you almost hurt Keeta Wee last night for calling you that word."

"I was raised to respect myself as well as my race. Using that word is degrading to me and our race. I don't like it, and I will not be called it, nor will I let anyone around me use that word."

"So, whoever says that around you, you just gon' go off and choke them out like you did Keeta Wee?"

"I normally give a warning first. Just like I did Keeta Wee. When you don't take heed to my warning, that's pretty much what will happen . . . that . . . or worse."

"You can't make people speak the way you want them to, honey."

"This is true. But it angers me to hear people use that word."

"Still, you need to control your anger, honey. You got issues," she said and smiled at him to take some sting from her words.

"There are many reasons why I have anger issues, Nola, trust me. I'm not out of control angry, and that's what matters most. A fool gives full vent to his anger, but a wise man keeps himself under control."

"Mmm, and you know your Bible. That comes from Proverbs, correct?"

"Yes. Proverbs 29:11 to be exact. I'm no one's fool, but I've been known to act like one. For the most part, I like to look at myself as a wise man."

"Again, you've impressed me, honey."

"I do try to impress those I deem worthy of impressing," he said with the hint of a smile on his face.

"If that's the case, then smile for me. You've yet to show me that smile of yours. Why?"

With a shrug, he answered, "Don't like to smile too often. Doesn't mean I'm not a happy man."

"That's understandable, but your demeanor gives off the impression that you are cold and distant. Even the music you listen to seems somewhat depressing."

"What's depressing about Tupac, B.I.G., or Eazy-E?"

She stared at him for a moment, then said, "Honey, there is one thing you should know about Nola. I am very observant too. Nothing is depressing about those particular rappers, but they are all dead. I noticed yesterday when we were leaving each mall you seem to have a fixation with musicians that are no longer living. Teddy Pendergrass, Marvin Gaye, Whitney Houston. Even when you listen to rap music, you went so far as to play Big Pun, Big L, Nate Dogg, and Mac Dre. While you were sexing me crazy, you were playing Minnie Riperton, Barry White, Luther Vandross, Gerald Levert, Teena Marie, and Rick James. Though their music is great, that had me wondering what has you on that. And that is what makes that music seem somewhat depressing to me."

"I've never really paid any attention to that. I like what I like. Again, I have my reasons, and if you stick around me long enough, I'll share them with you."

She smiled at him and said, "I like to think I'll be around you for a good minute. Like I said, you've impressed me greatly."

"That's a good thing for you blessing me with your presence. I will try my best to be more cordial.'"

Shaking her head, she said, "Uh-uh, honey. If you have to *try* to be more festive around me, it will come across as being fake, and nothing about a fake person impresses me. Stick to being yourself and everything will be fine."

"I like that. Like the Bible says, an honest answer is like a kiss on the lips."

"Proverbs again?"

"Yes. Proverbs 24:26."

"Never knew that a man who could quote the Bible would turn me on. You have many talents, Hot Shot."

"This is true."

"Can you answer a question for me?"

"Sure."

"Were you going to hurt Keeta Wee for calling you the N-word?"

"Yes, I was. He'd been warned, and if he had chosen to ignore me and fight back, he, along with his twin brother, would have been hurt. How bad would have depended on them. When I go there, I try to remain controlled, but at the same time, I will never let a man hurt me, Nola. Never. The reason I chose not to hurt Keeta Wee was because I didn't want to disrespect your brother. That wouldn't have been a good way to start a new business relationship," he said and grinned.

With a smirk on her face, Nola said, "Ya think? I told you about Tiny Troy being my brother, and that Keeta Wee and Weeta Wee are our cousins as well. Do me a fave, honey. If they try you or slip up and use that word again, can you let them make it with one more warning?"

"You got that, Nola. But please understand, if I feel any form of disrespect is being shown, I will turn up on them without hesitation."

Nola's sense of relief was evident in her tone of voice. "I understand, honey, and I will make sure that they know not to try you like that. My family means a lot to me, honey. I care for them deeply. They're all I have."

He stared at her lovely brown eyes for a full minute before speaking. "Not true, Nola. You have me now."

Chapter Seven

Nola had Lola come and pick her up from the parking lot of the post office after Hot Shot sent their money to the West Coast for their drug purchases. She still couldn't believe he was sending all of that money through the express mail. As long as it worked, she was cool with it, and she was sure her brother would be too. She hoped and prayed that everything went right with this new business venture with Hot Shot, because if things went wrong, it could get really ugly. She knew her brother and how dangerous he could be, and at the same time, she sensed a calm about Hot Shot that made her feel as if he was equally as deadly as her brother—if not more, and that thought scared her to death. Not only did she not want them to get into it, she actually feared that the man she was falling extremely too damn fast for would make her have to choose between her and her blood. And that thought was unbearable.

Thinking about Hot Shot made her feel queasylike in the stomach. He actually made her feel as if she were a teenager again with a mean crush. That man was doing something to her that she couldn't comprehend. Everything he did and said was right. He was intelligent, sexy, a body to kill for, and even was well versed in the Bible, for God's sake. Jeez, everything about him was perfect. He was gangster, and that tipped the scale in his favor entirely because she never wanted a man who couldn't stand on his own and demand respect. Sure, there were a lot of men like this who didn't have that gangster swagger in their lives, but that wasn't what she looked for in a man. She loved that gangster swag and mentality. It showed her strength, and she loved men like that. That's another reason why she chose to be single. She refused to fuck with just any man, and there was an extreme shortage of the type of men she liked in Dallas, Texas. Nola's zest for living was enticing nothing but the best at all times. Where Hot Shot was so calm and laid back, she was gregarious and vivacious. Her easy-to-get-along-with personality was infectious, and she could tell she had definitely affected Hot Shot in a good way. That thought made her smile as she relaxed inside of her sister's car.

With a smirk on her face, Lola told her twin, "Now you know damn well you need to take that 'I just got the shit fucked real good out of me' look off your face, Nola." They both started laughing.

"Honey, that man! That's all I can say. That! Man!"

"Whoa. He must be packing a monster between them legs."

"You can only dream of something that big and good, Lola; trust and believe me."

"You know you are making me way too jealous right about now. Come on, tell me more, because I know by that look on your face you are not going to share none of that fine-ass man with me."

Nola frowned at her sister and said, "You got that right. So don't you go there with him, Lola. I mean that shit."

"All right."

"I meant that shit, Lola," she repeated.

"I said all right. Damn. Now tell me more about this stud of yours. Is he vertical or what?"

"Straight up and down all the way. On the business side, I don't have a doubt in the world that he will handle up.

He doesn't strike me as a roach-type nigga. He has the connect, and he wouldn't play with our money."

"He better not because you know your brother would get stupid behind that."

"Yeah, I know. That's something else about Hot Shot. He is a no-nonsense type of man too. He won't play no games, and he damn sure won't let any be played with him. That nig—that *man* is dangerous, Lola."

"Look at you. What, you gon' stop saying the word 'nigga' now?" Lola laughed.

"As a matter fact, I'm trying. It's a matter of respect with Hot Shot, and I not only dig his sexy-fine-big-dick self, I respect his get down, and I will do my best to show and give him that respect. And I really think we need to stress that shit to Keeta Wee and Weeta Wee's asses because I know they are planning to try him at some point in time and that won't be good, Lola. Hot Shot ain't no punk."

"Damn, I've never heard you give a man that much props. He must have really put it on your ass last night."

Shaking her head, she said, "Not only did he put it on me great, he showed me that he's a real man. No faking with him. He speaks it as he sees it, and he ain't scared of shit. The man is a gangsta, trust and believe that."

"I believe you. You're right. We have to make sure that Keeta Wee and Weeta Wee don't try him. We don't need none of that mess getting in the way of the business."

"Exactly."

"Now tell me, did he eat you up too, or is he one of those types that likes to get knee-deep in the pussy with his tool only?" Lola asked as she licked her lips, eagerly waiting for some juicy details from her sister.

Nola smiled as she thought back how good Hot Shot's cunnilingus was, and said, "The tongue game is official,

Lola. Just as deadly as his dick game. A luxury like that once tasted then becomes a necessity. Trust and believe me when I tell you that it's now become definitely necessary for me to keep that man in my life."

"Damn, that's deep, Nola. You sound like you're in love with that nigga."

Nola frowned at her sister. With a sheepish look on her face, Lola corrected herself. "I meant that man."

Nola's frown turned into a smile when she said, "It's too damn soon to be using that L word, but I am feeling some kinda special way about his superfine ass, believe that."

"Damn, I am so jealous," Lola said, and they both started laughing.

Hot Shot pulled into the parking lot of Sweet Georgia Brown's Soul Food restaurant and got out of his Denali and quickly entered the restaurant and saw Cotton sitting at a table in the rear with two other young black men. After he was seated, he spoke to the men.

"What up, champs, y'all good?"

"Good as can be, dog," said one of the men who Hot Shot took notice as the leader and the man who he would be discussing the business with. He was a dark-skinned brother with a smooth bald head full of tattoos repping his Blood gang affiliation big time. Tattoos all over his head, face, and neck made Hot Shot think, *Damn, this man is really dedicated to his banging.*

The man reached across the table and said, "I'm Tone, dog. And this is my dog, Foe-Way."

After shaking both of their hands, Hot Shot said, "I'm Hot Shot. You can call me Shot for short. So, have you gangstas eaten already?"

"Nah, we just got here a few minutes before you came in," said Foe-Way.

"Well, let's order some of this good food, eat, and then we can roll out somewhere so we can get the specifics outta the way and make sure everything is everything."

"I'm with that, but I would like to touch on some thangs before we get to that, if that's all right with you, dog," said Tone.

"No problem. Can we at least order first? I'm starving, even though I had a big breakfast this morning. For some reason, I'm still in the mood for more food."

Tone gave him a nod and waved over a waitress. After they ordered and the waitress left them, he asked Hot Shot, "You from the West, huh?"

"Yep."

"Mind if I ask where in California?"

"Inglewood."

"Is that right? I got ties to the Wood, dog."

"Yeah?"

"Yeah. I'm from QSB. I got put on in Abilene back in the days, but I went to the turf to make it official and been going back and forth for years."

"Queen Street Bloods. I know some of your homies. Frog, rest in peace, Brad, Moon, Goonatick, and a few others from around my way," Hot Shot said in a nonchalant manner.

This brought a smile on Tone's face as he recognized the reputable names that Hot Shot dropped on him of his homeboys from his gang. "Yeah, those are the homies right there, for real. What part of the Wood you stay?"

"I'm from the Morningside High side of town. Not your side."

"Oh, you over there by the Center Park Bloods and the Crenshaw Mafias."

"That's right and the Avenue Pirus and the Imperial Village Crips, Watergate Crips, Legend Crips, Ten-Deuce Raymond Crips, and the Tongan Crips, but I don't do the bang thang, champ. I'm about my ends only. Though I grew up around it, that never really attracted me in any way. Red and blue makes green to me, and that's how I get down."

Tone nodded and said, "I can respect that. I'm good. I feel more comfortable now, at least knowing that you know some of my people from out that way. You know a lot of Cali fools come out this way and be straight pump faking. Making fools think they official just because they come from Cali."

"That's what's up. Glad you're all comfy with me. Now I have a few questions for you."

"What up?"

"Did my mans here tell you how I operate?"

Before Tone could respond, his homeboy, Foe-Way, spoke. "Yeah, he told us how you want half of the ends up front before we get what we are paying for. That shit don't really sit too well with us. We don't know you from shit. You could take our ends and vanish, and we'd be straight fucked."

"I understand those feelings, but I can only give it to you how I do it. If you guys don't want to deal with me on my terms, then we can enjoy our meals here, then go our separate ways because how I get down will not change. I don't play games, especially when it comes to getting this paper. I would never disrespect you two as men, nor what you rep. I try my best to avoid useless drama. Beating you guys out of those crumbs would only cause me more problems. *So,* are we to continue, or shall we disperse and go our separate ways?"

Tone stared at Hot Shot for a few seconds, and then gave Foe-Way a nod signaling for him to relax. "Nah, we good. You don't make me feel like you do the weak shit or a weak-type nigga. Just know—"

Cotton grimaced when he heard Tone use the N-word because he knew what was coming next from Hot Shot, and he was not mistaken.

"Excuse me for a minute, Tone. Please understand that what I'm about to say is not intended to disrespect you in any way. However, I would appreciate it if you would refrain from using the N-word with me. It's a distasteful word that I prefer not to be used in my presence."

Tone smiled and gave him a nod, then said, "My bad. No disrespect intended. I'm a Blood of principles, and I can respect your stance on that word. You got that." Cotton gave a soft sigh of relief. "Like I was saying, you don't strike me as the type of man who would beat us for our ends. Especially after knowing that I have ties to where you're from. So, I have no problem giving you half the ends up front for what we want to get from you. If this goes well, then we will be doing even more business. Things have gotten kinda sticky out this way with these Mexicans, and I have to make sure that my homeboys have the right amount of fire power. I'll be damn if I will ever let any Mexicans think they can run over my peoples."

"Understood. I saw the list, and you are asking for some serious weapons."

"Your man said you would be able to fade whatever we asked for," said Foe-Way.

"He was 100 percent accurate. You want fifteen HK G3 battle rifles. That will run you $2,000 apiece. Fifteen Steyr TMP submachine guns are a little more, so they will run about $2,500 each. And then thirty-five Skorpion SA Vz 61 machine pistols will run $3,000 each, and this is because my people will have to make some extra moves in order to get that many. You really seem to know your weapons because these are some of the best military weapons in the world."

"I fight for what I love. I love my family. I love Bloods. And I love Texas. I will fight to the death for all three. When in a fight, it's best to have the best weapons because I intend to win," Tone said seriously.

Before Hot Shot could respond, the waitress returned with their food and each man dug into their meals heartily. Thirty minutes later when they were all finished, Hot Shot spoke. "I won't be able to send the ends out until tomorrow because I have some other business to take care of, so I think it would be better if you guys hooked up with Cotton here, say around ten a.m. He will then come and hook up with me, and then I'll get your money headed west. Once my people get the money I'll have your order within twenty-four–forty-eight hours. Cool?"

"I don't have a problem with that," answered Tone.

Doing the math in his head, Hot Shot came up with the figures for them and said, "Okay, my math has the numbers at 172,500, so you guys bring Cotton 86,500, and then we'll hook up for the balance of 86,500 when I deliver the weapons. Cool?"

"We give the ends to your man here, but when the guns get here, you will be the one droppin' them off to us?" asked Foe-Way.

"Exactly. Unless something more pressing arises, then I'll have Cotton come get with you. Either way, I expect for the business transaction to go smoothly. I too am a man of principle. I don't play games at all, especially when it comes to my money. I trust this business will be handled accordingly?"

"No doubt," said Tone as he reached across the table and shook hands with Hot Shot. "I'll be back in Abilene by the time everything is everything, but I want you to know that as long as everything is good, we will be hooking up again, dog."

"I'll be looking forward to your business. Stay safe, Tone."

"That's the Damu way," Tone said and smiled as he and Foe-Way stood and left the restaurant.

After watching the two Bloods leave, Hot Shot frowned and said, "Well, champ, looks like you're going to get to see my work. Those fools are going to try to do some grimy stuff. That skinny one, Foe-Way, slipped and showed his hand just like I figured he would when I said I would be the one delivering the weapons. They think they dealing with something soft, and that's a big mistake on their part. So they got to get it."

"Come on, Boss man, if you think they on that weak shit, then why not just dead the deal? We don't need that shit."

"You're right, we don't. But money is money, and I may be wrong, I doubt it, though. Hit me when you got the money. What will be will be, champ." Hot Shot had a smile on his face as he stood and left the restaurant. He craved some action, so he hoped his assumption was correct. He needed some action in his life right about now.

Chapter Eight

Hot Shot woke up the next morning with a smile on his face when he turned and saw Nola sleeping peacefully in his bed. *I can really get used to this*, he thought as he got out of bed and went to get ready for his morning workout. When he came out of the bathroom dressed in his workout clothes, Nola was sitting up on the bed topless with a smile on her face.

"You do know that you don't have to go into the living room to work out, honey. I can work you out real decent right here," she said as she patted the spot on the bed he had vacated a few short minutes ago.

"I have no doubts whatsoever that you could give me a very good workout, but old habits are hard to break. If I skip my morning workout, I'll feel as if I've cheated myself. Give me an hour, and I'll be right back at you, and believe me, it will be I who will be giving *you* the workout."

"If you say so, Hot. Shot." She started laughing as she got out of the bed revealing that she was still naked from their night of lust the evening before and sashayed past him into the bathroom.

Cotton called Hot Shot just as he finished his last set of push-ups for the morning and told him that he had the $80,500 from Foe-Way and was ready to meet. After telling him to bring the money over, Hot Shot ended the call and was entering the bedroom when he received a text from JT informing him that he received the money he sent the day before. Everything was falling in line like clockwork. "I like that," he said to himself as he headed toward the bathroom to take a shower.

"Ahem, excuse me, Mr. Hot. Shot. Aren't you forgetting about little old me?" Nola asked as she pulled the comforter off of her, showing him all of her sexy body.

"I was going to take a shower first."

"No need, honey, we're both about to get real sweaty, so it doesn't matter. Bring your fine sweaty self here," she ordered seductively. He quickly followed her directive and kept his word and gave her a great morning workout.

Two hours later, Nola and Hot Shot were at a post office located not too far from Hot Shot's condo downtown. This time, Nola went inside of the post office with him and watched as he sent the money that Cotton had brought to him overnight express mail to his people in L.A. Still amazed at how easy it was for him to be sending that kind of money without a care in the world, she once again realized that he was one hell of a man. *Damn, what's happening to me?* she thought as she followed Hot Shot back to his truck.

When they were inside, she watched as he grabbed his phone and made a call to his people as he started the SUV and pulled out of the parking lot of the post office.

"You got something else headed your way, so be expecting it before ten a. m. your time tomorrow."

"I see you're making it happen, son. That's good. What's this one?" asked JT.

"Fire power. Needed back on this end ASAP."

"No problem. Is the list included?"

"Affirmative."

"Everything that was ordered on your first order will arrive late tonight, or should I say early in the morning your time. Same drop whenever you are ready."

"All right then, I'll be waiting for your text. Since the business has been handled, I think I'll enjoy some R&R."

JT was sitting at his desk reclined in his chair when Hot shot made that statement, and he instantly sat up in his chair and asked him, "What's her name, Hot Shot?"

"What are you talking about, who is her?"

"Don't play with me, boy, I know you too damn well for that. I can hear it in your voice. Some woman done got her claws into your ass. You sound a tad too happy right about now. Again, what's her name, son?"

Hot Shot glanced at Nola, grinned, and said, "Her name is Nola."

Before JT could ask him any more questions, he said, "I'm out, JT. Hit me when everything is everything." When he hung up the phone, he told Nola, "You must be making me happy. My people says he could tell that I was with a woman by how I sound. Do I sound happy to you?"

"Honey, you are always so serious I wouldn't know if you sounded happy or not. But I can tell you do look more comfortable with me than you did a few days ago. If your people in the West can detect something in your voice, it's because they know you way better than I do. And if you are sounding happy to them, then I should be damn proud of myself."

With a grin on his face, he said, "Ya think?" He then turned up the volume, and Tupac's "How Do You Want It" blasted through the expensive speakers as they headed back to Hot Shot's condo.

After undressing and getting back in bed, they had a quickie, then fell asleep wrapped in each other's arms. A couple of hours later, they woke up and took a shower together. When they finished, Nola asked him if he wanted her to cook him something to eat or if he wanted to go out to eat.

"It doesn't really matter to me. What you want to do?"

"You cannot answer a question with a question, honey. Now choose."

"I'm not really in the mood to get dressed and go back out. Let's chill, and you can cook something."

"Now, wasn't that easy?" she said as she went into the kitchen.

He followed her and sat at the island in the kitchen and watched as she opened the refrigerator and pulled out some chicken from the freezer. After placing the meat inside of the microwave to defrost she asked, "Did everything go right with the money you sent yesterday, honey?"

"Yes. Everything is fine, and the package should be here sometime early in the morning. When I get a text of its arrival, I'll go scoop it up, and we can make arrangements to drop it off to your brother."

"Should I give Lola a call and have her meet me with the rest of the money?"

He shrugged and said, "You can if you want. I'd rather hook up with them after everything is everything, though. Plus, when I deliver the product, I like to meet with the person I'm dealing with. That's how I get down."

"Well, I better let Troy know that. Normally, he would send me, Lola, Keeta Wee, or Weeta Wee to handle that type of thing."

"You definitely need to give him a call then, because I want us to have a chat after everything has been handled."

"I'll do that after the food is ready," she said as she pulled the chicken out of the microwave and began to cut and season it.

"I may need your assistance in a day or so on something, Nola. If you can help me out, I'll make it worth your time."

"My assistance like how?"

He then went on to explain what his gut feeling was about dealing with the Bloods in a few days when the weapons they ordered would arrive.

"When I go to drop the weapons to them and get my money, I may need an extra pair of eyes while I handle this. If they make a move like I think they will, I intend to be prepared for it. All I need you to do is watch my back from a distance. I'm going to have them be where I want them to be, but before I tell them the location, you will already be there along with Cotton lying in the cut. So, when they arrive, you can give me a call and let me know what you see. I'll take care of everything from there."

"I don't have a problem watching your back, honey. Shit, I love watching your back side anyway. Knowing that I will be helping you stay safe is more than enough incentive for me. It's all good, honey. But what did you have in mind when you said you would make it worth my time?"

"What do you want?"

She put a manicured fingertip on her bottom lip and said, "Hmmmm, let me see." She then snapped her fingers and said, "I got it. I want a whole bunch of *that.*" She pointed toward his dick and added, "What I mean by a whole bunch is whenever and wherever for a week straight. If we're having dinner at a restaurant, and I say gimme, you got to find a way to give it to me. Whenever and wherever. All right?"

He shook his head and said, "You are loony, you know that?"

"I do not contest that one bit, sir. You've made me this way. I haven't experienced feelings like I'm feeling for you in a long time. Honestly, I've never felt this way about a man. You've come into my life and totally rocked my world, Hot Shot. And I ain't talking about the sex. This," she said as she waved her arm around the kitchen and continued, "is really fucking foreign to me. The only men I have ever cooked for are my brother and my cousins. I had an ex who was so caught up in hustling that he never once even spent the night with me. So to be here at your place for the third right in a row feeling as if I belong here, totally comfy and all like we're a longtime couple, is weird to me. A good weird, mind you."

He stared at her with a serious look on his face for a minute and then said, "I don't know what's going on here either, Nola, but I do know I like it. I do know that I like you. I do know that it makes me smile to see you in my bed when I wake up every morning. I do know that I don't want it to stop anytime soon, if at all."

"Whoa, you smile every morning you wake up and see me in your bed? Shit, when will I be able to be blessed to see that smile? All your ass gives me is a smirk or a grin with a little hint of a smile. If I make you smile, then let me see that smile, Hot. Shot."

He slid off of the stool he was sitting on at the island, stepped to her, wrapped his arms around her small waist, and kissed her neck, her earlobe, her cheek, and then her lips. He slid his tongue inside of her mouth. Their tongues did a private dance meant only for them. One minute and thirty seconds later, he pulled away from her face and said, "You do know you're my woman."

"Are you asking me to be your woman, Hot. Shot?" she asked breathlessly.

"Nope. I'm telling your fine ass, you are mine. I'm digging you like I've never had a woman in my life. It's not the sex either; it's everything about you, Nola."

She placed her hand on his heart and said, "I feel exactly the same way, honey. But you can't just tell me to be your woman. You need to ask me. And your ass better ask me with a smile on your face." She stepped back from him and put her hands on her hips as she waited for him to comply with her request.

He gave her what she wanted. He smiled brightly and asked, "Nola, I know it's just been a few days, but this feels right, and I am more than anxious to see where we can take this. I will never play any games with you. I will never disrespect you. I will always keep it real with you because I know no other way. I want you. I want you every minute of every day. Will you be my woman?"

Staring at his handsome face and beautiful smile, she gave him a slight nod of her head and whispered, "Yes. Yes, I would love to be your woman, honey."

The smile left his face, and in a stern voice, he said, "Good. Now hurry up and cook my food, woman. I'm hungry."

She raised her right hand that held the spatula she was using to fry the chicken with and said, "Just because I've agreed to be your woman don't mean you can get stupid, mister. You're my man now, and you can get it."

He smiled at her and said, "Baby, I want it, so if I can get it, then you will keep me a very happy man."

"Shit, let me hurry up and finish this damn food. We got some fucking to do." They both started laughing.

Chapter Nine

Nola woke up and saw that Hot Shot was gone, so she knew he was in the living room working out. She got out of bed and went and took a shower. By the time she was finishing, Hot Shot entered the bathroom and joined her, and she quickly began to help him clean himself. Which, of course, ended up with them having some soapy sex with Nola bent over with Hot Shot standing behind her, giving her some early-morning dick doggie style.

After they both came, they again bathed each other and were finally able to cleanse themselves properly. As they each began to get dressed, Hot Shot wondered if there was such a thing as having too much sex. If there was, he knew that he and Nola were well past that mark. He couldn't help it, though. He was addicted to her. And this was one addiction he didn't want to be cured of. He shook the thoughts of too much sex out of his head and focused his attention on the tasks at hand.

He received the text from JT letting him know that everything was ready for him. Nola gave her brother a call and informed him of her new relationship status and was surprised, yet pleased, with her brother's response.

"Are you fucking kidding me? Damn, Nola, that's kinda fast there, girl. You don't even really know that dude. You don't have to get all caught up just 'cause the sex is good, little sister."

"It's much more than sex, Troy. It's feelings that neither of us can describe and neither of us want to fight them. We're rolling with it to see where it takes us."

"What if he shakes the spot? What you gon' do? Go with him back to Cali? You know how those Cali niggas are. He may have a wife and kids out there somewhere. I don't want you to get hurt, Nola."

"I know, Troy, and trust me, we've talked intensely. He doesn't have any kids or a wife. There's no lying in Hot Shot. He's the realest man I've ever met in my life."

"Ouch."

She smiled at the screen on her phone since they were having a SKYPE call and said, "Other than you, of course, my loving big brother."

Laughing, Tiny Troy said, "Yeah, right. If you happy, I'm happy. Now, what's what with that other thing?"

"All is good. We're about to make that happen in a minute. The thing is, Hot Shot doesn't want to do the last part with anyone but you."

"You know I don't move like that, Nola."

"I know, but what can I do? He wants to hook up with you for the last part of this and says it's either that way or a full refund; no harm, no foul."

"What does your gut tell you about him? Is he really as solid as he seems?"

"If he wasn't, he wouldn't have impressed me enough to fuck him, Troy."

"I trust your instincts, Nola. So, this is how we're going to play this. When he's ready to rock, bring him out here. I'm not taking no risks with that shit. You know I don't get down like that. So, bring him to the house and we'll handle everything like that."

With a shocked expression, she said, "Okay. Honestly, I feel that would make things a whole lot easier for all of us."

"Plus a whole lot safer."

"I'll give you a call when we're on our way," she said as she ended the SKYPE call. As she replayed the conversation in her head, she knew that her feelings for Hot Shot had affected everyone close to her, and so far, that was yet to be seen if it was a good thing or a bad thing. She stared at her man as he slipped on a pair of new Jordans and said, "You ready, honey? I know you looking good, so you got to be ready to get that money."

"I always look good, Nola. And I'm always ready to get money. Always."

"Have I ever told you that you're a cocky motha?"

"You know you love my swag. It stays on a thousand watts at all times."

"Ugh! You need to smile for me, honey, because that's the only thing that can stop me from feeling yucky about you and your swag one thousand right about now.'"

He started laughing and said, "Anything for you, Nola." He then gave her a smile that made her heart skip beats.

She fanned herself with both hands and said, "My God, that smile does me in every time. Seriously, Troy wants me to bring you to our ranch out in Rowlett. He doesn't want to meet in Dallas anywhere, and he feels it will be safe if we did it that way."

"I don't have a problem with that. I'll go scoop everything, and then hit you when I'm ready. We can meet, and I'll follow you to Rowlett."

"Perfect. Since I'll be in your Audi, I'll be able to pack some of my stuff when I get home to bring back here. I'm tired of going back and forth getting clothes every day."

"Are you moving in with me, Nola?" he asked with a grin.

"Do you want me to move in with you, Hot. Shot?"

"You can't answer a question with a question, Nola."

"That's my line, mister."

"Answer me, woman."

She stared at her man and sighed. "You consume me. I've never been this hungry for a man in my life. When we're not together, all I think about is what you're doing and if you're safe. I am in no way a clingy woman, but all I want is to be right next to you all day, every day, and damn sure every night. Am I scaring you off with these feelings?"

"Nope. That's pretty much the normal effect I have on women," he joked with a straight face.

"Ugh! You and that damn swag!"

"I'm still waiting for you to answer my question, Nola."

She pointed her index finger at him and curled it, signaling for him to come to her. Once he was standing right in front of her, she licked her lips and said, "Yes. Yes, honey, I'm moving in with my man so I can be here for you twenty-four, and some more for you. For us."

They kissed each other and shared a tight hug that felt so right to the both of them. He pulled from the embrace and said, "I can dig it. But you do know since I've been in Dallas I've met a few friends that have shared that bed."

She shrugged and said, "So what? That's a wrap for them ratchet-ass broads. If they show up unannounced, they will get put in their place . . . respectfully. If they act after that, then I will let my ratchet side be seen. Don't let this slim, goody figure and pretty face fool you, Hot Shot. I ain't nothing to be played with."

With his hands raised in mock surrender, he said, "Oh, I believe that, Nola."

"Good. Now tell me something before you go. This has been irking me since the very first night I spent the night over here."

"What's up?"

"Why don't you have any type of security system in place here? Remember when I got up while you were asleep and took your car to go meet Lola?"

"Yeah."

"You were straight slipping, honey. You can't be doing that. If I would have been on some ratchet shit, you were good as got. I don't like that, and I refuse to let my man slip like that. Especially since these grimy Dallas syrup heads are thirsty and would love to catch a Cali man like yourself slipping."

He gave her a nod of respect for her genuine concern for his well-being and said, "That's another reason why you've captured my heart so easily, Nola. Your concern for my well-being is touching and so sincere. But let me tell you something about your man. I don't slip. I watched you as you got out of bed, grabbed my pants, and left the bedroom. If you would have taken anything else, it would have broken my heart, but I would have gotten up and put you out of my place.

"Now, as for a security system, I don't feel the need for any of that. Mainly because in order to get to the sixth floor, you would need to be able to get past my doorman downstairs first, then you would need the key to my home to insert into the elevator in order to be brought to my floor. Last, if a man or woman did make it that far, they had better be well armed because I am." He then walked her to his side of the bed and showed her a nine-millimeter pistol that was stuck under the mattress with the butt of the pistol sticking out barely visible. He then took her into the bathroom and showed her another nine-millimeter pistol that was on the side of a small trash can that was next to the toilet. He took her into the living room and pulled another gun, this time a Glock 17 from under the sofa and said, "Remember this? This is the pistol I pulled on you when you entered the house while I was working out."

She nodded in complete awe of what he was showing her. He then led her into the kitchen and reached under the island and showed her another nine-millimeter handgun. Last, he took her to the closet in the front room, opened it, and came out with four MP5 submachine guns, each equipped with sound suppressors.

"I stay ready, Nola, and like I said, I don't slip. Ever."

"I am so wet right now. Can you please hurry up and go handle that business 'cause if you don't leave like right now, we aren't going anywhere anytime soon, Hot. Shot," she said fanning herself.

He laughed as he went back into the bedroom to get his keys to the Denali. "Be ready to roll within the next thirty minutes. Rowlett is off Interstate 30, right?"

"Yes."

"I'll be headed in that direction when I hit you, so it'll be easier for us to hook up, and I'll follow you the rest of the way."

"Okay, honey, be careful," she said as she gave him a quick kiss.

Everything went smooth for Hot Shot as he picked up the drugs from the drop that JT arranged through some of contacts affiliated with the Frito Lay franchise. All he did was pull into the warehouse parking lot, and ten minutes later, he was leaving with his SUV filled with the drugs that had been ordered forty-eight hours previously. *Smooth, JT, real damn smooth*, he thought as he headed toward the highway. With his Bluetooth in place, he called Nola and told her that he was about to get on the highway heading toward Interstate 30. She told him that she was already approaching I-30 and would be looking for him. Fifteen minutes later, he saw his Audi S8 about seven car lengths in front of him and called Nola back.

"I'm coming up on your bumper now, baby."

"I see you, honey, but don't you think you should slow it down some? You are kind of dirty."

"You worried?"

"I'm always worried about my man's well-being. Slow down, honey."

"I got you. Lead me to your home."

"Um, excuse me, don't you mean my *former* residence?"

He laughed and said, "Yes, that's *exactly* what I meant."

"Good, 'cause I like the sound of that better. Now, I just have to hope and pray that my family doesn't go snap the fuck off on me for making this decision."

"Last I checked, you were grown. What's the problem?"

"Family is family, Hot Shot. Especially a close-knit family like mine."

"Trust me, I understand the familial bond thing." *More than you'll ever know*, he said to himself. "It's all good, baby, what will be will be, you know?"

"I know, honey. Okay, we're coming up on the B. Tulane exit. That's our exit."

"Lead on, and I shall follow."

Ten minutes after exiting off of Interstate 30, Nola pulled into the driveway of what looked to be one enormous ranch-styled home. From Hot Shot's estimates, the home had to be every bit of 7,500 square feet. As they got out of their vehicles, he noticed that their spacious driveway looked like a mixture of an old-school Chevy car lot and an expensive luxury vehicle car lot. Everything from Mercedes, BMWs, Porsches, Ferraris, and even a Rolls-Royce were parked in different areas of the driveway. He took all of this in as Nola led him toward the front door.

As they were approaching the home, the front door opened and Keeta Wee or Weeta Wee, Hot Shot was not certain which was which, was standing there with his tough guy look on his face. That instantly told Hot Shot that that was Weeta Wee because he still felt slighted because of what Hot Shot did to his brother. The look on Weeta Wee's face also told Hot Shot that he was going to have to put some hands on him—or worse. He hoped his gut was wrong, but most times his gut remained on point. *Sorry, Nola*, he thought as he stopped and waited for Weeta Wee to make a mistake.

"Where the work at?"

Hot Shot stared at Weeta Wee without saying a word, then gave Nola a look that said, "You better handle this because you won't like how I will."

"Move your big ass outta the way, Weeta Wee," she said as she pushed past him and told Hot Shot to follow her.

Hot Shot wore a small grin on his face as he walked past Weeta Wee. When they were inside the home, Hot Shot was impressed even more than he was of the size of their home. It was richly furnished and immaculate. Shiny, marble floors where he could see his own reflection told him that Tiny Troy spared no expense when it came to where he rested his head.

Nola, who was dressed casually in some skinny jeans and Nikes, kicked off her shoes and grabbed him by his hand and said, "Come on, I want to show you my room." The twinkle in her eyes told him that no one had ever been to her room before. At least not a man.

He stopped her and said, "Let's handle the business first, baby. 'Cause I know when you get me in your bedroom you are going to try to be bad."

"Try? Since when do I have to *try* to be bad, honey? But you're right. Business first." She turned from the direction they were headed and pulled him into a spacious living-room area that had even more impressive furnishings. "Have a seat while I go get Troy," she said as she pointed toward a comfortable-looking sofa.

After he was seated, she smiled at him and shook her head before leaving the room. Just as he was seated, Weeta Wee came into the living room and stood in the doorway with that tough guy look still on his face. Hot

Shot sighed and said, "Let's keep this business and not personal, my man. You do that, and everything will be all good. You don't have anything to prove to me or your family. You make the mistake of trying me, you're only going to get yourself hurt. That's the only warning you're going to get from me." Hot Shot made this statement while staring directly into the chubby man's eyes.

Though Weeta Wee was trying to remain in his tough guy stance, Hot Shot saw weakness, and that bothered him because he knew for certain that this big man would definitely try him sooner or later. Damn.

"You think you like that, huh? But you not. I'm not my brother. Try that choke out shit with me, and I'm breaking your fucking hands."

With a slight roll of his eyes, Hot Shot replied sarcastically, "Sure, whatever you say. Now be a good boy and go get your cousin so we can get this business handled. I got better things to take care of than sitting here having such an intelligent conversation with a 290-plus pound weakling. That is, unless you're ready to try me now? If that's the case, I'll make sure Nola or Lola are ready to call an ambulance for your fat ass." Hot Shot stood after that statement and asked, "So, what's up?"

Before Weeta Wee could come up with a response, Tiny Troy, Lola, Keeta Wee, and Nola entered the living room. Keeta Wee noticed the look on his brother's face and frowned. Nola took notice of Hot Shot's demeanor and thought, *Uh-oh.*

"My mans, what it do?" asked Tiny Troy as he reached out his hand and shook hands with Hot Shot.

"I'm always good when I'm getting money."

"I know that's right. Let's get that out of the way, then we can chop it up a little bit." He stepped aside and Keeta Wee stepped up and Hot Shot noticed the medium-sized Gucci bag he had in his hand. He went in front of the marble coffee table that was in front of the sofa and slowly pulled out stack after stack of one hundred-dollar bills. Hot Shot could tell when he was finished that that was the remainder of what was owed for their order. He was quite good at eyeing money and telling how much it was.

"The Denali is unlocked. Everything you ordered is in the back."

Tiny Troy gave both of his twin cousins a look, and Keeta Wee and Weeta Wee acknowledged the silent command with a nod of their heads as they turned and left the room to go retrieve the drugs from Hot Shot's SUV.

After they were out of the room, Lola smiled and said, "Boy, they really don't like you, Shot. That's going to make things kinda awkward for us while doing business. You can't make nice with them?"

Staring at Lola was eerie to him because now that he had seen Nola naked and touched her in all of her most intimate places, all he could see when he looked at Lola was her body which was exactly the same as Nola's, and that was somewhat unnerving to him. He snapped out of his daydream and said, "I'm not here to make nice with anyone other than your sister. I hope you will keep your cousins in line because I don't have time for pettiness."

"Don't worry about that. I got them. They won't give you any problems, Shot," said Tiny Troy. "Let's head to the back and relax and chop it up. I may have some business you might be interested in." Tiny Troy turned without waiting for a reply, so Hot Shot followed him to the back of the large home.

Troy led them to a spacious room that Hot Shot took was a large den or recreation room. Several pool tables, ping-pong tables, and flat-screen televisions were mounted all over the room with music blasting from hidden speakers. What caught his attention most was the fact that there were over twenty people in the room, mostly women, and each one of them was completely naked, walking around the room as if they didn't have a care in the world. Some were playing ping-pong, some were shooting pool, and some were watching rap videos on the many flat-screen televisions. Some were just lying around on the many couches that were placed in different parts of the room, while others were playing video games as if them being naked was the most natural thing in the world to do. Hot Shot took it all in without changing his normal cool and calm demeanor.

Tiny Troy smiled and said, "Nothing seems to shock you, I see, my man. Welcome to Tiny Troy's world. This is my playroom. You like?" Hot Shot let his eyes roam around the room some more at the many different faces: white women, black women, exotic-looking women from nationalities he couldn't decide from where right off and grinned.

"Yes, I can see you have some very good taste."

That comment got him an elbow in his side. "Watch it, mister. You're taken, remember?" said Nola with a playful smile on her face.

"Taken? Don't tell me you done went and got sprung already, Nola?" asked Lola.

"Yep. That's right, y'all, this is my man. As a matter a fact, I'm moving out of here today. It's official," Nola stated proudly, though she was scared to death of their reaction.

"Damn," said Lola.

Tiny Troy shook his head and said, "You always did like to do shit fast. I ain't mad at you, sister. I just hope you don't make me have to hurt Hot Shot here. I can tell he's a man not to be taken lightly."

Before Nola could speak Hot Shot said, "As long as your sister is my woman, we will never have any problems. I know how to respect a queen. We won't ever have any problems, Tiny Troy."

With a nod of his head, Tiny Troy said, "Cool. Come on, let's talk business. You may be interested in what I have to tell you."

Lola stared at her sister and said, "I am so fucking jealous of you right now. Ugh!" They both started laughing as they followed the men as Tiny Troy led them outside to the patio.

Chapter Ten

Hot Shot had to suppress a smile when he saw even more naked men and women as they came and took a seat on the patio chairs in the backyard facing an Olympic-sized swimming pool. It looked like one big freaky swim party filled with naked people. Before he could say a word, Nola grabbed his hand and said, "There's a lot to what you are seeing, honey."

"I bet."

"I'm sure there's a lot of questions swirling around in that sexy bald head of yours."

"Not really, I see this type of stuff all the time," he deadpanned. She slapped his hand lightly.

Laughing, Tiny Troy said, "I wouldn't be surprised, you being from Cali and all. This type of shit ain't nothing to how they rock out west. Before I get to breaking thangs down for you a little bit, would you like something to eat or drink?"

Before Hot Shot could answer, his cell phone rang. He checked the screen and didn't recognize the number but answered anyway. "Yeah."

"Is this Hot Shot?" asked a female voice.

"Yes."

"My name is Meosha. I'm, uh, I'm a friend of Cotton's. He's in some trouble and told me to call you for him."

"What kind of trouble, Meosha?"

"He's in jail."

Hot Shot sighed and asked, "What's he in jail for?"

"Driving under the influence with a loaded firearm and some unpaid traffic tickets."

"When did this happen?"

"Around four a.m."

"All right, thank you for calling me, Meosha."

"He told me that he needs to hurry up and get bailed out because he has something of yours that you really want and he would hate to lose it. He wanted me to tell you that, and you would know what he was talking about."

"Yes, I understand. If he calls you again, let him know that the process has already begun for him to be bailed out and to give me a call just as soon as he is out."

"Okay, I can do that."

"Thank you for calling me, Meosha," he said and hung up the phone and turned toward Nola. "I have to go. Cotton is in jail, and I got to get him out of there ASAP."

"Do you have a bail bondsman?" asked Tiny Troy.

"Not out here, but my people in the West can take care of things from there."

"If you want, I can have my man in Dallas get right on it, and your mans will be out within an hour or so."

Hot Shot thought about that and figured why not. It would save some time, and he needed that time in order to get that money that Cotton obviously has stashed inside of his stash spot in his car. That was the hidden message that Cotton had sent him through Meosha. The joker was slipping driving around drunk with the money he had got from the Bloods.

My fault, though. I should have gotten with him, and he wouldn't have had this opportunity to screw up, he silently admonished himself.

"Thank you. If you could do that for me, you would save me an enormous amount of time on my business."

"Give me his full name and charges, and I'll get my mans right on it," Tiny Troy said as he pulled out his smartphone.

After giving him Cotton's full name and the charges that Meosha told him he was charged for, Hot Shot watched Tiny Troy as he made a call and spoke with someone for about five minutes. When he hung up, Hot Shot stared at him for a moment, and then asked, "Is everything good?"

"Yep. Your man should be out within the hour. He's being held in DeSoto."

Hot Shot stood and said, "Let me know what the bail amount is, and I'll take care of it."

With a smile on his face, Tiny Troy said, "Don't trip on that small stuff. We're good. I got a feeling we're going to be doing some good business together, so it's nothing."

"That's what's up. I got to go, though, 'cause this joker has some things of mine that I got to get ahold of and time is of the essence."

"I understand. I would like for us to hook back up so we can chop it up about some serious moves I'm making. With your connections in the West, I think we can make a whole lot of paper."

Hot Shot nodded and said, "Let me handle this, and I'll get back with you." He turned toward Nola and said, "Let's switch. I'm going to take the S8. I need speed right now. Plus, you need the truck for your stuff. Give me a holla when you're on your way to the condo."

"Will do, honey."

"Keep that and bring it with you for me," he said as he pointed down toward the Gucci bag that held the money that Tiny Troy paid him for the narcotics he purchased.

"Okay. Don't be driving too fast. The highway patrol has plenty of speed traps on the 30."

"I'm good." He gave her a quick kiss, then turned and faced her brother and twin sister. "I appreciate the service, Tiny Troy, and we will definitely get together again soon. You have piqued my interest with all of this," he said as he waved his right hand around indicating the many naked people walking around his backyard.

Laughing, Tiny Troy said, "I'm sure I did. It's all good. We'll get together, and everything will be put out there for you to check out."

"Can't wait. All right, let me go," he said as he let Nola lead the way to the front of the house. When they made it outside, he smiled at her and said, "You do know that there is no way I'm going to wait for your brother to break all of this down to me, right?"

She smiled at him and said, "I kinda figured that, honey. Go on and handle your business, and when I get to the condo, we'll talk about everything. One thing I need you to keep in mind, though."

"What's that?"

"Everything isn't what it seems to be."

"One thing for sure, that's something I've grown accustomed with in my life. Nothing is *never* what it seems to be."

"See you in a little while. I got to go pack," she said with a smile and gave him a kiss and slipped some tongue on him. "Mmmmmmm, you do something to me, something special, Hot. Shot. You know that, right?"

He gave her another kiss quickly by pecking her lips with his and winked but didn't answer her question as he turned and stepped quickly to his Audi and sped out of the driveway.

Thirty-five minutes after leaving Tiny Troy's ranch in Rowlett, Hot Shot was sitting in his living room talking to JT on his cell phone. After JT confirmed that everything was set in motion and gave him the time for him to pick up the weapons the next day for the Bloods, Hot Shot told him about what he had seen in Rowlett. That sparked plenty of JT's interest.

"What do you think they got going on out there, son, some super kinky shit?"

"I don't have a clue, but I'm going to get at Nola and have her give it to me raw. It may be something worth being a part of."

"Let me know. You know we can never turn down anything that's good for us."

"My thoughts exactly."

"Okay, back to this drop. You need to make sure that you're right on time because we are pushing it real close. The furniture store is located right off of Interstate 20. When you pull into the back, there will be two trucks with your package. Pull up beside them and pop the rear and the people there will load you up. In and out, so be on time."

"Affirmative."

"Is there a need for concern with your helper's incident out there?"

"I doubt it, but I'll check things out to make sure."

"Keep me informed."

"Always," Hot Shot said as he ended the call. He then stood and went into the kitchen and got a bottled water. Just as he was unscrewing the cap, he received a call from Juan G.

"What's up, Señor Juan G.?" Hot Shot asked when he answered the phone.

"You play a mean game, Hot Shot. I thought we were going to handle some business together."

"We were supposed to, but you chose to hold court for your entourage and that type of stuff tends to frustrate me. Once frustrated, I tend to move in a different direction. Your money, from what I've heard, is long. I would love to deal with you, but I don't jump through hoops for anyone, no matter how long their paper is."

"I respect that, man, I really do. My bad. I was in the moment and was sorta feeling myself. When can we hook up and make some progress?"

"Right now, I have some pressing stuff on my plate, but everything should be taken care of within a few hours."

"That's cool. Why don't we meet up at Exposures around five?"

"That's the strip club over there on Storey Lane, off of Northwest Highway, right?"

"Yeah, that's it."

"I'll get with you then. Make sure you be ready to handle business this time, Juan G., 'cause if you're not, we won't be having any other business meetings."

"I feel you. Trust and believe after we speak, things will be good, and we will make that bread together."

"I hope so. See you around five," Hot Shot said as he pressed the end button on his phone. "Looks like it's time to turn up," he said aloud as he drank some of his bottled water.

By the time Cotton was released from DeSoto city jail, he had sobered up tremendously from the alcohol he consumed at the club. He wasn't worried about the hangover he had, he was more concerned about what Hot Shot was going to do to him for being so careless. That's one of the things he knew Hot Shot hated: carelessness. He got inside of Meosha's car and gave her a kiss.

"Thanks for coming to get me, babe. Did you get at Shot for me?"

"Uh-huh. How else do you think you got out?"

"Did he sound pissed?"

"How in the heck am I supposed to know how he sounds when he's pissed, Cotton? I don't even know that man. I do know he was very polite to me. I'm surprised you got out this fast because I just spoke with him a little over an hour ago."

"He doesn't play any games when it comes to business, and he most likely used some of his high-powered connections to get me right out of there. Shit, I messed up. Take me down to the impound so I can get my car. All I can do now is pray they didn't figure out about my stash spot."

"What do you have in there?"

"Just some money. But its Shot's money, and I am in no way trying to have to pay all of that money back."

"How much is it, Cotton?"

Her last question made him realize that he was doing something that Hot Shot constantly reminded him not to do: talk too much. He ignored her and pulled out his phone and called Hot Shot. When the phone was answered, Cotton took a deep breath and said, "I hope you're not too salty at me, Boss man. I fucked up."

"Yes, I'd say you did. Where are you now?"

"I'm on my way to the impound to get my car."

"Come straight here after you get your whip. We'll talk more then."

"Everything should be good. I—"

"Cotton, be quiet. Get your car and come to my condo," Hot Shot said and hung up on him.

"Shit, he's pissed with a capital P."

"He won't hurt you, will he?"

Cotton gave her a look like she was stupid and said, "Nah, babe, everything is good. Look, after I get my car I got to go take care of some business. I'll be gone for a minute, so I'll hit you up later after I've had time to get fresh and get myself together, all right?"

"Okay. Will you still be able to give me that money you said you were going to give me, Cotton? I really need it for school."

"Don't worry about none of that stuff. I said I got you, Meosha, and I stand on my word. You just make sure you keep your word to me and give me all that good pussy whenever I want it."

She smiled at him and said, "Don't you worry about that. I keep my word too, baby. I'm going to put this pussy on you so damn good you won't want any other pussy in Texas." She meant that. She would fuck him for all it was worth to get that money from his extra flossy ass. She wished she could have gotten her claws on this Hot Shot guy. He seemed to be the real man. *Shit, if I could get at him, I could shake this lame-ass, small-time nigga. I'll keep him around, though. Maybe I'll get lucky enough to meet Hot Shot, then shit gon' change for the better,* she thought as she continued to drive with a smile on her pretty face.

When the doorman of Hot Shot's condominium called up and told him that Cotton was on his way up, Hot Shot was somewhat relieved. He knew that all was well with his money because if it wasn't, he felt Cotton would have tried to come up with some weak excuse. He opened a seat on the sofa. Before Cotton could say a word, Hot Shot received another call from the doorman informing him that he was on his way up to his place with a female who asked him to help her with some of her bags and luggage.

"Thanks, Barry," Hot Shot said and hung up the phone. He turned and faced Cotton and asked, "How could you be so stupid to go out and get drunk when you knew you had all that money on you? What were you thinking, Cotton?"

"I wasn't thinking, Boss man. My bad. When I saw the red flashers on me, I knew I was screwed because I had been downing Patrón shots. Thanks to my tint, I was able to get the money in the stash spot before I pulled over without them noticing me. Trust that shit won't ever happen again, Boss man," Cotton said as he reached in his waist and pulled out four thick stacks of money and set it on the coffee table in front of Hot Shot. "There's all the ends. Have you heard from your people on when everything will be good?"

"Yes. I'll get the call tomorrow when to go get everything. Then we'll proceed to put together how we're going to make the transaction complete."

"Do you still feel like those Bloods are going to try something grimy?"

"Without a doubt."

"What are we going to do then, Boss man?"

Before Hot Shot could answer him, Nola entered the condo, followed by Barry, the doorman. Hot Shot stepped to Barry and slid him a twenty-dollar bill and thanked him for helping Nola and told him that she would be staying with him so he wouldn't have to call him every time she came into the building. After Barry left, Hot Shot led Nola to the sofa and sat down next to her.

"I'm glad you're here while he's still here. I need you two to listen on how we're going to take care of this business tomorrow with those Bloods." He then explained exactly what he needed them to do. When he was finished, he asked, "Any questions?"

"You're going to have them meet you out South? Why? Isn't making that kinda move in the South in broad daylight kinda risky?" asked Nola.

"Yes and no. No way will anyone try to make an aggressive move on me in broad daylight in the parking lot of Big T's Bazaar."

"That's true, but what about security at Big T's? They're known for tripping sometimes," Cotton said.

"That's where you two come in. I want you there at least an hour before the set time so you can scope the scene and make sure all is good. I also want Nola to make sure that the security stays out of my way."

She smiled and said, "I can do that. You just make sure that you don't forget what you said."

"What did I say, Nola?"

She shot a quick glance at Cotton, and then said, "Fuck it. After I assist you with this, *that* belongs to me whenever and however I want it," she said, pointing toward his manhood.

He rolled his eyes and said, "Nola, you now reside in the same place as I do. How can this not belong to you whenever and however you want it?"

Shaking her head, she said, "Uh-uh, mister, that's not what I meant, and you damn well know it. Whenever and however means just that. It may not mean here at the condo. We may be at a restaurant. We may be driving down the street. We may be at Target. We may be at a club. Whenever, wherever, and however I want it, Hot. Shot," she said with a wicked grin on her face.

"Damn," Cotton said as he stared at Nola. "Wait a minute, Boss man, did I hear you correctly? Nola has moved in here with you?"

"Yes. Now can we get back to going over what I need for you two to do tomorrow?" They both gave a nod of their heads, and he continued. "Thank you. I'll be armed and ready for any weak moves. I just need to know ahead of time the numbers and what I will be up against. You two remain inside and away from the parking lot while it's going down. Even if I'm outnumbered, do not come get in the way. I will not need your help. You will only make things more difficult. Understand?"

"Whatever you say, tough guy. You know I don't have any problems staying out the way of any danger. Why not let me have Troy send someone to help you out with this? Nothing wrong with having more muscle, honey."

Shaking his head, he said, "Who would he send? Chubby guy one and Chubby guy two? I'll be fine, Nola, trust me. Now that that's out the way, Cotton, I want you to go get changed and freshen up. Meet me at Exposures at five. I'm meeting Juan G. so we can see if we can finally get that business in order."

"That's what's up. I'll be there, Boss man," Cotton said as he stood and left the condo.

Nola checked her watch and saw that it was a little after two p.m. She smiled and licked her lips seductively. "Since we have some time, we might as well have some fun, honey."

He smiled at her and said, "You read my mind!"

Chapter Eleven

For it to be five minutes to five, the parking lot of the strip club known as Exposures was packed when Hot Shot pulled his car into the valet parking area. Dressed casually in a pair of jeans, Nikes, and a black tee, Hot Shot got out of his car and watched as the valet parked his vehicle. He stepped inside of the club and began to survey the scene before him. Though he'd heard a lot about this particular strip club, this was his first time there, and from what he saw he liked. The females walking around half-naked were working that exotic look and had the type of country thick-boned bodies that most Texas women were known for. As he stepped deeper inside of the club, he thought about how glad he was that he didn't bring Nola with him. She tried to get him to bring her with him, but he refused because this wasn't fun time; it was business time, and he had to make sure that she understood that when it came to his business, he was serious at all times.

Even though she almost made him lose his resolve by giving him that pouty look that drove him nuts, he still remained firm and told her to stay and get her stuff together so she could be organized.

Now that he was here and watching all of the lovely ladies, he intended on enjoying himself. Cotton was nowhere to be seen, but Juan G. was easy to spot. He was located at a table in the rear of the club with his normal entourage of two sexy Latina women, and three

young Mexican men who were trying to look extra
hard core to give some the impression that they were
the menacing types. Hot Shot deduced, instantly, that
they were not hard core at all. He shook his head as he
strolled slowly toward Juan G.'s table while taking in all
of the lovely ladies' beauty he passed along the way.

When he made it to the table, he gave Juan G. a nod.
Juan G. smiled and waved a hand in the air flamboyantly
and said, "What it do, my hombre? You good? Glad to see
that you made it. A little late, but at least you're here. So,
now we can take care of the business and have some fun,
eh?"

Shaking his head, Hot Shot said, "Business and fun
don't mix with me, Juan G. If you're ready to chop it up
seriously, then we can definitely do that. But you will
need to give the crowd here some time to themselves
if we're going to chop it up about anything. I don't do
crowds all that well, especially when it comes to business."

Juan G. stared at Hot Shot for a moment thinking
about how he would love to bash his face in. *Who the
fuck does this arrogant fuck think he is? If I didn't need
his plugs on the ice and weapons, I'd have his cocky ass
smashed,* he thought. To Hot Shot, he smiled and said,
"No problem, Shot. It's very important to me that we do
good business, and I feel we can make a lot of money with
each other."

He then turned toward his men and in Spanish ordered
them to give him some time with Hot Shot so they could
take care of business, but to make sure that they kept a
close eye out for anyone and anything that looked out of
the ordinary. He then turned and faced his female com-
panions and gave each of them a handful of ten-dollar
bills and told them to go up to the stage and have some
fun feeding the dancer who was performing while he
took care of things. Each of the gorgeous Latina women

smiled happily as they accepted the money, stood, and went to the stage to do as they were told.

Once they were alone, Hot Shot took a seat and asked Juan G., "Now, how can I be of service to you, Juan G.?"

"Right to the point, huh? No drink for you or nothing? Come on, hombre, you need to loosen up some. We got plenty of time to take care of business; relax a little. I want to get to know a little about you before we jump right into the business."

"It's a little too early for me to be drinking. But if you have any questions, then ask away, and I'll see if they're worth me answering."

"Damn, you serious like this all the time, hombre?"

"When it comes to business, yes, pretty much."

Juan G. shrugged his broad shoulders, sipped his drink, and stared at Hot Shot. *This hombre may just be a problem,* he thought as he continued to stare at him. He then smiled and said, "So, you're from the West Coast, eh?"

With a bored expression on his face, Hot Shot nodded but didn't speak.

"Let me get straight to the business since you not trying to be cordial and shit."

"Glad you're feeling me now. Let's do that."

With a frown creasing his Spanish Don Juan-like handsome looks, Juan G. said, "I need a plug on some Ice. Built myself a nice clientele over the last year, but here lately, the connect I have is having problems getting what I need on a regular. You think you can get at me with enough to hold me down?"

"How much is enough to hold you down?"

"How much you got?"

"How much do you want?"

Laughing, Juan G. said, "At least fifteen pounds a month."

"What you paying for that like, seventeen–eighteen a pound?"

Juan G. shrugged and asked, "What will you charge me?"

"Fifteen thousand a pound, plus my expenses for getting it here, which will run another twenty-five hundred every five pounds you buy. You want fifteen pounds a month, that will be 225,000, and with my expenses added, that will be another 7,500, so the total will be 232,500."

Doing the calculations in his head, Juan G. smiled a minute later and said, "So you'll give them to me for fifteen a pound for real?"

Hot Shot gave him a nod yes.

Damn, with his taxes, I'm still paying less than I was fucking with Simon's people out there in Houston, Juan G. said to himself. To Hot Shot he said, "I can do that."

"I figured you could. I can only assume you were paying seventeen–eighteen a pound. That's why I dropped the ticket somewhat so you would like that. That way, we both make money, and we can get that money. I have one rule when I do business, though."

"What's that?"

"You got to give me half of the money for the purchase up front before I make the order. You will then pay the other half upon arrival of your purchase. Your money is protected at all times just in case anything happens."

"I don't know about that, my man. I don't know you well enough to give you that kind of bread."

Hot Shot gave a nod in understanding and started to rise up out of his seat.

"Say, hold up. Where you going?"

"Our business is concluded because the rule I just told you about is not negotiable. Either we get down my way, or we don't get down at all."

"Have a seat, Hot Shot. We are definitely going to get down."

After he was back seated Hot Shot said, "Okay. When do you want to get this started?"

"As soon as possible."

"Give me a call, and I'll have Cotton get with you to pick up the 116,250 on the 232,500 you want to spend."

"How long will it take to get the work?"

"Twenty-four to forty-eight hours tops after I receive your deposit."

Juan G. nodded and said, "That's cool. You do know that if something happens to my money I expect to get mines. If not, we will have a serious problem, hombre."

With a grin on his face, Hot Shot said, "Yes, I can dig that. Save the threats, though. I don't play any games when it comes to business. Like I said, if something was to go wrong, your money will be protected."

Before Juan G. spoke, he looked up and saw Cotton as he entered the club, looked around for a moment until he saw them, and started walking toward their table. "Here comes your man now, hombre."

Hot Shot nodded, though he already saw Cotton when he came into the club by staring at the mirrored wall in front of him. Since the club walls were mirrored all around the club, it made it real easy for him to watch his back. He made a mental to have many more business meetings here at Exposures because the mirrored walls gave him an extra sense of security. Even though he knew if anything ever got hectic he would tear shit up like no one in Dallas had ever seen, it was still an added luxury security-wise. He shook those thoughts from his mind and watched as Cotton came toward them. When Cotton was seated next to him, Hot Shot told Juan G., "Is there anything else that you will be needing my services for?"

After taking another sip of his drink, Juan G. said, "Yeah, I need weapons, a lot of them. Been having some beef with those Bloods out on the North. I got a feeling they're going to try to make a move on the South, and that's something I cannot allow."

Cotton was about to say something, but Hot Shot tapped his leg under the table to stop him and said, "What kind of weapons are you looking for?"

"Something heavy, like, you know, some fully auto shit."

"You may need to be a little bit more specific."

"Can you get me whatever I want?"

"As long as you have the money there isn't a weapon short of a nuclear bomb that I cannot get for you."

"Then I want fifty MP9s and fifty MP5 submachine guns, fully auto."

"No problem. That will run you 3,000 apiece, which comes to 300,000. My expenses will add another 5,000 to that, so it will be 305,000 total for your weapons order, which will make your total order 537,500. Half of that will be 268,750. When will you be able to get with my mans here with the half needed to get this put in play?"

Juan G. smiled and said, "I like fucking with you, Shot. Shit, if you can kick it here with me for a little bit, I can have the ends brought here within the hour."

Hot Shot turned in his chair toward Cotton and asked, "You got anything pressing on your schedule?"

Shaking his head, Cotton said, "I can chill here if you want me to, Boss man."

"In that case. I guess we're good. I'll have that drink now."

Laughing, Juan G. said, "You are one calm and cool dude, hombre. I like that shit." He then signaled for a waitress and ordered some more drinks for himself, Hot Shot, and Cotton. Not asking either of them what they wanted, he ordered a bottle of Patrón for them all. He then signaled for his two men to come and join them back at his table. Once they were at the table, he gave them orders in Spanish to go get the 268,750 that was needed for Hot Shot. They both nodded their heads quickly and left the strip club.

Hot Shot watched them leave and said, "You must feel comfortable with me since you've sent your security away which leaves you all by yourself."

"My security? Who, those two who just left? No, hombre, they are my cousins, not my security. Those two lovely ladies over there tossing those strippers all my money are my security. If you take a closer look at them, you will see that they have never taken their eyes off us once since they went over to the stage to watch the dancers dance. See, the obvious is most often unseen. To those who don't know any better, it would look as if I was by myself now with you guys. But, nada, if something was to jump off, you would see how ruthless and deadly trained those two gorgeous women are."

"Smart," Hot Shot said as he watched as the waitress came and set a bottle of Patrón onto their table along with some shot glasses and sliced lemons and a salt shaker. After taking a shot of Patrón, Hot Shot asked Juan G., "You said something about a beef with the Bloods out north? I thought you ran the South. Why would you have beef with them and they are posted north?"

After downing a shot of the tequila, Juan G. grimaced from the strong liquor and said, "If they would stay north there wouldn't be any problems. Lately, they've started crossing the lines trying to get money on the South. That's something that can't happen. Everything in South Oak Cliff from South Camp Wisdom to downtown is mine, and when they try to get money within those boundaries, I have to put a stop to that shit immediately."

"I see. Looks like a war is brewing then, huh?"

Juan G. shrugged and said, "I doubt it. But I'd rather stay ready, just in case. I don't think those Bloods really want to fuck with me. If they do, then, it will get real bloody for them." He started laughing and said, "Now, *that* was funny."

Hot Shot shook his head and said, "I don't find anything humorous about war. War is not good for business and could bring a lot of heat around the town. I kinda like it out here. Would hate to have to up and leave because of your turf battle."

"You're right. Like I said, I doubt if anything happens. I'm meeting with one of their top men to see if we can find a peaceful solution to this, and, hopefully, all will be good."

"How can you find a peaceful solution to this if they are trying to get money within your boundaries?" asked Cotton.

"Easy, hombre, they got to get the fuck out of the South. I don't touch the North, so they got to respect that and stay away from the South. They don't do that, then it's whatever," he said as he poured himself another shot of Patrón.

Definitely not good, thought Hot Shot as he stared at the head Mexican of South Oak Cliff. *Thought you were smarter than that, Juan G., but I guess I gave you more credit than you were worthy of,* he said to himself.

"Since the business has been taken care of, let's have some fun," Juan G. said as he signaled for his two sexy security guards to come and join them. He then got the attention of several of the dancers by waving a large stack of bills toward them. The exotic dancers flocked toward the table and without saying a word, began giving Juan G. a table dance. He laughed and said, "Hey, don't forget my friends here. They want in on some of the fun too!"

Hot Shot smiled as he watched a sexy white dancer who had a body like a sister pull his chair away from the table a little and began to gyrate her thickness all over him. He was *definitely* feeling Exposures. The quality of dancers there were a tad bit better than DG's.

Cotton also had a scrumptious-looking dancer on his lap getting him extremely hard by putting some serious moves on his lap. "Damn, baby, where you learn to twerk like that?" he asked the dancer as she got to popping her ass cheeks together so loud that it sounded as if several people were slapping their hands. Cotton slapped her on her big ass a few times and started laughing, truly enjoying himself.

Though Hot Shot was also enjoying himself with the dancers, he was also chastising himself for not peeping out how the two gorgeous Latina women were actually Juan G.'s personal security. He was slipping. *Should have spotted that,* he thought as he now watched each of the women through his peripheral vision. Now that he was onto them, he was very impressed. Neither woman took their eyes off of Juan G. for longer than sixty seconds. They kept everything around him under a strict surveillance, and he respected that. He appreciated their professionalism.

He had to give Juan G. credit for that move right there. He was on point. He kept his safety at his advantage by having these women protect him. Hot Shot could also tell that not only were they good at their job, they were women who could handle their business if things did get ugly.

Though they seemed relaxed and casual with their movements, he could tell they were ready to strike at any given moment like a coiled rattler ready to hit for the kill. Female warriors who could kill some shit up quick. *Mmmm, yes, Juan G., you get much kudos for that move, my man,* Hot Shot thought as he poured himself a shot of Patrón and continued to enjoy the dancers as they continued to earn their money by entertaining them with their bodies.

Chapter Twelve

Hot Shot woke up the next morning, finished his morning workout, took a shower, and went to go pick up the weapons that had arrived from the West Coast. By the time he returned, Nola was up and dressed. Looking good as always in a pair of black skinny jeans and a white tee that had the words typed in bright red capital letters that said I'M A TECHNICIAN on the front of it. On the back of the tee was a picture of the rapper Tech N9ne. Hot Shot went into the kitchen and returned with a bottled water in his hand and asked, "So, you're a Tech N9ne fan, huh?"

"No question. That man is so underrated that it makes no sense. I respect his grind because he works nonstop. I love all of his music as well as everything he and his clique put out under his Strange Music label. You know they're coming to Dallas next week, right?"

"Nope, didn't know that."

"You should, 'cause I want to go see him, and I expect to have some good seats."

"Thanks for the heads-up. I'll see if I'll be able to accommodate your request."

"No, honey, that wasn't a request. That was a demand. I needs to see me some Tech N9ne."

"Gotcha. But the demand thing kinda makes me want to go to L.A. next week, Nola," he said as he stared at her pretty face with the hint of a smile playing on his lips.

"Hot. Shot. Would you, *please,* find a way to get us some tickets to Tech N9ne's show next week? From what I've heard, it's already sold out," she said in a seductive tone. "I'd be very, very, very, *very* grateful, honey."

"Mmm, since you've changed the tone of your voice, I think I may be able to come up with something. But right now, I need to get at Cotton so we can get ready to go handle this business with those Bloods. You ready?"

"I stay ready, honey. I understand your plan, but I still feel you may need more than just us on the lookout for you. That shit might get too heavy for you to lift alone, Hot Shot."

Shaking his head, he said, "Trust me, when it comes to this type of stuff, I'm good. If you or Cotton tried to assist me, you would only serve as a distraction instead of an asset to me. I got this, Nola. I'm about to hit the post office so I can mail this money off for Juan G. By the time I'm done with that, you will need to head on out south to Big T's Bazaar and post up. I'll give Cotton a call, and he'll be there when you get there. Remember, I need the numbers as well as the positions on those Bloods."

"I got you, honey. As long as Cotton can identify them, then we will let you know. Not trying to sound game goofy here, but are you sure you'll be able to get me into the Tech N9ne show next week, honey? I mean, it's a sold-out show. It's not like you can call out to the West Coast and make it happen way out here in Texas."

"Ye of so little faith. You haven't realized or accepted the fact that I am a go-getter of the highest order. When I say I can make it happen, you need to trust and believe that I can make it happen. Though I haven't really listened to any of Tech N9ne's music, I do know some people who deal with him directly. A good friend of mine from Inglewood just happens to be the head of his security detail. I'm pretty sure when I call Mugs, I'll be able to acquire a backstage pass for you."

"For *us,* honey. I want you to take me. You need to start listening to some real shit instead of all of those old classics from dead musicians. That stuff has started to play on my mental a little. Even when you sleep you like the music on throughout the night, and all that plays are songs by musicians who are no longer alive. I mean, I agree with your choice of songs because you be on point there, but the thought that *every* song that comes on was made and sung by dead musicians is kinda creepylike."

"Good music is timeless and never dies. I enjoy those classics, and I appreciate those musicians for creating great music. The fact that they are no longer alive makes me appreciate them even more. Since it is 'creepylike' to you, then I'll be open to some change—not much, but some. I like what I like, Nola."

"I understand. Give Tech a chance because I'm sure you'll like his music and style. He is wicked with his verbiage."

With a grin on his face, he said, "Sure, Nola. Now put your game face on while I go send this money to the West."

"Will do," she said as she gave him a kiss and went into the bedroom to finish applying her makeup.

After leaving the post office, Hot Shot got into his SUV and headed toward Big T's Bazaar, a popular local flea market type of setting that sold everything from urban clothing, CDs, rims, stereo equipment, and anything else you could think of for a cheap price. This was what was called the hood Walmart. In California, a place like Big T's Bazaar is called a swap meet. Hot Shot grew up getting a lot of his gear and shoes from swap meets, so he was well accustomed to places like Big T's. He pulled out his phone and called Cotton to make sure that he had hooked up with Nola.

After he confirmed that they were together and all was good, he said, "I'm about to make the call, so keep your eyes open and don't only pay attention to Foe-Way. Make sure you check for anyone you even think may be with him or affiliated with the red team. That means if they look like a Blood, then I need to know their position. Got me?"

"Got you, Boss man. You just be safe."

"Will do. Remember, no matter what happens or how rough things may look, do not, I repeat, do *not* try to come and assist me. I'll be fine."

There was a pause, and then Hot Shot asked, "Did you hear what I just said, Cotton?"

"I heard you, Boss man. Not feeling that shit, though, but I hear you."

"Good. Now get your eyes on alert. I'm making the call now," he said and hung up the phone and called Foe-Way's cell. When Foe-Way answered the phone, Hot Shot wasted no time with greetings. "Listen, I'm on the clock with this. Meet me in the parking lot of Big T's Bazaar in fifteen minutes."

"That's pushing it kinda tight for me. I need at least twenty-five minutes to get that far south. You forgot I'm from the North?"

Hot Shot knew he would say something like this and was ready for it. "All right, twenty-five minutes then. Hit me at this number when you're there."

"That's what's up, dog," Foe-Way said and ended the call.

Hot Shot called Nola this time because he wasn't in the mood to deal with Cotton again. "Hey, baby, I just made the call, and the guy I spoke with wants twenty-five minutes before he arrives, but my gut tells me he'll be there most likely within the next fifteen minutes, so you make sure Cotton is on point."

"I got you, honey. We're standing right in the front so we can see whoever pulls into the parking lot. When Cotton spots any of them and lets me know, I'm going to go outside and walk the parking lot like I'm going to my car. When I have their positions locked down, I'll come back inside and give you a holla."

"Very good. Talk to you in a little bit," he said as he continued to drive the speed limit on I-35. No way in hell did he want to get pulled over with a truck full of brand-new guns. He had enough guns in his SUV to make the gun case the rapper T.I. caught seem like a misdemeanor charge of the lowest order. Twenty minutes later, his cell rang. He checked the caller ID display and saw that it was Nola.

"Talk to me baby."

"They just got here, honey. Cotton spotted Foe-Way and three other SUVs. One is parked right next to Foe-Way who is sitting inside a burgundy old-school Chevy with some twenty-six-inch rims. The other two SUVs are pulling away right now, and it looks like they are positioning themselves so they can box you in when you get here. One is parked about five cars and two rows behind where the guy Foe-Way is parked. The other car is parked at the rear of the parking lot backed in his parking space."

"Okay, I got it. One SUV is five cars and two rows behind Foe-Way's position, and the other is parked in the rear of the parking lot, and he's backed in the parking space?"

"That's it, honey."

"All right, I'm on my way. If anything changes or some more men come, make sure you hit me."

"I will. Be careful, Hot Shot."

"Affirmative," he said and hung up the phone. He then reached across to the passenger's seat and checked both of the MP5 submachine guns to make sure they were cocked and locked. Both guns were fully automatic, and each had sound suppressors screwed tightly on their barrels. If gun play had to be used, he wanted to make as little noise as possible because there was no way he was going to jail. Just as he set the guns back on the passenger's seat, his cell rang. It was Foe-Way.

"I'm here, dog, where you at?"

"Less than three minutes away. What you in?"

"I'm in a burgundy '72 Cutlass. I'm parked in the second row from the front next to a black Suburban. How you want to do this when you get here?"

"I'll pull in front of your whip and get out and come get the money. Then you can follow me so we can go somewhere else so we can unload the guns from my truck to you. I assume you have someone else with you in a bigger vehicle for all of these boxes?"

"Yeah, we good on that. I got my homies with me for all that. Everything is all good, so let's make it happen."

"I'm pulling into the parking lot now. Let's do this," Hot Shot said as he ended the call, set his phone on the console between the seats, and grabbed one of the MP5s. When he pulled in front of Foe-Way's car, he saw Foe-Way standing on the side of his car with two other men standing next to a Chevy Suburban that was parked next to Foe-Way's Cutlass. He couldn't see their hands, but he was pretty sure they were holding guns. He took a deep breath to calm himself and said, "Time to get this money. They chose to play rough, so I will play rougher."

When he stopped his truck in front of Foe-Way's car, Foe-Way was smiling as he raised his pistol and aimed it directly at Hot Shot.

"Kill your shit and raise them hands, Blood. This shit ain't going down how you thought it would. We taking that shit for half price."

Without saying a word, Hot Shot did as he was told. Once the truck was off, he stared at Foe-Way and said, "Now what?"

"Get the fuck outta your shit and help my niggas put them guns in they shit."

Hot Shot smiled and said, "Remember what I told you about the use of that word around me, Foe-Way?"

Laughing, Foe-Way said, "Nigga, you are in no fucking position to be telling me a mothafucking thang. Now get the fuck outta that truck so we can get this shit loaded up and get the fuck out of here!"

Hot Shot inhaled deeply and said, "No problem, Foe-Way. You got the best hand, my man." He then opened the door and watched as Foe-Way and his men seemed to relax as if they actually did have the best hand.

Wrong. That mistake could have cost them their lives.

Instead of killing them, Hot Shot was going to make sure that they would receive some severe pain for their stupidity. As soon as his feet touched the ground, he dropped to the ground with one of the MP5s in his hand pulling the trigger at the same time, spraying the tires of Foe-Way's old school and the suburban, as well as hitting each man in his ankles, shins, and calves. Each man screamed as he fell to the ground. Hot Shot wasted no time. He jumped to his feet and rushed Foe-Way who was writhing in pain from the multiple bullet holes in his legs.

With his gun aimed directly at Foe-Way's head, Hot Shot calmly asked, "Where's my money?"

"It's in the front seat, dog. Take it, Blood, just don't kill me."

With a quick glance to his right, Hot Shot saw three men as they jumped out of the SUV that was parked five cars and two rows back from his current position. He aimed his gun at Foe-Way, smiled, and shot him three more times in each of his thighs, then raised his weapon, and let out a lengthy volley of gunfire that stopped the three men in their tracks who were advancing toward him. They ducked for cover, terrified from the type of fire powder they were facing. Though each held nine-millimeter pistols in their hands, they were no match for the fully automatic MP5 submachine gun Hot Shot was using.

Hot Shot then ran to the side of the suburban where the other two men who had been shot in their legs were on the ground crying out in pain from their wounds. Wasting no time, he shot both of them with a short burst from his machine gun. He then opened the passenger door on Foe-Way's car and grabbed a red duffel bag and quickly opened it to check and make sure that the money was inside of it. A quick glance told him it was all there. He scooped the bag up and ran to his truck. Once he was inside of the truck, he threw the duffel bag in the backseat, along with the now empty MP5 and quickly grabbed the other submachine gun from the passenger's seat and started the truck.

As he was speeding toward the exit at the rear of the parking lot, he saw the SUV's running lights come on that was backed into a parking space, and that told him that the SUV was started and was most likely going to try to stop his departure from the parking lot. *Another mistake made by the Bloods this afternoon,* Hot Shot thought as he slammed on the brakes of his truck just as he made it to the SUV that started to pull from its parking space. Hot Shot was out of his truck in a flash with his machine gun blazing, spitting heat into the SUV. He watched as the driver and the passenger inside of the SUV ducked, trying to avoid being hit by the barrage of bullets that were tearing into their vehicle. Hot Shot ran to the side of the SUV, opened the driver's side door and let a short burst from his weapon go, severely injuring the men inside of the SUV. They were extremely lucky he wasn't in a murderous mood or every one of those Bloods would have died on this day.

He took a deep breath and quickly looked around the parking lot, then told the men he just shot, "Tell your homeboy Tone that he fucked up if he authorized this dumb stunt. Come at me again and you all *will* die." He then ran back to his truck, jumped inside, and sped out of the parking lot of Big T's Bazaar with a lot of blood from the Bloods spilling in the parking lot. He checked his watch as he eased into the traffic and saw that the entire scene that had just taken place lasted a little over three minutes. Though his guns were silenced, he wasn't taking any chances. He was not going to jail, so he put the pedal to the metal and got the hell out of South Dallas.

Chapter Thirteen

Hot Shot made it safely to his condominium and was sitting down on his sofa watching the news when Nola and Cotton entered. Before either of them could speak, he held up his hand to stop them as he listened to the news reporter as she gave her report on the shooting that and taken place in South Dallas.

"This is Jazmine Champion here broadcasting live from South Dallas where something truly bizarre has happened here at Big T's Bazaar, the local flea market in South Dallas. Approximately twenty minutes ago, a 911 call was made to the South Dallas Police Department reporting that several men had been shot here in the parking lot of Big T's Bazaar. By the time the authorities arrived, there were no victims to be found, but there is a tremendous amount of blood on the ground, as well as a large number of shell casings from some kind of firearm. Though there are no witnesses that can actually say for certain they saw the shooting, there are some people who heard several men screaming out in agony in the parking lot. I have also learned that the men who were screaming each helped one another get into their vehicle, and then fled the scene. What's so bizarre about this situation is that no gunshots were heard.

"This leads the authorities to believe that whoever did this shooting used a weapon with a sound suppressor. I spoke with one officer, who couldn't comment directly, but he did say that all local authorities have been alerted

and are focusing their attention at every hospital in the area for any gunshot victims. Hopefully, some leads will come from one of the hospitals because all of the blood on the scene would make one think that surely one or more of the victims will seek medical treatment. We will keep you abreast of any new developments as we remain on the scene here at Big T's Bazaar in South Dallas. This is Jazmine Champion reporting live for Fox News KDFW," the reporter said as the television camera zoomed in on the spent bullet casings from Hot Shot's weapons and all of the blood splattered in the parking lot of Big T's Bazaar.

Hot Shot turned the flat screen off and tossed the remote control he held in his hand next to him on the sofa and sat back. "Looks like I wasn't spotted, so that means all is good. I will definitely have to stay out of my truck for a while, though. I'm going to need you to get me another SUV that we can use so we can move the guns somewhere until I can find a way to get rid of them," Hot Shot told Cotton.

"Why not get at that Mexican and see if he wants them? He just ordered all those guns, and he may want more."

"That makes sense. It's not like I can't show him some love for them since I got all of the money for the weapons the Bloods were buying anyway," he said as he gave a nod toward the floor where the red duffel bag sat next to his feet.

"Damn, you got the bread too? You done came up for real, Boss man!"

"But will this come up at a costlier price?" asked Nola.

"Those fools tried to get slimy, and it backfired on them. Now they lose their money, and it's their own fault, not mines, Nola."

"I understand that, honey, but will it be worth the drama that's going to come behind all that mess? You not hurting for no money. I think you should give them what they paid for and move on with your business. You keep their money, they gon' want beef for that. And that kind of heat you don't need behind your name out here. Guns and drugs equal the feds, and when the alphabets enter the equation, things get real ugly, honey."

After a few minutes of processing her words, Hot Shot gave a nod as if he made a decision and grabbed his phone and made a call. When the line was answered, he said, "Give your man this line and tell him to call me in ten minutes."

"Fuck you, Blood! You shot the wrong niggas, fool! You're a dead man, you bitch-ass nigga!" screamed Foe-Way.

"You already know how I feel about the N-word, yet you still insult me, Foe-Way. That's not good. The next time I pull my gun, I won't give you and your homeboys limps. I'll take your lives. So think about that the next time you call me that N-word. Now, do like I said and be a good soldier. Call Tone and tell him if he wants his money or what he paid for, he needs to call me within the next ten minutes. If not, then it's a wrap, and we can handle things however he wants to," Hot Shot said and pressed the "end" button on his phone.

"Aww, come on, Boss man, don't tell me you gon' give them fools they money back or the damn guns? They did that shit. They deserve to lose everything. They will take you as being weak if you do that shit," whined Cotton.

With a smirk on her face, Nola smacked her lips and said, "Do you *really* think they will think he's a weakling after the demonstration he put down in that parking lot? That is some silly shit you talking. He got the best of five men without so much as a scratch. There is no way they will take him as being weak. If anything, they will respect his gangsta more, as well as how he conducts his business. That's the right thing to do, honey. In the long run, it will pay off in your favor."

Before he could respond to Nola, Hot Shot's cell started ringing. He looked at the caller ID and saw a West Texas area code and frowned.

When the phone was answered Tone said, "I want you to know that that move was not authorized. My homeboys thought they could come up and did that shit without my approval. I don't get down like that at all, and that's on Bloods."

"Understood. I don't have time for games, nor do I play any, so this is how we'll proceed. You and I will meet, and I will give you what you paid for, and that will be that. I don't need the heat from this mess, nor do I care to have beef with you and your homeboys. I'm only concerned about my money."

"I respect that."

"Do you? You give your word that after we handle this business there won't be any type of revenge moves made against me by your homeboys?"

"Yeah, you got my word on that shit. I'm in Abilene right now, but I'm on my way to Dallas, and after those fools are patched up, I'm lining they asses up for disciplinary actions for that stupid shit they did. Like I told you, I don't get down like that. I don't condone grimy shit from my people, especially when it comes to business."

Tone's words seemed sincere enough, so Hot Shot said, "All right, you got my number. Call me when you get to town, and we'll meet, and you can get what you paid for."

"I should hit the town no later than seven p.m."

"I'll be waiting for your call," Hot Shot said and ended the call.

He stared at Cotton and said, "All right, that's that. I want you to make sure that you stay strapped and watch yourself whenever you are handling business from this point on. No slipping, Cotton. Wherever you go, no matter what you are doing, I want you to watch your back. They may not try me, but you are out there more, and they may want to get at you. I don't want to have to get at these fools again, because if I do, then it's murder instead of a few fools getting their legs shot up."

"I got you, Boss man. You don't have to worry about it. I don't fuck around on the North too much anyway. I won't slip."

"Good. All right, then, you can go on and handle your business. I made the order for more work for you, so when everything arrives for the Mexican, I'll have things ready for you as well."

"That's cool 'cause those fools in Denton been sweating me all morning for some more X and oxy."

"Tell them to give you forty-eight hours and you'll be at them."

Cotton stood and said, "Gotcha, Boss man." He smiled and added, "You told me that you were a fool with it, then it came to the gangsta shit, and you damn sure showed that shit today, Boss man."

"That was nothing spectacular, Cotton. Trust and believe things can get a lot worse. I try to keep this gangsta toned down, but when it comes to my money and my well-being, I will do whatever it takes. You stay safe and make sure you watch your six. Don't make me have to show Dallas, Texas, my murder game."

Cotton smiled brightly at his mans and said, "Don't trip, I won't. Holla at me," he said as he left the condo.

After the door was closed, Nola smiled at Hot Shot and said, "You do know that watching you put that shit down had me scared to death, right?"

He shrugged and said, "There was no need for you to be scared, baby. I had everything under control. That's why I didn't need you or Cotton in the way when I got down. Trust me, I've been in way more serious situations than what happened today."

"Believe me, I can tell. You moved with such speed and precision it was like you were trained or some shit, honey."

"Anyway, we need to talk, Nola."

"About what?"

"About all of those naked men and women walking around your former residence."

"Oh, that."

"Yes, that."

"I think you should wait until you can get with my brother and let him break all of that stuff down to you, honey."

Shaking his head, Hot Shot said, "Nope. I'd rather hear it from you first. What, you can't lace me on this business, Nola?"

"Of course, I can. I'd rather you get with Troy, that's all."

"Why?"

"It's his business to discuss, honey, not mine. Me and my sister sit back and make sure that the money is right and everything is handled properly. That's it, and that's all. Keeta Wee and Weeta Wee make the moves with the drugs. Troy oversees everything else, as well as handles the other business."

"What is the 'other business'?"

She sighed heavily and said, "You're not going to gimme a break on this, are you?"

"No way. Look, it's like this, if we are going to do this relationship thing, you're going to have to trust me all the way and keep nothing from me. I trust you now only because my gut tells me too. I'm following my heart and my gut with you, and honestly, that's not the intelligent way to go about handling my business. It's definitely not the gangsta way at all. There's something about you that has gotten under my armor and touched me deep, real deep. This hesitation on your part to put me up on your brother's moves is making me feel as if I've made a mistake. I have to feel totally comfortable with you in every aspect of this, Nola."

"It's really not that serious, honey. You're making way more out of this than you realize. I too have gone against all that I'm accustomed to. You have touched me in ways I've never thought possible. Not only that, you have gotten into my heart deeper than anyone has in my entire life. The speed at which we've moved is fucking amazing to me. I mean, look at us. I fucking live with you already! Talking about crazy, you could up and fly back west and forget about me, and I'd be left here looking like a damn fool to my family. Yet, here I am living with you, feeling you, and ready to kill for you. You don't know how close I came to running out of Big T's with my gun blazing at those Bloods when I saw them trying to get at your earlier. I realized right there and then that my feelings for you are real and as deep as I thought they were. Don't doubt me, Hot Shot, because you don't have to. I *am* your woman, and I am with you all the way."

"Then put your man up on this business with your brother, Nola."

She smiled and said, "You got that. Anything to make you feel as comfortable with me as I am with you. Troy has aspirations of being the next Larry Flynt. He knows the drug thing won't last, and his run at sending dope outta town isn't going to last too much longer, so he wants to start his own porno moviemaking business. He even wants to start a porno magazine based solely here in Dallas. Dallas talent only. All those women and men at the house are his porno actors and actresses. His 'future porno stars' is what he refers to them as. He has turned the home we all grew up in into a damn porno farm. He's in the process of training them in every form of freaky sex he can think of. And I do mean *every* form.

"To be totally honest, that was another reason why it was so easy for me to want to come and move in here with you. I'm tired of walking around the house seeing naked men and woman all the damn time. Not only that, but when they get to fucking, it's like all night long. Troy has spent hundreds of thousands of dollars on moviemaking equipment, as well as taken online cinematography courses on filmmaking. He is dead serious with this, and he is giving it his all, honey. I'm proud of his dedication toward doing something legal, but at the same time, it's like he's not paying attention to how anyone else feels about this.

"Our mother and father were killed in an explosion at the oil refinery where they worked and left us that house. That's the only home we've ever known, but now, it's nothing but a damn freak house, and I just couldn't stand it any longer. I had to get out."

"What about Lola?"

"That witch loves it, because she's a superfreak. She actually wants to star in some of the movies Troy intends to make. Right now, they have been filming some, but nothing to put out. He feels he's not ready yet. Plus, this venture is costly and sucking up money while not bringing anything into the kitty. That's why he has to get the work thing going strong by sending the drugs to Oklahoma."

"Why does he get down in Oklahoma and not Dallas?"

"He feels it's safer to send work to another state. He used to get down out here, but the feds and how niggas got to telling spooked him out. Since we got family in Oklahoma City and Tulsa, as well as a few other small country towns in Oklahoma, he came up with the idea to get down out there, and that's where the money has been made, thus far. But things have been slowing up and not being as consistent as it was. It's still good, but he needs more in order to get this porno stuff off the ground and running fully."

"That's why he wanted to get at me? What, he thinks I'd be interested?"

She shrugged her shoulders and said, "That's a question only my brother can answer for you, honey. The only thing he said to me about you was he needed your plugs, and he hoped we could do some good business together. I told him I felt we could do good business with you because, though it hasn't been long, I feel I know enough about you, and I trust you. If I can trust you, then I know he can too."

That put a smile on Hot Shot's face. The smile that Nola loved to see. "What makes you think you know me so well, Nola? I could be a wolf in sheep's clothing, baby."

Shaking her head, Nola said, "We've talked and shared things during our pillow talk that makes me feel as if I've known you my entire life, honey. I think I know you pretty well. There's no lying in you. I know your heart and what motivates you."

With his smile still in place, he said, "Do tell then."

"You are a very closed person to anyone who you do not trust. You have a large network of people you deal with but just on the surface. There are very few people you allow to get close to you for many reasons. One, your past. There's something there that you haven't shared with me yet, something deep, something that hurt you. Two, you guard your heart and thoughts because you believe they are sacred and should be earned. Three, you are used to being on your own and taking care of yourself. Meaning, you believe that no one has your back better than you do, and that fact was proven earlier by your actions with those Bloods. Four, you have been hurt by someone, either friends, family, a past lover, or homeboys, numerous times, and there are piles of examples you reference, but rarely does anyone get to see that they have physically or emotionally scarred you. That's why you have that 'never let them see you hurt' attitude about yourself. It's like a tough guy façade, but it's more real too.

"You want more than someone to say they love you. You want to believe it to your core that the person you choose to live your life with is just as much invested and sincere about loyalty, love, and life as you are. That is the main attraction I have toward you. Your passion is so calm yet so damn strong, it's magnetic to me. You've pulled me to you, and there's no letting go, Hot Shot. Loyalty is your main and only point of reference when you rank individuals in your life. The more loyal they are to you, the higher the status becomes on your personal hierarchy. That's why you care so much for Cotton. You know he's loyal to you, and for his loyalty, you will go all out for him, even though he seems somewhat careless at times. You sense the loyalty I have toward my family, and that too has helped us with our connection.

"More than all of these things, you are at a point in your life that you want to not have to be so guarded all the time and not have that fear of being hurt. That pain factor is lingering, though, and until I know more about that, I can only sit back and continue to observe and listen. You have a woman in your life that you can be your normal, ultra-calm self with and remain relaxed, safe, corny, abstract, and carefree without being judged. You want to be taken care of mentally and emotionally as well because you have the financial part locked down and in total control.

"I'm your fan, Hot Shot. I'm your friend. I'm your lover. I'm your woman. I can be your everything if you let me, because I've felt pain. I've felt a pain that no one in life should ever have to feel, and that's the pain of losing both parents at the same time. I don't know exactly what your pain is, honey, but believe me, it can't be worse than the pain I've felt. We're together for a reason, honey, and if you let me, I can share all of your happiness as well as all of your pains. Because together, there won't be anything that we wouldn't be able to overcome. How did I do?"

Wiping tears from his eyes, Hot Shot gave her a kiss and said, "You hit me hard right here, Nola," he said as he thumped his fist against his heart. "I don't know how you've been able to read me this well, but you are on point so accurately that you have me feeling as if you're inside of my head, as well as my heart. This has to be fate, baby, it has to be."

"What's meant to be will be, Hot Shot. God knows the outcome of our lives. We're just living to get to what he already has designed for us."

"Predetermined."

"Exactly."

"Damn."

"What?"

"Pain. That pain you spoke of. I feel it every day, all day, Nola. No matter what I do or what I'm into, the pain never leaves me."

"Talk to me, honey. Tell me about it, and maybe I can help you with your pain."

He shook his head and said, "No, you can't until you can get over the pain of losing your parents. That's the only way you could ever be able to help me and give me the answers I seek."

"You're right, then, because I will never be able to get over that pain. Tell me, though, who have you lost that causes you so much pain?"

"You lost your mother and father in an accident, correct?"

"Yes."

"Predetermined?"

"Sad but true. God's will, God's way."

"It's not right to ever question God, I know this. Yet, I question him every single day, Nola."

With tears sliding down her face, she said, "I do too, Hot Shot, I do too. I ask God every single day why he took my mama and daddy from me and my sister and brother. They were such good God-fearing people. They didn't deserve to die so young."

He grabbed her hands and squeezed them. "We share the same type of pain, Nola, and I feel that's why we're connected so strongly. My mother, father, and my little brother were brutally murdered. I ask God why every single day. The people who did this have not been apprehended, nor do the authorities have a clue about who did this to my family. So asking why is the norm for me. Why did they have to die like that? Why did someone do this to my entire family? Why? Why? Why? Why, Nola? Why did God let my family be killed like that? Why do I have to live with this pain every single day of my life? The pain is real. The pain is so real that no matter how much money I make, and no matter how much material stuff I acquire, it will never go away. There is one thing that I must have that I feel will at least help me cope with the pain of losing my family."

With tears streaming down her face as she relived the day she watched as her mother and father's caskets were being lowered into the ground, she asked him, "What, honey? What can help you deal with such a devastating loss like that?"

He stared at her with tears of his own blinding him and said, "Finding the people who did this to my family.

Finding them and punishing them slowly for the pain they caused me. Punishing them for taking away everyone whom I ever loved. Punish them for my beautiful mother, my loving father, and my innocent little brother who didn't deserve to be brutally murdered. But before I punish them, I have to know why. I need to know why. Why? Why? Why? Why did they take my family away from me?"

Chapter Fourteen

"Okay, honey, this has been way too emotional for both of us right now. I don't know about you, but I need a drink, and I think we both need to get some fresh air. It's been one hell of a day, thus far. Let's go somewhere and lighten up this mood, 'k?"

"I'd rather chill here and relax, baby. I have some business that still needs to be taken care of. Not really trying to get out and about until it's time for me to go make the drop with those guns for Tone. I still have to check in with my people and make a few other calls. We can get into something later if you want, but right now, I need to stay on schedule."

Wiping her eyes, she said, "I understand, honey. I want to thank you, Hot Shot. Thank you for sharing your pain with me. That shows me that this is as serious with you as I felt it was."

"I feel exactly the same, Nola. What's so crazy is that I've never spoken on my feelings to anyone and never thought I would. For some reason, I am totally at ease when it comes to talking to you. You've come into my life and broken down some serious barriers, baby."

With her hands on her hips, she smacked her lips and said, "Well, smile and act like you're happy about that then. 'Cause, honey, Nola ain't going nowhere."

He smiled as he stood and gave her a kiss. "Hot Shot ain't either. Now, let me go get to this business, okay?"

"All right. I'm going to go out to the house and get some more of my things, so by the time I come back, we can maybe do dinner or something tasty."

"What you mean by tasty? Like you teaching me some porn star moves?"

Laughing, she said, "See, that's why I didn't want to share that bit of information with ya' ass, Hot Shot. Now I got to get the porn star jokes all the damn time. Ugh! I am so not no porn star, and the only man who gets to see me naked is my man. You got that, buddy?"

With a smile on his face, he said, "Got it, Nola. I wish I could say you won't be the brunt of anymore porn star jokes, but I'd be lying to you, and you said it yourself, there's no lying in me!" They both started laughing as she rolled her eyes at him, grabbed her purse, and marched out of the condo.

As soon as the door closed, he grabbed his phone and called JT in California. After giving him a play-by-play of the day's events, he then informed him that he had sent the money for the order for Juan G.

"You think this Mexican is going to be a valued customer? Meaning, will he be long term?"

"I don't know. As far as the weapons go, I think he will need us. He has beef with some Bloods out here who are equally serious about their beef, so that is a plus from both angles. From the Ice standpoint, though, he will definitely get at us for a minute. He's loving that ticket I gave him. I can see him wanting more and more 'cause he'll never be able to get better figures than that."

"That's good. I want to get stuff locked in so we can make as many moves as possible and hopefully get you up out of there before the town gets too hot. Nothing lasts forever, son. We got plenty of moves to make."

"I agree. But there's more." Hot Shot then went into detail about what he learned about Tiny Troy's operations. When he finished his conversation with JT, he sat back and wondered how good things could get if he was granted the opportunity to join Tiny Troy's pornographic movie endeavors. He smiled as he went into the bathroom to take a shower and try to wind down. Everything was going just fine in Texas, and he was loving that.

Nola arrived in Rowlett to see Lola and Tiny Troy arguing in front of the house just as she pulled into the driveway. She quickly got out of her car and got in between her siblings and asked, "What the hell is wrong with you two out here yelling and acting like some zip damn fools?"

"Your crazy-ass twin has lost her damn mind. She has taken this shit to the extreme, and she doesn't understand that I cannot accept how she is getting down, Nola," fumed Tiny Troy.

"This man, your fucking brother, fails to realize that I'm a grown-ass woman and can do whatever the fuck I want to. And as long as I'm a key component to this business we're doing then I will do whatever the fuck I want to!" screamed Lola.

"Stop! Both of you need to calm the fuck down first. Second, please tell me what you two are talking about exactly."

"I've been downtown securing shit so we can have different locations for the movies we're about to start shooting instead of doing all of them here. I come home and walk into the back, and who's lying down getting double penetrated by two of the biggest dicks in the fucking house? Your crazy-ass sister, that's who! I understand you're a freak and you get off on this shit, but I cannot be looking at shit like that, Lola. That shit just ain't right!"

Nola shook her head but remained silent as she waited for her twin to speak. In a calmer tone, Lola said, "I understand how you feel, Troy, I honestly do. But this is something I *want* to be a part of, not because of the freaky shit, well, mostly because of that, but I always wanted to do something like this. You came home earlier than expected and weren't supposed to see all of that. But for real, I'm glad you did. I mean, if you're going to be the director as well as the producer of these movies that I am going to be in, then you might as well get used to seeing me get fucked. It's not like you're a pervert getting off on that shit. It's business, brother, just business."

Shaking his head, Tiny Troy said in a serious tone, "I can't, and I won't let that shit go down, Lola. I'll slam all of this shit down and dead everything before I have to look at that type of shit going down with my little sister. I just can't take that."

"Nola! Will you tell him this is *my* decision, not *his*?"

"How can you expect me to tell him that, honey? He has the right to feel how he wants on this. We're family, and there is nothing I can say to make him change his mind, Lola."

"This ain't right. I should be able to do whatever I want to do. It's my body. I'm a part of this hustle too! Troy, we're going to have to find some kind of agreement on this because you and I both know we have way too much money invested in this to be stopping now."

"She's right, brother, there has to be a way that we can make this happen where the two of you can get what you want out of this."

Shaking his head, he said, "There is no way I'm going to make porno flicks with my sister getting fucked all kinda ways. Not gon' happen. No fucking way!"

"How about the films I do, I produce and someone else directs? That way, you can be somewhere else when we film, and whatever we make we still split it like we normally do? I respect how you feel, brother, but I won't lie to you, I want to do this bad. I like the sex and the freaky taboo shit with all of this. It's totally safe. Hell, you've made sure we have the best doctors on deck. Everyone is tested every other week. We're totally good on the safety, Troy. It's just sex. You need to stop tripping," Lola pleaded.

Tiny Troy looked from one twin to the other and shook his head.

"One sister done went and fell in love with a stranger from L.A. and left the nest. That shit alone has me stressed. The only reason why I'm semi-okay with it is because my gut tells me that Hot Shot is solid . . . that, and the fact I think he has the connections that can help us get where we need to get faster than we anticipated."

"Lightweight pimpin' me, huh, brother?" Nola said with a grin.

"You know better than that, Nola. Then my other sister wants to live out her fucking porno star fantasies fucking as many dicks as she can. This shit is totally nuts. You two are going to send me to an early grave, I swear."

Both Nola and Lola screamed in unison, "Stop that, Troy!"

"You know better than talking that way," Nola said with her eyes watering.

"We lost Mommy and Daddy. We'd be crushed if something ever happened to you, so don't you ever even think about saying something like that," added Lola with her eyes watering just like her twin.

Seeing that his words caused a traumatic response from his sisters made him feel like a jerk. He gave them both a tight hug and said, "We all we got, and best believe I'm not going anywhere, and I'm going to do whatever it takes to take the very best care of both of you. I'm sorry.

I love you two with all of my heart and just want what's best for you both. You want to do this, Lola, then we'll make it happen. It's hard, though. I won't lie, it's going to be extra hard dealing with this. I understand separating personal from business, but damn, Lola, seeing you like that drove me fucking crazy."

"I know. It's business first, brother, always remember that."

"I'm not totally with this either, but this one here always has been a damn freak, so it fits her. We may not like it or care for it, but she is in charge of her life. All we can do is support her and continue to make sure that she remains safe. What she said makes sense, Troy. You've gone above and beyond to make sure everyone is safe. The actors and actresses are tested twice a month and have the best doctors. Lola will be safe, and at the end of the day, everything else is just business. If you look at it from a business standpoint, it's a damn good business tactic."

"Why is that?" asked Tiny Troy.

Laughing, Nola said, "Because whenever your freaky-ass sister here does a movie, you will be saving ends from having to pay one of these locals you've been training for the last six months! Shit, it's a win-win because she gets her rocks off, and we all get the money from that while saving in the process!"

Shaking her head, Lola said, "Only your cheap ass would find a way to save some coins out of this shit."

"What. Ever. Now, is this a dead issue or what?"

"It's all good, I guess. Still not feeling this, but I guess it is what it is," said Tiny Troy.

"Good. How did things go with the locations you're looking for?" asked Lola.

"It's all good. Got everything set up for next week. What's up with Keeta Wee and Weeta Wee? Y'all heard from them?"

"Keeta Wee sent me a text this morning and told me all was good and they should be back by the end of the week with more than half of the money," said Nola.

"Good, really good. Gon' need them ends to get the last of the equipment we're going to need to get things ready to start shooting the first few movies. What's up with Hot Shot? He good?"

"Uh-huh, he's fine. That man is something else, I'll tell you that. He had a little incident today at Big T's, and let me tell you, he handled that shit like a gangsta."

"Are you talking about that shooting that happened out South?" asked her brother.

"Uh-huh."

"That was Hot Shot's work?"

"Yep. He had a deal with some Bloods for some guns, and they tried to rob him for the guns instead of paying the rest of the money for them. He handled they ass and kept the guns and took the money too."

"Damn, he is a fool with it," said Lola.

"I was downtown and saw all kinds of lawmen rolling out hard out south. I was listening to the news station on the radio and heard about it and thought somebody was taking they ass to jail today. Then they said there were no clues or witnesses. What that fool have, some silencer or something?"

"Yep. He has so many damn guns that if anybody tries him, they are going to regret that decision, trust me."

Troy smiled and said, "I like how he handles his business. When you get back home, tell him that we need to have that talk. I want to get at him and see if he wants to join us with the movie thing. Plus, it looks like we're going to need some more work for Oklahoma."

"I'll let him know. Tell me something, where have all of the X pills and oxy been going?" asked Nola.

Lola and Troy exchanged glances with each other that Nola didn't miss at all. She crossed her arms and waited for her question to be answered by one of her siblings, knowing by their looks that she was not going to care for the answer she received.

Troy sighed and said, "These little freaky broads like staying in the sky while they practice for the movies, sister."

"Yeah, and some of the studs we're using like poppin' a pill or two to stay superhard while getting it in. No big deal, really," said Lola knowing that Nola was about to go off on her and her brother.

Nola inhaled deeply and said, "I'm not going to go off on you because my head has started to hurt. I am going to calmly speak my mind, and I expect for the two of you to take heed to what I'm saying. When you came up with this plan for the porno filming thing, I got right behind it because I was happy to see you looking ahead and getting away from the drug life. When you told me about bringing these people into our home, I still stuck with it, even though I feel it has Mommy and Daddy doing flips in their graves. Now to hear that you not only have these sex-fucking training sessions and filming in our home, you are feeding these girls oxy and X-pills, it is totally a different ball game. If these people can't perform without the drugs, then get rid of them, Troy. If I even think that *you*," she said pointing a perfectly manicured finger at her twin sister, "are doing any kind of drugs, I will beat the living shit out of you, Lola. Stop it. Stop the usage of drugs in our parents' home. Respect this house better than this. Respect their memory. I. Mean. That. Shit."

Both Troy and Lola gave their sister a nod yes and watched as she stormed into the house and left them standing outside. As soon as the door closed, Troy sighed and said, "I told your ass she would be pissed when she found out we been feeding them that shit."

"So what? We just got to make sure she stays away from the filming and shit. She don't want no part of that anyway."

"What about when we need some more and get at Hot Shot with another order? She now knows what we will need it for. She's going to go the fuck off on us."

"We'll deal with that when the time comes. Right now, we got enough to last for a good minute, so we're good."

"Okay. I do agree with one thing she said, though, your ass needs to back off them X-pills, Lola. You like that freaky shit fine, you want to do the movies fine, but taking the X stops or all deals are off. You hear me?"

"Yeah, yeah, I hear you. Come on, I'm hungry. Let's get something to eat," she said as she led the way inside the house.

Chapter Fifteen

There was no way that Hot Shot was pulling his Denali out of the garage and back on the streets in Dallas anytime soon, especially with a truckload of guns. So he chose to bring out his Ducati for the meeting with Tone. If everything met his satisfaction, then he would call Cotton and have him bring the guns to the designated meeting place, which was the parking lot of Beamer's nightclub. Even though Cotton had informed him that the previous Saturday night there had been a shooting inside of Beamers, he still felt comfortable with meeting Tone there. No way would anyone think someone would be crazy enough to do a gun drop in the parking lot of a well-known club that had just had a shooting incident there a few days prior. The location was perfect for Hot Shot, and he was determined to get this business handled and out of the way.

He slipped on a pair of black leather gloves and climbed on his Ducati. It had been a few weeks since he rode his bike, and he was looking forward to the ride. He had a smile on his face as he slipped on his black helmet and started the powerful motorcycle. After revving the engine several times, he was satisfied and eased out of the underground garage of his condominium. Less than fifteen minutes later, he pulled into the parking lot of Beamers nightclub and saw a black F150 parked at the rear of the parking lot. Hot Shot gave a quick flash of his high beams from the headlight of his bike and waited to see if the man inside of the Ford would do the same.

When he did, Hot Shot spoke into his Bluetooth and asked Cotton if Tone was alone. When Cotton told him that the Ford had arrived about ten minutes before Hot Shot did and came alone, Hot Shot nodded and ended the call as he rode the Ducati toward the back of the parking lot where the Ford was parked.

When he was next to the truck, he took off his helmet and killed the engine to his motorcycle and waited. Tone rolled the window down of the truck and smiled.

"You are a real one, I'll give you that, dog. No slippin' with you, huh?"

"Slippers fall, Tone. I don't have any time to be falling. There's too much money to be made for that type of stuff. Since we're good, I'll have my mans bring you what you paid for. Before I do, though, I want you to know that the only reason why this is going down is because I feel you're a stand-up Damu. If I didn't, you would have taken this loss for the disrespect your homeboys displayed by that weak move they tried to put down. Please don't take this as a sign of weakness because that will be a grave mistake on your part. I'm a businessman, and I do good business at all times. I hope we're good and won't have any other issues behind this situation."

Tone climbed out of the truck and stepped to Hot Shot. "We're good, and like I said before, I didn't green-light that move because that's not my way when I do business. This is dead, and those involved will be dealt with accordingly. As for me and you, hopefully, we'll be able to do some more business. I'll make sure the next time that it will be the two of us so this type of goofy shit won't ever pop again."

Hot Shot gave him a nod and reached out his hand. They shook hands, then Hot Shot spoke into his Bluetooth and told Cotton to bring the guns. He then told Tone, "Two to three minutes from now and your weapons will be here.

We'll help you load them in your truck, then I'll give you an escort out of here to the highway. If anything looks out of order lawman-wise, I'll get wicked on my bike and draw them to me so you can make it on your way."

"That's the business. You do more than just the gun thang, huh?"

"Whatever you need I can get, just holla at me."

"I'll give you a call in a few days. May need some oxy and Kush."

"No problem."

"Prices?"

Hot Shot grinned and said, "Fair. My taxes is where I earn my coins. We'll get into all of that when you're ready. Right now, let's get this handled," Hot Shot said as he stepped off the motorcycle and stepped quickly to Cotton's Chevy which had just pulled on the opposite side of Tone's Ford. They worked quickly and loaded all of the boxes of guns into the back of the F-150. When they were finished, Hot Shot told Tone, "Your business with the guns is no business of mine. Since I'm about to drop another load of guns off to Juan G. within the next few days, I thought it would only be fair to give you that heads-up."

Tone's eyes grew wide. "Are you fucking serious? What would make you tell me some shit like that, Shot?"

"Juan G. likes to speak on his business."

"What did that wetback tell you?"

Shaking his head, Hot Shot said, "Come on now, that's not how I rock."

"I feel you. Can you at least tell me what that fuck he ordered from you?"

With a grin on his face, Hot Shot said, "He made a similar order as you did here. For what it's worth, your order was heavier than his. Be safe, Mr. Tone. Get at me when you ready to do some more business," Hot Shot said as he

got back on the Ducati, started it up, and waited for Tone
to get inside of his truck.

Once Tone was ready, Hot Shot led the way out of the
club's parking lot with Tone right behind and Cotton
bringing up the rear. Hot Shot led Tone to the highway
without any problems, then sped off, leaving him to make
it to wherever his destination was. Twenty minutes later,
he pulled into the parking lot of IHOP restaurant. He
was hungry, plus he wanted to use this time to have a
discussion with Cotton. After they were seated and had
ordered their food, Hot Shot sighed and said, "Okay,
that's a done deal. Now we can focus on Juan G. next and
get some more work for you. You good?"

"You know it, Boss man. Ready to get that bread and
more bread."

"That's right. There's more to getting that bread, Cotton.
It's all about being safe as well. You have to pay more
attention to things. I would hate for something to happen
to you out there in them streets. Be more selective on
how and when you handle your business. I feel you have
enough people on your line now where you don't need to
add to your plate. There's no need to be greedy because
then, that will open doors for the unnecessary stuff to
enter the equations."

"I feel you, Boss man. Don't worry, I'm on top of
everything."

"Hope so. Also, I want you to never forget this . . . You
got what they want, so never, and I mean *never*, let
anyone dictate how you move. If they want to meet you
here, you tell them no, let's meet there. You feel what I'm
saying? Remain in control at all times."

"I got you. It will be where I want to meet at all times, or
we ain't meeting at all."

"Exactly. And if you don't want to meet when they want
to meet, then you're not meeting at all."

"I like how you had me get to Beamers first to watch and see if Tone would be on any shady shit or come with a posse. You don't slip at all, Boss man, and I am going to make sure to move the same way whenever I'm handling business."

"Good. As long as you do that, you will remain ahead of the game, and that's all I want for you. When you win, I win too, Cotton. But the main thing in all of this is safety. What good is all of this money to you if you end up cold and stiff under the ground?"

"No good at all, Boss man."

They were interrupted by Hot Shot's phone ringing. He checked the caller ID and saw Nola's face on the screen and answered. "What's good, Nola?"

"Just made it back home and I'm ready to do something. Where are you, honey?"

"At IHOP off of 635."

"Ugh. How you gon' get something to eat without me? That's selfish, Hot Shot."

"No, it isn't, Nola. I was hungry, and I didn't know when you'd be back. Why don't you come and join me?"

"I'm not in the mood for any breakfast food."

Laughing, he said, "So why make a fuss about me getting something to eat without you?"

"It's the thought that counts, sir."

"Tell me what you're in the mood for, and I'll go pick it up for you."

"I'm about to make me something to eat here. You just finish up your business and come home. I miss you."

"That's what's up."

"I said, I miss you, honey."

"You should. I'm worth missing."

"Ugh! Hurry up and come home!"

"I will. See you in a little bit," he said and ended the call.

Cotton stared at Hot Shot while the waitress returned and set their food in front of them. After she left, he started eating because something told him that it would be wise not to speak his mind about how close Hot Shot and Nola had become so quickly.

As if reading his mind, Hot Shot said, "Nola is good for me and my pockets, Cotton. You don't have to worry about her. I'm a pretty good judge of character."

With a smile on his face, Cotton said, "Yeah, I guess you are, Boss man. Hell, you chose to fuck with me, so you got to be knowing what you doing!" They both started laughing and continued to eat their food.

Chapter Sixteen

Since that one mishap with the Bloods, everything went extremely well in Dallas, and Hot Shot was very pleased with the money he had been making. Even more pleased with the progress in his relationship with Nola. It seemed as if they were falling deeper in love with each other as each day passed. Hot Shot was thinking about his day and what needed to be taken care of while showering, and he couldn't help but smile when his thoughts turned to Nola. She had become so intertwined with his business that she considered herself a partner. He laughed aloud at that thought, because she should be a partner with how she spent the money he made. It didn't bother him one bit, though, because she did her share in helping the business continue to progress. The money that came from her brother's business alone brought in a nice monthly gross for him. That, combined with the money he invested with Tiny Troy in his pornographic movies, made the nest egg he was stacking grow faster than he ever anticipated. That was the best 500,000 he ever spent.

So far, Tiny Troy had given him his money back with a $250,000 profit. He didn't know what Tiny Troy was doing, but whatever it was, he was glad he was doing it so well. The money from that business was stupid crazy! He never thought that kind of money could be made in the porno business. Definitely a good move, and it made Nola happy that he was doing good business with her brother, so all was good all the way around.

Juan G.'s business had increased dramatically as well. All of the Ice he purchased monthly served to make JT one happy man back in California. Cotton had stepped his game up tremendously, where he was doing higher numbers monthly too. *Yes, everything is all good,* Hot Shot thought as he turned off the shower and stepped into the bathroom. As he was drying himself, he heard his phone ringing in the bedroom. He stepped into the bedroom just as Nola was answering his phone. He smiled at her and said, "You are just too comfortable with me answering my phone like you running something around this piece, Nola."

"Just a moment, Cotton, here he is," she said into the receiver and gave Hot Shot the phone. "If you think I'm not running thangs around this piece, honey, you're sadly mistaken." She started laughing as she went back into the living room so he could have his phone conversation in private.

Shaking his head, he said, "What up, champ, you good?"

"I'm great, Boss man. Just came back from the car lot."

"You got it, huh?"

"Yep. The brand-new Raptor, and, man, this thang is sweet. The rims I ordered arrived, so I'm on my way to the South to get them put on."

"What size?"

"Some 30s."

"You getting your swag on big time, I see, my man, that's what's up. You ready to see me since you spending all of that money?"

"I been ready for you, Boss man. You're the one doing all that lovey-dovey stuff with your girl. You could have gotten at me last night."

"Whatever. Me spending time with my woman has nothing to do with you or the business. The Tech N9ne concert was a must. I went through a lot to secure those backstage passes, and I wasn't missing that show for anything."

"I hear you. I heard it was crazy too. Is it true he be having all those becky broads wilding out, taking their clothes off and shit?"

Laughing, Hot Shot said, "What the heck does becky broads mean?"

"Come on, Boss man, you playing, right?"

"You know better than that. If I asked a question, I want an answer."

"White girls! A becky broad is a white girl, Boss man."

"Oh. In that case, yes. Tech got them to take their clothes off. His show was interesting, to say the least. His music is on the wild side for my tastes, but Nola loves it. And to be honest, I dig his flow. And that surprised me."

Laughing, Cotton said, "Don't tell me you and Nola are about to become a part of the juggalo subculture. I can see Nola being a juggalette, but I cannot see you being a juggalo, Boss man."

"What? What are you talking about, fool? I just said I liked his flow. I don't even know what a juggalo subculture is."

"Juggalo is a name given to fans of Insane Clown Posse or any other psychopathic records hip-hop group. Juggalos have developed their own idioms, slang, and characteristics. Tech N9ne has like a cult following. That's how he gets them to take they clothes off during concerts and shit."

"That's wild. I thought he was in charge of his own label called Strange Music."

"He is, and he's the boss, as well as the main artist on the label. But his style of rap falls under the Psychopathic Records category. You know the lyrics, which are often violent in nature as a catharsis for aggression. Wearing the face paint, generally like a clown, making the whoop whoop calls comes from his affiliation with the Bloods in his hometown. One thing for sure, though, that dude is getting his bread like in a monster way. He stays on the road damn near all year-round."

"Don't I know it. Nola already has asked me to take her to OKC next month when he performs out there. She loves his stuff. I won't front, that one joint called 'Caribou Lou' had me vibing to it."

Laughing, Cotton said, "You done got hooked! You are a Technician now, like your girl! That's some funny shit right there."

"No, not funny at all, Cotton. Now, back to the business, what's up out there?"

"You know, since the beef with the Bloods and Juan G.'s people has slowed down, things are so-so on the streets. For real, it feels like eggshells and razor blades, to be honest. If you slip and fall, you gon' get cut the fuck up. Me, I'm straight, though, slipping in and hitting and moving. Staying away from all the sucker shit because it's at an all-time high around Dallas right now. They act like fake is the new real. It's hard to look past this shit sometimes, but I think about what you told me, and I smile because I am more focused on this money. I'm seeing this shit for what it is and missing all the madness."

Nodding into the receiver, Hot Shot said, "Good, real good. You keep that up and you'll be able to get away from this game unscathed with your paper right. You keep the desire, dedication, and discipline, and you will win. Never forget, success is measured by effort. The more work you put in, the more money you make. You are responsible for your own actions, so you basically dictate the course you will take to obtain success. Remember, for success, attitude is just as important as the ability to make money."

"I feel you, Boss man, and right now, my attitude is fuck these suckers! I'm handling my business with no times for games."

"I like that."

"Speaking of games, I saw that fool Foe-Way the other night when I was leaving Beamers."

"Why you still going to that spot? Heard it's gotten wack with all of the shootings taking place there. They have lowered their standards by letting youngsters in there now. You don't need any of that, Cotton."

"You right. I was there for business, though. I met someone there and wasn't there for more than twenty. Plus, I had Meosha with me, so you know I wasn't gon' be at that spot with her for too damn long."

"You two have gotten kind of close, I see."

"Yeah, I've been thinking about wifing her up. She's a good girl with her head on straight."

"A man always needs a good woman by his side."

"That's real. But like I was saying, I saw that fool Foe-Way, and he shot me the tough guy mean look as I was waiting for valet to bring my wheels to me. I noticed the limp he had and smiled at him and asked how his legs was feeling. You should have seen his face. The look he gave me was priceless. Uberpissed off," Cotton said laughing loudly.

"Uber, Cotton? Really?"

"You know, like superpissed."

"I know what you're saying, just shocked at your vocab. It seems as if Meosha is definitely rubbing off on you. You seemed to have raised the bar with your vocabulary, my man."

"Any. Way. That shit was too funny to me."

"Not feeling that. You make sure you keep an extra eye out for him or any of his homeboys. No need to throw salt on an open wound that could come back and haunt you."

"I doubt that. With how we get down with Tone now, he knows better than to try anything goofy."

Sighing loudly, Hot Shot said, "That may be true; just make sure you stay on point."

"I will."

"All right. I'll be out in Rowlett for most of the day taking care of some business. When I get back, I'll hit you up so you can show me your new toy, and we can make things right so you can be good for a minute."

Understanding his words as they would hook up later so he can re-up with more drugs and pay what he owes, Cotton said, "I got you, Boss man. Oh, man, can you hook me up with some of those new videos? That indie with your girl's twin is superhot! I want to check it out for myself."

Hot Shot groaned and said, "Good-bye, Cotton," and hung up the phone. After he was finished dressing, he stepped into the living room to see Nola sitting on the sofa watching Jerry Springer. He shook his head and said, "*Jerry?* Really, Nola?"

She shrugged and said, "Bored out here waiting on your slow tail, honey. Can we go now? Troy has called me twice asking me if we were on our way yet."

"I'm ready if you are."

She looked him up and down checking out his choice of clothing and said, "What's with the extra bling today? You trying to impress anyone in particular at the house?"

"Do I detect a tad bit of jealousy, Nola?"

"Humph. For what? I wish one of those ratchet hoes would blink at you twice. They will get something they cannot deal with. You take that into account with all of your diamonds and shit on today, Mister Hot Shot."

"Stop it. I haven't worn this stuff in a minute, so I decided to sport a few pieces, that's all."

"I like those earrings. How many carats are they?"

He smiled and said, "Two carats each."

"So you rocking four carats, two in each ear. That's a nice chunk of change you got in them earlobes, honey."

Laughing, he said, "I think I can afford it. Now, come on, let's get going. Oh, and you're driving too. I'm not in the mood to bring the S8 out today."

"No problem. I'm not in the mood to be listening to any of that depressing-ass music you like to listen to anyway."

"I don't know why you insist on calling my choice of music depressing, Nola. Just because the musicians are no longer alive doesn't make their music depressing."

"Your . . . choice of music makes me think of death, and death makes me think about my mommy and daddy."

He held up his hand and said, "Stop. So my music makes you think about death, and that depresses you?"

"That's what I said."

He started laughing and said, "That is one huge contradiction, Nola."

"How is that?"

"Because all you like to listen to is Tech N9ne's music. And from what I've just been schooled on, when it comes to Tech N9ne's music, or should I say the juggalo subculture, death is all they rap about in a roundabout way. Tech N9ne's music doesn't seem to depress you, so how can me listening to musicians who are no longer alive depress you? That makes no sense."

"Totally two different types of deaths, Hot Shot. Come on, I don't wanna talk about this anymore. Let's go," she said as she stood and led the way out of the condo. He knew that he scored the winning point, but he knew better to speak on it, so he remained quiet as he followed her out toward the elevator with a smile on his face.

Once they were on their way to Rowlett, Nola made it a point to turn the volume up extra loud bumping Tech N9ne's song "Am I a Psycho?" while singing along with her favorite rapper. Again, Hot Shot knew to remain silent, but her actions confirmed that he scored a good hit and pissed her off.

When they arrived at the ranch-style home, Nola noticed that Keeta Wee and Weeta Wee were there. Since they had been getting more and more cocaine from Hot Shot, it had been at least three months since they had last seen Hot Shot, and she hoped and prayed they wouldn't get into it.

"Looks like Keeta Wee and Weeta Wee are back from Oklahoma City. That means they may need more stuff."

"That's a good thing 'cause I have a few on deck that I was about to let Cotton push. But if they need it, they can have it, and I'll make a call and get Cotton right later in the week."

"That should be cool," she said as she turned off her car and got out. When Hot Shot was out of the car, she said, "Please be good, Hot Shot."

"What do you mean be good? You act like I'll be the one to start something with your cousins. You know better than that, Nola. I won't start anything with them."

"Promise?"

"Promise. But, if they start some stuff with me, I also promise you I will be the one to finish it."

She sighed and mumbled, "That's what I'm afraid of," as she led the way inside of the house with Hot Shot following her with a smile on his face.

Chapter Seventeen

As soon as they entered the house, Lola rushed up to them and gave them both a hug. "Hey, you two, what it do?"

"Why are you so dang happy, Lola?" asked Nola with a smile on her face.

"I'm happy 'cause my movie is a smash! Girl, they are blowing me up on Twitter and Facebook like crazy! Everyone loves my shit! I was born to be a porno star!"

Hot Shot and Nola shared a look and both groaned.

"Now you need to change those looks on y'all's faces and be happy for me. You don't have nothing to worry about either, Nola. I wore a bright red wig and no one will mistake you for being me."

"Whatever. You know no damn wig is going to help change how you look, honey, so stop that."

"Wait until you see it, then you'll understand what I'm saying. Come on, Troy is about to show the sequel he just finished editing."

"Is that why he wanted us to come out here, to watch your new movie?" asked Hot Shot as he followed Lola toward the back room.

She shrugged and said, "I don't know. Maybe. Either that or he wanted to talk some business with you. What, you don't want to watch me get fucked on screen, Hot Shot?" Lola teased as she smiled at him and Nola.

Nola rolled her eyes at her sister and walked right past her with a grin on her face. Hot Shot said, "I don't have a problem watching you on screen like that, Lola. I mean, after all, I do have the more mature version at my home every day and night."

"Whatever, hater," she said with a smile.

When they made it to the back room, Hot Shot was surprised at how many people weren't there. Normally, whenever he came out to Rowlett, there were more than thirty naked men and women around. Today, it was just Tiny Troy, Keeta Wee, Weeta Wee, and two very young-looking white girls sitting down on one of the many couches scattered around the room watching a porno on that flat screen that was in front of them. When Hot Shot stared at the two young white girls who were half naked sitting up under Tiny Troy, the first thing that came to his mind was the term Cotton had used earlier describing the white girls. Becky broads. He smiled and went and shook hands with Tiny Troy and said, "What's good, my man? I see you, as usual, got the best hand."

"Me? I wish. You're the man with the best hand in this house, dog," Tiny Troy said with a smile.

"I wish. I'm barely making it out here in this tremendously hot state of yours."

"If Texas is so damn hot, then why don't you take your ass back to the West Coast?" Weeta Wee said with a frown on his face.

Hot Shot sighed, but chose to ignore the slick remark and said, "What up, Keeta Wee? You good? Hope so, 'cause it seems like your brother is in one of those moods of his."

"Fuck you, Hot Shot," replied Keeta Wee.

"Yeah, that's right. Fuck you, Hot Shot," added Weeta Wee.

"Oh my God, what's wrong with you guys? You got your panties all in a bunch today for real."

"Men don't wear panties, fool."

"That *is* correct. *Real* men act like real men and show respect to men. That way, they get respected in return," Hot Shot said as he stared the twins down. When they dropped their eyes, he grinned and said, "Anyway, what you got going on today, Tiny Troy?"

Troy was frowning at his cousins when he said, "Business as always, Hot Shot. Don't pay these two any attention. For the life of me, I don't know why they can't let shit go and stay focused on all of this fucking money we getting."

Staring at Nola who had a look of fear in her eyes, Hot Shot smiled and said, "It's all good. One day, they will see that staying on my good side will be good for them, 'cause if they keep trying me, it's going to get ugly eventually."

"Hot Shot, stop that, honey," said Nola.

He gave her a nod okay.

"Yeah, one day, we may get tired of the weak shit and just give you what you been begging for since we first saw your punk ass," said Weeta Wee.

"Weeta Wee! You need to dead that shit, fool."

"Whatever, Troy. Let's get the business done so me and my brother can rock up outta here. We got better shit to be doing than to be going back and forth with your mans."

Not caring for the tone of voice he was hearing from his cousin, Tiny Troy felt it was time to check this situation once and for all.

"Look, you niggas don't run shit here." He turned toward Hot Shot and said, "Excuse me, Shot, this ain't toward you."

"Understood."

Tiny Troy turned back toward his cousins and continued. "You two think you can run my shit here, then you got shit twisted. You run shit in Oklahoma—not here. When you are in *my* house, you will respect the people I am dealing with. You don't like him, then that's cool. I can't make you like this man, but you will show him respect. If you don't or can't get that through your fat-ass heads, then we gon' see what we gon' do to end this shit, because you two are acting stupid as fuck. This is business, and business means money. More money than the fucking crumbs you two are bringing in from Oklahoma. So either calm the fuck down or get the fuck on! Am I understood?"

"You don't run us, Troy. We can do what the fuck we want to. And for real, that nigga disrespected us, and we don't care for the fact that you still fuck with him. We want to get at his ass, but you stopping shit and that ain't cool," said Weeta Wee, furious at his cousin.

"I don't run you? I'm not stopping you two from getting at Shot. You can do whatever you want to do. You must be out of your fat fucking-ass mind! One, this here," he yelled as he waved his arms around the room, "is all *my* shit! You fucking right I run your ass! Neither of you fat fucks would have shit if it wasn't for what me and my sisters here put down. The shit you doing in Oklahoma is because of me! That's *my* money that pays for that work, and all the shit you getting belongs to *me*. Now, if you think you two can take this and do your own thing, then that's cool. Take your fucking crumbs you made from me and get your own connect and go make it happen. I don't have a problem with lightening my load by getting rid of your asses. Trust and believe my shit gon' keep right on popping.

"As for me letting this man disrespect you, that is even more stupid of your ass to say. The man gave you a warning about respecting him by not calling him a nigga. When your brother called him that and got his ass choked the fuck out, I vaguely remember your fat ass sitting still in your chair with a bitch look on your face. But now you say *I'm* stopping you from getting at him. That's some stupid shit. I'll tell you what, though, since you're feeling yourself so fucking strong today, this is what we're going to do. Y'all want to get at this man, then do whatever it is you feel you need to do. I'm positive that Shot here can handle himself."

"No, Troy, I am not going to stand here and let them do anything to my man," Nola said with a fierce expression on her face.

"Calm down, Nola. Weeta Wee here is smelling himself today, and it's time for him to put up or shut the fuck up. And I mean for good." He turned back toward his cousin and said, "What up, cousin? Why you ain't made your move yet? You have the green light to get at this man you feel has dissed you so bad. I know you ain't just bumping ya gums, huh?"

As Weeta started to stand, Hot Shot gave a quick glance toward Nola and shrugged. "If they start it, I'm finishing it, Nola."

Before she could respond, Weeta Wee charged Hot Shot with more speed than Hot Shot figured he possessed. Though Weeta Wee was faster than he expected, he was still big and clumsy and nowhere near as agile as Hot Shot was. Hot Shot sidestepped his charge, reached in the small of his back, and pulled out a .380-caliber pistol in his right hand and a nine-millimeter pistol in his left. Without hesitating one second, he shot Weeta Wee three times. Once in the stomach, once in the shoulder, and once in his right thigh. Nola, Lola, and the two young white girls all screamed in fear and disbelief over what they were witnessing. Tiny Troy was extra calm as he sat back on the couch and held the two young white girls while he watched as this situation played out. Keeta Wee was on his feet and was about to charge Hot Shot as well—until he realized what Hot Shot had done to his brother.

Hot Shot turned toward him and said, "You can try to be tough like your brother here and end up feeling just as much pain as he is right now, or you can be smart about this and take his fat ass to the hospital so he won't bleed out. I hit him in the gut with this .380 'cause I know the shot won't be fatal. The bullet is lodged in a shitload of fat, so he'll be fine. The shoulder shot should have gone through, and the thigh shot is causing more discomfort than pain right now. I didn't hit any vital organs or arteries, so he should be fine. It's your call on how we shall proceed, Keeta Wee."

"Man, just let me get my brother to the hospital," said Keeta Wee with obvious fear written all over his face. Hot Shot gave him a nod and stepped aside and watched Keeta Wee as he went to his brother and started helping him to his feet.

"This has to be the end of this now, because if I have to use my gun again, it won't be this .380. It will be this nine, and the shots *will* be fatal. Am I understood, gentlemen?" asked Hot Shot as he waved his nine millimeter at the twins.

Neither twin responded to what Hot Shot said, so Tiny Troy eased his arms from around the young white girls and said, "You need to answer the man. Is this shit dead or what, tough guys?"

Wincing in pain, Weeta Wee gave a nod yes.

"It's over," said Keeta Wee as he continued to help his brother toward the door so he could take him to get some medical attention.

Lola was feeling some kind of way about what she witnessed and really didn't know how to process her feelings. She was mad at her brother for allowing this to happen. She was shocked that Hot Shot actually shot her cousin, and she was tripping out because she was becoming sexually aroused by how calm he had been while shooting Weeta Wee. This was like a scene in a movie to her. She shook her head and said, "Family first, Troy. You just put this man before family, and that was wrong. I know Weeta Wee was wrong, but you don't put anyone before family."

Shaking her head, Nola said, "Uh-uh, sister. What he did was give Weeta Wee a choice to make, and he made it. He did what he chose to do because his big-ass mouth boxed himself in a corner. This isn't on Troy; it's on Weeta Wee. Hot Shot could have easily killed him, and he didn't. Let it be."

"This shit needed to happen. They needed to get put in they place. You heard how cocky Weeta Wee fat ass was acting. Now I didn't think he would get shot, but the point has definitely been made here. It needed to happen, Lola." He turned toward Hot Shot and said, "Thank you for not killing my cousin, Shot. Now, can we sit down and get to the business, because after I break this shit down to you, I'm sure you're going to be very interested."

Hot Shot gave a small smile and said, "I'm always interested when it comes to making money."

"Good. 'Cause what me and Lola about to break down for you should put you in a real good mood.

"The money we've made so far ain't nothing compared to what we're about to make with this next move."

"You guys can handle all of that. I'm going to the hospital and sit with Keeta Wee while Weeta Wee gets patched up," said Nola as she stepped to Hot Shot and gave him a quick kiss. "You finished it, so let it be now, you hear me? I don't think they will try you again. Still, I'm not trying to stand and watch you hurt my family, honey."

He gave her a nod in understanding and said, "I hear you, baby. Go check on your family. It's all good."

She smiled and left the room.

Hot Shot sat down next to Lola and said, "Okay, Tiny Troy, what you got for me now?"

Tiny Troy began rubbing his hands together with a smile on his face and pointed at the two young white girls sitting next to him and said, "You see these two young white tenders right here?"

"Yes, and?"

"This is what the porn world wants and craves the most. Young pussy. Young white pussy. These broads and plenty more that I have on my line are about to make us filthy rich."

Hot shot gave a nod of his head and said, "Interesting. Please continue."

When Nola arrived at the emergency room of the hospital, she rushed inside to see a nervous Keeta Wee pacing back and forth outside of the waiting room. She stepped to him quickly and asked, "What did they say?"

He stared at her as if in a daze for a moment before answering. "Nothing. They haven't told me shit, but the police have been notified, and I'll have to answer some questions when they get here. Then they rushed off to do whatever they have to do for my brother. I'm telling you, Nola, if Weeta Wee dies in there, I'm going after that nigga Hot Shot, and I don't give a damn what happens to me. One of us will have to die, because I ain't taking no shit like that."

"Nobody is going to die, so you need to calm yourself down some, honey. I understand your anger, but everything is going to be all right."

"You can't say that for sure, Nola. Weeta Wee was in some serious pain. When we were driving here, he made me promise to get that nigga if he didn't make it, and I swore to my brother I would. And that brother of yours better not try to stop me either, or he'll get it too."

She pulled on his arm and said, "Come on, let's go outside in the parking lot and talk for a minute." Once they were outside standing next to her car, she said, "Listen to me, Weeta Wee is going to be fine. I'm no doctor, but I trust Hot Shot. He said he would make it if he got here in time, and I believe him. There's something about that man that has me believing everything he tells me. There's no lying in him. He could have easily killed your brother, but instead, he chose to wound him to hopefully get his point across to both of y'all."

"Fuck him, Nola. I can't stand that nigga!"

"You know what? After what he did to your brother, you have every right to feel that way about him, Keeta Wee. But honestly, your brother brought all of this on himself. Don't get me wrong here; I'm mad as fuck at Hot Shot too. He hurt my family, and that's something I don't accept. We will have our falling out about this, that I promise you."

"Falling out, huh? Yeah, right. It ain't like you gon' leave that nigga for what he did to my brother. You love that nigga, Nola. We all can see that plain as day."

"And y'all are 100 percent right. I do love him. But that doesn't mean I will not go the fuck off on him and let him know he was wrong for hurting my cousin like this. Regardless, you, your brother, Troy, and Hot Shot are all equally responsible for this macho bullshit. It has to stop, Keeta Wee. If y'all don't want to fuck with him, then stay away from him, and I'll make sure he does the same. If and when you do be around him, give him the same respect he gives you, and there won't be any more problems, honey. The business has to continue, and the business is what's really important here. Don't let your anger cloud your judgment, cousin."

"I hear you, Nola. You don't let your love for that nigga cloud yours either. I'm going back inside now and wait for the police to come, and then be there for my brother when he comes out of surgery. You coming or are you going back to the house to be with your man?"

"They're talking business back at the house. I'm here to be with my family. This is where I need to be right now, honey. Come on, let's go," she said as she grabbed his hand and led the way back inside the hospital.

Chapter Eighteen

Hot Shot sat stunned as he listened to what Tiny Troy and his sister proposed to him. He couldn't believe that they were actually getting at him with this. They wanted him to invest more money into their porno productions because they felt that child pornography would make the money they've made thus far seem like chump change. He felt disgusted toward both of them but kept his poker face on as he continued to listen to them as they took turns trying to convince him of this next move.

"I'm no creepy dude on some child molestation shit, Shot, so let me be clear up front on that. When I say child porn, I'm merely talking underage girls like these two here," Troy said as he pointed toward the two young white girls sitting silently next to him.

Hot Shot stared at the two girls and quietly asked them, "How old are you two?"

When they hesitated to answer him, Tiny Troy gave them a nod and said, "Go on, girls, tell him. It's all good."

"I'm seventeen, and my cousin is sixteen. We do this because we want to, and we love to have sex. If Tiny Troy is going to pay us to make movies and keep us safe, there's nothing wrong with it to us," said one of the young, naive white girls with a defiant look on her young face.

Hot Shot stared at them for a moment and said, "I don't know about this one, Troy. I mean, there's a lot of risk factors here, dude, that could come back and bite us. Young girls, drugs, sex . . . Man, is it really worth the risk?"

"Hell, yeah, it's worth the risk!" screamed Lola. "My movie made us some cool change because we did everything from the production to the directing as well as distributing. We are eating great from that one flick. From this move, we will eat damn near ten times better! These hot little thangs gon' burn the screen up, and we gon' get mad bread from that shit. They get all the black dick those little tight white pussies can handle, and we get a whole bunch of fucking money. All you got to do is continue doing what you been doing as far as our other moves and invest your money. Then sit back and watch how we make you even more money. Don't worry about what's going on; just let it do what it do, Shot. It's that simple."

"Does Nola know about this get down?"

Lola sighed and answered him honestly. "Nope. She would be totally against it. That's how she is. That's why you cannot speak about any of this with her, whether you're with it or not."

"Yeah, my sister wasn't with the porno thing from the get. She accepted it because she saw I'm trying to get some legit money here. She would throw a monster fit if she knew about this part of thangs," said Tiny Troy.

"All it will be is these two females in your movies?" asked Hot Shot.

"For starters, yes. Once it pops like we think it will, then we'll add more to the stable and make more moves."

With raised eyebrows, he asked, "Such as?"

"More girls, Shot, just more girls. I'll make sure that they all will be no younger than sixteen. We won't get outrageous with this shit," said Lola.

"All right. I need a minute to process this fully, and I'll get back with you. Remember this, if I do sign on, I expect for things to be run real tight, 'cause like I said, this is a dangerous move, and I got a lot of irons in the fire out here and can lose way more money than what we got going on here if things go left with this."

"Understood. I respect that, and believe me, I only know one way to run my business, and that's tight as can be," said Tiny Troy with a smile on his face.

"One more thing."

"What up?"

"If your cousins get in my way again, I'm going to kill them both." Hot Shot made that statement crystal clear to the two of them, and they knew that he had just told them the absolute truth.

"I'll make sure that they don't step on your toes or even think about getting at you in any way, Shot," said Tiny Troy.

Laughing, Lola said, "Shit, you already made sure that they won't try your ass again. I can't believe you actually shot Weeta Wee. You are one crazy, sexy-ass man! I wish I would have been the one you chose that night at the club," she said flirtatiously.

Tiny Troy rolled his eyes at his sister and said, "Anyway, don't worry about them. You won't have any more problems from them, that's my word."

"I'm not worried about them at all, Troy. I just want it clear and understood right now. If we're going to get this money, then we can get this money, but I don't have time for the extra stuff. I did what I did today because Weeta Wee pushed that line. I try to let that side of me remain dormant, but when it's time to get wicked, no man in Texas can get as wicked as I can."

"Damn, that cocky-ass macho shit gets me wet!" said Lola as she squirmed in her seat.

"Me too," said one of the white girls as they both started giggling like the teenagers they were.

Troy and Hot Shot both shook their heads.

***

Nola gave Hot Shot the silent treatment all the way back to the condo, and he knew that he was in trouble. He waited until they were inside and changed into something more comfortable before speaking.

"I take it I'm not on your good side at this time, huh, Nola?"

"Damn, honey, sometimes your intelligence simply amazes me. You hurt my family today, Hot Shot. You could have killed my cousin."

"I could have, but I didn't."

"Don't. Don't do that. I know he was wrong, and I meant what I said. He chose to get what he got, but you didn't have to shoot him. The doctor said he's going to be laid up for at least a couple of months in order to get right from that gut shot you gave him."

"Would you have rather me let that huge cousin of yours harm me, Nola? Though I am pretty good with these," he held up both fists. "I'm no fool to try to go up against two men who weigh close to three hundred pounds each."

"It wasn't two, Hot Shot, it was just Weeta Wee."

Shaking his head, he said, "If I would have gotten in a tussle with Weeta Wee, it would have been only a matter of seconds before Keeta Wee would have joined the fray, and I would have gotten hurt. I don't get hurt, Nola. I did what I did to control the situation. I knew once Keeta Wee saw his brother had been shot, all of the fight would have been taken from him. I told you if they started it, I would finish it, and that's exactly what I did. I don't want any issues with your family, Nola, but my safety comes first. I don't want you upset with me. I do understand your anger, and I respect your loyalty to your family. That's one of the many admirable traits you possess."

"Don't. Don't you give me compliments trying to woo me, honey. I'm still mad at ya ass!"

With a grin on his face, he asked, "What can I do to stop you from being mad at me, Nola?"

"Will you do whatever I tell you to do?" she asked with a hint of a smile on her lovely face.

He groaned and said, "That depends, Nola. Spit it out and I'll tell you if I can or can't."

"More like if you will or won't."

"You say 'tamaytoe,' I say 'tomahtoe.'"

"Mm-hmm, same thing, honey."

"Exactly."

"I want three things. One, since it looks like Weeta Wee will be out of the way for a minute, I'll have to make a few trips to Oklahoma with Keeta Wee, so I want you to come along with me when I have to go."

"I can do that. Are you sure Keeta Wee will be able to deal with that? You know, being around me while we're out that way?"

"That won't be a problem because we will be hitting up the different towns in Oklahoma where they get down. So, you won't be around him as much as you think."

"Done."

"Two, I want you to go see Weeta Wee at the hospital and apologize for shooting him. Though he was wrong, you were too, Hot Shot. I want you to tell him that as long as he doesn't trip on you, you won't trip on him."

"Tell me the third one while I let that one marinate for a few minutes, and I'll get back to it."

"Fair enough. And three, I want you to tell me exactly what it is about me that has made this work between us thus far. I know what I like about you, and I've told you several times how much you impress me. You have only given me a little of what you like about me. So, spit it out, Hot Shot."

"That's easy, Nola. You possess qualities that I love for a woman to have. You're confident. You're intelligent. You're spontaneous and outgoing. You're cool and laid-back yet playful and silly at the same time, which is a perfect blend in my eyes. You exude sensuality. You have an air of sexuality that draws my eyes to you whenever you enter a room. You're honest. You're independent. And you're supportive of me and my every move. Even when you felt I was wrong today, you stood behind me to your family. You waited until we got here to air your grievances about my behavior earlier, and I respect that so much about you. And, of course, you are sexy as I don't know what. You turn me on with words, you turn me on with your looks, your body, and your scent. Everything about you excites me sexually. You're the woman for me, Nola. I love that. I love you."

Fanning herself she said, "Whew! Okay, Hot. Shot. You done real good with number three. Before I give myself to you for making me so damn hot, I need an answer to number two, honey."

He sighed and said, "When he gets out of the hospital I'll go see him and give him a heartfelt apology, Nola. I respect his courage, so I have no problem apologizing."

She smiled happily at him and said, "You told me you loved me! Do you know how wet that made me? Do you know how *good* you have made me feel just now? You are about to get some of the best pussy you have ever had in your life, Hot. Shot," she said as she stood and pulled down her shorts and sat at the end of the bed with her legs spread open. "Now, come here, get on your knees in front of me, and taste me. Eat me, Hot. Shot."

Without saying a word, he did as he was told. He dropped to his knees and stuck his face between her thighs and began to slowly suck and lick her pussy. She held his head with both of her hands tightly against her clit as he sucked and nibbled on it. She came so hard and fast that she felt as if she were seeing stars. When he came from between her legs, his nose, lips, and chin were shining with her juices. She giggled as she licked some of her pussy juice from his chin. He stood and began to slide off his thigh-high boxer briefs, but she stopped him.

"Let me do that, Hot. Shot." She then pulled his underwear down to his feet and let him step out of them. While on her knees now, she put his dick inside of her mouth and began to suck him slowly. While greedily bucking his dick, she stuck her right hand between her legs and began to play with her soaking wet pussy. He could actually hear how wet she was as she played with herself. Hearing that wetness drove him to the brink of orgasm so he stopped her and pulled back. He gently pulled her to her feet and gave her a passionate kiss . . . A kiss that made them both feel as if their souls had become one. Neither of them realized that they had somehow lay down on the bed and had begun making soft, slow love to each other. Two people in perfect sync with each other. Two people madly in love with each other. Two people reaching their peaks at the same time as nirvana overcame them both.

Chapter Nineteen

"This is really some ridiculous stuff right here, JT. I mean, for real, child porn! That's something I don't want to have my name attached to at all. I am *so* not feeling this move, and I couldn't care less about how much money it can bring in, so don't even try to play that card with me," Hot Shot said as he sat back on the couch and waited for the response he knew he would receive from JT.

JT sighed heavily into the speaker of his smartphone and said, "You just don't seem to understand the bigger scheme of things when it comes to getting this money, son. You're not out there to be on some high moral shit. You are out there for a purpose, and a part of that purpose is to get money in every facet of the game. You aren't a dope boy. You aren't a one-dimensional type of hustler out there. You are multifaceted, and you were designed to be that way. A hustler is about getting the money any and every way that you can. And that is what you're going to do. If investing in Tiny Troy's porno shit will bring you more money, then that's exactly what we expect for you to do. It's not like you will be hands-on with all of this. You are merely an investor. Sit back and let that bounce around your head before you turn down this money. Granted, I do share your views on the creepy shit. No one likes to think about that sort of thing. Again, it's not our place to give moral judgment on this shit. It is our place to gain from this and make that paper. So stick to the script and be the hustler that you are and get that money. Am I understood, son?"

Hot Shot sighed and answered, "Affirmative. Still don't like that stuff, though."

"Sometimes we don't like what's best for us. It's the end result that matters most, son; never forget that. The end result. Now, is there anything else you need to bring to my attention, or are we done?"

"We're good for now. Cotton has been handling up real good and has slowly built up a solid clientele around the town. My little helper is getting that bread."

"That's what I like to hear. Okay, son, do what you do and stay safe. I'll be coming that way in a week or so to speak with some important people. When I get there, we'll do lunch."

"That's what's up. Holla at me when you get here."

"Will do. Later, Hot Shot," JT said and ended the call.

After the call with JT, Hot Shot sat back and thought about what had been discussed with his main man, and he still didn't feel any better about being a part of Tiny Troy and Lola's child porn movie operation. Even though it wasn't like they were using babies, they were still using kids. Sixteen- and seventeen-year-olds were kids who didn't know any better, whether they liked the sex or not. No grown-ass men should be having sex with kids like that. Thinking about that made him feel sick to his stomach. He was glad to have learned that Nola had no part in that part of the business. It made him feel real good inside about her to know she wasn't with that disgusting and despicable hustle that her brother and twin sister were putting together. That made him feel real good about his woman.

She is the woman I thought she was, he thought and smiled. *Sexy, intelligent, loving, caring . . . Everything I want in a woman she has. It's going to get crazy when it's time for me to leave this place. Wonder how that's going to play out,* he thought just as his phone started to ring. He picked up the smartphone and saw Cotton's face on the screen and answered. "What up, champ? You straight out there in them streets?"

"I'm good. Just chilling right now with Meosha, about to go get something to eat. You busy? If not, why don't you and Nola come and join us somewhere, Boss man?"

"I'm good. Taking care of a few things in a minute with Juan G. Nola is out at the hospital visiting her cousin."

"I heard on the streets that Weeta Wee got shot up. Why you didn't get at me on that one, Boss man?"

"Not my business and none of yours as well. We have more important stuff on our plates than worrying about Weeta Wee's issues, Cotton."

"From what I heard, though, someone pretty close to me had something to do with that incident. That's why I asked. Anything that happens with that particular person does concern me and my business, Boss man."

"True. But you can't believe everything you hear, Cotton. Remember, all lies start with either 'they said' or 'I heard.'"

Laughing, Cotton said, "You are something else, Boss man. Something else for real. All right, just checking in on ya. I'll get at you later on then."

"That's cool. And remember to do as I told you with these new phones we got."

"I got you. Everything is as you wanted it. Never can stay too safe, right?"

"Right. Talk to you later," Hot Shot said and ended the call and sat back in his seat and thought about what Cotton had told him about the rumor of what had happened to Weeta Wee. Something like that on his name could be good in a sense and bad in another. He made a mental note to make sure he had Cotton keep his ear to the streets on that issue.

***

"I'm telling you, Troy, he's not going to go for it. I could see in his eyes what we're trying to do disgusts him," Lola said as she watched as their two newest female recruits were making out on the bed in the back room trying their best to impress her and Troy with more moaning and groaning than was necessary.

Not responding to his sister's comments, Tiny Troy was more concerned with what he was watching. "Uh-uh! No way! Y'all are doing way too much damn moaning and groaning and not enough sucking and finger fucking each other! Suzy, I want you to lick Barbie's pussy like your life depends on it. Make her come so hard that she sees stars, babe. And, Barbie, I want you to put your fingers as far as you can in Suzy's asshole and pussy. Got me?"

"Yes, Tiny Troy," the two white girls said in unison. He then faced his sister and said, "My gut tells me he'll be with it, Lola. He may not dig the get down, but he will definitely be with the payout. So relax. Shit, with these two new white girls combined with Melody and her cousin Kamden, we're good. I'm sure we can have a nice run with them before adding more to the team. They will be eighteen in a minute, and that's barely legal but still legal. Shot won't trip, trust me."

"I don't know, maybe we should bring Nola into the fold because then, she could get at him and make sure he gets with us. That man is stone gone in love with her. I don't think there's no way he would ever deny her anything."

Shaking his head emphatically, Tiny Troy said, "No way! For one, there ain't anything in this world that would make Nola roll with us on this. You know better than that. She is stuck on the high and mighty road for real. This would piss her the fuck off and put everything we have in place in jeopardy. Two, though Hot Shot is loving our sister, he doesn't strike me as the type of man that would let a woman sway his decision on anything pertaining to his business. He's not built that way. He's about his paper, though, and that's why I know he'll roll with us." As if on cue, Tiny Troy's phone started ringing. He smiled when he saw that it was Hot Shot calling him. "Here he is now. Let's see who's going to be right on this one," he said as he answered the phone. "What's good, Shot, you straight?"

"I'm always straight, Troy. What about yourself?"

"Chillin', just waitin' to hear what you gon' do with this move we presented to you."

"I spoke with my people in the West, and they want me to roll with you simply because it sounds like a good business move, and they're always with good business. Personally, I'm against it. But that's me and my feelings. I'm a hustler by nature, so getting bread is my primary concern. Wit' that said, I'm in."

"Good."

"There are some conditions, though."

"Holla at me."

"Nola. You're keeping this from her is something I not only agree with, I feel it's a must that she never finds out that I'm a part of this with you."

"No problem there at all. Anything else?"

"Yes. I never want to be around for any filming of the movies. I never want to be around any previews of the movies, and I never want to even see a cover of these movies. I am solely an investor. I know what you're doing, but I don't need to see nothing but the numbers and the money that comes from what's being put down. Agreed?"

"Agreed. When will you be able to drop that 1.5 million I need to get everything in place?"

"Nola is at the hospital with your cousin, so the best time for us to get down would be now. I have a run to make real quick, but I'll be back here within the hour. Why don't you have Lola come over and pick it up."

"That's cool. I'll have her leave here in say, forty-five minutes. By the time she gets to your crib, you should be back from handling your business."

"Perfect. I'll get with you later, Troy," Hot Shot said and ended the call. After setting his phone down, Tiny Troy smiled brightly at his sister and said, "See, I told you he would rock out with us. This shit is too big to pass, Lola."

"I guess you're right. Shit, we about to make some major bread with this stuff."

"Yes, my sister, yes, we are," he said as he continued watching the two teenagers make out on the bed.

Hot Shot arrived at Exposures and stepped straight toward Juan G.'s table and took a seat after greetings were made. Juan G. smiled at him and said, "My man, Hot Shot, you know you've helped me elevate my game, right?"

"If you say so, Juan G. You've been spending a nice chunk of change, so I guess I can say you've helped me step my game up a few notches as well."

"We're good for each other, dog. You should maybe think about fucking with me exclusively. We could cake out all the way and lock Dallas all the way down."

Shaking his head, Hot Shot said, "That's not how this works for me. I'm good with how things are right now. Is this why you called this meeting? Because if it is, I can tell you now, I am not interested, and I have more pressing things to take care of, Juan G."

"You won't even give me an opportunity to break things down to you? I mean, I got a real live plan that can make what we're doing turn into a monstrous move, Shot."

"I've heard enough when you said lock all of Dallas down. That's not my forte, Juan G. When you get on that type of time, things tend to get heavy, and what I mean by heavy is people tend to want beef. Kinda like Biggie Smalls said, more money more problems. I don't need that kind of weight on my shoulders. The beef and the extra drama that comes along with locking a town down is something that could destroy all that I got going on, and it's just not worth it to me."

"I respect what you're saying, Shot, but like I said, you haven't given me the chance to break what I have on my mind all the way down to you. If you give me a moment, I think I can convince y'all to see things from my eyes, and you just might roll with me."

"I doubt that very seriously. But go ahead and shoot your shot and we'll take it from there," Hot Shot said as he sat back in his seat and folded his arms across his chest.

"With your connects behind me, there is nothing that could stop me from locking the town down. I have the manpower and the resources to move every type of drug that's popular in town. You have the plugs on everything, and that alone can gain me even more power. The fools who's getting the weight will have no other choice but to want to fuck with me. That will up the ante to enormous heights for both of us. I'll be spending more and more every time out. You will be making even more money, and I'm sure your people in the West will love how things will take off. You won't ever have to worry about the beef or the petty jealousy type shit because I'm getting that weak shit all the time anyway. As for the beef, I dead all beefs because I got the soldiers that will go all out and handle whatever. Just like that beef with the Bloods. Why do you think it got squashed so easily?"

"I thought because you guys worked out a truce or something to that effect."

Shaking his head, Juan G. said, "Nah. Those fools knew they were about to get that heat brought to they ass. Yeah, they about their work and can put in a little work here and there, but when it came to the major work, they knew that they were lacking in numbers. Not only did I have my people ready to get on they ass, I also had an added bonus with the Crips in the South who fuck with me. Dropped the numbers on the yay yo to them as well as hooked them up with some of your high-powered weapons, and they were ready to rock all out with me. It didn't take long for those Bloods to know to back the fuck up before they got faded."

"I understand all that, but do you really think they've backed off for good? They could be regrouping and trying to figure out another way to get at you."

"That may be true, but if they do, they will still lose. This is why I'm telling you we need to hook all the way up. With you fucking with me exclusively, the town will be forced to go through me for everything."

Now with the entire picture in front of him, Hot Shot understood the play Juan G. was trying to make. And he didn't like it at all. *This man has become extremely dangerous to me and everything I've worked to build out here. I need some time to think on this and get at JT,* Hot Shot said to himself. He waited a moment, and then told Juan G., "I feel what you're saying, but this still seems like something I don't really want to deal with. What I will do is run it by my people and see what they have to say. I'll get back with you and let you know how they feel in a couple of weeks."

"A couple of weeks? Damn, Shot, can't you get at me faster than that?"

"I have other obligations at this time, Juan G. Like I said, give me a couple of weeks and I'll get with you after I holla at my people."

Juan G. sighed like a spoiled child who had just been told he could not have a cookie and said, "All right, Shot. Get at me when you're ready."

"Will do. Cheer up, there's still plenty of money to be made in the town."

Juan G. stared at Hot Shot with a serious expression on his face and said, "See, you don't get it, hombre. I've always made money out here, and I always will. I'm at the stage of the game where it's all or nothing. I'm ready to take the entire city. You need to really understand that, 'cause it's going to happen whether or not you're with me."

Hot Shot didn't respond. He just stared at the cocky Mexican drug dealer and once again thought, *Yes, this joker is definitely going to be a problem.*

Chapter Twenty

Hot Shot wasn't in the best of moods this morning. Actually, his mood was downright foul. Over the last month or so, Cotton had turned slowly into a swagged out monster. First, a new truck, and now, he went and bought Meosha a brand-new Benz. His flossing had become an irritant to Hot Shot in a major way. Mainly because his productivity had begun to decline. He was busier flossing in the streets and clubs than he was into getting money, and that was a huge no-no in Hot Shot's eyes. Not only did he have to have a sit-down with Cotton, he also had to deal with Nola and the promise he made her. Thus, his foul mood as he sat next to her as she drove toward Rowlett.

"I don't understand why you won't let me send your cousin a text telling him that I apologize for the shooting thing, Nola. I mean, do you really think he's going to accept my apology anyway?" Hot Shot asked as he stared at the passing cars on the highway.

"You know damn well that sending an apology by text is flat-out wrong, honey. If you ever tried to apologize to me that way, it wouldn't be accepted in no way, shape, or form. A man looks a man in the eyes when he has wronged him and gives him a face-to-face apology. You are a man in every sense of the word, honey. You're my man. I want my man to be the man I know he is and face my cousin and give him a sincere apology. Whether he accepts it really isn't my concern. I want him to see that you're not as bad as he makes himself think you are."

"Whatever. I gave you my word, and I will stand on that. When are we heading to Oklahoma?" he asked, changing the subject.

"I'm glad you asked because I was thinking, if you didn't have a full plate, we could get out there tonight or tomorrow morning. Now that Weeta Wee is out the hospital, Keeta Wee is ready to make that move. We kinda fell off since the shooting stuff because Keeta Wee wasn't feeling right about going back outta town with his twin still laid up in the hospital."

"No need for that added guilt stuff, Nola, I get your meaning. All I need to do this evening is get with Cotton, then we can go on and head out there. How long will we be staying?"

She shrugged her shoulders and said, "Not that long; maybe two, three days tops. Just long enough for Keeta Wee to check all his traps and for us to handle Weeta Wee's load. Keeta Wee said that his people have been getting at him, and they're ready with what's owed to him. So this new batch they just got should go pretty fast."

"That's what's up. Let me get at Cotton real quick to make sure he's around because we need to have a serious discussion."

"What has that boy done now, honey?"

"Way too much to talk about, for real," he said as he pulled out his phone and dialed Cotton's number. When Cotton answered, Hot Shot told him, "I'm on my way to Rowlett to take care of some business. I should be back in a couple of hours. We need to meet and have a talk."

"About what, Boss man? Everything good?"

"No, everything ain't good. Meet me at my spot around two, I should be back by then."

"Okay. I got something for you anyway, so that works well for me."

"Later," Hot Shot said as he ended the call just as Nola was pulling into the driveway of her former home. When they entered the house, the first thing Hot Shot noticed was there were even more young white girls there than the last time he had come out and saw Tiny Troy. He wondered if Nola really was in the blind about what her sister and brother were up to. She seemed to pay the white girls no attention as she led the way to the back room. When they entered the back room, Tiny Troy was laughing and talking to Weeta Wee who was lying on one of the many couches being pampered by two very young-looking Spanish girls.

This fool done went from white girls to young Spanish girls, Hot Shot said to himself as he let his eyes roam all over the room. That's when he noticed even more young girls who looked to be no older than seventeen tops. Some looked even younger! He groaned and thought, *This is nuts.* Without any greeting, he stepped quickly toward the couch where Weeta Wee was sitting and held up his hand in a peaceful gesture when he saw how wide Weeta Wee's eyes grew when he saw Hot Shot approaching him so quickly.

With his hands still raised, Hot Shot smiled and said, "I come in peace, my man. I want you to know that I have no problems with you and that I apologize for what I did to you. I regret that day because I could have dealt with it in a different manner. Like I've told you, I'm a man that demands respect because I give respect at all times. I have become seriously involved with your cousin Nola. Straight up, I love her. That, combined with the fact I'm doing some real good business with Tiny Troy means I will be around for a long time, hopefully a very long time. I don't want to have beef with you or your brother over there. So I hope you will accept my apology so we can get past this and make some serious money. All I ask is that you respect me as I will give you the same respect you deserve as a man."

Weeta Wee's facial expression went from a hard frown to a soft smile as he stared at Hot Shot for a few moments without speaking. He looked over to where Keeta Wee, Lola, Nola, and Tiny Troy were sitting and could tell by the looks on their faces that they wanted him to accept Hot Shot's apology. Though he was still undecided on how he felt about Hot Shot, he respected how he got at him. As he gently stroked the arm of one of the Spanish girls who was beside him, he said, "I respect how you just got at me, Hot Shot, and I accept your apology, man. I apologize for getting at you sideways like you were weak. I was wrong for that. We good. I just need one thing from you, and I can pretty much say we'll never have any issues again."

"What's that, Weeta Wee?"

"Don't be so damn quick to pop off if I slip and use the N-word at you or in your presence. Because if I do, best believe it was a mistake and not intentional in any damn way!" Everyone in the room started laughing, and the tension was broken. All was cool.

Hot Shot grinned at the chunky man lying on the couch and said, "You got that, Weeta Wee, you got that, dude." He reached out his hand, and the two men shook on it.

"Now, *that's* what I'm talking about! Now we can get focused more on the money and remain a solid family all the way around," Lola said with a smile as she stood and walked toward Hot Shot. When she made it to him, she whispered in his ear, "I think you really need to get Nola out of here before she pays attention to her surroundings."

He gave her a nod and said, "Gotcha." He turned toward Keeta Wee and said, "That apology also goes to you as well, Keeta Wee. We good too?"

Keeta Wee nodded his head and said, "Yeah, Shot, we good. Let's get this bre-ded."

"Bre-ded? What's that?"

"Bread, fool. That's how that brew rapper outta New York says bread when he be talking about getting money."

"You heard that single that's out right now, honey. 'Get Dat Bre-ded,'" said Nola.

"I heard it, but I hadn't really paid much attention to it."

"I don't know why. It's the hottest single out right now. That New York dude is popping. It features that other new rapper dude called Da Plug."

"Oh yeah, I definitely heard about him. He's from somewhere in South Carolina, right?"

"Yep, and he's the truth too. I heard him and that New York dude I. V. L. were in the feds together. That's where they met and started writing rhymes together."

"That's a crazy way to meet, but it looks as if it paid off for the brothers."

"I know that's right. Wish I could rhyme like they ass," said Keeta Wee.

"Shit, all we got to do is practice that shit and we could be the first set of twin rappers," said Weeta Wee. Laughing, Tiny Troy said, "Hell yeah, then we'll be able to make even more bre-ded!" Everyone started laughing.

"All right, since the business has been taken care of, I need to get back to town. I got some other stuff that needs to be checked on," Hot Shot said as he started walking toward Nola.

"Keeta Wee, when are you going to Oklahoma?" asked Nola.

"I was about to leave in a little bit. What's up?"

"Me and Hot Shot will be on our way sometime this evening. I'll give you a call when we leave. You make sure that you call me to let me know you made it safely, ya hear me?"

"Will do. I'll be in Guthrie by the time y'all get there, then I'm hitting up Lawton. I'll be able to let you know where I need you to go by tomorrow afternoon."

"That's fine, honey."

"Anything we need to discuss, Tiny Troy?" asked Hot Shot.

"Nope, everything is on auto pilot, Shot. We good all the way around, my man," Tiny Troy said with a huge smile on his face.

"That's what's up. All right then, be cool and stay safe," Hot Shot said as he led Nola out of the back room toward the front. Once they were outside and walking toward the car, he asked Nola, "Are you happy now, baby?"

She smiled at him and said, "You always make me happy, Hot Shot. That's why I'm so in love with you. Now, I need you to tell me what did my ratchet-ass twin whisper in your ear when we were in the back room."

He stared at her and said, "Business stuff."

"You gon' be that vague with me, honey?"

"If it was anything else you already know I would tell you, Nola."

"So far, you've never given me reason to doubt you, but right now, my bullshit meter is humming like crazy, honey. Don't fuck us up over some weak shit. Love is wonderful, honey, but at the same time, it can be real destructive. Always be honest with me, and we will always be good. I can respect honesty, but I will never respect a lie."

Hot Shot sighed heavily as he got inside of the car. When Nola joined him, started the car, and was pulling out of the driveway, he said, "I don't do lies. That's not my way, Nola. Now, I may not reveal all of my business, but I don't lie. Your sister got at me on some business stuff, and that's the truth."

"I believe you, honey, but there's more to this than you're telling me. I can feel it. I have the right to know, Hot Shot. Don't I?"

"If you feel you're not knowing something business-wise, then I think you should have a sit-down with your twin and your brother. It's not my place to interfere with what you guys had in place long before I entered the equation."

"They have been lying to me for Lord only knows how long. I stopped asking them questions just as soon as I left that house. I fell for you in a major way for many reasons, honey, and all of them are good. I chose to move in with you so fast because I needed to get the hell away from that house. It's tainted with what they're doing there, and I feel we're disrespecting our parents' memory. But at the same time, I want Troy to realize that he has to become legitimate sooner or later, because the game don't last forever. He's so caught up into this porno making stuff he has become less interested in the drugs. Which is definitely a good thing, in my eyes. I know my brother and sister, though. They are always up to something, and when I saw my sister whisper in your ear, I knew then that my man was now a part of whatever they are into. Now that brings you into the equation in a major way with me. It gives me the right to ask you what the hell is going on, and I deserve the truth because I am asking my man for it."

Nola had him boxed in a corner, and he knew that there was only one way for him to get out of it, and that was to tell her the truth.

"Before I answer your question, I want your word that you will listen before asking me anything else."

"You got that."

"You will not judge me behind this, because I feel cruddy enough as it is about this."

With raised eyebrows, she nodded and said, "Okay."

"Your brother and sister love how the money came in from the porno movie Lola did. It was better than they ever imagined. Their noses are wide open now, and Troy sees a way to be able to make even more money from this business. That's why there are more girls at the house now. If you paid attention, you would have noticed that mostly all of the girls there are all underage. Your brother and sister are using these underage girls to make child pornography. Not the kiddie porn but still kids, sixteen and seventeen years old. They got at me and asked me to invest some more ends so he could get more top-notch equipment for better quality that would help with the distribution side of things. Not only DVDs, he wants to go straight to the Blu-ray deal and market his own line of porno movies using all of those young girls. I wasn't with it. Honestly, it disgusts me. But when I brought it to my people in the West and broke down the numbers that could be pulled in from this, they wanted in, so I agreed and gave your brother the money he needed.

"They know that you wouldn't be with that, and they told me to keep it away from you because you would go off on them. Lola whispered to me that I needed to get you out of there before you paid attention to all of the young girls there in the back room. She feared you would notice that they were all teenagers and not the older women that had been there before. That's it, and that's the entire truth, Nola," he said as he sat back in his seat and waited for her response. He saw how her hands tightened around the steering wheel and thought, *Oh crap, she is salty for real.*

"Humph. Always up to something. Those two have been that way their entire life. They have to do things the goofy way all the time. Lola's freaky self is probably freaking off with those little girls too, and that's just plain sick. My sister and her abnormal sexual desires, and my brother and his greedy get-money schemes have been something I've had to deal with all my life, and even more so after my parents died. We only live once, and we should enjoy life, but not at the expense of selling our souls. Using teenagers is wrong, honey, even if they're with it. It's still wrong, and I don't give a damn how much money is made from it. That's a sin I'm not willing to face God for."

Hot Shot felt ashamed because he felt exactly the same way, but his hands were tied, and he couldn't say a thing but sit there and feel like dirt.

"The money has gotten the man I'm in love with caught up in this mess. Three of the most important people in my life are caught up in some smut child pornography shit, and I'm supposed to sit back and accept that shit? That is fucked up in the highest order, honey. And I mean that."

"You weren't supposed to know any of this, Nola. They were respecting you enough to keep it away from you."

"Don't! Don't you dare try to use the word 'respect' in this. Respecting me would have been to *not* have started the shit in the first place. They were *hiding* it from me and being deceitful because that's their way. That's the only way they know how to be. They then brought you on board to help advance their sick desires, honey. At least I can respect you for being honest with me. Even though you kept it from me, you didn't lie to me, and that means more to me than you will ever realize."

"I told you I don't do lies, Nola. That's not my way. So, what do we do now?"

She stared straight-ahead as she drove and remained silent for a few minutes before answering, and then said, "We continue to live and let life take its course, honey. I'm too tired of battling my brother and sister. I'm going to start distancing myself from them more and more until I'm outta the way. I refuse to get caught up in any of their mess. It's time for me to take my life in an entirely different direction."

"What about us? Will this affect you and me?"

She smiled at him and said, "We're good, Hot Shot. You are a man that I respect and love dearly. The way you make your money is the way you choose to live. Promise me you won't let the way you make your money get me caught up. I'm about to get away from the hustling life and do right. I want to live righteously and be happy. Can you promise me that you will protect me from any of the bullshit that comes with the hustling lifestyle you're a part of, Hot Shot?"

He stared at her and realized how much he loved Nola. He respected what she was saying and appreciated her honesty. "I am so in love with you, Nola. I give you my word you will never get caught up in anything that comes with my business. I'd die before I'd ever let that happen."

She smiled as she continued to drive, a smile that was so sincere, a smile that was genuine, because she knew that her man was telling her the truth.

Chapter Twenty-one

When they made it to the condo, Nola told Hot Shot that she needed to get some therapy, which, in her eyes, meant to go do some serious shopping. So off to the mall she went to try to get some peace of mind. He laughed as he watched her drive off. He then went upstairs to wait for Cotton to arrive. Cotton made it to the condo about twenty minutes after Hot Shot. Hot Shot wasted no time getting right at him about his newfound attitude and swag.

"What's up with all the extra stuff you on, Cotton?"

"What you mean, Boss man?"

"What I mean? Look at you—big diamonds in both ears, big nasty diamond-encrusted watch, big fat new platinum Jesus piece. Why you getting all flossy with it all of a sudden? That's not your get down. What's up with that? Who are you trying to impress out there, Cotton?"

Cotton shrugged and said, "Enjoying the fruits of my hustle, Boss man. I'm handling my business, and I thought it was time that I enjoyed some of the bread I've been making for us. I mean, why are you tripping? You're the one that's way more swagged out than I am. You're the one pushing the whip for 131 Gs. You're the one that has way more diamonds than little old me. What's up with checking on me for trying to step my swag game up a little bit?"

"'Cause there're levels to this game, Cotton. You can't skip levels. You got to gradually rise to them. If I thought that was your MO, then I would have no problem with you raising your levels like this. But that's not your MO. You don't move like that, and I want to know the reason for the sudden urge to make these changes. You're an intricate part of my business out here, and it's a must I know all, and I mean *everything* that you do, and why you do it. You screw up out there, it can potentially screw up me and my business, and that's something I will not tolerate or ever let happen. So, if you wish to further our business arrangement, I suggest you get at me with the real, or this will be the last time we speak. Talk to me, Cotton, and stop wasting my time," Hot Shot said with a stern look on his face.

Cotton sighed and gave one word for his answer. "Meosha."

"What about her?"

"She's the baddest broad I've ever had as a woman, Boss man. I'm so caught up with her that all I think about is keeping her happy. She told me how she felt I was carrying myself as a flunky instead of carrying myself like a boss. She told me that I needed to step my game up and look like a man getting money instead of a chump making money for someone else. She said that my business arrangement is cool, but that didn't mean I shouldn't have the best of everything. As long as my money was right and my business has been handled, then I should enjoy what I got, so that's what I've been doing, Boss man . . . enjoying what I got."

Fuming and feeling his anger mounting, Hot Shot asked him a serious question. "What does Meosha know about our business, Cotton?"

"Nothing. That's the truth, Boss man. She knows I get down for you, and that's it. She knows no more than any of the other people I deal with out there in the streets. Everyone knows I fucks with Hot Shot, and that in order to get at you, they got to go through me, and that's all she knows; nothing else. I love that girl. She has me gone, but I'm no fool. I will never put your business out there like that with her or anyone else. I'm not trying to get cut off. I'm trying to continue to eat and live good, and fucking with you guarantees that, Boss man."

Accepting his words as being truthful, Hot Shot's anger slowly dissipated, and he began to somewhat relax. "All right, I can understand you trying to impress your girl and all that, but don't you see how you're putting yourself out there for the haters? For the jack boys that may want to try you? I appreciate your honesty here because I can tell you are keeping it real with me. But you ain't looking at this picture clearly. Getting all the extras is cool, but that comes with a price. You say you're not slipping, but actually, you are. You're bringing more attention to yourself than needed. From the haters as well as the snitches, you have to think for yourself and not let your woman dictate how you move out there. Love is good, trust me. I know how good it is and how good it feels. But love won't get you out of jail. Love won't bring you back from the grave. You have to control what love does to you instead of letting love control how you get down. My moves are cool because I'm not out there like you are.

"Again, levels to this game, Cotton. Yeah, my name rings, and thank God I haven't had to put anything serious down out there. Yet and still, I'm prepared to go all out if I have to. That's me, though, not you. You have to be safe and watch yourself and give the impression that you're out there making yours like everyone else in them streets, grinding. You start acting brand-new looking like you're on some boss time, then you open an entire new can of worms that you're not really capable of dealing with. I won't let nothing happen to you. I will do what needs to be done if anyone ever got at you, and that's my word, but what good is that if you get twisted out there all because you wanted to impress Meosha? See what I'm saying, Cotton?"

"Yeah, I feel you, Boss man. I didn't look at it like that."

Laughing, Hot Shot said, "I know you didn't. You were too busy trying to show your girl that you the man. Beating your chest and swanging your piece so she can smile and be all on you with that, 'Yes, Daddy, stuff'! That's cool, and I understand that. You care about your girl and you want her to be happy with you. But in order to be truly happy with you, she has to be happy with you as you are, not as she wants you to be. She's not out there, and the risks of her getting twisted out there is minimal. You are the front line, and it's you that must do what needs to be done in order to maintain out there. I ain't mad at you for spending your ends the way you want too. That's cool. Actually, I agree with Meosha. You needed to step up your swag game some. I don't want no one affiliated with me not looking their very best anyway. Your reasons for doing so were wack, though. Go have a sit-down with Meosha and let her know that you are a boss in your own right. Spending money on the extra stuff is cool, but you got a money management thing going on, and nothing can get in the way of that."

"What if she asks me what that money management plan is?"

"You tell her to sit back and watch, and she will learn all in time. But for now, let you do what needs to be done."

"I feel you, Boss man. Thanks. You always gon' keep it real with me, and I respect that."

"I know no other way, Cotton. Like I said, you are representing me out there, and I can't afford to let you be out there slipping."

"Fools out there know better to even think about stepping to me on some slimy shit. The word around the town is you're not to be fucked with, so that transcends to me. I'm not to be fucked with neither. That demo you put down on the Bloods has turned wanna be jack boys away from even thinking about trying us."

"That may be true, but you can never say what a desperate man will, or will not, do. Keep your eyes open and make that money, Cotton, and everything will continue to be good."

"I know that's right."

"All right. Look, I'm about to be gone out of town for a couple of days. Three at the most. You good, or do you need something?"

"Nah, I'm straight. I got enough to hold me off until you get back."

"Cool. I'm about to make some runs before I leave. Remember what I said. Do you, just be safe about it."

"I will, Boss man. I'll holla at you when you get back," Cotton said as he stood and headed toward the door.

After Cotton left, Hot Shot sighed loudly and prayed that he wouldn't have to get out there in the streets and get crazy behind Cotton. The game was a wicked one and could chew a man alive if he didn't remain on his toes at all times. Cotton, though sharp as a tack, was still easily distracted, and that could be a potential danger. Meosha was definitely a distraction that Hot Shot felt he would have to pay close attention to for both of their sakes. He would not let her get Cotton twisted. *No way, no how,* he thought as he grabbed his phone and called JT on the West Coast.

Nola knew she was pissed, but she didn't realize how pissed she actually was until she got to the mall and didn't feel like doing any shopping. If she didn't feel like shopping, then she knew that her feelings toward her

brother and sister's actions had her to the point of hurting someone. She walked around the mall aimlessly for
over an hour before she realized that she was wasting her
time, even after seeing some simply-to-die-for stiletto
heels by Jimmy Choo at the Nine West shoe store. *Yep,
they done went and ruined me,* she said to herself as
she walked briskly toward the mall exit. As soon as she
stepped out of the mall, it started raining so hard that
she was instantly soaked by the time she made it to her
car. This only added insult to injury she thought as she
sat inside of her car trying to dry herself off with a scarf
she had in her purse. She then started the car and said,
"Fuck this, I need a drink!"

She drove to a nearby bar she used to go hang at back
in her wilder days. Luckily, by the time she made it to
the bar, the rain subsided enough that she didn't get
drenched again as she got out of the car and entered the
bar. She went straight to the bar, waved to get the bartender's attention, and ordered a double shot of Peach
Cîroc Vodka. After the bartender set her drink in front of
her, she smiled and held up her hand signaling for him to
wait a moment. She then downed the drink quickly and
said, "Ahhh, now you can bring me another, please."

The bartender laughed as he went to do as he was told.
Nola sat down on the bar stool and turned away from the
bar in her seat so she could look around and check out
her surroundings, something she knew she should have
done as soon as she had entered the bar. Her brother,
as well as Hot Shot, told her numerous times to make
sure to be aware of your surroundings at all times. Never
know when someone could be lurking or trying to make a
move on her. Though she thought they were being overly
protective, she still took heed to their words because
she knew they would never tell her anything that wasn't
for her safety. She received her second drink and was

sipping it when she saw someone that instantly made her regret the decision to come and have a drink at this particular bar. *Damn, I'm having a really bad day,* she said to herself as she watched as her ex-boyfriend, Simon, start walking toward her with a devilish smile on his face.

At six foot two, with a honey-brown skin complexion, the man was so handsome that he knew he could have any woman he wanted. In fact, he did have any woman he wanted. That's why he was no longer with Nola. There was no way she would ever let a man carry her the way he tried to. He actually thought because she was really feeling him, along with his extraordinarily good looks, he could do and say whatever he wanted to her. That, or the fact that he was supplying her brother with the drugs he needed when they were together. Boy, was he wrong on all accounts because when she found out that he not only had a wife tucked away out in the city of Grand Prairie, he also had two other baby mothers set up nicely in North and South Dallas. He received the shock of his life when Nola told him to kick rocks. He thought that since he was doing business with her brother that that would give him some leverage and help him remain in her life. Wrong. Everything happened for a reason because once Tiny Troy saw that she was no longer comfortable with Simon being around them, he slowly stopped conducting business with him, and that was something she knew pissed Simon off tremendously. That thought put a smile on her face as she watched as Simon approached her. He obviously mistook her smile as her being happy to see him because when he stood in front of her, he tried to give her a kiss on the cheek. Nola frowned as she eased her head back and said, "Whoa, what's with all that? A hello would have been just fine."

"You know you need to go on with that shit, Nola, with your fine ass. You know you miss Simon just as much as Simon has missed you. Now give Simon a kiss, girl."

Craving another drink but deciding against it because she knew she would need all of her wits to deal with the man standing in front of her, Nola sipped some more of her drink and said, "You still don't get how irritating it sounds when you speak in the third person."

Laughing, he took a seat on the bar stool next to her and said, "Same old Nola, never hesitating to speak her mind to Simon, huh?"

She rolled her eyes and said, "I speak my mind not only to Simon, honey; everyone gets it straight from me. Anyway, you can excuse yourself. I'm waiting for someone, and I would hate for him to get here and misconstrue this conversation for something it's definitely not."

"That's cold, Nola. You act like you can't spare a few minutes of your time with Simon. Who you waiting on? That California nigga I heard you been fucking with?"

She stared at him without letting the shock that he knew her business be seen on her face.

He laughed and said, "Look at you. You know you wondering how I know about you and that nigga Hot Shot. Yeah, that's right. Simon does his homework, baby. I also know that that's your brother's connect too. That's real fucked up how you got your brother to dead fucking with Simon, all because you found out about my wife."

"You got it really twisted, don't you, Simon? One, I didn't get my brother to do anything. He makes his business decisions on his own. I don't have shit to say about any of that. Two, it wasn't just your wife that I found out about, Simon. It was those other two women who have kids by you as well. And three, I could care less about you knowing who my man is because Simon can never be as good for me as Hot Shot is. He's a man that knows how to treat a woman. More important, he knows how to respect a woman by being totally honest with her *at all times*. Now, like I said, could you please leave before he arrives? I don't want this to turn into something ugly."

Simon started laughing and said, "Yeah, I know that's right, 'cause I'd sure hate to smash that punk-ass nigga if he came in here acting like he was in Cali-some-fucking-where."

Hot Shot tapped Simon on his shoulder and said, "I would appreciate it if you wouldn't use that N-word in my or my woman's presence. And as for smashing me, I don't think that could happen, you punk peon of a man."

Nola was staring at her man as he stared Simon down with a look so deadly that her only thought was, *Oh shit!*

Chapter Twenty-two

Simon started laughing and said, "Oh, you do got nuts, huh? I heard about your incident with the Bloods out South, plus the rumor of how you supposed to have hit up Weeta Wee. All of that's good and dandy, bruh, but what you working with when it comes down to those hands?"

"All you have to do is make a move and you *will* find out," Hot Shot said as he continued to stare directly into Simon's light brown eyes.

"Come on, honey, let's go. There's no need for any of this. We don't have time for weak shit."

"I'd rather let Simon make that decision, Nola." He then asked Simon, "So, what's it going to be, champ? You ready to see how I get down in Texas? Believe me, it's way worse than how I rock it in the West. The stuff you've heard ain't nothing compared to how I get when I'm *really* turned up. So either make that move or get to stepping, chump." Hot Shot hoped by goading Simon he would let his pride push him to act, and he was absolutely correct. Simon tried to throw a left jab toward Hot Shot's face that he easily avoided and countered with a solid right hook that connected to Simon's nose, breaking it upon impact. Wasting no time, Hot Shot then proceeded to beat the daylights out of Simon, hitting him everywhere he wanted with ease. The right eye, the nose again, the side of his jaw, two powerful uppercuts to the stomach, and the coup de grâce blow to the temple that dropped Simon to the ground dazed heavily but not knocked out.

Standing over Simon, Hot Shot smiled down at him and said, "That right there was my Floyd Mayweather impersonation. Broke you down like a real fighting tactician. If you get up, I will show you my Iron Mike impersonation and knock you out, Simon. Do you understand?"

Simon looked up at Hot Shot and stared into his cold brown eyes and knew that he was dead serious. But he refused to go out weak like that in front of all of the people who were inside of the crowded bar watching. More important, he couldn't let Nola watch him get punked like this. No-fucking-way.

"Fuck you, nigga!" Simon screamed as he reached in the small of his back for his gun.

Bad decision, Simon, thought Hot Shot as he pulled his pistol from his waist way before Simon even had a chance to touch his gun. He put the barrel of his nine millimeter on the tip of Simon's rapidly swelling broken nose.

"Don't make me kill you, Simon. I really don't have time for that in my life right now. But if you wish to die today, then by all means, continue to reach for your weapon."

Simon stopped and brought his right hand from behind his back without anything in it. He then held up his hands and said, "You got the best of Simon, Hot Shot. I can't win. But you really should go on and handle your business because we got beef now. You better do Simon now because the beef won't end until one of us is dead, nigga!"

Upon hearing the N-word, Hot Shot lost it. Such disrespect would never be tolerated by him. It was time to get an example. Without hesitating, Hot Shot pulled Simon to his feet and slapped him three times in the face with his gun, and then kicked him in his groin, folding him over like a rag doll. He then slapped Simon on the back of the head with his pistol, dropping him to the floor again. After kicking him viciously several times in the ribs, Hot Shot screamed, "Do! Not! Ever! Call! Me! That! N! Word! Simon! If it's beef you want, then so be it." He then knelt over Simon's body and put the pistol to the back of his head.

"No! Hot Shot! No!" screamed Nola. "Let's get out of here, honey. I'm sure someone has called the police already. Let's go home, baby," she pleaded.

Realizing that he'd totally lost it, Hot Shot let Nola's words calm him some. He stood and kicked Simon once more and said, "Catch you in the streets, Simon." He then turned toward the bartender, reached into his jeans, and pulled out several hundred dollar bills and placed onto the counter of the bar and apologized. "I'm sorry for this disturbance, sir." He then grabbed Nola by her hand and led her out of the bar with everyone inside staring at them, awe-struck by what they had just witnessed.

When they made it to the condo, Hot Shot went straight to the kitchen and returned to the living room with a bottle of Peach Cîroc in his hand, clearly vexed. Without saying a word, he opened the bottle and took a swig. He groaned as the vodka burned its way down his throat to the pit of his stomach, and then took another swig. He started pacing back and forth, and this scared Nola. She'd never see this side of her man before, and she hoped that he would be able to regain his composure because he had the look of death in his eyes something terrible.

"Hot Shot, come here and sit with me, honey. You need to calm down. All that pacing you doing ain't doing nothing but keeping you amped all high. You got to calm down, honey," she said as she reached out her hands toward him. "Come here, honey."

He stopped and stared at her for a moment, took another swig from the vodka bottle, and slowly went to her on the couch where she was seated. He set the bottle of vodka onto the coffee table and grabbed her hand.

"I apologize for spooking you like that, Nola. It's just when I get in this mode, it's not easy to turn down. I can't just turn it off when I get like this. It takes me a minute. All I keep hearing is that joker telling me that we got beef now, and the beef won't end until one of us is dead. He threatened my life, and I don't play that at all, Nola. He has to die," Hot Shot said as he reached toward the bottle of vodka on the coffee table.

Nola stopped him by grabbing the bottle before he could and said, "Don't you dare let Simon's simple self get you like this. His bark is way worse than his bite. Trust me on that, honey. He's a weak man that was beaten and embarrassed. He was just trying to save face, honey."

"Reaching for a weapon looked more to me like he was trying to handle his business than save face, Nola."

"Simon don't have that kind of mentality for real, honey. You forced his hand, and he tried to act, but that's all that was—an act. Let it be and keep doing what you been doing. No need to let that weakling mess up all of what you got going on out here."

"If I don't, what I'm supposed to do? He may get at me. When it comes to this type of stuff, I do what I feel needs to be done, and that's that. End of discussion, Nola."

The finality in his tone told her not to push any further. She had to let her man be the man that he was. She hoped and prayed that he would come out of this mess unscathed. Sighing loudly, she chose to change the subject. "Tell me, how in the hell did you find your way to that bar? I was so shocked I couldn't even speak when you stepped up behind him."

"I was on my way to make a quick drop on the North when my cell rang. When I answered it, I could only hear you singing along to that Tech N9ne song you like to play from his CD, all 6's and 7's. I think it was that song 'Delusional.' I kept saying hello over and over, but you couldn't hear me. I started laughing and realized that you must have called my phone without knowing it, so I hung up. Then a few minutes later, you called me back, but this time, I could hear you telling a bartender to give you another drink. A few minutes after that, I heard you sigh, and then start a conversation with that prick, Simon. Once I heard the start of that conversation, I continued to listen as I pulled up the GPS on my phone to your GPS so I could see where you were. Luckily, I wasn't more than four minutes from your location. I made a beeline toward the bar, and that's how I found you."

She was shaking her head as she pulled her phone out of the pockets of her skinny jeans. She checked it and saw that she had, in fact, called Hot Shot twice like he said she had. Somehow, with the phone inside of her jeans pocket, she must have accidentally pressed the "send" button, and the phone dialed Hot Shot's phone. *These damn smartphones,* she thought.

"Then you heard him say that slick shit, and the rest is history, huh?"

"Yes, that's about it. As for the history part, I don't know about all that. I do know that that fool has to go."

"Stop that talk for now, please, honey."

Before he could respond, Nola's phone rang. She saw the picture of her brother on her phone and suddenly remembered how pissed off she was at him and her twin. She got even madder because if she wouldn't have been so pissed off at them, she would never have ended up at that bar, and this incident with Simon and Hot Shot would never have taken place. *Ugh,* she thought as she answered her phone.

"What do you want, Troy? I'm busy."

"I imagine you are. Is Hot Shot all right? I just got a call from a friend of a friend who told me you and Hot Shot got into it with that buster Simon. What's up, sister?"

"Nothing is up. We're fine over here. Simon started something he couldn't finish."

"Yeah, that's what I heard. My peoples told me Hot Shot put them paws on that boy something fierce. Said he even pistol-whipped him right there in the middle of the bar. Is that true?"

"Mm-hmm."

"That's not cool, Nola. You know that fool Simon will try to make a move on Shot. He will look like a superhook if he didn't."

Staring at her man, Nola said, "Tell me something I don't know, Troy. Is that all you wanted?" she asked with much attitude in her tone.

"Damn, what's with all shitty tone for? What I do to you?"

She sighed and remembered that she told Hot Shot she wouldn't speak on what he told her about the kiddie porn stuff and said, "Nothing. This shit got me bent all out of shape right now, Troy. I'm fine, though. My man made sure of that," she said proudly as she smiled at Hot Shot.

"All right. Tell Shot I said to make sure he watches his back. If he needs any info on how to get at that mark Simon, tell him I said to let me know."

"I will not pass that along for sure. It's all good, Troy."

"You're tripping and not having your man's best interest at heart if you don't pass that along, Nola. Simon may not be the hardest, but he is far from the weakest too. This type of shit will make him try to get at Shot. Keep your man on point and tell him what I said," Tiny Troy said seriously.

"Trust and believe he's already aware of all of that, Troy. Hot Shot is far from a rookie at this kind of shit. Bye, brother," she said and ended the call.

"Your brother heard what happened already, huh?"

"Mm-hmm."

"And he wanted to warn me to look out for Simon, huh?"

"Mm-hmm."

"You do know that I'm about to get at Simon and end this, right?"

She stared at the man she had fallen madly in love with and sighed loudly, then answered his question. "Mm-hmm."

Chapter Twenty-three

Hot Shot and Nola returned to Dallas from Oklahoma City with more than $200,000, and Hot Shot had to admit that he was impressed with how Keeta Wee ran things in Oklahoma; so impressed, in fact, that he was actually giving some thought to adding some more weight to his workload so he could score some of that easy money they were making out there. But right now, his mind was on things in Dallas. Getting with Cotton to make sure that his figures were right would be the first order of business. After that, he would have to get with Juan G. and let him know that he wouldn't be joining forces with him for his mighty plan to take over Dallas. He hoped that this decision wouldn't interfere with what they had in place because that would put a serious dent in his pockets since Juan G.'s consistency had become so good that he feared he would feel the decline if anything switched up.

Third on his to-do list was to go out and end the Simon situation. Cotton had called him while he was out of town and told him that the streets were buzzing, and the current buzz was Simon was telling any and everyone who would listen that he was going to get at Hot Shot the first chance he got. That was not good news. As a matter a fact, it was horrible news for Hot Shot to receive. He knew then that he would have to find another way to deal with Simon because killing him was now out of the question. He would be the number one suspect, and he didn't want or need that kind of heat in his life. JT would go nuts if that were to happen. Thinking about JT made him realize that he was supposed to be in town, so he grabbed his phone and called JT while Nola was busy showering.

"What's up, champ? You out this way yet or what?"

"Yep, just got in this morning, son. Thought you were out there in Sooner country."

"Was. Just got back about thirty minutes ago."

"How was things out that way?"

"Pretty decent. They got a nice setup working out there. I might send something down there if they accept my offer."

"Aren't your hands full enough out here in Dallas to be adding more to your plate?"

"My hands are never too full to get this money, JT. Anyway, what you got going on out here?"

"A few meetings with some key people to make sure everything continues to be good for us. I'm on my way to one of those meetings now, so let me go. I'll give you a call this evening. You're taking me to dinner tonight with your lady. It would be a shame if I came all the way to Texas and didn't get to meet the woman that has made Hot Shot the loner, the ladies' man, fall all weak kneed," JT said laughing.

"Ha-ha. And who am I going to tell her you are? My uncle from Kentucky?"

Still laughing, JT said, "That sounds fine with me, son. Hell, you can tell her whatever you want. Why not tell her the truth?"

"You clowning right now, right?"

"Of course, I was, stupid. Tell her I'm a good friend and you're taking me out to a fine Texas dinner. So pick somewhere where they have good steaks."

"This is Texas, JT. Damn, near every place you go to eat has good steaks."

"That's right, huh. Okay, son, let me go, I'll give you a call around six, and you can tell me where to meet you guys," JT said and hung up the phone.

When Nola came into the bedroom, Hot Shot couldn't help but smile as he watched her sit on the end of the bed and begin to lotion her luscious body. *This woman is supergorgeous,* he thought as continued to watch her.

Nola was grinning as she watched him staring at her through her peripheral vision. "You keep staring at me like that, you know we're going to end up getting this bed full of wet spots, honey. That there hungry look you got in those sexy brown eyes of yours is getting me moist over here, and you know when I get like that, we have to take care of thangs, so if you got something to do, you better quit it, honey."

Laughing, he said, "Yeah, well, maybe I have time for a quickie."

Shaking her head, she said, "Nope. No quickies happening today, so go get your business handled so you can come home and handle me properly later on tonight."

"Speaking of tonight, we have a dinner date."

"With who and where?"

"A good friend from the West Coast is in town for some business, and he wants us to take him someplace that has great steaks."

"This is Texas, honey. There ain't too many places out here that don't make great steaks."

Laughing, Hot Shot said, "That's exactly what I told him. So where do you want to take him? He should be getting with me around six, so I figured we'd scoop him around seven and go eat."

"That's fine. I think we should take him to Cattlemen's over on Skillman. They have some real good steaks, and they're huge, so if your friend wants to be impressed by steaks, Cattlemen's is the right place."

"Cattlemen's it is then," he said as he stepped to her and gave her a quick kiss, then tweaked her right nipple and said, "After dinner, I'm going to serve you something huge as well."

"Now you know I'm gonna hold you to that, Hot. Shot."

He was laughing as he grabbed his phone and left the bedroom. When he was inside of his car, he called Cotton and told him to meet him so they could see what was what on the business side of things.

"That's what's up, but I got Meosha with me. I need to drop her off, then we can hook up, Boss man."

Since she knew most of the business anyway, he didn't have a problem with her joining them for their meeting, plus he wanted to see this Meosha and see what she was working with that had his little helper so gone. "Nah, I'm on the clock right now, so you might as well bring her with you. Have you guys had lunch yet?"

"We just finished eating. That won't matter, though. Where you wanna meet at?"

"You know me. Meet me at the IHOP off 635. I'll be there in less than ten minutes."

"We should be there at the same time then. See you in a minute," Cotton said and hung up the phone.

Hot Shot and Cotton both pulled into the parking lot of the IHOP restaurant at the same time. Hot Shot hopped out of his car and watched with a smile on his face as Cotton got out of his truck and went around to the passenger's side and opened the door for his girlfriend.

Mmmm, such a gentleman all of a sudden. Wonder what happened to the wannabe mack daddy. This is going to be interesting, thought Hot Shot as he stepped toward them. He shook hands with Cotton and smiled at Meosha. "Hello, there, Meosha. We finally get to meet. I'm Hot Shot."

"Pleased to meet you finally, Boss man," she said with a smile as she grabbed Cotton's hand and let him lead the way inside of the restaurant. After they were seated, she took a sip of water and said, "I hope I won't be in the way with the business you guys need to discuss. I told Cotton he could have dropped me off at the mall while you guys met, but he said it would be all right if I joined y'all."

"Yes, it's no problem. We need to discuss some figures, not anything top secret or newsworthy," Hot Shot said as he smiled at the lovely brown-skinned young woman. She was definitely a looker. A nice, slim body that made the jeans she was wearing look real good. Her caramel complexion was smooth, and her long hair a shiny black which instantly made Hot Shot wonder if it was real or an expensive weave. Either way, she looked good, and he could tell she knew it. Her figure was rich and firm, but it was the combination of her dimples and her midnight-black eyes framed by long, heavy lashes that completed a look that screamed *sexy!* She was wearing an open-necked creamy silk blouse that showed an ample amount of cleavage. It took Hot Shot only a moment to figure out how Cotton had become so enamored by this beautiful young woman.

"Okay, great. Let's get to business then," she said happily.

Laughing, Hot Shot said, "Let's. Tell me, Cotton, are you ready for me? I need to get everything wrapped up tonight, because my people are in town, and it would be convenient for me to drop that bread on him."

"I'm good, Boss man. After I drop Meosha at the house, I'll swing by your place and drop that off to you. How long will it take for us to get back on?"

"The usual, no more than forty-eight hours."

"I'm good then. I was thinking about going down to San Antonio for a day or so and kick it out there with some family I want Meosha to meet."

"That's what's up. So tell me, what's the word out there in the streets you were speaking on about that Simon guy?"

"Like I said, he's running his mouth like he's trying to look at you. From what I heard, you put hands on him kinda decent-like, and he wants to see you for that."

"I guess I didn't put my hands on him decent enough then, huh?"

Cotton shrugged and said, "I guess not. From what I've heard about him, he's more talk than about that business. I didn't know that he used to mess with Nola though. Was that the reason why you got at him?"

"Nah, he was disrespectful, and you know how I feel about disrespect."

"True. What's the next play?"

Hot Shot watched as Meosha tried to feign as if she was not interested in their conversation, but he could tell that she was paying close attention to everything that was being said. "What do you think I should do about this guy, Meosha?"

Shocked to be joined in their meeting, she stuttered and answered, "I don-I, um, I mean, you should handle it the best way you can. I mean, in a way that won't let it interfere with your business out here. Do you really think he's worth your time and trouble? Is he worth going out of your way? If he is, then I think you should be as aggressive as needs to be to bring this to a close."

"Sound advice. I like your girl, Cotton. She seems to know the business when it comes to this type of stuff."

Cotton stuck out his chest a little and proudly stated, "Yeah, this here is my right hand, Boss man. She's good people."

"I see. As for this joker Simon, I may need to go and handle this, but first, I want to see if I can bring this to a peaceful conclusion by having Tiny Troy get at him and let him know that I don't want any problems with him."

"Won't that come across as showing weakness?" asked Meosha.

"If Simon has any sense, he will take this as a way out and let it go. He already knows there's nothing weak about me. If he takes it, then cool. Everything will be everything, and we can move forward."

"And if he doesn't?" she asked.

"Then he gets what he deserves for being an idiot," Hot Shot said in a tone that told her he was not the boss man for nothing. He was a man that was not to be taken lightly. Though she was really feeling Cotton and proud of the fact that he chose to listen to her and step his game up some, Hot Shot turned her on more than his voice had when she called him that time. She knew she was wrong for feeling this way, but she couldn't help it. There was something magnifying about him.

"I say we just serve him and keep it moving, Boss man. That way, we'll make a point to the streets so they will know what it is with us," said Cotton.

Shaking his head, Hot Shot said, "We don't need to make a point to anyone. Who cares what the streets think? All I'm concerned about is the money and our well-being. The rest of that stuff is useless to me, as it should be to you. You can look the part all you want, Cotton, but you have to understand that there's levels to this business. Looking good won't do you any good if you're no longer breathing. Pick the battles that need to be fought. If any weak stuff can be avoided, then avoid it. If it's time to get wicked, then believe me, we will get wicked like no one has ever seen before. Money first. We're working at a high level, so if you want to continue to raise the bar, I need you to think, use your intelligence, and make sure your decisions are based on what's beneficial for the business. Feel me?"

"Yeah, Boss man, I feel you."

"Good."

"You really seem to know what is right in this situation. That's exciting. It makes me feel even more comfortable knowing that my man deals with you, a man who knows what he's doing," Meosha said and smiled at Hot Shot.

With a grin on his face, Hot Shot said, "That's nice to hear. Thank you. You being my man's woman seems to have made him raise the bar to his business. I respect that. But, you have to understand that him looking extra with his new toys and accessories will only draw more attention to his get down. That can work for him as well as against him. What works for him is good for me and my business. The same goes for what doesn't work for him. Either way, I'm affected by the decisions Cotton makes. I refuse to lose, so you two need to think about every move you initiate out there in them streets. Your man listens to you, which is cool. Make sure you don't steer him in the wrong direction. Be good for him in more ways than one. Am I clear, Meosha?"

"Crystal clear, Hot Shot."

"Good. All right, I'm about to finish eating my meal, and then go and make a few runs. When will you get at me?"

"I'll go out to Meosha's now and get the ends counted, then give you a holla within an hour or so."

"All right, do that. It was nice meeting you, Meosha. You have worked wonders for my mans here. You two look good together. I wish you both all the happiness you deserve," Hot Shot said sincerely.

Right then and there, the outlook she had toward Hot Shot switched from him turning her on to looking at him as if he were her big brother. She liked the feeling of security he gave her, and it all came from the way he carried himself with such authority and confidence. She smiled at him and said, "I'm glad you approve of me, Hot Shot. I won't let Cotton or you down. I promise."

He smiled at her and said, "I know you won't. Cotton wouldn't let you 'cause he's the mannnnnnnnnn!" They all started laughing.

Chapter Twenty-four

Simon was parked across the street from the IHOP restaurant in his Chrysler 300 in a gas station with Foe-Way sitting on the passenger's side watching the restaurant where Cotton had entered with his girlfriend, along with Hot Shot.

"See, I told you. Follow the worker bee and he will lead you to the boss. Now, this is what I want you to do. I need you to follow that nigga Cotton when he leaves. I'm pretty sure if you follow him until he goes to his resting spot, you'll be able to come up with a nice amount of ends, work or both, as well get a little get back at him for what his boss did to you and your homeboys," Simon said and laughed.

"Fuck that getting-at-Cotton shit. I'm trying to look at that punk-ass nigga Hot Shot. That nigga fucked up my leg for life! He needs to feel the same type of pain," Foe-Way said heatedly.

Shaking his head emphatically, Simon said, "Nah, he's all mine. Don't worry. I'll make sure he dies painfully for you, though. Plus, you can't get at him or Tone will hurt your ass. You already got faded for the goofy move you pulled to get all of this shit started anyway. You pissed Tone off so bad, you're lucky he didn't kill your ass."

"Tone is my relative. He would never have took me no matter how mad he get at me. He was mad, and I accepted the fact, but fuck that shit. I'm still a man, and when a nigga gets at me, I have a right to gets back at his ass."

"True. That's why I'm going to get at Hot Shot, and you can take some of your revenge on Cotton. Everyone will be satisfied, and you won't have to worry about any repercussions from Tone. It's a win-win."

"What about you? Tone will be salty at you for fucking up his connect with that nigga Hot Shot."

"Tone and I are friends, not business partners. He can't speak on my shit like he can you and the rest of your homeboys. He may be salty, but he knows how Simon gets down, so it's whatever." Seeing Cotton and Meosha step out of the restaurant stopped Simon's words. "Okay, there that nigga Cotton goes. You and your homie stay on that nigga until he takes you to his vault. From what I've heard, he is all goofy in love with that broad he's with. Odds are the money is at her spot or his. Either way, you should be able to come up after smashing that nigga."

Foe-Way smiled as he thought about how Cotton had looked at him with that cocky-ass smile on his face when he saw him at the club and said, "Yeah, you know what? I'm gonna have a ball fucking that black-ass nigga off."

"You do that. Just make sure that it's an even split with whatever you come up with from his spot."

"I got you," Foe-Way said as he got out of the car and climbed into the passenger's side of a black Dodge Durango and told his homeboy Dank, "Follow that truck that's pulling out the IHOP right there and make sure you don't get too close. We might have to be on they ass for a minute before we make our move."

"What kinda move you talking about making, Blood?" asked Dank as he eased the Dodge out of the gas station and got a safe distance behind Cotton's truck.

Foe-Way pulled out a nine-millimeter pistol and said, "The best kind of move, nigga. Some money and some mothafuckin' revenge," he said as he racked a live round into the chamber of his pistol.

***

When he was finished eating, Hot Shot made a few rounds to some of his other people in Dallas letting them know that he would be back on within a few days and if they needed anymore, now was the time to get at him. By the time he made it home, he felt as if he'd accomplished a lot for the day. He went into the bedroom and saw that Nola had clothes scattered all over the bed and floor. He shook his head as he stepped over the clothing articles and went into the bathroom where he saw her standing in front of the mirror admiring a light blue blouse she had on.

"Looks good, babe. Can you tell me why you have all these clothes out scattered all around the bedroom?" Hot Shot asked as he leaned against the bathroom door.

"Trying to figure out what I'm wearing to dinner, honey. You know you have to be dressed to impress when you dine at Morton's."

"Morton's? I thought we were going to Cattlemen's?"

Shaking her head, she said, "Nope, change of plans. I want to impress your friend, so I made us some reservations for Morton's. Their steaks are top of the line, and it's a classier place to eat, honey. So, you need to get with it as well. I can't wait to see how you clean up. You got a mean urban swag, but I want to see what your grown-up dress game is talking about."

"I'm sure my grown-up swag will impress you just as much as everything else about me has impressed you, Nola," he said with a grin.

She rolled her eyes and said, "You do know how much I hate when you get extra cocky with it, right?"

"I thought that was one of my attributes you liked most, my swag."

"Humph. You know that's some bull. Your best attribute is that long schlong thang between them legs, honey, and don't you ever forget."

With a frown on his face he said, "So, you love me only for my tool, Nola? That's cold. You're using me for my body, and that ain't right."

She stared at him for a moment to see if he was teasing, and when she saw that damn grin again, she sighed and said, "You need to quit it."

"All right, tell me the truth. Is it my tool or my tongue?" he asked as he stuck out his tongue and flicked it real fast, then licked his lips slowly.

Laughing, she said, "You're terrible! Would you go in the room and start getting yourself together? It won't be long before your people calls."

"I will. I got to wait for Cotton to get at me, then I'll start getting ready. I already know what I'm wearing, so it won't take me long."

"Wish I could say that, but it's going to take me a minute to get everything together, so, shoo, be on your way, honey," she said, turning her back toward the mirror looking at her blouse, trying to decide if she liked how it fit her.

Hot Shot was shaking his head as he turned and reentered the bedroom. He checked the time and saw that it was pushing close to five p.m., and he still hadn't heard from Cotton. He grabbed his phone and gave him a call. When Cotton answered the phone, Hot Shot said, "I thought you would be getting with me within the hour. That was almost two hours ago, champ. What's up?"

"Got caught up, Boss man. I'm heading toward Meosha's house now. A few people hit me, so I needed to go on and pick up that loot and drop off the last of what I was working with. Give me like thirty and I'll be there. Cool?"

"That's straight. You just make sure you're on time 'cause I have something to do. If it looks like you won't be on time, then hit me, and we'll hold up until later or just hook up tomorrow."

"That's what's up, Boss man," Cotton said as he ended the call and set his phone on his lap as he turned into Meosha's neighborhood in DeSoto. "Check it out, baby. We need to hurry up and get that money counted so I can go drop it off to Hot Shot. Then when I come back, we can find something to get into for the night."

"I'm not in the mood to get into much tonight, baby. Why don't we stay in? I'll cook us something to eat, and we can Netflix it and chill here. You don't have any business out in the streets, so let's relax and enjoy this break," Meosha said, then added, "Plus, I wanna sex you real good tonight. No need to go out, baby. I got everything you need right here," she said as she pointed between her legs.

Cotton started to become erect instantly as he stared at her firm thighs as he made a right turn off of Hampton onto Richard Circle in the Mantlebrook Farms neighborhood. He didn't realize he had slipped big time until he pulled into Meosha's driveway and saw the black Dodge Durango pull in quickly right behind him and watched as two men jumped out of the car with guns in their hands. When he saw Foe-Way's evil smile, he knew that he had colossally fucked up. Before either man reached each side of the truck, the only thing Cotton thought to do was grab his phone and quickly push the "send" button to call Hot Shot back. He then put his phone in his pocket and prayed that his boss man would hear what was about to go down.

Damn!

After hanging up with Cotton, Hot Shot decided to do as Nola suggested and went to get his clothes together for their dinner with JT. He went to his closet and picked a pair of gray Armani slacks and a black, short sleeved mock neck silk tee shirt. He then grabbed a black Tom Ford blazer and set it on top of his slacks. "Mmm, yes, that should do," he said as he stepped back to the closet and grabbed a pair of black Italian loafers. He paused as he stared at the shoes and wondered if he should do the gators instead. He turned toward the bathroom and yelled, "Nola! Should I wear alligators or loafers to Morton's?"

She came into the bedroom and said, "It depends. Let me see them." When he held up the loafers in his right hand and the alligator shoes in his left, she stared at each pair for a moment, and then looked at the gray slacks and black silk shirt and blazer, then said, "The loafers will be perfect, honey."

He nodded and said, "Yes, that's what I was thinking too," he said as he turned and returned the alligator shoes back in the closet.

His cell phone started to ring when he grabbed it. He saw that it was JT. "What up, champ? You finished with your business meetings?"

"That's right, son."

"Everything good?"

"Pretty much. We'll talk more during dinner, or should I say, after dinner?"

"Definitely afterward."

"Affirmative. Tell me, where are you and your lovely woman taking me to dine this evening?"

"Morton's. Very expensive and very classy. The best steaks in Texas from what I've been told."

"I love it! *All* that time living in Los Angeles, and I've never had the time to go eat somewhere as good as Morton's, so this will be a truly memorable experience. I'm glad I brought some of my best digs. Looks like I'm gonna need them for this dinner, boy."

"That's right, champ, dress to impress. Where are you staying so I can come and pick you up?"

"I'd rather meet you. No need to expose my where-abouts. I know you trust your new girlfriend and all, but I don't know her yet."

Nodding into the receiver, Hot Shot said, "I feel you. We're getting dressed now. We have a 7:15 reservation."

"I'll be there on time, son," JT said and ended the call. Just as Hot shot set his phone down, it rang again. He grabbed it and saw that it was Cotton and hoped that he would be telling him that he was on his way. When he answered the phone, his heart froze and felt as if it had stopped beating when he heard Meosha telling someone to "please don't hurt" them. When he heard Cotton say, "Come on with this shit, Foe-Way. What you on, man? This shit ain't even cool!" He knew instantly that Cotton and Meosha were in some serious trouble. His heart beat faster as he continued to listen.

"Shut the fuck up, nigga, and lead the way inside of the house before you and this cute bitch get it right here," said Foe-Way.

"Man, you don't have to do this. Ain't shit here at my girl's house, dog. If you trying to jack, take me to my spot, and I'll give you whatever you want," pleaded Cotton.

Though Hot Shot was scared and worried about his little helper, he had to smile because Cotton had just given him what he was hoping for. They were at Meo-sha's house. He quickly began tapping his iPhone S5, thanking God he'd let Cotton talk him into purchas-ing the newest smartphone with him so they were on the same plan. Once he pulled the GPS app up on Cot-ton's phone, he was instantly relieved as the directions to Meosha's home came on the screen. He didn't have time to tell Nola where he was going so he rushed and grabbed his guns and ran out of the condo down to the garage. He didn't have a minute to waste, and he knew that he was going to have to go all-out to get to them in time.

Without any hesitation, he ran toward his bike. When he was on the Ducati, he quickly put his helmet on and was out of the garage in a flash. So fast, in fact, that he didn't notice Simon as he was getting out of his car about to enter the condominium complex to see if he could locate the exact condo in which Hot Shot lived. Things were turning up all around Hot Shot, and he didn't realize it at all.

"Come on, Foe-Way, man, you don't need to do this shit. We don't got beef. That shit was squashed by your mans and Hot Shot."

"Nigga, I got a permanent fucking limp from that nigga. I don't give a fuck what Tone said. Ain't shit over with until that nigga dead. And from what I know, that will be happening real-fucking-soon. So since I won't have action at handling that nigga, I get the pleasure of taking care of your soft ass. Now, where is the bread, nigga? I'll make this shit quick for you and this pretty-ass bitch here. Slow play me and this shit gon' go slow and nasty. Your choice, Cotton," Foe-Way said and smiled.

Staring at Meosha for a few seconds and seeing the fear all over his girl's face broke him down. There was no way he would ever risk her going through any more pain than was necessary. He knew he had to stall because if Hot Shot answered his phone, there wasn't a doubt in his mind that he was on his way to save the day. At least, that's what he was praying for. "You don't have to do this, Foe-Way. I'll give you what you want. Just take me to my pad out north and you'll be straight."

Shaking his head, Foe-Way said, "Nah, fuck that weak shit, Cotton. You think I'm a chump, nigga? I know the bread is here, so you need to give it up, or like I said, it's about to get nasty in this bitch." Knowing he couldn't risk letting anything happen to Meosha, Cotton sighed heavily and said, "All right, man, I'll give you what you want but let my girl go. She don't deserve to be caught up with this shit. Let her go, Foe-Way, dog. I ain't giving you shit until she's gone."

"Nigga, you act like you running shit in here. Let her go? This bitch is about to die with your ass!"

"Fuck you, nigga," screamed Meosha. "Don't give this crippled bitch shit, baby. They gon' kill us anyway. Fuck him!"

"Dank, duct-tape this loudmouthed bitch up. She got a slick mouth, so let's see how slick this bitch will be after we serve her some dick in that big ass of hers." Cotton's eyes grew wide, and Foe-Way started laughing. "Yeah, nigga, I told you it's about to get nasty in this bitch. You could have made it easy for you and this pretty bitch. But, nope, you had to go out the hard way."

"Fuck you, punk-ass nigga," spat Cotton as he watched in horror as Foe-Way's accomplice came back from outside with some duct tape in his hands. *Come on, Boss man. I know you're on your way. Hurry the fuck up,* he prayed silently.

Laughing lewdly, Foe-Way said, "Yeah, that's right, duct-tape that bitch's dimples. I'm about to enjoy this shit. Stupid fuck nigga, you about to watch me fuck the shit out of your bitch, and I do mean that literally." Foe-Way then stepped to Meosha and snatched her from Dank and slammed her onto the floor next to Cotton. After Cotton's hands were secured behind his back with the strong tape, Dank pushed him on his back, and he lay there with tears in his eyes as he watched as Foe-Way began to pull down his pants. "What's so crazy about all of this is, after I fuck this bitch in that ass, I'm going to let my nigga Dank here get some of that pussy. Then you will still tell me where the money and dope at. You don't, then I'll have to think of something really fucked up to do to the both of you. I promise, before it's all said and done, you will give me what I came for. Then it's curtains for you and your bitch. Don't trip, though, you'll be meeting up with your mans Hot Shot, because Simon's in the process of handling that wannabe-ass Cali nigga."

When he heard Simon's name, Cotton realized that it had to be Simon who was pushing Foe-Way's buttons. *That nigga Tone is a stand-up Blood. He would never go against his word to Hot Shot. This is so fucked up,* Cotton thought as he turned toward Meosha and let the tears fall freely from his eyes and said, "Close your eyes, babe. Don't look at these cowards. Close your eyes and think about how Hot Shot is gonna kill these bitch-ass niggas. Everything is gon' be all right one way or the other, I promise you that, baby."

"Nigga, you making promises you cannot keep. You a dead nigga, just like this bitch is a dead bitch. Now, watch my work." Foe-Way then grabbed Meosha roughly and pulled her slacks down and ripped off her blouse. He then bent her over and stroked his dick until he was fully erect and placed the head of his dick on her asshole and rammed his dick as hard as he could into her ass. Though she had duct tape taped tightly over her mouth, her screams sent chills through Cotton's body as he watched as Foe-Way anally raped his girlfriend for ten straight minutes before pulling his bloody dick out of Meosha's ass and spraying his come all over her back. He pushed her onto the floor on her face and laughed. "Yeah! That shit was the fucking bomb. Come on, Dank, come fuck this bad bitch, Blood. The pussy may not be as tight as that ass, but I'm sure you gon' enjoy that shit."

Shaking his head, Dank said, "Nah, Foe, that ain't me, dog. Let's rough this nigga up some so he can give us what we want so we can get the fuck outta here. I ain't with no raping shit, Damu."

"That is the smartest decision you've ever made, my man. Because of that intelligence, I'll spare your life," Hot Shot said as he stood in the doorway with two nine-millimeters pistols in each of his hands aimed directly at Dank and Foe-Way.

The terrified look on Foe-Way's face was priceless to Cotton. "Yeah, nigga, you about to get fucked now, and I do mean that literally!" screamed Cotton.

Hot Shot frowned at Cotton's use of the N-word, but under the dire circumstances, chose not to speak about it. The relief on Cotton's features made him feel real good inside. But when he focused on Meosha lying on her stomach, naked and bleeding from her behind, he became very angry.

Chapter Twenty-five

Hot Shot watched as Dank did as he told him to and took the duct tape off of Cotton. He saw the pain in Cotton's eyes as he got to his feet and quickly scooped Meosha up in his arms and carried her into the bedroom. He returned a few minutes later with a furious look on his face as he stared at Foe-Way, and then at his homeboy Dank.

"You two fools came with the intent on killing me and my girl. Now you die by my hand." He spit on Foe-Way and said, "Bitch-ass coward, you get to watch me blow your brains out." He then turned and reached his hand out toward Hot Shot and said, "Give me that lighter, Boss man, so I can light both of the fools up. You don't even have to be here. You saved me and Meosha. I got it from here."

Shaking his head, Hot Shot told Cotton, "Wait a minute. We need to make sure this will be the right move to make."

Then Cotton screamed, "That bitch raped Meosha! He hurt her bad, Boss man. This is the only move to make. She didn't deserve that, man. She didn't deserve that at all. This is the best move. It's the only move. Now give me one of those lighters and let me handle my business. If anything goes left, I will gladly take everything that comes with it. Please, let me handle my business for my girl, Boss man. Please."

Before Hot Shot could respond, Meosha stepped out of the bedroom with a dazed look in her eyes and tears streaming down her face. She had put on some sweatpants and a Dallas Cowboy sweatshirt. "No, Cotton, you don't have to do anything to those bastards. I got this, baby. I got this," she said as she stepped quickly toward Foe-Way with that same dazed look in her eyes. Before either Cotton or Hot Shot realized what was about to happen, she raised a small .380-caliber pistol from behind her back and shot Foe-Way one time right between the eyes at near point-blank range. She turned before his body hit the floor, then aimed her gun at Dank. She paused, tilted her head to the side slightly as if in thought, like whether she should kill him too. Then she nodded as if making that decision and shot him once in the head. She stood over his body, crying and shaking uncontrollably. She turned around slowly and stared at Cotton and Hot Shot for a moment, then said, "They hurt me, baby. He made me feel like dirt, a piece of trash, baby. I'll never be right after this, baby. I'll never be right!" she screamed as she turned and stepped to Foe-Way's dead body and shot him two more times in his face.

"Come on, baby, it's over now. Everything is going to be all right. We'll make it through this now. We'll make it through this together, Meosha," Cotton said, trying to calm her down as he stepped toward her.

Hot Shot was staring at her, and he knew she was in a highly traumatized state and could do anything at this time, so he too tried to calm her down. "Don't worry, Meosha, Cotton's right. We're going to make everything good. We'll take care of you, and in time, everything will be good."

She shook her head and started sobbing even harder. "No! No! No! I'll never be any good for you, Cotton. You saw what he did to me! You saw it! I'm nothing no more!"

With tears sliding down his face, Cotton screamed right back at her. "You *are* something! You're my *everything!* That will never change, baby! I love you, Meosha! Everything will be all right. Come here, baby, let me make everything right for you . . . for us," he pleaded.

His words seemed to have a calming effect on her. She slowly stopped crying and regained some control as she stared at him. She smiled at him and said, "I love you too, Cotton, I really do. You believe me, don't you?"

"Of course I do, babe. I know you love me just as much as you know I love you. Come on now, put that gun down so we can get this shit situated. Everything is going to be just fine."

"You will be just fine. Boss man over there will always be there for you. You're a good man, Boss man. Keep looking out for my man, 'k?" Hot Shot knew instantly by her words what she was about to do. As he took a step toward her, he watched in horror as she raised the small gun to her head and pulled the trigger.

"Nooooooooo!" both Cotton and Hot Shot screamed as they watched as Meosha's body fell to the floor just as dead as the two men she had killed.

Fuck!

Nola was sitting in the living room wondering where in the hell Hot Shot was. She heard him leave and thought he had to make a quick run somewhere, but that was close to an hour ago. Now she was beginning to worry. Especially since he wasn't answering his phone or returning any of her texts. Here she was dressed to impress in a sexy black Chanel dress, some black satin Manolo Blahnik heels with a single strand of white pearls to complete an outfit she felt was on point for sure. Her instincts told her that something was wrong, and she couldn't shake the feeling that her man was in some kind of trouble. She grabbed her phone and called Hot Shot again, and this time, he answered on the first ring. "Where are you, honey?" she asked when he answered.

"I'm with Cotton. Some heavy mess has happened, Nola. I mean, really heavy. I've already called my people. We won't be going out to eat dinner. I got a lot to do right now. I'm sorry I didn't call you sooner, but this is so wild I haven't had the chance."

She heard Cotton in the background sounding as if he was moaning and crying, and her heart began to beat faster as she asked, "Are you okay, honey? Please tell me you're okay."

"I'm fine, Nola," he said in a stern voice showing her that he was in total control and all was good with him. She sighed and said, "Okay. Do you need me to do anything?"

"I might, so get changed and stay ready for my call. Right now, I got to sort some things out. I'll explain everything when I see you."

"Okay, honey. I love you."

"I love you too," Hot Shot said as he ended the call and stared at Cotton as he sat on the floor holding on Meosha's lifeless body in his arms while crying and moaning loudly. He didn't want to interrupt him during this tragic moment, so he stepped toward the front door and leaned against it as he stared outside thinking. Thank God he had made it in time to save Cotton and Meosha, but for what—for her to kill Foe-Way and his man, along with herself? *This is totally screwed,* he thought as he continued to stare outside of the glassed door, wishing he would have made it sooner so maybe things could have turned out differently. *Now, what am I going to do to clean up this mess?* he asked himself.

He sighed heavily and called JT back. When he answered, JT asked him what he needed from him because he could hear it in Hot Shot's voice that he needed his partner big time.

"I need to figure out how I'm gonna handle three dead bodies, JT."

"Give me the address of the location of this crime scene and get the hell out of there, boy. I'll take care of everything."

"But how?"

"You don't worry about how. Just do as I say. Get Cotton and get the fuck out of there. I'll give you a call later after everything has been taken care of, son. Trust me," JT said in a serious tone. "Trust me."

"Cotton is gone, JT. I mean, man, he's really gone behind this."

"That's not my concern. My concern is making sure you don't get caught up for three dead bodies. Now, do what I said. Get your man and get the fuck out of that house!"

After giving JT the address to Meosha's home, Hot Shot disconnected the call and went back into the living room where Cotton hadn't moved. He was still sitting on the floor cradling Meosha's body in his arms, rocking back and forth, crying. Hot Shot sighed and said, "Cotton, we have to get out of here. I need you to shake it off, little man. We got to go."

Cotton didn't stop doing what he was doing. He kept right on rocking and crying as if he hadn't heard a word Hot Shot said. Hot Shot knew he was in shock and that was only going to make things more difficult for him. He took a deep breath and stepped toward Foe-Way's dead body and went into his pants pockets searching for the keys to the Dodge Durango that was parked in the driveway behind Cotton's truck. When he didn't find the keys on Foe-Way, he quickly stepped over to

Dank's body and found them. He then turned toward Cotton and shook his head sadly. He really felt for his mans, but he had to get things handled so JT could manage the situation. There was no doubt in his mind that JT would, in fact, take care of things, so he had to do his part. He stepped over to Cotton and grabbed him roughly by his shirt and yanked him to his feet, then slapped him hard several times in the face.

"Wha-what the fuck you doing, Boss man? What I do, man? What I do?" screamed Cotton.

"You lost it on me, Cotton, and I need you here with me. We got to get out of here. And I mean now! Do you understand me?"

"What about Meosha, Boss man? What are we going to do about my girl?"

"She's dead. There's nothing we can do for her now. We'll figure things out in detail later, but right now, we got to go; now come on. I need you to help me put my bike in the back of your truck."

Cotton gave him a nod, and Hot Shot could tell that he was back in the now and was relieved as he watched as Cotton knelt and gave Meosha a kiss and whispered, "I'll always love you, babe." He then stood and stared at Hot Shot for a moment and said, "This ain't over yet, Boss man. One more man has to die today."

With a puzzled expression on his face, Hot Shot asked, "What are you talking about, Cotton?"

"Simon sent Foe-Way and his mans to do this to me and Meosha. Simon was supposed to be getting at you while they were here getting at me and my girl. We got to get that fool Simon, Boss man."

Somewhat confused by his words, Hot Shot stood there staring at Cotton for a moment, and then as if replaying everything in his mind as he left the condo, he saw a tall man dressed in all black walking toward the entrance of his building when he left. He quickly pulled out his phone and called Nola. He sighed when she answered, then said, "Listen to me, Nola, and do not question anything I'm about to tell you."

"Okay, honey."

"Remember the weapons I showed you around the spot?"

"Mm-hmm."

"Grab you some of them and go sit in the living room and keep one in your hand aimed at the front door until I get there. I will call you before I get to the door so you will know it's me. If I don't call you and anyone else knocks on that door, I want you to start shooting the gun you have in your hand until it's empty, then grab another. Do. You. Understand. Me. Nola?"

"I do," she said and hung up the phone and went to do exactly what her man instructed her to do.

After he ended the call, Hot Shot told Cotton to follow him. He went outside, and they loaded his Ducati in the back of Cotton's truck. He then jumped into the Dodge Durango that Foe-Way and Dank arrived in and sped away, headed toward his condo, praying that that fool Simon wasn't there about to try to hurt Nola.

Nola took a few deep breaths to calm her nerves as she sat down on the sofa in the living room with one of Hot Shot's Sig nine millimeters in her right hand and a second one lying beside her on the sofa. She prayed that she wouldn't have to do what he told her to, but she knew without a doubt that if someone knocked on that door, they would be filled with every bullet that was loaded in the gun she held in her hand. Though Hot Shot tried to remain his usual calm self, his words scared the shit out of her, and that only made her more determined to make sure she did exactly as she had been told.

"Okay, Nola, everything is going to be all right. Hot Shot is on his way home, and he'll take charge and all will be just fine," she said aloud as she stared at the front door, praying to God that she wouldn't have to murder anyone. Her phone rang at the exact same time that someone knocked on the front door. The only reason she didn't start shooting was because she saw Hot Shot's face on her iPhone. She sighed with relief and set the gun down on the table, grabbed her phone as she stood, and started walking toward the door . . . then stopped suddenly and answered the phone.

"Please tell me that you're right outside the door knocking right now, honey," she said as she felt her stomach start to do flips.

In the calmest voice he could muster, Hot Shot said, "Please tell me you have the guns in your hands right now like I told you to, baby. If you don't, then do so now."

Nola stepped back to the sofa quickly and grabbed one of the guns, set her phone on the coffee table, and hit the speaker button so she could talk to Hot Shot while she aimed the gun at the front door. "I have my gun aimed at the front door right now, honey. What do you want me to do, shoot?"

Hearing that she had him on speaker, he said, "No, ask who is it. It may be Barry. Would hate for you to kill our doorman," Hot Shot deadpanned.

"How far away are you, honey?" she asked nervously.

"Less than five minutes, Nola. Come on now, hold it together for me, baby, and ask who it is."

She inhaled deeply and asked, "Who is it?"

"It's Barry, ma'am. I need to speak with you real quick."

Hot Shot heard Barry's words, but something wasn't right so he told Nola, "Tell him to give you a moment. You need to get decent, Nola."

"All right, Barry. Give me a minute to put something on."

"Okay, ma'am."

"Now what, honey?"

Hot Shot made a right turn onto his street and said, "Go into the bedroom, put your back against the wall, and wait for me. I'm on our street now. I should be up to the door in under two minutes. If anyone tries to enter the house, you know what to do," he said and hung up the phone as he came to a screeching halt in front of his building. This was one time he hated living in a sixth-floor condominium.

He jumped out of the car and ran as fast as he could toward the elevator. Cotton was right behind him. "Come on, come on! This elevator is taking too long. Cotton, wait for it and ride it up. I'm taking the stairs. If you see that joker Simon, you know what to do," Hot Shot said as he turned and ran toward the staircase.

He hit the stairs hard and took them three by three, racing toward the sixth floor, praying that he was wrong but fearing he was right by thinking Simon was standing outside of his door with Barry. By the time he made it to the fifth floor, he heard gunshots and knew that he had been right. With an extra burst of speed, he ran faster up the last flight of stairs to his floor with his guns in each hand. He came out of the stairwell and saw Barry lying on the floor right in front of his door, which had been kicked in.

Without any hesitation or fear for his life, he ran straight through the door ready to face whatever he had to in order to save Nola. He came to an abrupt stop and stared at Simon as he was laid out in the doorway of his bedroom slowly dying from several bullet wounds in his chest and stomach. Hot Shot took a deep breath and said, "Nola! I'm standing in the living room with my guns trained on this joker you shot. He doesn't have a gun in his hand, and he's dying. I want you to come out of the bedroom to me. Do you hear me, baby?"

"I-I-I, shot him, hon—honey. Is, is he de-dead?"

"Nola! Come! Out! Here! Now!" he screamed as he continued to stare at Simon as he gasped for breath.

When Nola came to the doorway, she had her gun pointed at Simon and was shaking uncontrollably. Cotton came to the front door, and Hot Shot told him, "Watch my back." He then stepped to Nola, grabbed her, and picked her up and carried her over to the sofa and set her down. He then stepped to Simon and leaned over his body to see if there was anything he could do for him. He really didn't want or need for this man to die in his home. That would be way too much light shined on his darkness. He shook his head as he stared into the eyes of a dead man. Simon's time on earth had just expired.

Hot Shot then went back to Nola and sat down next to her and wrapped his arms around her tightly trying to calm her down some.

"This has to be the most fucked-up day of my entire life," Cotton said as he stared at Simon's dead body. "What the fuck are we going to do with all of these dead bodies we keep accumulating, Boss man?"

As he rocked his woman in his arms, Hot Shot looked up at his mans and said, "I don't have a clue, Cotton, I truly don't. Fuck!"

That response totally shook Cotton because that was the first time in over nine months of knowing Hot Shot that he'd ever heard him utter a curse word. *Damn, this is really crazy,* he thought as he continued to stare at Simon's body, wishing that it had been him who murdered the bastard who was responsible for Meosha being raped and her committing suicide.

Fuck!

Chapter Twenty-six

Hot Shot's mind was racing, trying to figure how he was going to deal with the dilemma before him as he continued to rock and console Nola. He had two dead bodies in his home, and he didn't have a clue about how he was going to be able to get this situated without involving the police. That kind of attention with all of the money and weapons he had in his condo was not good at all. He stared at Cotton and saw the mixed emotions on his face and knew that he had to remain calm and in control or everything was going to continue to be twisted.

"Look, champ, I know this has been one crazy day, but we need to keep our wits in the game, or we'll soon be finding ourselves in a Dallas jail cell, and that's one place Hot Shot is not trying to be. You feel me?"

"Yeah, I feel you, Boss man, but I'm hurting. I'm hurting bad. Every time I blink, I see that fool Foe-Way raping Meosha, and I feel sick. That girl didn't deserve any of that, and it's all my fault, for real," Cotton said with tears sliding down his face as he stood there staring at Simon's dead body.

"Wha-what is he talking about, honey? What happened to Meosha?" Nola asked as she raised her head off of Hot Shot's chest and stared up at him. After he told her what had happened at Meosha's home, she began to cry softly.

Just what I need, more emotional crap. Think, Shot, think, he ordered himself as he started rocking Nola back and forth, consoling her. He knew he was pushing it, but he had no other choice but to call JT again. He was about to grab his phone but stopped when he saw some movement at the front door that was still slightly open. He eased his arm from around Nola, stood, and pulled out his pistol and slowly stepped toward the door. When he saw Barry, the doorman, turn on his side and groan, he sighed with relief. *Thank God he isn't dead,* he thought as he put his pistol in the small of his back and knelt down next to Barry to see if they would have to rush him to the hospital. After checking him out, he saw that Simon didn't shoot Barry like he thought he had, but must have slapped him real hard across the back of his head with his gun and knocked him out cold. That's why there was so much blood. Head wounds always bled heavily.

Thinking fast, Hot Shot stood and told Cotton, "Come here, Cotton. I need you to help me get Barry downstairs to your truck so you can rush him to the hospital. Parkland is less than five minutes from here. He needs some medical attention badly. Hopefully, we won't be too late." Cotton didn't say a word. He just helped Hot Shot carry Barry to the elevator. Once they were on the elevator, Hot Shot said, "I want you to stay there with Barry and when they ask what happened, tell them that you found him laid out in front of your friend's place."

"That's only going to lead to more questions, Boss man. The best move would be for me to carry him inside and make sure they have him, and then slip right back out that mothafucka. At least we'll know he's getting some help, 'cause I don't need to be questioned by nobody right now. Ain't no telling what the fuck I'd say. I'm twisted for real, right now, Boss man. Straight running on fumes for real."

Nodding in understanding, Hot Shot said, "You're right. That makes sense. Do that, then I want you to go to your spot and lie down. Try to get some rest, and I'll get at you once I've figured things out."

"What you gon' do about Simon's body, Boss man?"

"I don't have the slightest idea, but something has to be done. I'm glad I'm the only occupant on the sixth floor. Doesn't seem like anyone else heard the shots fired by Nola since no police have been called. Luck has been on our side."

"Yeah, I'm feeling real fucking lucky right about now," Cotton said as the elevator stopped on the lobby floor. They carried Barry out to Cotton's truck that was parked right behind the Dodge that Hot Shot drove to the condo. Once they had Barry inside of the truck, Cotton said, "I got him, Boss man. Go on and handle shit. Give me a call and let me know what's what."

"Will do. You make sure you text me when you leave the hospital to let me know you're good."

"All right," Cotton said as he sped off toward Parkland Hospital.

Hot Shot got inside of the Dodge and drove it across the street and parked it correctly so it wouldn't draw any attention. He then went back into his building and went up to his condo. As he walked inside, he saw Nola standing in the kitchen drinking a glass of wine. When she saw him, she downed the rest of her drink and quickly poured another. After taking a sip, she sighed and said, "Thank you for hurrying up. I don't know how much longer I can stay in this place with a dead man in the other room, honey. Can you please tell me that you came up with a way to deal with this situation? 'Cause you do know that I am in no way trying to have any police contact, right?"

"Yes, baby, I know. Looks like I'm going to have to deal with this one solo. Since I've already got at JT, and he said he would handle that mess at Meosha's, I don't want to get at him again. That would be putting him and his resources on major blast."

"I've pretty much figured out that JT is a major force in your life, so I won't even question that. But, honey, can you please tell me how in the hell is he going to handle such a messy situation as the one at Meosha's house?"

He shrugged and said, "Honestly, Nola, I don't have a clue. I didn't ask anything, and it's best for you not to either. Now listen to me, baby, I need for you to go on and get out to Rowlett until I have everything handled here. I'll give you a call, then you can come back when everything is everything."

Shaking her head, she said, "I wanna help you clean up this shit, honey."

"No. I'll deal with it, Nola," he said firmly. "You've been through too much to even think I'm going to let you be a part of this disposal. I got this."

"I don't feel like going to Rowlett. I don't want to be around all that, Hot Shot."

He sighed and said, "All right, go get a suite somewhere and call me when you get there. When everything is done here, I'll come and we'll spend the night there and relax, okay?"

She nodded and went into the bedroom to change clothes and get some of her things together. When she stepped over Simon's dead body, she felt a shiver go through her entire body. She made the sign of the cross across her chest and kept it moving.

After Nola left, Hot Shot sat down in the living room and thought about his next move. He needed to address this situation correctly, and he knew in order to do that properly, he had to inform JT of all of his moves. He sighed as he grabbed his phone and called him. When JT answered, Hot Shot quickly filled him in on the events that had taken place at his home.

"Damn, son, you done had yourself one hell of a day now, haven't ya?"

"You can say that. Now, how do I play this here at my spot?"

"Touchy situation you got there, boy. I've already made some serious calls to get that one situation handled. I don't know if I could, or if I should, try to pull another fave. At this rate, I'm going to put myself in some serious debt dealing with your shit."

Knowing he would have to hear it from JT, Hot Shot ignored him and said, "Don't worry about this one then. I got it."

"How?"

"I think it's best you don't know. So tell me how is that going to play out at Meosha's?"

"A call was made, and the police have arrived and found the bodies at her home. That's all you need to know. I'm sure if you watch the evening news, you'll be informed properly on what happened there. I think it may be time to start wrapping up our business out here in Texas, son. Things have gotten sticky, to say the least."

"Ya think?"

"I know."

"Me too. But there's stuff that needs to be handled still. When I get everything taken care of, then I guess I'll be ready to bounce back to the West."

"You guess?"

"It's going to be a complicated departure, JT."

"Damn, boy, you done went and fell head over heels for this woman, I see. Crazy. You know there's no room for love in what we got going on."

"Too late for that, don't you think?"

"You know she's going to be hurt, boy."

"Maybe, then again, maybe not."

"That right there gives me cause for some serious concern. I trust you, son, and I know you know how important our business is. Nothing and no one can interfere with that, Hot Shot."

"Right. You know that I know that, and you should also know that I'm never going to let you down. Let me go. I got some work to do."

"Be careful."

"Always," Hot Shot said as he ended the call, took a deep breath, and went into the bedroom. He grabbed the plush comforter from the bed and shook his head because he was about to ruin the expensive comforter. *Oh well, Nola will love shopping for another one,* he said to himself as he stepped to Simon's dead body and began to wrap him up in the comforter.

The hard part about what he was doing would be taking the body from his condo downstairs to the Dodge. Luckily, no one was on the elevator, or the elevator hadn't been summoned to any other floor during the ride down to the garage. Once he had the body inside of the back of his Denali, he went outside and brought the Dodge into the garage, then transferred Simon's body from the Denali to the Dodge. After that, he drove the car back across the street and parked it, then he went back upstairs to his place and gave Cotton a call.

"Is everything good with you?" Hot Shot asked as he stepped into the kitchen and grabbed the bottle of wine Nola had been drinking and took a long swig straight from the bottle. With loud music blaring in the background Cotton slurred, "Yeah, Boss man, I'm straight."

"Thanks for texting me to let me know that," he said sarcastically.

"Come on, Boss man, don't be salty at me right now. You know what I'm going through here, man."

He inhaled deeply and asked, "Where are you, Cotton?"

"Up at DG's throwing back a few."

"Yes, I can tell. I assume everything went cool with Barry?"

"Yeah, it's all good. Before they got to asking me all types of questions I told them I needed to go turn my car off and left. I called back up to Parkland and checked to see if they had a patient who had been dropped off with a head injury, and they told me yes and that he was being attended to and looked like he would be okay."

Hot Shot sighed and said, "That was smart. Check it out, I want you out of the way for the rest of the night. Toss back another drink, then head on home. I need you to be ready for the calls you're going to receive in the morning concerning Meosha."

"What calls? What's going on, Boss man?"

"Just get home and watch the news and you'll see, And this time, text me within the hour letting me know you're at home," Hot Shot said sternly and ended the call. He then walked into the living room and stared at the front door wondering how in the hell he was going fix that. He then grabbed his phone and Googled some information on a locksmith. After making a few calls, he found one he thought would work and was now waiting on him to arrive so he could fix his front door.

Next on his agenda was to call Tone. When Tone answered the phone, Hot Shot told him, "We need to talk, my man. If you're out the way, then you really need to get this way as soon as possible."

"This gotta have something to do with Foe-Way and Dank, huh, Hot Shot?" asked Tone.

"What makes you say that?"

"I haven't heard from neither of those fools, and that's not like them. They ain't returning my calls or texts. What's up?"

"Some foul play that ended badly for both of them, Tone."

Tone sighed heavily and said, "I am out the way, but I'll be there in the a.m. Where you wanna meet at, Blood?" Tone asked with anger lacing his words.

"Give me a call when you get here, and I'll tell you where to come. And, Tone, it's not what you're thinking, so calm down some."

"Foe-Way isn't only my Blood homeboy, Shot. He's family. So whatever you got to tell me, I sure hope I'll be able to make this right."

"It's a messed up situation that Foe-Way brought on himself with some help from Simon."

"Simon? What that snake bitch have to do with shit?"

"Like I said, get here and hit me up and we'll talk, and all will be explained, Tone."

"In the morning then," Tone said and ended the call with tears sliding down his face. His anger and pain was getting the best of him. He hated the fact that he would have to call his sister and let her know that her only child was no longer living.

Chapter Twenty-seven

Nola wasn't in any shape to be driving for too long, so she went to the first hotel that came to her mind, which happened to be the very expensive W Hotel. The W was located downtown right off of I-35 North less than five minutes from the condo. Once she checked in and paid cash for a suite, she went straight to the bathroom and began to run some hot water in the huge Jacuzzi tub. She then undressed because all she wanted was to get in the tub and soak and hopefully succeed in erasing from her mind the murder she committed. Even though she knew it was in self-defense, she was still shaken. She had taken a life, and that terrified her. Not only was she scared that she may get caught for doing what she did, she was worried that this could only lead to more problems in her life. Simon was connected with the Mexican gang, Tango Blast, and when they found out that he had been murdered, there was definitely going to be drama.

She sighed as she stepped into the tub and let the hot water begin to soothe her. Hot Shot would take care of everything, that she was positive of. But would he be able to deal with the Tango Blast if shit really got heavy? He's a strong man, but he's just one man, and the Dallas faction of Tango Blast was large in numbers and could summon thousands of members from all over Texas if need be. *Damn, this is going to get crazy before it'll get better,* she thought as she leaned her head back and continued to soak.

Then, all of a sudden, she smiled as she remembered that Hot Shot did a lot of business with Juan G. *Everything might just be all right,* she thought, and grabbed her cell from the side of the tub and sent a text to Hot Shot letting him know that she made it to the hotel. She told him where she was and gave him the suite number. He responded right back telling her that he would be there within the hour and she felt relieved. That meant everything had gone smoothly with the removal of Simon's body from the condo. *Thank God,* she thought as she closed her eyes and relaxed.

Hot Shot paid the locksmith who came to the condo and repaired his lock, and then went downstairs and brought his bike back to the underground garage and covered it up. With that done, he went back outside and got inside of the Dodge Durango and went to the W to join Nola for some much-needed rest. He shook his head as he thought about her choosing one of the most expensive hotels in Dallas to relax. The lady definitely had class. Even in the midst of a disaster, she had to have nothing but the best at all times. Funny, he thought as he drove the few blocks to the hotel.

He parked the car in the parking lot choosing not to use the valet. Wouldn't be a good look if the valet chose to see what that lump wrapped up in an expensive comforter was. That would definitely cause a problem, he thought as he got out of the car and went into the hotel and headed straight to the tenth-floor suite Nola had for them.

When he knocked on the door, it took Nola a couple of minutes to come answer because she was just getting out of the tub. She opened the door and smiled at him, still wet from the bath she had been taking.

Stepping inside of the room, Hot Shot smiled at her and stared at her incredibly hot body and said, "Answering the door butt naked is something you normally do when you stay at hotels, Nola?"

With a smirk on her face, she said, "I looked through the peephole, honey. When I saw it was my man, it seemed appropriate to open the door while being butt-ass naked. I mean, you *have* seen all of this before, right?" she asked as she raised her hands and pointed toward her luscious body.

Laughing, he shook his head as he followed her into the bedroom of the suite and watched as she sat at the end of the huge bed and began to dry herself off. With a serious tone of voice, he asked her, "How are you feeling, baby? Better?"

"Somewhat. But I can't get Simon's face out of my head. That, plus I feel a little nauseated, like I want to throw up."

"Nerves, baby. Taking a life is never easy, and seeing something like that has traumatized you some. You're a very strong woman. I'm surprised you haven't already thrown up. That's a normal reaction after what you've been through tonight."

"Did you get rid of him?"

"You can say that."

"Huh?"

"Don't worry, he's out of the condo."

"What about Barry? Is he going to be okay?"

He told her what Cotton told him about Barry's condition and then said, "Now we got to figure some things out. JT feels it may be time for me to depart Texas."

"So, this JT is your main connect from the West?"

He nodded but didn't speak.

"And now, with all that has happened, he wants you back West? Are you going to leave me, Hot Shot?"

"If I asked you to come with me, would you, Nola?"

She looked up at her handsome man, the man she had fallen madly in love with, and smiled as she reached back and put her hair into a ponytail and said, "You can't answer a question by asking one, honey."

"In order for me to give you a proper answer, I need to have the proper information, Nola."

"I'd follow you around the world if I had to, Hot Shot. I don't ever want to be without you. I'm all in, honey. You got all of me. I'm gone in every way. There's no doubt in my mind that you will take nothing but the very best care of me."

He nodded his head and said, "Good. Then when I leave, you leave."

"Do you have any idea when that might be?"

"There's some business that still needs to be handled. I need to get with your brother and let him know that with all of this sudden extra stuff, I need to shake the town for a while, and if things seem cool, I can return and resume the business. After we get things settled, I have to take care of some more things with a few other business associates. Once all of that has been tied up, then we can head west. Are you sure you can take being away from your family like that?"

"I've been waiting to leave that nest ever since my parents died. It's way past time, honey. Plus, with what Lola and Troy are into sickens me, so it's an easy good riddance as far as I'm concerned. I think I'd like tearing up the malls and Rodeo Drive in Beverly Hills," she said with a grin on her face.

Hot Shot groaned and said, "I almost forgot how expensive you're going to be. We may have to rethink this decision, Nola." He ducked as she threw the towel she was using to dry off at him and started laughing. "It's all good, baby. Everything is going to be all right. I need to get with Tone in the morning so we can handle some things and clear the air. After that, I'll set up a meeting with Juan G. He is in no way going to care for hearing about my upcoming departure from Texas."

Nola patted the spot next to her on the bed indicating that she wanted him to sit next to her. When he was seated, she said, "There are some things I think you should know about Juan G. He's the plug for Simon. Simon moved a lot of weight for Juan G., as well as handled a lot of other business stuff for him. I don't know how things are going to be when Juan G. hears about Simon's, um, disappearance. I don't know if you know or not, but Juan G. is hooked up strong with Tango Blast."

"The big Mexican gang out this way?"

"Yeah."

"That's strange."

"What, honey?"

"Juan G. had off and on beef with the Bloods, right?"

"Yeah, but I heard they finally squashed all of that when the Bloods agreed to not come south."

"They did. But what gets me is how Simon could be plugged in with Juan G. and have a strong enough relationship with the Bloods."

"What makes you think he had a strong relationship with the Bloods, honey?"

"It had to be a strong enough relationship if he was able to get Foe-Way and that other guy to get at Cotton and Meosha like they did."

"You're right."

"I still can't believe Simon had the temerity to have them get at Cotton and Meosha that way. I mean, was it really that serious? He couldn't take the L you gave him; he had to get grimy like that? Then to have the nuts to come to my home and try to get at me." Shaking his head he sighed heavily. "That man was a fool, and he deserved to die."

"I won't disagree with you there, honey. I do have a question for you, though."

"What up?"

"What does 'temerity' mean? I'm just a lowly high school graduate, honey. You lost me with that one there," she said and smiled.

"It means reckless boldness; rashness, baby."

"Oh. Well, yeah, he's that type of dude. Or should I say *was* that type of dude. Back to Juan G., Simon, and the Blood connection."

"So you think Juan G. may have an issue when he finds out that Simon is no longer among the living?"

"When the word gets out that he is gone, dead, or whatever, I'm sure Juan G. will feel you had something to do with it. I mean, I'm quite sure he knows about what you did to Simon at that bar."

Hot Shot sighed again and said, "More problems. Yes, it's definitely time to shake this state. I'll give Juan G. a call tomorrow after I've gotten at Tone. Right now, all I want to do is take me a hot shower and clean the stink of death off of me," he said as he stood and went into the bathroom.

"Do you want me to order you something to eat from room service, honey?"

"Yes, that would be nice, thank you. A steak and baked potato will suffice," he said from inside the bathroom.

By the time he was finished with his shower, the food had arrived, and Nola had everything set up for him in the bedroom. She had his plate and a bottle of white wine set on the bed while lying beside it. She smiled a mischievous smile and said, "Come here, honey, and let me feed you."

"You have that look in your eyes, so I guess it's safe to assume you have overcome your traumatization from earlier."

"It's still there, but I've chosen not to think about death right now. Instead, I'm thinking more about life. Life with my man on the West Coast. Life with my man who I love so very much. Now, come eat before your food gets cold."

He got on the bed and let Nola feed him some of his juicy steak that was cooked just as he liked, medium rare, nice and chewy with a little red in the middle. When he finished eating, he sighed and smiled at her. "If you treat me this good when we get west, I'm positive all will be well."

"I have more than just food to feed you, honey," she said in a seductive tone as she shrugged off the terry cloth robe she had put on and climbed on top of his chiseled chest. She then eased up on top of him until her pussy was hovering right over his lips. Wasting no time, he began to slowly lick her pussy lips and clitoris. She moaned loudly as he reached and grabbed her firm ass cheeks and gave them a squeeze. The smell of clean pussy and lemon burst invaded his nostrils as he put a finger between her outer pussy lips to separate her wetness.

She tightened her legs a little because it tickled her. He then put a finger inside of her now soaking wet pussy and started fingering her deeply. With his other hand, he reached up and found one of her titties and began to squeeze her nipples. With a loud scream she shuddered and came, and he happily swallowed all of her juices as they poured out of her pussy. He then eased from under her and turned her so she was now lying on her back with her legs spread wide open. He smiled as he stared at her and licked his lips wanting more of her. He bent between her legs and went back in for seconds. He stuck his tongue back inside of her pussy and swallowed and licked and sucked while he took his thumb and lifted the top portion of her pussy so he could have direct access to her clit which bulged out as he gently licked it. He began to flick it faster and faster with his tongue while fingering her faster and faster, driving her mad. She came ten times harder than the first time and swore to God that she loved Hot Shot. His dick was so hard that he felt uncomfortable. He needed release, and he needed it fast. He slid inside of her hotness and got primal inside of that pussy. No tenderness at all; it was like an animal sexing her, and she loved every bit of it.

"Yes! Yes! Give it to me fast like that, honey. Take this pussy! Work this pussy! Take it! Work it! Take it! Work it!" she yelled over and over as she felt yet another orgasm mounting. The pussy was feeling so damn good to him that he felt as if he could stay inside of her for a real long time, and he intended on doing just that. He paused and pulled his dick out of her, much to her displeasure. But it didn't take him long to submerge his dick back inside of her pussy. This time, he had her on her hands and knees on top of the bed, and he was behind her giving her every inch of his dick from the doggie-style position. She clenched the sheets tightly as he slapped that ass and went as deep as he could inside of her.

"Oh! My! God! Hot! Shot! I'm! Coming!" she screamed as her body began to shake and shiver. She squeezed her pussy muscles together tightly and clamped down on his dick which caused the effect she was looking for. He moaned loudly. "That's right, honey, that's right. Come for Nola. Come for me, Hot Shot! Come. For! Me!" Her words combined with the tightness of her pussy gripping his dick caused him to explode while screaming her name at the same time.

"Nola! I love you! I love you, Nola!"

Chapter Twenty-eight

The next morning when Hot Shot woke up, Nola was lying right next to him already awake. He smiled at her and said, "Excuse me, baby, I got to piss." He jumped up and went into the bathroom and handled his business. When he returned, Nola was smiling at him. "Please don't tell me you're ready for some more because all I want to do is go back to bed for a couple of more hours. A lot needs to be taken care of today, Nola. Don't wear me out, baby, okay?"

"We can put it off until later, but you better believe I want some more of this luscious piece of meat you possess, honey. I love how you make love to me. You have that longtime staying power, you're tender when needed, and rough when I want it like that. All that combined with your double Snicker-like thickness and long ten inches has totally hooked me, honey."

Shaking his head, he asked her, "How do you know that I'm ten inches long, Nola? I don't even know my exact length. I've never measured myself."

Smiling at him while licking her lips she said, "Trust me, I know. Since you need to go back to sleep, here, let me help you, honey," she said as she dipped her head under the covers and slid down to his dick and inserted him inside of her mouth. She began sucking him deep and long. Sucking, licking, sucking, licking. Licking, gag, suck, gag, lick, gag, suck. Sucking up and down using lips and tongue going extra deep, deep throat all the way, gag, then all of a sudden, *Boom!* He exploded inside of her mouth in less than three and half minutes, a personal best for Nola's masterful head game.

"Oh my God, Nola," he moaned as he curled in the fetal position and closed his eyes.

With a smile on her face, she wiped some of his semen from her lips with her index finger and stuck it inside of her mouth. "Mmmm, I do love the taste of my man. Nite nite, honey. Sweet dreams," she said as cuddled close to him and went back to sleep feeling totally relaxed and comfortable with the man she was in love with. Their journey together had just begun.

A few hours later, Hot Shot felt Nola shaking him telling him that his phone was ringing. He opened his eyes and groggily accepted the phone from her and answered it. "What up, champ?"

"It's almost eleven in the morning and you're still asleep? You need to get up, dog, so we can chop it up. I gotta get up outta Dallas within a couple of hours," said Tone.

"Had a rough night, you know what I'm saying?"

"Yeah, I had one of those myself. So, where you wanna meet me at?"

Not feeling like getting up and dressed, Hot Shot decided to have Tone come to the suite so they could talk. "I'm at the W. I got a suite on the tenth floor, 10554. Come on up and we can chop it up here."

"You always do big thangs, huh, Shot? I'm feeling that. But look, I've been on the road since early this morning. Order some of that good room service. I need some substance in my body, dog."

"You got that. Any preference?"

"Yeah, some good food," Tone said and started laughing as he ended the call.

Hot Shot sighed and lay his head back on the pillow not really wanting to move. It had been a real long time since he'd felt this out of it. Everything that had taken place yesterday had definitely taken a toll on him. He thought back and saw how Meosha shot herself, and he quickly opened his eyes. *No more time for those thoughts. Time to get things together and get this exit plan in order,* he thought as he slowly got out of the bed with Nola staring at him.

"Are you okay, honey?"

"I'm fine. Do me a favor, baby, and order some breakfast from room service for me. Make a large order for three, okay?"

"No problem. I'll take care of that for you, honey. You go on and get showered."

He nodded and went into the bathroom to get himself together while thinking about all that needed to be taken care of later on in the day. After making a mental note of what he needed to handle, he sighed and wondered how things were going to end for him in Dallas. He hoped it all worked out as planned.

Twenty minutes later, Hot Shot came into the living room of the suite to see Nola sitting on the couch watching the flat screen with a pale look on her face. Before he could ask her what was wrong, there was a knock on the door. He stepped to the door and checked the peephole to see Tone standing outside of his room. He opened the door and let Tone inside and quickly stepped back toward the living room without saying a word to Tone who followed him. They both stood next to each other and watched what Nola was watching on television, both having their own thoughts haunt them as they listened to the news reporter from KDFW Fox News give her report while standing in front of Meosha's home in DeSoto.

"So far, there hasn't been any more word or details given to us on this grisly triple homicide here in DeSoto. What we have learned is that the woman who lives here at this home, Meosha Davies, and two men, Jackson Barnes, aka Foe-Way, and Daniel Weaver, aka Dank, were found dead when a neighbor saw that her door was left wide open in the middle of the night and decided to come and check on Ms. Davies. We've been told that Ms. Davies was a quiet, young lady who recently graduated from North Texas University and was well liked in the neighborhood. When we have more, we'll be sure to keep you posted on this terrible crime here in DeSoto. This is Jazmine Champion reporting live from DeSoto. Back to the studio."

Nola, dressed in a pair of shorts and one of Hot Shot's wife beater tee shirts, stood and stepped into the bedroom without saying a word with tears sliding down her face. Hot Shot started to follow her but changed his mind. He was just as messed up as she was. Especially, when he saw Cotton in the background speaking with the authorities and crying loudly. This sucked. This really sucked, he said to himself as he turned toward Tone and said, "Have a seat so I can break all of this down."

After they were seated, he told Tone everything that happened at Meosha's house, and then finished with what had taken place at his condo, except he left out the fact that Nola was the person who shot and killed Simon. Just as he finished, there was a knock at the door. Hot Shot went and let the waiter in who brought them their breakfast. After tipping the room service waiter, he went to the cart and began to make himself a plate of the breakfast food Nola had ordered for them. Tone joined him and began to pile food on his plate as well. Hot Shot made a plate of bacon, eggs, toast, and grits and poured a glass of orange juice, then took it into the bedroom and gave it to Nola who was sitting on the edge of the bed crying softly. He set the food down next to her and said, "Hold it together, baby. Eat something. Let me handle this with Tone."

She held up her hand to stop him and said, "Go on and do what you have to do, honey. I'm fine. Seeing that on the news just made everything that happened yesterday come back to my mind is all. Go. Take care of your business."

Not knowing what else he could say or do for her he nodded, turned, and went back into the living room where Tone was busy tearing into his breakfast. When he was seated next to him, he too started to eat. In between bites of his pancakes, he asked Tone, "You don't have anything to say about this mess?"

Tone swallowed and said, "Dog, I got a lot to say about this crazy shit. I don't understand how that fool Simon could get Foe-Way and Dank on that stupid shit. But the more I think about it, the more I understand. That fool was still salty at you, so that made it easy for Simon to sic him on your mans and his girl. I want to apologize for that, Shot. I told you before I don't condone stupid shit. I never saw this coming, dog."

"How could you? There's no need for you to apologize, Tone. This mess is all because of Simon not being able to accept the L he took when he tried to get at me. I had just decided to get at him through Juan G. to see if we could squash the matter before all of this went down. Guess I was a little too late."

"It wouldn't have mattered. That clown had his mind made up to do you something, dog, so it was gonna go down regardless. Simon was about his paper, but he was a goofy clown, gung ho to the point where he thought his money and connects to that fat-ass Mexican gave him more power than he really had."

"That's something else that puzzles me. How can you be hooked up with both Simon and Juan G.? The beef you had was squashed with Juan G., I know, but wasn't that like playing it real close?"

Tone smiled at Hot Shot and said, "Dog, I'm a G. with this thang, and I've been around a long time. One of my best moves is to always keep those I don't trust real close and wait patiently for them to expose their hand. Yeah, I fucked with Simon and Juan G. It served a purpose. I knew sooner or later it would be time for me to make my move, so I was positioning myself to be in the right place of power when it was time to act. With Simon done, things are about to get weird out here for real. Speaking of that prick Simon, I still can't believe he had the nuts to get at you like that," Tone said shaking his head.

"Me neither. Never thought he would make a move on me at my spot."

"Resentment kills a fool, and envy slays the simple. Damn."

Hot Shot grinned and said, "Job 5:2. Didn't know you were a man who read the Bible, Tone."

Tone smiled and said, "There's a lot you don't know about me, Shot. I've banged all my life for Bloods, so best believe I bang even harder for God."

With respect and admiration for him, Hot Shot said, "I know that's right."

"So, what's the next move with this mess?"

"I'm about to get at Juan G. and set up a meeting and see if we're good. After that takes place, then I'll know how to proceed. What about you?"

"I'm going to head back to Abilene and get at my sister and deal with this Foe-Way situation. Before I head out, I'll get at Dank's people and drop them some bread. That's about all I can do. If things don't go as you want with that fat Mexican, make sure you holla at me, dog.

We may be able to form a strong team and move on that sucka."

Shaking his head, Hot Shot said, "Not my get down, Tone. But if it looks like things will get wicked, I will deal with it. And when I deal with wicked things, they normally turn out bloody."

"I see. You seemed to have handled this deadly situation quite well."

"I've seen and dealt with way worse. I've been known to respond accordingly in complicated situations. I'm icy when things get heated and deft when it comes to my survival as well as my money."

Laughing, Tone said, "I know that's right."

"I need to ask you for a favor, Tone. If you deny me this, then I will totally understand under the circumstances, and I wouldn't blame you one bit."

With raised eyebrows, Tone said, "What's up, dog?"

Hot Shot smiled sheepishly as he explained that Simon's body was downstairs in the parking lot in Dank's Dodge Durango. With everything he had on his plate, he didn't have enough time to deal with the disposal of Simon's body.

"You mean to tell me you actually drove to this fucking five-star hotel with a dead body in the fucking back of Dank's load? You are fucking nuts. You trying to kick the damn door down to the fucking penitentiary, Shot."

"That's one thing I'm not trying to do. Can you help me with this, Tone?"

Tone pulled out his phone and made a call. When the other line was answered, he said, "What's up, Damu? Blood, I need you to come meet me in the front of the W Hotel downtown. How long can it take you to get here? . . . Okay, that's what's up. That's just enough time for me to finish my breakfast. When you get about five minutes away, text me and I'll meet you in the front.

Bring a homie with you 'cause I'm going to need one of y'all to roll my whip. I'll explain everything to you after we handle this shit. . . . Yeah, I know what happened to Foe-Way and Dank. Just get here and we'll talk," he said and ended the call. He then pointed toward his food and said, "Mind if I finish my breakfast before I go dispose of a dead man for you?"

Hot Shot smiled and said, "Not at all. Good looking out, Tone."

With a mouth full of eggs Tone nodded, chewed, swallowed, and then said, "You owe me big-fucking-time for this shit, Shot."

"I'd figured you would say something like that."

"Damn right."

Chapter Twenty-nine

When Tone left the hotel, Hot Shot went back into the bedroom to find Nola standing in front of the mirror looking sexy in a multicolored silk dress with a low neckline and matching multicolored sandals on her small feet. She smiled at him, and that smile made him feel real good. *This is one strong, black woman,* he thought as he stepped to her with his arms open. She stepped into his embrace and let him give her a warm, tight hug. She inhaled his cologne and sighed. "I love how you always smell so good, honey. I love you."

"I love how you love me, baby. I love you more."

"Don't you ever stop, Hot Shot. Please don't ever stop loving me."

"I won't." He gave her a soft kiss so he wouldn't mess up her lipstick. "Okay, this is the plan for the day. I need to go check on Barry and take care of that end of things. After that, I'll go back by the condo and make sure everything is cleaned up. Then I have some stuff to take care of, so I'll be caught up until the evening time at the latest. I need for you to get out of the way, Nola. Go out to Rowlett and chill until I can get at you."

"That's exactly what I planned on doing. But before I head home, I'm going to the graveyard to put some flowers on my parents' grave. In one of those moods, you know."

"Yes, I know," he said as he thought about his parents and his little brother. He quickly shook those thoughts out of his head and slapped her on the ass and said, "Let's get going, baby."

"Oww! Boy, you better be careful with that. You know how I do like to get rough at times," she said smiling.

"Later for that, you freak!"

"Your freak!"

He smiled. "Always." They then grabbed their keys and went downstairs to Nola's car.

She dropped Hot Shot off in front of the condo and sped away with her family on her mind. She needed to talk to her brother and twin sister. As she drove, she wondered how they were going to feel when she told them that she was leaving for California with Hot Shot soon. She grimaced as she thought about their reactions to that bit of information. Ouch!

Hot Shot went upstairs to make sure everything was okay in his place. He then sat down and called Cotton. Cotton informed him that he had just left the police station from being questioned, and everything seemed to be okay. The police are still baffled as to how Meosha was able to kill Foe-Way and Dank, then take her own life.

"That's going to remain a mystery to them, I guess. So, how are you holding up, champ?"

"Holding on, Boss man, holding on as best as I can."

"That's all you can do right about now, Cotton. Hold it together as best as you can."

"What about you, what you got up?"

"Business as always with me, Cotton. About to get at Juan G. and let him know what's what. After I check his temperature to make sure he's not on nothing grimy, I'll determine how things will proceed from there."

There was a brief pause, then Cotton said, "Honestly, I think you need to give Juan G. some of the same thing Simon got."

"What? For what? He hasn't done anything to me or us."

"I just feel things are going to get worse, and he may be a key factor in shit, Boss man."

"You need to calm down. Get you some rest and leave that type of thinking to me. You got me, Cotton?"

"Yeah, I got you, Boss man. I got you loud and clear," he said and hung up the phone.

Hot Shot stared at his phone and didn't like what he was feeling at that moment at all. He shook his head as he grabbed his phone, keys, and went downstairs to the garage. It was time to go check on Barry.

One hour later after visiting Barry at Parkland Hospital and making sure that he was taken care of as well as assuring him that as long as he kept his mouth shut he would be well compensated, Hot Shot was back inside of his Audi headed toward a strip club called Onyx which was right around the corner from DG's. He shook his head and had to smile at how Juan G. seemed to love to meet at strip clubs. This dude was one seriously freaky Mexican, he thought as he turned on N.W. Highway and a minute later pulled into the parking lot of the Onyx cabaret. This strip club was huge and made DG's look miniscule in comparison. Not only was it a strip club, but it was a barbershop as well. Now, who in the hell combined a barbershop with a strip club? That is a way-out combo right there, Hot Shot thought as he got out of his car and stepped inside of the humongous strip club. As soon as he entered, he saw Juan G. with his normal cronies and the two sexy female security guards he kept with him at all times posing as some groupie females. When he was standing in front of Juan G., he smiled at him and said, "What's good, Juan G.?"

"Everything is good, Hot Shot. I got money, I got hoes, I got the world by the balls, hombre. God, I love Texas! God, I love America!" Juan G. said and laughed loudly.

Hot Shot took a seat across from the obnoxious Mexican and said, "I'm glad you're in such an exuberant mood. I hope that mood remains after I've shared what I need to speak with you about."

"I got a funny feeling I'm not going to be in an exuberant mood after you speak. From your tone of voice, it sounds as if you're about to deliver some bad news for me."

"Could we have a few minutes alone so I can speak freely?"

"My people here know all of my business; no need for that."

Hot Shot shook his head no and said, "They know your business not mine. This involves me more than it actually involves you."

Juan G. gave him a nod of understanding and dismissed his two cronies as well as his sexy protection detail. When they departed, he said, "Now, you can speak freely. What's up, my friend?"

"Glad to know you consider me a friend. We've done some good business, Juan G., and, hopefully, we will be able to continue to do good business together. I recently got into it with an associate of yours, and that incident has now caused things to spiral somewhat out of control."

"Which associate, Shot?"

"Simon."

"Ahhh, so you're the one who put the hands on Simon at that bar."

"Yes."

"Don't tell me Simon has tried to get at you behind that shit?"

"That's exactly what I've come to tell you, Juan G.," Hot Shot said with a serious look on his face.

Juan G. stared at him for a minute, and then let his words sink in. "Oh shit! Don't tell me that Simon is no longer breathing because of that incident at the bar?"

"That's exactly what I've come to tell you, Juan G. Except it wasn't because of the incident at the bar, at least not on my end of things." He then went on to tell the Mexican drug czar what Simon did by invading his home. When he finished, he stared at Juan G. trying to gauge his reaction to what he had just told him.

Juan G. sighed heavily and downed what was left of his drink and said, "This is not good, Shot, not good at all. Simon and I did a lot of good business, and I do mean a whole lot. He got connected with me through my people. When they hear about his demise, they're going to be very upset. Keeping it all the way real, they are going to want your head for this."

Tango Blast, that Mexican gang Nola told him about, thought Hot Shot as he stared at Juan G. with a blank expression on his face as if he didn't give a damn about what he had just told him. "You need to let your people know that both occasions when he got at me he was in the wrong and was the aggressor—he just wasn't aggressive enough. You know how I get down. I don't have time for nothing but getting money. In fact, when I heard he was still wanting beef, I had intentions on getting at you to see if you could have deaded the situation before it got wicked."

"I wish you would have, Shot. Damn, I wish you would have. I can get at my people, but I doubt they'll be trying to hear anything I have to say in your defense. They lose a lot by losing Simon. However, there is a way I think I could get things smoothed out here."

Knowing where he was headed Hot Shot started shaking his head before Juan G. could continue and said, "If you think this will give you some leverage on me to hook up with you on your offer, you're mistaken. I got at my people, and they are not with any of that takeover type stuff. So if there's more drama to be dealt with, then I guess it is what it is."

Shaking his head sadly, Juan G. said, "You don't get me, Shot. The drama that Simon tried to bring you is nothing what Tango Blast will bring your way."

Hot Shot stared at him as if he was stupid because of the way he said the name of his people, like by merely mentioning Tango Blast that would strike the fear of God in him. It didn't. "Look, your people may be strong and have the power in Texas, that's fine. Don't forget I'm not from Texas."

"True, you're not from here, but you *are* here. As long as you try to get money in Texas, you will face problems when everything comes out about Simon. You're just one man, Shot. There is no way you can handle this type of funk."

"You keep warning me of this; yet, you say that you would try to assist me on this matter if I agree to what you want from me. Which I won't. So that tells me that our business relationship has come to an end, Juan G.," Hot Shot said as he stood.

"You really need to reconsider my offer because that way, you can save yourself all the bullshit and still win and get that bread, Shot."

"No, thanks. There's nothing to think about. I already told you what my people said. And trust me, your people may be strong and all that rah-rah you talking, but my people are stronger. Stronger here in Texas as well as the West Coast. So, let's see who's actually the strongest. I hate that we will have to take it there, but you aren't trying to give any peaceful way out of this, so I guess it's war. And for real, though I love money and enjoy living peacefully, the thought of some action excites me. You've peeped my money game, and you see I play to win always.

My murder game is about fifty times more intense than my money game. So tell your Tango Blast homeboys that when they get at me, they better get at me right and don't miss. If they do, then I'm about to tear Texas up worse than anyone has ever seen. That's my word."

Juan G. stared at Hot Shot's back as he turned and left and wondered if he was really cocky enough to try to go to war with the Dallas faction of Tango Blast, the biggest Mexican gang in Texas next to the Texas Syndicate.

When his cronies returned along with his lovely personal security detail, Juan G. quickly informed them about what was said between him and Hot Shot. One of the gorgeous Latina women smiled sadly and said, "That man is a confident one. Confident men are dangerous, Juan G. You should tell the Tango Blast to let this go because it may not be worth it. Simon was a pawn who's time expired because he underestimated a dangerous man. Don't let your devotion to Tango Blast cloud your judgment and cause you to make the same fatal mistake that Simon made. Be smarter than that."

Juan G. poured himself another drink and downed it quickly, then gave his security guard a nod. He then grabbed his phone and made a call to the top man of Tango Blast. "Yogi, we have a problem, jefe."

Chapter Thirty

When Hot Shot made it back to his place, he went straight to the bedroom, changed into his workout clothes, and began to stretch and warm up before starting his normal morning workout routine. Though it was the middle of the day, it didn't matter to him. He needed to think and working out relieved his stress. He felt he thought more clearly while working out. After an hour and a half of push-ups, sit-ups, and calisthenics, he went and took a long hot shower. By the time he finished and was dressed again, his mind was made up. It was time to definitely end his run in this part of Texas. War brought heat, and he was in no way trying to get caught up like that. A part of him wanted to smash Juan G. and give those chumps from Tango Blast more than they'd ever seen, but he knew that would be detrimental to the overall plans, and JT would go nuts. Thinking about JT made him smile as he grabbed his phone and dialed JT's number.

When he answered, Hot Shot wasted no time informing him of the conversation he had with Juan G. When he finished, he said, "So, I think it's best to wrap this up and head back home, regroup, and get things ready to hit another state."

"After what happened yesterday, I've already come to that same conclusion. I got a mind to let you get at those Tango Bash guys just to show them they aren't as strong as they think they are."

Laughing, Hot Shot corrected him. "It's Tango *Blast,* JT."

"Who gives a flying fuck. Them sum bitches think they tough, and they're nothing but some prison gang that got lucky and made some good connects. Fuck'em!" He sighed to calm himself down and said, "All right, let's start the close out preparations. How long will it take for you to get outta there, son? And I do mean pronto."

"I can have everything tied up and situated in forty-eight hours. I'll have Cotton get my place wrapped up for me. I might let him keep it and send me my vehicles and bike. That will save me some time."

"True. What are you going to do about the love of your life, son?"

"We've already discussed everything. Where I go, she goes."

"These are some special circumstances, you do know that, right?"

"I love her, JT."

"But do you trust her?"

"If I didn't trust her, I could never love her, so that goes without saying."

"You know this is a big gamble on your part, son?"

"Yes, champ, I know. It's a gamble I'm willing to take, though. Like I said, I love her, and I know she loves me. What will be will be."

"That's the truth. All right, I'll expect to hear from you in forty-eight hours when you're either headed west or already home. Speaking of home, how's that going to work for you and the love of your life? You gon' keep her cooped up in a hotel and live like you were living while you were there?"

"I haven't given that any thought. By the time we get there, I'll have something figured out."

"Why not go to your home and get that situation taken care of?"

"I'm not ready to go there yet, JT. If things go as planned, I won't be in the West that long anyway, right?"

"You better believe that. I plan to have you in a new state within ninety days. So you better use that time to get everything settled for the lady of your life so she can be comfortable while you're gone back on another mission."

Shaking his head no as if JT was there with him and could see him, he said, "You must have not heard me when I said, where I go, she goes."

JT started laughing and said, "Well, I'll be damn, son. She's just become a part of the damn team then, huh? What, do I need to start reading her in on all of our business too?"

"I'll holla at you in forty-eight hours, champ."

"Do that. And Hot Shot?"

"What up?"

"Make it back west in one piece. If you see anything remotely out of whack, then do what you do best."

"Affirmative," he said and ended the call, then relaxed back on the bed. It was time to get the hell out of Dodge.

Nola couldn't believe how her brother and sister had turned the home they were raised in into a damn freak show house. Almost every room she went into inside of the seven-bedroom, ranch-style home was occupied by either two or more couples having some kind of freaky sex, sleeping, or doing drugs. She was so upset by the time she made it to the back room that she felt as if she was going to hurt somebody. When she saw Lola lying on one of the many couches in the back room with her legs spread wide open while some young, white man ate her pussy sloppily and noisily, she felt like she wanted to throw up. What disgusted her most was her damn brother was on the other side of the room with a small camera-like thingy in his hand and was busy filming two young white girls as they were giving some big black guy head simultaneously, one sucking his dick while the other was sucking his balls. Weeta Wee was in the far corner of the room talking to a few other young, white girls, so she headed in that direction. *At least they aren't involved in any of that freaky shit,* she thought as she stepped quickly toward her cousin. When Weeta Wee saw her, he smiled and said, "What's good, cuzo? Where ya been, stranger? Heard you been having some issues with Simon?"

"You could say that. That's nothing. How you feeling?"

"Cool. Almost good as new. Been getting the very best care here with all the ladies," he said smiling.

"Yeah, I bet."

"Where ya man at? Heard he served that fool Simon something special."

"You could say that. Look, I need to talk to old Mr. Flynt over there. Do me a favor and get him and my whorish-ass sister's attention for me. I'm not going anywhere near that disgusting shit they doing. Tell them I said to come in the kitchen because I have something I want to talk to them about that's important. Where is Keeta Wee? Still in Oklahoma?"

"Yeah, he's coming back at the end of the week. What's going on with you, Nola? You okay?"

"I'm fine. Just get them and bring they ass to the kitchen," she said as she walked quickly out of the back room because the smell of sex and drugs was making her sick. She went into the kitchen and poured herself some water from the faucet in the sink. After emptying her glass, she sat down at the kitchen table and sighed. *This is going to be easier than I thought. I got to get away from this crazy shit,* she thought as she sighed again and

tried to rid her thoughts of her sister doing all of that
freaky mess in the back room.

Ten minutes later, Lola, Weeta Wee, and Tiny Troy
entered the kitchen. Each spoke to Nola as they took a
seat at the kitchen table with her.

"What's good, sister?" asked Lola.

"Changes, that's all. Changes," Nola said as she stared
at them.

"What's on your mind, Nola?" asked Troy. "Talk to us."

"First, I want you to know what I feel you all know
already. I love you to death. We family, and we all we got.
That will never change. But what y'all are doing is just too
damn turned up and ratchet for me. I cannot be a part
of it any longer. I'm done. I'm moving to the West Coast
with Hot Shot."

"You got to be fucking kidding me! You don't know that
man well enough to up and move to another state with
him, sister," said Lola. "What's wrong with your ass?"

"What's wrong with *me?* Ain't that a joke! What the
fuck is wrong with *your* freaky ass? That shit you doing
ain't cool, Lola. You doing this porno shit doing God
knows what ain't fucking cool at all. But it's more than
that. I don't feel none of this shit. I mean, we were getting
money just fine from the Oklahoma thing. Then, Troy,
you wanted to get some legit money, and you know I
supported that totally. But why bring this shit into our
home? The same home that our parents provided for us.
I went up to my room, and what the fuck do I see? Two
white bitches who don't even look old enough to be into
this shit! I head toward the bathroom, and I hear giggling
and some silly shit going on, open the damn door, and I
see what . . . Two more white girls smoking weed
and snorting powder—in our fucking home. You guys
have taken this shit way too far. You don't shit where
you sleep, remember? You got drugs and a bunch of

underage white girls in this mothafucka! Y'all tripping and trying to go to fucking jail and make us lose the one thing our parents left us, and that is something I cannot, and will not, be a part of. I can't stop this shit, so I'm out."

Troy sighed and stared at his sister and thought, *Damn, she is pissed.* "Calm down some, Nola, and listen. I know shit looks crazy, but it's all good, for real. I'm in the process of getting us our own studio so we won't be having this shit at the house no more. A month or so from now, it'll be back to normal around here."

"In a month or so, I'll be getting adjusted to my life with Hot Shot in California, brother. It's not just the house, it's the life we're living, and I'm tired of it. I'm ready to go to school and take my life in an entirely different direction."

"So going to California with Shot is going to help you make all of these changes, Nola?" asked Lola as she frowned at her twin.

"Yes."

"It ain't like he's living a squeaky clean life, Nola. He's knee-deep in this game too," said Weeta Wee.

Nodding her head, she said, "I know. But how he gets down and how this shit is on totally different levels is huge. He'll support me with any move I make, and I'll stand by him with all that I have."

"What, we don't support you, sister? I mean, damn, you're acting real brand-new, Nola. You just gon' up and abandon us like we ain't family?" Lola said, realizing that Nola was dead serious, and the anger combined with the hurt was making her feel some kind of way, and that was something she was not accustomed to.

"You know what? If being with that man makes you happy, then go on and be happy. Just know I'm the bitch that will say I told you so when you come back home with a broken heart. Them California niggas ain't no good. Yeah, they good for getting that money, but when it's all said and done, they don't care about nobody but themselves. You're just some in-town ass for that nigga, and you so blinded by the dick, you can't even see that shit!"

"Watch your mouth, sister. I love you to death. That will never change, but don't you dare disrespect the man I'm in love with."

"Fuck him! And fuck you too if you leave us!" screamed Lola.

Before this turned into a major catfight, Troy stepped in between the twin sisters and said, "Stop it! I'm not going to let this turn into some weak shit. Nola, you want to go west, then so be it. You know we want only what's best for you. You feel Shot will make you happy, then go be happy, sister. If it don't work, then you come right back home. Don't be out there all ashamed to come back to where we feel you belong, you hear me?"

She smiled at her brother lovingly and said, "I hear you, brother. If it don't work, I'll be the first to call and let you and this 'I told you so' sister of mine say it, that you both were right and I was wrong." She stepped around her brother and stared at her sister and said, "I love you. You doing what you want, and you're happy with that freaky shit. Let me be happy doing what I want to do, 'k?"

With tears sliding down her face, Lola nodded but couldn't speak, so she gave her twin sister a tight hug, then turned and left the room.

"On some other shit, though, since you and Shot are about to shake us, do you know what he's going to do about the business we've been conducting?" asked Troy.

"He told me he was tying up some loose ends, and he would get with you. I get the impression that he's still going to keep everything as it is, just on some long-range shit."

"Why is he going back west? What, the money out here ain't good for him no more?" asked Weeta Wee.

Though she heard his question, her mind was on how she had shot Simon. She shivered and said, "He don't want beef out here. He feels that ultimately that will interfere with his business. That issue with Simon and some more stuff has made him decide that it's best he leaves."

"You watch that fool, Nola. Watch him close and take nothing for granted. He doesn't strike me as the type to ever disrespect you. Even though I'm still not really feeling his ass, he is a stand-up-type dude. But never think it's all good. Always keep those pretty brown eyes of yours wide open," Weeta Wee said with genuine concern for his cousin.

She smiled at him lovingly and said, "Ahh, give me a hug, honey." After they finished hugging, Weeta Wee left the kitchen and left her alone with her brother.

"You know I don't want you to leave us."

"Yeah, I know. But you got to know that the direction y'all going isn't for me. Look at it like this, I'll be keeping the plug in order for you guys. You just keep making that paper and stacking it up. Get it and get out, brother. No—"

He cut her off and finished her sentence for her with a smile on his face. "Nothing lasts forever. Get it while the gettin's great!"

With a smile on her face, she gave her brother a tight hug and a kiss on the cheek and said, "That's right, honey. So, get it. And stay safe."

"I will."

"I love you, Troy."

"I love you too, sister. So, when you leaving?"

She smiled brightly and said, "Just as soon as my man is ready to go!"

Chapter Thirty-one

Hot Shot felt as if he'd been on the phone for hours after he ended a call with the last person he had dealt with over the last year in Dallas. He felt it was only right that he let them know he was out for a minute. He didn't inform them that it was highly unlikely he would ever return to Dallas to conduct any business. Instead, he told them that things had gotten somewhat hectic for him, and his business in the West needed his attention. He added that if they needed him, to give him a call and he would see what he could do for them. Now that he'd made that last call, he had to do something he felt somewhat bad about. Telling his little helper man, Cotton, that it was time for them to part ways. Though Cotton was a new acquaintance, he had become closer to Hot Shot than he cared to admit. Especially after what had happened to Meosha. Hot Shot didn't want anything to happen to Cotton behind any of his decisions, so he devised a plan for him. He just hoped that Cotton wouldn't be hardheaded and go against what he was about to propose to him. He sighed heavily as he again grabbed his phone and made another call. As soon as Cotton answered the phone, Hot Shot told him, "I need you to get here as soon as you can."

"That's cool, Boss man, 'cause I'm about five minutes from your spot now. I was just about to call you and ask can we hook up for a sec. Got some thangs I want to talk to you about."

"So do I. See you in a minute then," Hot Shot said and ended the call. He stood, stretched, and then went into the kitchen and grabbed a bottled water from the fridge. As he came back into the living room, his phone rang. He checked the caller ID and saw that it was Tone. Tone had been his first call to all of the people he had dealt with in Dallas, so he was curious about him calling right now. "What up, champ? You straight?"

"Yeah, dog, I'm good. Out the way for real. Just wanted to get at you on some real shit. You making that move back west for a minute is a damn good move. That fat fuck Juan G. just got at me and told me that I'd better find a new connect 'cause your time was just about up in Texas. He didn't go into any specifics, but he hinted that the Tango Blast are salty at you, dog. Real salty."

"Figured that. It's because of Simon."

"How did they find out about that business?"

"I told Juan G."

"Why?"

"That's how I get down, Tone. Good looking on the heads-up, though. I figured it would get like that, so it's time for me to make my move."

"Never figured you to be the type who would run from beef, dog. Shit, with the action you got at getting the heavy artillery, you should be getting ready to take all those punk-ass Mexicans to war."

"War don't make money; only causes death. I don't have time for death if it's not about making my money. This could get real ugly, and it's just not worth it. If the Tango Blast really want it, then they will have to come to the West to get it. And trust me, they hit the West looking for me, I'll know it just as soon as they enter the Pacific standard time zone. Then they will get their issue."

Laughing, Tone said, "I feel you, dog. If you need any-thing from me just holla. These numbers ain't changing no time soon."

"That's what's up. Thanks again for the heads-up. You didn't have to do that, Tone. I really appreciate that."

"I'm a black man, dog. Before I ever let a Mexican get a step on another black man, I'd rather be dead. I live with honor out here on these cold Texas streets, and I'll die with it. That's the Damu way."

Laughing, Hot Shot said, "I know that's right, Blood!" They both laughed. "Stay safe, Mr. Tone from QSB."

"Always."

"Oh, Tone."

"Yeah?"

"What did you do with that package that was in the back of the Durango?"

"I was going to have it burned and disposed of that way. But after speaking with that fat fuck Juan G., I decided on something else."

"What's that?"

Laughing, Tone said, "Stay safe, Mr. Hot Shot!"

Hot Shot ended the call and set the phone back on the table when Cotton knocked on the door. After letting him inside, they sat down and were quiet for a minute before speaking. Cotton sighed and said, "This shit has me real fucked up right about now, Boss man. I keep seeing what Meosha did to herself, and I feel like the weakest man in the world. I let that coward Foe-Way do that to her, man. I should have did something. She didn't deserve to have that done to her."

"You're right, she didn't. But what's done is done. As much as it hurts, there isn't a thing either of us can do about that. She did what she felt she had to do. We may not agree with it, but it was the decision she made. What we have to do now is stay focused and keep it moving. Easier said than done, I know, but it still has to be done. It's time for you to take a nice vacay somewhere for a minute, Cotton. I want you out of Texas by the morning, do you understand what I'm saying?"

"Where do you want me to go? I was born and raised right here in Dallas, Boss man."

"Why don't you hit Atlanta for a minute? Spend like a week or so out that way. Enjoy some of that Southern thickness you like so much. If that tires you out, you can always hit South Beach and really get it in out there. Either way, I want you out of here. It may get crazy around here soon, and I don't want you to get caught up."

"What's going on, Boss man? What about you? What you gon' do? 'Cause if you not leaving, then I ain't leaving."

Touched deeply by his loyalty, Hot Shot smiled. "Nola and I are out of here, champ. It's time to move on for a minute. When things cool down, we'll pick right back up where we left off."

Cotton stared at him for a moment and smiled. "You are one real dude, Boss man. So real, in fact, that you come off as plastic when you lie. I've been with you for almost a year. You think I don't know it when you're serving me some bullshit?" Before Hot Shot could answer his question, Cotton continued. "I ain't tripping, though, because I agree with you. I do need to get out of Dallas for a little bit. I need to get my head on straight 'cause I'm twisted right now. The ATL and the MIA both sound like some good spots to go cool out and regroup and get my mind right. The thing is, though, my ends ain't that damn cool. Not trying to spend my vault while getting some P therapy."

"What the heck is P therapy, Cotton?"

With a bright smile, Cotton said, "Pussy therapy, Boss man. 'Cause you already know if I hit the ATL and the MIA, all I'm gonna be doing is fucking and fucking and fucking."

Shaking his head, Hot Shot said, "You stupid." He then stood and went into the bedroom for a minute and returned with a Crown Royal pouch in his hand. He tossed the pouch to Cotton and said, "That's 150 large. Your bonus for a job well done, my man. No questions. I need you out of here no later than in the morning, you got me?"

"Yeah, yeah, I got you, Boss man. When we gon' hook back up and make some more money, though?"

Hot shot smiled and said, "When the time is right I'll call you." He then went on and told him that he was leaving his condo to him as well as his Denali. He gave him instructions on sending his vehicle to the West and then finished with, "Stay out the way for at least two months. Then I want you to come back here and chill. Keep your eyes and ears to the streets and check the temperature for me. When I think it's right, we'll make it happen again."

"What if it don't get right, Boss man?"

Hot Shot shrugged and said, "Then we hit another state and make it pop off there. Texas isn't the only state that we can make that bread in, Cotton."

"You'd take me on the road with you?"

Hot Shot stared at Cotton for a minute and said, "Yes, you're a good dude, and you are loyal. I think it's best I keep you with me. That way, you won't get twisted out here in this cold, cold world." They both started laughing. "Now, get on and get packed. I want you gone ASAP."

"Don't worry, Boss man. I'm outta here. I'm going to make some calls and get everything set up to have the S8 and your bike shipped to the address you just gave me. After that, I'm on the road. I should be in the A. late tomorrow night."

"Why are you going to drive? Why not fly out and move around in a rental?"

"Nah, I need this road trip. Give me time to think more, you know? Plus, I ain't got no damn money to be wasting on no rental or plane ticket. This here bonus money is my P-therapy money, and believe me, Boss man, I'm going to have some of the best pussy therapy this money can buy!"

"Trick."

"Call it what you want. It's therapy to me!" Both men gave each other some dap, and then Cotton surprised Hot Shot as he gave him a tight manly hug and said, "Thanks, Boss man. You're one stand-up dude.

"You know you're like my big bro, right?"

"Yes, li'l bro. Now get out of here. The numbers I gave you will never change so when you need me, you get right at me. No matter what, if you change any of your numbers, make sure I get them."

"Gotcha."

"And, Cotton."

"Huh?"

"Make sure you keep condoms." They both started laughing as Cotton left the condo.

Across town on the South in Oak Cliff, Juan G.'s controlled area was rocked by Simon's dead body being found on the front porch of Juan G.'s main trap house. A little "fuck you" gift from Tone on behalf of Hot Shot. Tone was laughing so hard tears were sliding down his face as he headed back home to Abilene.

"Yeah, you fat fuck, how the fuck you gon' explain that shit to the Dallas PD?" Tone said aloud as he continued to laugh as he pressed his foot down on the accelerator, and his powerful V-12 engine seemed to take his SL600 soaring down the highway.

Chapter Thirty-two

When Nola entered the condo, she was shocked to see that all of her clothes were packed in several Gucci suitcases piled in the living room. She set her purse down and asked, "Where are we going, honey? 'Cause I know we're not going where I think we are. Are we?"

Hot Shot stopped packing his clothes and said, "This is real life, Nola, not the movie scene-type stuff where we hold off on making our moves and something happens to stop us from living happily ever after. We're out of here on a six a.m. flight to Los Angeles. That is, if you are going with me to California," he said as he stood there, hoping she hadn't changed her mind.

Her heart was beating so fast that she could barely breathe. "Now you know I'm not changing my mind. I'm with you all the way, honey. I thought we would at least have a week or so before we left. . . . You know, with all of your business dealings and all."

"Everything has been handled. I spoke with everyone I deal with, and it's all good. I spoke with your brother and let him know that we can still make the same moves we've been making. He'll get at me with my end from the porno stuff so everything is ready. There's no need for me to be here any longer. It's a wrap for me out here in Dallas."

She stared at him with a smile on her face and said, "For *us*."

He nodded. "Yes, Nola, for us." He then started back packing his suitcase and gave her instructions for what he needed her to do while he finished packing. He also told her about the beef with the Tango Blast Mexicans. He didn't want to keep anything from her. He wanted her to be up on everything that was going on. By the time he finished packing, he was dead tired and real hungry.

"I'm going to take our bags down to the truck and go get us another suite at the W. After that, I'll bring the truck back here for Cotton."

"You're not leaving me here. I'll go with you, then when we come back, we can take my car back to the hotel. I'll call Lola and let her know where they can come and get my car. We'll catch a cab to the airport in the morning."

"That sounds like a better plan. Come on, the quicker we get this done, the quicker we can get something to eat. I'm starving!"

Hot Shot loaded all of their bags inside of the Denali, then stepped to the Audi and opened the trunk and placed a suitcase full of his weapons inside. He closed the door and stepped quickly back to the Denali, where Nola was already sitting on the passenger's side.

They went and got another suite at the W and had a bellhop take their suitcases to their suite. When they were on their way back to the condo, Hot Shot received a phone call from JT.

"Tell me you're on schedule to be out of Texas within forty-eight hours as we agreed, son."

"I can do you one better. We'll be touching down in LAX around nine a.m. tomorrow."

"Good. Have you made up your mind on how you're going to handle this situation? Because things will get dicey, to say the least, son. We have things ahead of us that no one can interfere with, not even the love of your life. So make sure you got your ducks all lined in a neat row."

"Affirmative. What about you? Is everything lined up for your moves?"

"Yep. I will admit I'm going to have a ball watching this all unravel. You did good, Hot Shot. Now, come on home so we can regroup and get ready to do some more good."

"That's right, champ, you know I'm with getting this money," he said and hung up the phone.

To say Juan G. was angry would be a monster understatement. He was *furious*. He couldn't believe that Hot Shot would disrespect him this way. Not only did he disrespect him, he disrespected Tango Blast by this blatant act. That, combined with the heat it was bringing to his main trap house, had Juan G. seeing red. He wanted Hot Shot's head served on a platter, and he was going to make sure he was alive when it was being cut off. He marched into his living room and ordered his two cronies to go get Hot Shot. "I want him brought out to the house on Camp Wisdom. That *mayate* dies this night. Do *not* return without him."

Both men smiled as they left the house to do as they had been ordered. After they left, one of Juan G.'s gorgeous security guards stepped to him and asked him a question. "Do you really think it was wise to send those two after Hot Shot? Hot Shot has shown he is not to be taken lightly. You should have sent someone better trained and equipped to deal with a man like that."

Letting her words sink in, Juan G. nodded and pulled out his phone and quickly called his cronies and told them to forget the order he just gave them and ordered them to return. He hung up the phone and smiled at his two gorgeous security guards. "I assume that you two feel you're better trained and equipped to handle this situation for me, huh?"

They both returned his smile but didn't speak.

He gave them a nod and said, "Go get him and bring him to me."

Without a word being said, they left the room to go do what they had been ordered.

Hot Shot and Nola returned to the condo and dropped off the Denali. They switched cars and got inside of Nola's 760 BMW, not realizing that that simple tactic saved both of their lives. When they pulled out of the underground parking garage, they drove right past Juan G.'s two gorgeous security guards who had just pulled in front of his building on their way to his condo to abduct him. While Hot Shot and Nola were on their way to have a nice dinner served to them from the W's room service, Juan G.'s security guards were inside of Hot Shot's condo discovering that he no longer resided there. After a careful search of his bedroom, they saw that the closets were bare, and that told them that Hot Shot had been one step ahead of them. They each had a frown on their face as they left the condo. Once they were back inside of their vehicle, the lead security guard, Pia, pulled out her phone and called Juan G. to deliver the bad news, how Shot was in the wind. Just as she expected, Juan G. was not pleased one bit.

"What the fuck you mean he's gone?"

"Do not curse at me as if I'm one of your minions, Juan G. Like I said, he's gone. We picked the lock to his condo with the intention of catching him slipping. Once we were inside, we found that he was not there, and he isn't coming back."

"How do you know that? He might be out running around or some shit."

"The closets are empty, the bathroom essentials as well. No cologne bottles, no nothing. Hot Shot is most likely already in California by now, or on his way at the very least."

"Fuck! That fuck nigga thinks he can just say fuck me and get away with it, he got me fucked all the way up. What, he think I won't go to Cali and get at his ass? I'll be damned. That nigga is a dead man. Hurry up and get back here," Juan G. said, clearly pissed off, knowing that in truth, there was nothing he would be able to do to get at Hot Shot.

There was no way he or the Tango Blast would try to go to the West Coast to get at Hot Shot. *Fuck!* he thought as he stepped to the kitchen and grabbed a bottle of Patrón and took a long swig straight from the bottle. "One thing for sure, your bitch ass better never step a foot back on Texas soil. You do and you're a dead man, Mr. Hot Shot," Juan G. said aloud as he took another swig of Patrón.

Hot Shot and Nola were lying side by side after finishing off a nice dinner of crabs, lobster tails, and shrimp, each full and somewhat sleepy. Hot Shot knew that they should get some sleep so they could be well rested for their early flight out to California in the morning. As he stared at Nola's sexy body, he felt himself getting aroused. What better way to end his last night in Texas then by making love to his woman? He smiled at her and ran his hand on her stomach. She moaned and turned on her side to face him. No words were needed. They both knew what was about to happen. Hot Shot began to take her clothes off slowly while staring at her beautiful body as she reached and started to rub his dick. When he had her naked, he quickly removed his clothes and stood at the end of the bed and told her to play with her pussy to get it nice and wet for him. She smiled at him seductively as he watched her finger herself slowly while he watched with his dick standing at full attention. Not being able to take too much more of this erotic show, he eased onto the bed between her legs and slowly slid his dick inside of her soaking wet pussy, inch by inch, until he filled her completely.

"Yes, honey, all of that. Give me all of that dick, honey. Oh yes, oh yes, just like that!" She kept her eyes open as he started to kiss her passionately. When he pulled away from her face, he opened his eyes and saw her staring at him, and for some reason, the look in her eyes turned him on even more. He really loved this woman and knew that there wasn't a doubt in this world that he could spend the rest of his life with her. He was in love, and it felt so right, so special, so good.

She reached and pulled him back to her, and they started kissing again, and she began to suck his tongue as he continued to stroke her pussy slowly, feeling all the wet walls and creamy coating of her pussy all over every inch of his dick. Though they made love plenty of times, it was still somewhat difficult for her to take all of his dick, but she loved the hurt and ache that he caused her pussy as she absorbed every stroke as he gradually picked up the pace going in and out of her faster and deeper with each stroke. His staying power was such a turn-on, and she kept her pussy wet for him, totally aroused, trying her best to resist the feeling of coming, yet the tingle inside of her pussy was so intense that the mini comes she felt had her aching to have a full-blown orgasm. All she could do was lie back with her legs tightly around his waist and take every bit of the man meat he was serving her. He groaned loudly, signaling that he was almost there. His dick seemed to get harder and grow another inch as she gasped loudly.

"Give it to me, baby! Give me all of that nut! Bust!" she screamed as her orgasm finally came and rocked through her body. She was trembling extra hard when she felt his orgasm explode inside of her. His sperm felt as if it shot like a missile inside of her, filling her pussy totally with that warm, sticky, wet sensation. She pressed her pussy closer to him trying to make sure she got every drop. She then realized that this was the very first time he had ever come inside of her. They were having unprotected sex for the first time, and it felt right. So right. Perfect. "Mmm-mmmm," she moaned as he pulled out of her and rolled onto his back and sighed. She wasn't done by far. She turned on her side and began to lick and suck all over his body until she reached his dick and inserted it inside of her mouth. She could hardly get all of it in her mouth, but she put forth one hell of an effort to deep throat all of him. He was harder than before, and that excited her to no end. She wanted more. She needed to have him back inside of her. She stopped sucking his dick, turned over, and put all of that big ass she was packing in the air for him.

She slapped her ass hard and said, "Come fuck me now, honey. Fuck this pussy good from the back."

He got behind her without saying a word and gave it to her just as she requested. He eased his dick inside of that pussy and slapped her ass real hard, causing a stinging sensation that made Nola gasp. "God, that feels so damn good! Fuck me! Fuck me, Hot! Shot! Fuck! Me!" she screamed, and fuck her he did. He fucked her hard and long while placing his hand over her clit driving her crazy. After close to thirty minutes of this, they both screamed and came at the same time, swearing how much they loved each other. Once their orgasms subsided, Hot Shot barely had enough energy to grab the phone and call the hotel operator to make sure they had a four a.m. wake-up call so they wouldn't miss their flight from DFW to LAX. By the time he finished speaking with the operator, Nola was knocked out snoring lightly. He smiled, kissed her softly on the lips, and put his head on the pillow. Within minutes, he too was sound asleep.

Chapter Thirty-three

It had been over a month and Nola was still having the time of her life. Every day seemed to be a new adventure for her. Hot Shot was spoiling her by making sure that she enjoyed everything there was to enjoy about California. *My God, the weather!* She could never get enough of being able to walk outside in that sunny, beautiful, California weather. She was in heaven on earth. They did everything from walking on Malibu Beach to shopping at some of the most expensive stores on Rodeo Drive to personal boutiques in Hollywood. He even took her around where he grew up in the hood and took her to a few swap meets. That was funny to her because in Texas, they called them flea markets. They ate everywhere from Mr. Chow's to the famed Fatburgers, the famous hamburger stand in South Central. Since the Dodgers were in the playoffs, they caught a game, and she got to eat peanuts and hot dogs and scream like she was a die-hard Dodger fan. What was so crazy, after the game, she *had* become a die-hard Dodger fan.

Hot Shot laughed as he realized his woman was, in fact, a little crazy! He truly enjoyed her company and the time they were spending together. It all felt so right to him. But a part of him wondered if it would last. He knew for a fact that he was in love with Nola, and that love caused him to have tremendous fear. Fear of losing her. He knew he would be crushed if that ever happened. He also knew if it did ever happen, it would be all his fault.

Everything done in the dark always finds its way to the light. This thought made his mood somewhat dark as he got out of bed and went into the living room of the suite at the W where they'd been residing since their arrival in Los Angeles. He saw Nola sitting on the couch talking on the phone to Lola. He stood in the doorway with his early morning hard-on poking out of the slit of his boxers. Nola turned and saw him standing there and shook her head with a smile on her face.

"Honey, let me tell you, you got to hurry up and find a way to get your ass out here so I can show you around. . . . Girl, I know my way around. I got a drop-top Beamer, and I be driving myself around when Hot Shot's busy handling his business. Trust me, Lola, Cali is the place to be, but listen, honey, I have to go take care of something kind of important, so let me go. I'll give you a call later, okay?" Nola said as she hung up the phone not waiting for a response from her sister.

Hot Shot was now standing right in front of her with his dick sticking a mere inch from her lips. Nola smiled, licked her lips, and said, "Hello, there, Mr. Dick." She then kissed the head of Hot Shot's dick and swallowed him whole. She gave him some extraordinarily great head that made him come within three minutes. His legs almost buckled from the monster orgasm she made him have inside of her mouth. After swallowing every drop of his semen, she smiled and stood up. "Mmmm, nothing like a real protein shake from my man to start the day."

Trying to regain his senses, Hot Shot smiled and said, "Yes, you can say that again. Listen, Nola, you're going to be on your own today. I have to get with JT and take care of some business. I don't know how long I'll be, so I'll hit you later when everything has been taken care of."

"That's fine, honey. I wanted to go find me a beauty shop anyway. I need to get my hair done, I've been rocking this ponytail for way too long. So that should take up most of the day. Plus, I was wondering when we were going to start looking for a place of our own. We can't keep staying in this expensive-ass hotel, honey. That makes no sense."

"I thought you liked being catered to."

"Oh, don't you get it twisted, if you can handle this, then I'm with it. But at the same time, there's no place like home, Hot Shot. We need to find us that home," she said seriously. "*Our* home."

He nodded and said, "All right, we'll get right on that. You do know that sooner or later I'll be on the move again? JT's working out some things now for me on a new out-of-town spot."

"So when you go outta town what am I supposed to be doing out here, Hot Shot?" He stood there silently thinking about that because he never thought about it before. "Exactly. If you think I'm going to be stuck way out here in this state by myself, then you are loony, sir. When you go outta town, I'm right there with you, buddy. Ya dig? You'll need me to watch your back anyway. Four eyes are better than two, especially out there in them cold streets."

"What, we're going to work that Bonnie and Clyde theme now, Nola?"

Shaking her head, she said, "Uh-uh, honey, that's not my thing. I'm no gangsta nor killer. I do know how to watch my man's back and look out for his best interests at all times, though. And that's exactly what I intend on doing. Wherever JT sends us, I'll play my part and be the good woman staying in the cut while playing my role. Where you go, I go, Hot Shot. It's that simple."

He smiled and gave her a kiss. When she tried to stick her tongue in his mouth, he pulled away from her and said, "Ugh, you got nut on your tongue and breath. You not sticking your tongue in my mouth!"

She punched him on the chest and said, "If I can kiss your ass after you eat me, you damn sure can kiss me when I swallow your nut, boy. You better give me a kiss!"

Laughing, he screamed, "Noooooooooooo!" and started running around the suite as she chased after him. When she finally caught him, he smiled and said, "You know I love you, right?"

"You better."

"Where I go, you go. I wonder how JT is going to feel about that piece of information."

"Do you want me to tell his ass? Shit, I've been here a month-plus now and still haven't met him. What, he scared of me or something?"

Hot Shot started laughing and said, "JT is fearless, Nola. He's just been real busy getting everything ready for the next mission. I'll make sure to tell him you're ready to meet him."

"You do that. As a matter a fact, you tell him he's invited here tonight for dinner, and I expect him to show his ass up. Am I understood, Hot Shot?"

"Yes, ma'am."

"Good. Now gimme a damn kiss so I can go shower and get ready to go out and find me a beauty salon to get these naps whipped up."

Hot Shot frowned but relented when he saw the scowl on Nola's face. They shared a kiss that was meant to be brief but turned intense quickly. After a full two minutes, he pulled from her embrace and said, "Ugh, you still taste like sperm."

"It's your sperm, so what?"

"That's nasty."

Laughing, she said, "Get used to me being nasty, then, Hot. Shot."

"Freak!"

She stopped in the doorway of the bedroom, turned, and looked back over her shoulder and said, "That's right, I'm your freak and don't you forget it!"

He was smiling as he watched her go into the bedroom.

Hot Shot arrived at JT's home in the city of Pasadena, home of the famous Rose Bowl Stadium. He smiled as he got out of his car and saw JT standing in his front yard watering the grass, dressed in a pair of shorts and a wife beater with some Nike flip-flops on his pale feet and a Marlboro stuck between his lips.

"Damn, you look nice and relaxed out here in the city of the Rose Bowl. This what you get from all of my hard work?"

"I wish. Come on inside. We got a lot to go over. Everything is in place out in Texas," JT said as he turned and led the way inside of his modestly furnished but well-kept home. Once they were inside, JT asked Hot Shot if he wanted a beer. He gave him a nod, and JT went into the kitchen and returned with two bottles of Coronas. He tossed him one and said, "Okay, son, before we get to the business, it's time you tell me exactly how you wish to proceed with the business."

"What do you mean? I'm going to handle everything just like we planned; nothing changed, JT."

"Nothing's changed? A lot has changed, boy. You now have a girlfriend, a woman, a significant other, whatever the hell you want to label her. Nola is here, and she's with you. How is that going to work and coincide with the business plans, son?"

"I just had this conversation with her, and she's with me, JT. She's going to move when I move wherever I move. She's my ride or die. And for real, I think it won't hurt things one bit."

JT took a sip of his beer and stared at Hot Shot. "I know you trust her, but do you trust her enough to tell her *all* of the business?"

Hot Shot had been pondering that question for weeks now, and he still didn't have an answer.

His silence was answer enough for JT. "That's what I thought. Son, I know you care for that woman, but she can hurt you. If you really love her, you'll get at her with the real and let the chips fall as they may. That way, if she chooses to proceed to be your ride or die, it'll be all good. You can't have her with you not knowing the entire truth; that's a recipe for disaster. There is no room for any form of that type of disaster for us and what we got going on. So while we go over this business, I want you to think about that and make a decision before you leave. Understand?"

"Affirmative."

"Good."

Hot Shot smiled and said, "Oh yeah, Nola said she wants to meet you, and she's not taking no for an answer. Since our previous dinner date was canceled due to unforeseen circumstances, she feels it's a must that we have dinner at our suite at the W this evening."

"Might as well get it over with, especially since she seems to be a keeper."

"Might as well."

"What time?"

"Any time after six should be fine."

"I understand your feelings for this woman, but we're breaking a lot of rules with this, son. By right, she should be charged for the same federal crimes that the Northern District of Texas is filing against her brother, cousin, and her twin sister. Speaking of that, the warrants will soon be served against her family, along with everyone else that has been stung by your superb undercover work, Special Agent Jason Gaines.

"So I guess congratulations are in order for a job well done. I spoke with the director, and he told me to make sure to convey those exact sentiments to you from him. You did good, son, real good. Operation Cleanup has started off exactly like the director and I hoped it would. Now, we have to get ready and get things set up for your next mission."

"Where am I going to now?"

"Oklahoma. The director wants to tighten things up in both Oklahoma City and Tulsa. After reading the reports I gave him from your reports on how easy it was for the distribution of drugs in OKC, he felt that should be the next target state. When you really look at it, you being with Nola actually will help ease you into that situation. Nola may come in handy after all."

Shaking his head, Hot Shot said, "No way. I'm not using her in our mix, JT."

"If that's the case, then tell her the truth and let the chips fall. Stop trying to straddle the damn fence, son. You're going to lose doing it that way. If the love is as real as you think it is on her part, then she will accept it and still stand by your side, son."

"And if it's not?"

"She's going to leave you and hate you for the rest of her days."

"Thanks for making me feel good about this, JT."

"That's just it, I'm not trying to make you feel good, son. I'm giving it to you as I've always given it to you since we first met when you were a young know-it-all chump in boot camp. I saw your talent levels from the very first day we met. I knew you would be one of the best soldiers the United States Army would ever see, and I was right. When you became Delta Force's big dog, no one could have been prouder than me. I watched your career from afar and loved it every time I found out about how you continued to excel. You're a good man, son. You were born to do some good. What we're doing here with this operation is good. Good for our country. Good for decent and honest Americans who are living out there peacefully in the good old U.S. of A."

"That good has come at one steep price, JT. You and I both know the only reason why I signed on for Operation Cleanup was because of what happened to my family. Besides my cousins Hakeem and Holli, I don't have anyone."

"Not true, son, you'll always have me."

"You know what I mean, family wise, blood relations. My two cousins are the only blood-related family I have left. And I haven't spoken to them since we buried my parents and my brother. Before I hit Oklahoma, I need some time, JT. I need some time to look into things more. It's eating me slowly that no one can seem to find out anything about the murders of my family. I'm a time bomb ticking, JT. Sending me back into the fray too soon may not be the wisest decision right now."

Nodding, JT said, "I agree. If you want to take a break, then I don't have a problem with that. That'll give me more time to check out the target areas more carefully. So when you're ready, we can move full steam ahead."

"Cool. Tell me what your contacts have found out about my family."

"Nada. I'm working some other angles, but I want to have something solid before I get at you."

"That's fair. I have to get out there some and see what the streets have to say about it."

"It's been over eighteen months since those murders, son. The streets most likely have nothing for you."

"I thought that too because no one in my family played the streets. At least, that's what I think. Won't hurt to check out every angle, though."

"You have the best instincts I've ever seen, son, and so far, they've never steered you wrong. Follow them and see what comes from it. What are you going to do with Nola, though? Either tell her or keep it from her until she eventually figures out you're not Hot Shot, a major player in the game, but an undercover operative for the FBI assigned to me and the director of the FBI. Do you want to continue to live a lie with the woman you've fallen in love with, son? Or do you want to tell her the truth and see if you two have really found real love?"

"You're giving me permission to blow my cover, JT?"

"No way. What I am giving you permission to do is to do what's right here. Like I said, I trust your instincts. You'll know the right thing to do here, for both our business and your personal life. That's why I gave you the name Hot Shot back at boot camp. Your decision making is above average; always has been, son. Make the move that your gut tells you to make."

Hot Shot stared at his mentor/boss/father figure/and friend, smiled sadly, and said, "This is one crazy world we're living in, JT."

"Doing good comes at a price most times, son. You are a good man, and I know you want to continue to do some good."

"You're right, I do. Let's get this business handled. I got to get with Nola and hopefully do some good for both of us."

"The first order of business is Cotton. What do you want to do with your little helper?"

"Let him make it. I'm going to need him later. Since we're going to be right up the highway from Dallas, he'll be useful. He's been through too much with what happened to Meosha."

"I agree. The Blood guy from Abilene is one smart sum bitch. He was able to stay away from all of the weapons that they purchased with the transponders inside of them that led us to a warehouse in North Dallas. He isn't seen clearly on any of the video footage you made while meeting him that night, so he basically gets a pass."

"Actually, that's a good thing. He did me a solid, so I owe him that for now. Later in the game, we'll be able to bring him and his homeboys down. He's a stand-up dude, so he'll give further credibility to my cover. The respect he has on the streets can be helpful, very helpful."

"Again, I agree. Like I said, the warrants will be served tomorrow, and you will be responsible for over seventy-five federal arrests in Dallas, Texas. You gave the U.S. District Attorney for the Northern District of Texas the biggest busts of his career."

"Yes, I did."

"You ready to do some more good for your country, Hot Shot?"

With a smile on his face, he said, "You know my rule, JT: I can't stop, and I won't stop."

"My man. Get what you need to get out of your system, then get ready to turn up."

Hot Shot started laughing and said, "Turn up, huh?"

"That's right, son, you know I'm hop with it. It's time for us to turn up, this time, in Oklahoma City."

Chapter Thirty-four

Special Agent Jason Gaines, better known as Hot Shot, got to skip the FBI Academy in Quantico due to his special training in the Special Forces of the United States Army. His training and expertise in combat as well as with any gun made by man made him a valuable asset to the first African American director of the FBI. When Jack "JT" Tackett contacted the director and explained Hot Shot's skill set and his situation, they both knew that he was the man they needed to launch Operation Cleanup, a special operation that would be designed to place Hot Shot out on the streets of the urban communities across the U.S. and let him infiltrate every form of street crime, drugs, guns . . . Anything that made the community unsafe would be his aim. After surviving several tours over in Iraq and Afghanistan, Hot Shot was a warrior at the elite level. He collected more medals than anyone his age and was on his way to becoming the youngest major in the U.S. Army within the Delta Force.

All of that changed for him when he was on a leave of sorts taking a class at Fort Hood at their special sniper school. Hot Shot was trained to be able to shoot at any range and hit his targets with deadly precision. He knew the vital areas on the human body where he could kill or hurt without taking life if he chose to do so. A perfect marksman and an even deadlier soldier. But the death of his family changed his life forever. Before he destroyed himself chasing revenge, JT, his former drill instructor, stepped in and saved his life, along with the help from the director of the FBI.

Hot Shot was unpredictable in civilian life as he was on the battlefield, and that made him deadly efficient. His methods proved effective, and that's all that mattered to him. If he had to kill, then so be it. He never killed an innocent or anyone he deemed didn't have it coming. When it came to his life or some scumbag, the scumbag lost, hands-down. Being fearless wasn't what defined him . . . It was the thought of doing what was right that made him the man he was.

He was raised by a man who instilled honor, respect, and truth deep inside of his soul. And out of nowhere, that man was taken from him—Taken along with his wife and youngest son. Taken for reasons that Hot Shot had to find out. That was now his mission in life, to find the men or people responsible for taking his family away from him. In the interim, he would continue to live and do what he promised his father he would do . . . some good. His family was dead. Eighteen months later and his grief and pain were still acute. The case was now considered a cold case. That's because of the lack of attention by the Inglewood Police Department. He didn't blame them, though. He accepted the fact that it was going to take him to do whatever it took to solve this heinous crime that had been committed against his family. And as long as he had a breath to breathe, he was going to do whatever it took to find the killers of his loved ones. In his mind, all he thought was that he can't stop. That's the creed he now lived by and would die by. Can't stop, won't stop.

Now, here he was back in Los Angeles after completing his first mission for Operation Cleanup. He did some good and felt good about that. He hated the fact that such an innocent and sweet young lady had to die. Meosha's suicide made him lose more sleep than he cared to admit. When innocent people suffered at the hands of evil men, he felt even more empowered to keep doing what he was doing. Yes, he was making false friendships; yes, he was deceiving. Some would call what he and JT were doing for the director of the FBI as entrapment. What they called it was doing what others have failed to do: cleaning up the urban streets in all the hoods of America. These thoughts gave him more confidence as he rode the elevator toward the tenth floor of the W.

He was about to take the biggest risk of his life, and that was telling Nola the truth. She deserved the truth, and JT was right. . . . There was no way he could continue to be with her without letting her know who he really was. He was smiling because he was known as a fearless warrior on the battlefield, but right now, he was so scared he felt as if he were facing a hundred enemy soldiers over in Iraq. Scared to death. But he would do what he did when he was overseas and face the mission head-on, and deal with it the best way he knew how to. Win or lose, he had to tell Nola the truth. He knew deep inside of his soul, though, that he was going to lose her. Once she found out he was the reason for the charges being brought against her family she would never forgive him for his deceit.

I'm screwed, he thought as he stepped inside of the suite to see Nola sitting in the living room eating what looked like the messiest hamburger he'd ever seen in his life. He stared at the paper bag and saw the logo of a local hamburger stand in LA called Quick N Split and started laughing. "How in the heck did you come across a Quick N Split joint, Nola?" He asked as he sat down next to her on the couch and grabbed a few of her french fries.

"I went back to that soul food restaurant in Inglewood you took me to when we first got here, and while I was waiting to eat, I heard these guys talking about how tired they were from waiting to be seated and how they would rather have a Quick N Split burger. So when they stepped out of the restaurant, I followed them to the parking lot and asked them if they could tell me where that Quick N Split place was because I was hungry and tired of waiting too. They started laughing at me because they said I sound 'country.' After I told them I was from Texas, they laughed even harder at me. I then had to show them some Texas attitude and checking before they finally stopped laughing and told me to follow them, and they took me to Quick N Split and advised me to get this here Super Quick N Split burger. They even paid for my food. I didn't know how big this burger was until I got back here and warmed it up. Man, this is something else. Look at all this damn ground beef. It has—"

He cut her off and said, "I know, Nola, I'm from here, remember? I've been eating Quick N Split burgers since I was a teenager. It has pastrami, chili, cheese, and egg, all on top of a pound and a half of ground beef fresh out of the fridge and handmade. Well, after you eat all of that, I guess you won't be in the mood to have dinner with JT then, huh?"

"I guess not. You better not tell his ass that. I want him here tonight, though, so I can meet the man that is so close to my man."

"Told him to get here any time after six, so he should be here within the next hour or so."

"That's fine. So, how was your day?"

"All right. Found out that we may be going back close to Texas."

"Where?"

He smiled at her and said, "Oklahoma."

"Stop it."

"Seriously. I told JT about the money out that way, and he feels that may be a good look. Tulsa as well as Oklahoma City."

"I don't have any people that I know of in Tulsa, but you know my people are all over the city, so that can be real easy. I bet Keeta Wee and Weeta Wee are going to love having us out that way."

"Yeah, I bet. They just *love* me!" joked Hot Shot. They both started laughing.

They grew silent for a minute as if they were deep in thought. After a few minutes, they spoke at the same time. "Baby . . ." They laughed again.

"You first, Nola."

"Honey, I have something I need to talk to you about, something serious."

"That's funny 'cause I have some serious stuff to discuss with you too. Ladies first."

She nibbled on some of her fries and stared at him for a few seconds before sighing loudly. "I'm preggo, Hot Shot. When I was driving around looking for a beauty shop, I had the funniest feeling in my tummy. And for some reason, I knew instantly what it was. So I went to a Rite Aid and bought a pregnancy test. I didn't even wait until I made it back here to take it. I went right into the bathroom and did it there. And just like I thought, I'm pregnant, honey," she said as she stared at him to see if he was angry with her. When he didn't speak, she knew she had messed up, and her heart began to beat wildly. The last thing she wanted to do to him was to make him feel as if she was trying to trick him or stick him with a baby to try to lock him in for the long haul with her. "Talk to me, honey. Please, you're killing me over here."

Though he heard her, the only thing that was going on inside of his head was there was no way he could tell her what he did now. No way at all. He smiled at her and said, "We're having a baby, huh?"

Nola nodded and smiled as tears slowly slid down her cheeks from happiness. "You're not mad, honey?"

He grabbed her hands and said, "No way could I ever be mad at you for some news like this, Nola. You've just made me the happiest man in the world. You're about to give me a son."

"Ahem, excuse me, you mean a *daughter,* don't you?"

"I couldn't care less. A baby! Our baby! I love it! I love you, Nola," he said as he gave her a tight hug and a kiss. When they finished, he said, "You do know this changes a lot of things for us, right?"

"What do you mean, honey?"

"There's no way I'm letting you go on mission with me. We're going to find a nice spot out here so you can be nice and comfy while I go handle up."

With a smirk on her face, she shook her head no and said, "Now that is just plain goofy. If you think you're leaving me out here, you're out of your damn mind. Being preggo ain't stopping nothing. I'm going with you like I said I was. I'll play the back and watch your back. When it comes close to the time for me to give birth to our child, then we'll make the decision on where we'll have the baby."

"Nola, that's not good."

"How long will it be before we leave for Oklahoma?"

"I don't know. Right now, JT is giving me a minute because I got some things I need to handle out here."

"Okay. So, what did you have to talk to me about that was so serious?"

"After hearing your news, it doesn't seem as serious, but it's something that we have to discuss."

"Is everything all right, honey?"

Knowing he had to switch things up fast, he said, "Yes and no. Nola, I need to find out who murdered my mom, dad, and li'l brother. It's been eighteen months, and nothing has been done about their murders. I have two living relatives left, my cousins Hakeem and his li'l sister

Holli. I haven't seen or spoken to them since we buried my family. I got to get at them and get out there in the streets a li'l and see if I can find something out. It's a must that I find out why my family was murdered."

"Why? That's all, honey? Just why?"

He stared at her for a moment and then answered her honestly. "Why and who." Before she could ask what he knew she would ask him, he added, "Then kill them for what they did to my family. The day I find the people responsible for the deaths of my family is the day I'll commit cold-blooded murder, Nola."

She reached out to him and said, "Whatever you want to do, I'm with you, Hot Shot. Whatever you choose to do, I'm with you. You smile, I smile. You cry, I cry. I'm with you all the way, honey."

"I love you, Nola."

"I love you too, Hot. Shot."

He smiled. "There you go saying my name in that sexy voice I love. You know all that's going to do is make us go get busy."

She licked her lips seductively and said, "Bring it on then, Hot. Shot."

Before he could say a word, there was a knock at the door. He smiled and said, "Looks like JT saved you from getting wore out, Nola."

"Humph. He would have to be right on time now, wouldn't he? Go on and let him in so we can order his ass some food, and then make him kick rocks. We got some freaking to get to up in this piece!" They both started laughing as Hot Shot went and let JT inside of their suite.

JT, ever the suave one, smiled brightly when he set his eyes on Nola and stepped straight toward her without so much as a hi to Hot Shot. "Nola, it is my pleasure as well as honor to finally meet the woman that has made this knucklehead realize that there's more to this life than getting money," JT said as he shook hands with Nola, laying on the charm a tad too thick for Hot Shot's taste.

You slick jerk, Hot Shot said to himself as he watched the two people in this world who he was closest to converse.

"Well, I'm glad you finally found some time for me. I was starting to think you didn't approve of me and Hot Shot being together, JT."

"No way. My business tends to keep me and most of my time occupied, Nola. Trying to maintain everything as well as staying one step ahead is a constant for me. After seeing how beautiful you are, I understand totally now why Hot Shot has been struck by Cupid's arrow. You two make an absolutely perfect couple. I wish you well and long-lasting happiness."

That was about all Hot Shot could stand. "You really can take some of that swag off, JT. She likes you, jeez," Hot Shot said, slightly irritated by JT's extra charm.

Laughing, Nola said, "Please don't stop him, honey. If he's trying to impress me, then let the man do what he do!" They all started laughing.

Nola had to admit that she was impressed with JT, and she was more shocked to see that he was white. For some reason, she thought he would be this imposing-looking Suge Knight type. Instead, he was a middle-aged white man with a gaunt face, full beard, with a clean-shaved bald head with a thick neck that made her think he used to be a boxer. He looked to be in great shape as well. His personality was crisp and honest. She liked him instantly. "Now, come on, honey, and have a seat so we can order you some of the finest grub this hotel has to offer," Nola said as she led JT toward the living room.

JT noticed the Quick N Split bags and said, "Awww, that's cold. Y'all went to Quick N Split on me. Come on, no fair."

Nola told JT about her trip to Quick N Split and then said, "I didn't know it would be all this food, though. I thought I would be able to munch it and still be able to have a salad or something while you and Hot Shot ate dinner. But, honey, let me tell you that Super Quick N Split ain't no punk. Way too much food for me."

"I know that's right. I love those burgers, but my favorite food from there is their Lip Drippers."

Laughing, she asked, "Now, what in the hell is a Lip Dripper?"

"It's sorta like a soft taco with ground beef, pastrami meat seasoned real spicy, with lettuce and tomatoes. Super greasy and supe rgood."

"That's right, and super heartburn when you eat more than one of them," added Hot Shot.

"Yep. But you know what? That's what I'm in the mood to eat. So y'all can save the room service. I'm about to go around the way and get me a few Lip Drippers and head on out back to my home and chill and get my grub on. Don't you worry. Nola, we'll have plenty of time to get to know each other better since you're a keeper." He turned toward Hot Shot and asked, "She *is* a keeper, correct?"

Hot Shot ignored him and told Nola, "Tell JT the good news, baby." Nola was practically glowing when she smiled at Hot Shot, turned, and faced JT and said, "We're having a baby!"

JT's eyes bulged as he stared at Hot Shot speechless. After congratulating them both, he stood and gave Nola a hug and told Hot Shot to walk him down to his car. When they made it to the parking lot and were standing in front of JT's brand-new Jaguar, JT sighed loudly and said, "Well, son, I guess you didn't tell her what you really do for a living now, did ya?"

"Can you blame me?"

JT stood there and thought about it for a minute, and then said, "Nope. You just remember, everything in the dark will come to the light sooner or later. Let me go, my stomach is rumbling for some Lip Drippers. Talk to you later, Daddy!" JT was laughing as he got inside of his car and left.

Hot Shot turned and started walking toward the hotel entrance just as there was a deep rumble of thunder and rain started to pour down from the sky. "I wonder if that's a sign of things to come?" he asked aloud as he let the rain drench him before he entered the hotel.

Chapter Thirty-five

The next morning, Nola woke up and grabbed her iPad and went into the living room so she could watch the morning news in Dallas. Though she was enjoying living in California and being with Hot Shot, she was still somewhat homesick. Watching the morning news on her iPad became her morning ritual and helped fix her craving for missing Texas.

After turning on her iPad and logging on to the Web site for KFDW Fox News in Dallas, she sat crossed-legged on the sofa and watched as a breaking news alert came flashing across the screen. "Oh Lord, what done happened out there now?" she said aloud as the news reporter came on the screen.

"This is Jazmine Champion reporting live outside of the Federal Court Building for the Northern District of Texas where we have just been informed that Assistant United States Attorney Walter Long Jr. will be having a press conference momentarily informing us about the arrests of over forty-seven men and women here in the Dallas area. Arrest warrants have been served this morning in the cities of Oak Cliff, North Dallas, Desoto, and Rowlett. Charges range from cocaine distribution, illegal gun possession, and even a child pornography ring."

When Nola heard the city of Rowlett mentioned as one of the cities where someone had been arrested, she thought nothing of it, but when the reporter said "child pornography" was one of the charges, her heart began to beat wildly as she continued to watch the news, praying that she wouldn't see any of her family members.

FOX TV news cameras cut from a tight shot of their reporter to a wide shot of the U.S. Assistant Attorney.

"Good morning. We're proud to inform you all that after a lengthy undercover operation conducted by the FBI, there have been over forty-seven arrests made today. Some suspected heavy drug dealers have been taken off the streets of Dallas. We have also broken up what looks to be an extremely sophisticated pornography ring in the city of Rowlett. Since underage females were involved in this crime, I am unable to release any other information pertaining to that particular case. I wanted to have this press conference to let the citizens of Dallas, Texas, know that we are continuing the fight of illegal guns and drug activity that's plagued our state for so long. Today, we've made a big win for the team who wears the white hats. Thank you for your time. Have a great day."

The camera then zoomed off of the U.S. Assistant Attorney and showed several men and women being led into the courthouse handcuffed by FBI agents. Nola screamed when she saw Weeta Wee, Keeta Wee, Tiny Troy, and her sister Lola getting out of a black Suburban in handcuffs. "Oh . . . no. God . . . no!"

Hot Shot came running into the living room with two nine-millimeter guns, one in each hand aimed at the floor of the suite. "What's going on, Nola, are you okay? Talk to me!" he demanded.

She turned and looked at him with tears streaming down her face and pointed toward the screen of her iPad. She couldn't speak she was so choked up.

He checked the room quickly with his eyes to make sure everything was secure, then stepped to her and put his guns onto the coffee table. When he focused on her iPad and saw the KDFW news insignia on the lower part of the screen, he knew instantly what she was watching. *Jeez, here we go,* he thought. He felt like the jerk of the year for the deception he was about to embark on. He was stuck between a rock and a hard place and had no other choice but to put his poker face on and play it out. "What's wrong, Nola?"

Gasping for breath and trying to regain her composure, Nola wiped her face with her hands and said, "Th-the feds got'em, baby. They got my family. I just saw them taking Lola, Troy, Weeta Wee, and Keeta Wee inside of the courthouse. They said they were arrested for child pornography and drugs. Oh my God! This cannot be happening."

Rubbing her shoulders as he sat next her, he felt so stupid. Lies—he never lived by them. . . . Now it seemed that his very existence was a lie, and he didn't like how it made him feel. But there was nothing he could do about it at this time, so he did what seemed was his best trait of late.

He lied.

"Don't worry, baby, we'll get some people right on this and figure this out. You need to stay calm, Nola. Stressing right now can't be healthy for the baby. Let me give JT a call and see if he can get at some of his contacts out that way and find something out."

"Okay, honey. Do you think they'll be able to get bail? I know where the money is, and I'm sure no one was able to get it because one thing Troy was adamant about was not keeping any money at the house. No matter what it costs, we got to get them out of there, Hot Shot. My sister cannot be in nobody's jail. She'll lose her mind."

"Whatever it takes, Nola, we will do whatever it takes. You just try to calm down, please."

"I'm trying, honey, but it's hard. I knew this would happen sooner or later. I knew it! I prayed and prayed for them to quit, but they were greedy and too far gone. Now look at them. How could this happen? How could this happen to them, Hot Shot?"

He shook his head and lied with a straight face to the woman he was madly in love with. "I don't have a clue, Nola." Not caring how he was feeling, he stood and went back into the bedroom and grabbed his phone. He called JT, and as soon as JT answered the phone, he said, "The cat's outta the bag."

"Figured that when I saw your number on my phone this early, son. How are you going to play this?"

"I'm letting it play out as it will, JT. I need you to check and see if Nola's family will be able to get a bond. Let me know if they can. She needs them out. She cannot be stressing about this too much. It can hurt the baby."

"I know. That curveball was one that makes me feel real sick about this, son."

"You? How do you think *I'm* feeling?"

"I can't even imagine. Since there's going to be a nice break before we turn up, you might as well find a place to stay and try to bring some normalcy in your life with Nola. I figured we can put everything off until after the baby is born."

"Thanks. But that's not what I'm thinking about right now."

"You want to tell her the truth right now?"

"I can't live a life lying, JT. That's not my way."

JT sighed and said, "I know, son. Do what you have to do."

"I have no other choice."

Epilogue

Three months after the arrests of Nola's family in Texas, they were finally released on federal bonds, which meant they could not leave the state of Texas and had to wear leg monitors to ensure they obeyed the rules of their conditional release. Nola was feeling much better now that her family was free for the time being. Hot Shot thought it would be best if she went and spent some time with them to see what they were going to do regarding the charges that they were up against. It also gave him some much-needed breathing room, because every morning he opened his eyes and saw Nola lying next to him, the more the guilt ate at his insides. With her in Texas, he could focus on trying to figure out a way to tell her the truth—that he was a federal agent working on a major undercover federal operation. How in the hell would she ever forgive him was the question he asked himself repeatedly every single day. He shook his head as he pulled into the driveway of JT's home.

JT opened the door and didn't say a word as he turned and headed straight into his office.

Hot Shot followed silently, wondering what JT had on his mind. His not greeting him with some sort of smile or slick remark normally meant drama. *Just what I need, more drama in my life right now,* he thought as he took a seat across from JT who was sitting in his big leather chair behind his desk, staring at Hot Shot. "Don't hold me in suspense. What's up, champ?"

"A whole lot, son. I got a call last night from our Texas U.S. Assistant Attorney, and Mr. Long is very concerned about some of the information he has received thus far. Seems like everyone who has been arrested are singing like hummingbirds on any and everybody, trying to cut a deal to save their asses."

Hot Shot shrugged and said, "That's to be expected. What, you thought they would stay down and take their charges like real men and women? Telling is the new way of the land, champ. That's what they do out there. And that makes our job that much easier."

"True. But in this case, it looks bad, real bad, son. Everyone from Juan G. to Nola's family is screaming your name. Hot Shot this, Hot Shot that. One of those huge fucking twins are even claiming you shot him. He has the scars to prove he's been shot too. I told Mr. Long that was absurd because there was nothing in any of the many detailed reports you sent me monthly of anyone being shot. . . . Now, did I lie to that man, son?"

Hot Shot stared at JT and gave him a stone-cold look before speaking. "Whatever it takes to get the job done and stay breathing is what I'm willing to do when I am in the field, JT. Whatever I have to do."

"I understand that, son. Shit, those are the rules the director gave us, and I'm with you on this. But when you believe you can do no wrong is when everything you do will be wrong. There's a fine line here, son. Be careful, Hot Shot. We're backed by the director of the FBI, but that still doesn't mean you can fuck up."

Smiling, he said, "How can I screw up by shooting a bad guy who was trying to hurt me, JT?"

"You are in the field, and I understand you have to do what you have to do in order to survive out there. But you are one of Delta Force's youngest and best. Use that training and skill to remain safe. I cannot have it like you're some psychopath or sociopath out there on some vigilante shit."

"A psychopath is a crazy person. You know I'm not crazy, JT, though I have every right to be. A sociopath is a person with no conscience. After all of the death I've seen and now have had in my life, I think I am somewhat of a sociopath. After giving this further thought, I guess I'm both. Crazy to think I can get involved in this and maintain the sanity I need in order to complete this mission. No conscience at all because I've fallen in love with a woman while at the same time setting up her entire family so they can get a whole bunch of federal time. Yep, I fit the criteria for both psychopath and sociopath, JT. I can kill and not lose a bit of sleep. I can sleep with my woman and lie to her face like it's nothing. What a good guy I've become. I was better off back in the desert taking out Bin Laden's cronies than this mess you've got me a part of now."

"Stop it, son. You're doing a job you were born to do. To do some damn good. You did six tours over there and did them damn good just to make it back home. You're one of Fort Bragg's toughest. You're in the best top ten soldiers of the Special Forces. Technically, Delta Force doesn't exist since the army is notoriously known for denying the elite Special Forces unit. But you are the best among the best, and I expect for you to act like it, now and always. Remain professional and do what needs to be done to continue to do some damn good. Lies. That's life. You do what you have to do, and when the time is right, you make everything right."

"Make everything right, huh? How can I make everything right when we got assistant attorneys not understanding that it's a war we're fighting out there, and they have to give me the leeway needed to do what needs to be done? Yeah, I shot that guy, but there was no other choice. I used my training. That's why he's still breathing and not dead. I could have easily put two in his head and ended his creepy existence. Instead, he got a gut shot, leg, and shoulder wound that he fully recovered from. If I'm going to continue with this operation, I need you to be able to protect me in every way, JT. Call the director and let him know. I have no problem doing the good he expects from us, but I will not be compromised, nor will I ever let my life be threatened without responding accordingly. If I have to kill, I will kill. If I can wound a bad guy and control the situation, then that's what I'll do. But, it will always be my decision to make, JT. Mine. Not yours. Not the director's. Only mine."

"Understood. Though Mr. Long has given me some noise, he's not going to be too hard to deal with. We have the director behind us, and the director has the president behind him, so we're good."

"Okay."

"Back to what I was saying, your name along with that Blood guy Tone are the names that have been tossed into the fray. Mr. Long wants Tone and is acting as if he wants you just as bad to keep your cover intact."

"That's cool. I figured there would be a lot of telling, but I didn't think super hard Juan G. would run his mouth, especially with his ties to the Tango Blast."

"Juan G. is a chump just like the rest of them. He's given up some major people within the Tango Blast too. He's trying to save his ass any way he can. What surprises me most is the only person out of the forty-seven people arrested that refuses to cooperate is Lola. A damn female is stronger than the men in this case. Tiny Troy, the fat twins, all of the Bloods and Crips, along with everyone else, is telling like it's the thing to do."

"That's funny. Lola is a strong woman like her sister, so I'm not surprised. What about Cotton? Has anyone given him up?"

"His name was the first to come up when your name was mentioned. Mr. Long received instructions to ignore anything said about you or Cotton."

"Thank you for that, JT."

"No problem. You just make sure your little helper continues to pull his weight in our business. He does that and he'll remain free."

"Got you. You do know that that move you made by putting a felony charge on my name was brilliant, right?"

"I hate to toot my own horn, son, but . . . *toooooooot tooooooooot!*" JT screamed and started laughing. "I never thought any of the lowlifes you would be dealing with would have that type of clout or access to have a NCIC database check made on you. That list contains 50 million names, almost everyone who has ever been arrested, convicted, jailed, or paroled in the United States. Something told me to ask the director to give you some kind of trouble in your background to help authenticate your street credentials."

"Like I said, brilliant. Tiny Troy has that kind of plug, and it's a must that you remain on top of his moves. Who knows what else he has plugs into."

"I'm all over it. So, since everyone is telling on you, you can pretty much figure that the name Hot Shot is solidified out there in the streets. You ready to turn up now, son?"

Hot Shot smiled at his mentor/friend/father figure, and said, "You better believe it. I've got to get with my cousins. We're turning up out here in LA first. Hakeem found out that my little brother was into something in the streets. I need to know what, JT."

JT nodded, and then said, "Understood. Never thought to check that angle because I never believed James would ever play the streets."

"Neither did I. But Holli said one of her girlfriends knew he was getting some money for some people, but she didn't know who."

"Do you want to explore this while you wait for Nola to give birth, or are you ready to get back to work?"

"Both. You get on these streets out here for me and find out what you can about my little brother's business in the streets."

"And?" JT asked with a smile on his face.

"And I'll head to Oklahoma City and get turned up."

"I like that."

"Yes, I knew you would."

AUTHOR'S NOTE

Okay, another one in the bank. I hope you liked Hot Shot because he's not going anywhere any time soon. I've been thinking about making a crime fighter type for the hood for a long time, and now I've done it. I hope I don't make anyone mad at me, but I felt the urban books needed to step up their game. I mean, if we're going to portray real-life street stuff (of sorts), then we should make it seem more real by showing that there's more to the streets than just the bad guys. There are some good guys, and the hoods across the United States are about to find out that Hot Shot is one of them. *Can't Stop* is the first of a series. The next one in the Hot Shot Series will be called *Won't Stop,* so be on the lookout for it. I'm right back in the lab now working on it. I am striving every time to improve my game with the stories I put out. Trying my very best to raise the bar to our genre and show the world that I am a storyteller who can give the best at it a run for their money. Take care and may God bless you and yours. Time to make Hot Shot Turn Up! Lol.

Peace & Love

Spud